GIRLS GONE SOUTH

A TALE OF EARLIEST HOLLYWOOD

Bruce Lee Bond

MONTAG

First Montag Press E-Book and Paperback Original Edition September 2016

Montag Press

ISBN: 978-1-940233-36-9

Jacket and book design © 2016 Niall Gray

Montag Press Team:

Editor – Charlie Franco

Managing Director – Charlie Franco

A Montag Press Book

www.montagpress.com

Montag Press

1066 47th Ave. Unit #9

Oakland CA 94601 USA

Montag Press, the burning book with the hatchet cover, the skewed word mark and the portrayal of the long-suffering fireman mascot are trademarks of Montag Press.

Printed & Digitally Originated in the United States of America

10 9 8 7 6 5 4 3 2 1

Also by the author

Treasures of the Night	Montag Press
The Broken Coast	Montag Press
The Babysitter	Solstice Press
Honor Thy Father	*Slaughterhouse II* Sirens Call Publications
The Well of Souls	*Bones II* James Ward Kirk Publication
Midnight Lunch	*Blood in the Rain* Cwich Press
Girls' Day Out	*Girl at the End of the World II* Fox Spirit Publications

For Connie Ballenger, who ran away at seventeen and became the first of many girls I knew who didn't survive.

Contents

I.

The sun was a bloody smear melting in the Pacific as a pale figure bounded down ruddy sandstone cliffs to the beach. The breeze was a balm on hot skin as she strode through the sand onto the firmer surface soaked by the sea and launched her long body into the waves with a shout of exultation to scatter fish a hundred yards off shore.

She broke the top of a wave and rode it back in the falling dusk. The mansion on the cliffs was alight, so the servants had returned. Soon they'd find their employer's body stretched out on the gold satin sheets between the carved teak pillars of his bed. It would make ripples in the fabric of Hollywood, as those around him swarmed to grab pieces of his studio and his mistresses fought over the treasures and scraps.

She walked up the beach naked in the moonlight, shook out her long hair, and sighed. He'd been perfect for her purposes. She'd intended to keep him for the winter, but he was such an arrogant cad. Everything he did was a dare, a taunt as he flaunted his pride and prowess and she'd been much too hungry. At least he'd enjoyed it and didn't seem that surprised, but now she had to find other accommodations.

Lorelei sprang up the cliff and snatched her suitcase from his room before the maid entered, leapt to the roof, and put on her dress gazing inland at the Hollywood Hills across the scattered buildings of Los Angeles. The moonlight lit the high walls of the abandoned movie set of Babylon along a gravel stretch of Sunset Boulevard, like a castle of lust and avarice towering over its minions.

A high-pitched shriek came from the bedroom below that was followed by a long plea in Spanish to the Virgin of Guadeloupe. It was time to go.

* * *

Sarah's cardboard suitcase split apart when the train jerked to a stop in the little town of Lankershim. The laminated leather handle came off as it burst, exposing a red velvet jacket, crumpled silk hat, and a few precious silk underthings in the brilliant southern California sunshine streaming through the windows.

"Here, Miss." It was the man with the owl glasses and walrus mustache who'd been watching her since Oakland. He was standing behind her.

Sarah stiffened, ready to fend off an exploring hand. Her face grew warm as she tried to stuff her clothes back in the disintegrating suitcase and she glanced over her shoulder. A shiny new silver dollar was in the man's stubby fingers. She imagined her fair countenance red as a beet as she smoothed her rumpled beige jacket and skirt. "Sir, I cannot take charity."

"Pshaw, you ain't eaten since King City. I saw the look you had when other folks did. I been hungry before myself. There's a store on Lankershim Boulevard where you can get another suitcase and a café next door where the grub's good. All you can eat soup and crackers for a dime. Try the Mulligan stew. Chalk it up to luck and pass it on. God bless ya lass." The man pushed the heavy coin into her palm with a callused thumb, tipped his straw hat, and stepped onto the station platform.

"Thank you, sir!" Sarah called at his retreating back. She brushed a damp strand of hair from her forehead and lugged her worldly possessions toward the end of the coach.

The heat was something for October. Having grown up on Vancouver Island, Sarah was used to rain. She considered herself familiar with hot weather from summers in the Okanagan Valley of British Columbia, but the area around Los Angeles squatted in a smoky brown haze that seemed to grow as the heat did. The heat pressed against her face. Her chest felt tight. Sarah closed her eyes, and the sounds of rain on a cedar shake roof returned along with the pale face of her sister. Her fingers twitched. She rubbed them together at a memory of wiping sticky blood from Angeline's mouth and the hollow cough of influenza that had taken her sister into the damp ground.

She returned to her surroundings, fanned herself with a tattered copy of *Photoplay* magazine, and sat on a hard wooden bench in the shade of the platform's roof. On the magazine's cover were the fair hair and red lips of Lillian Gish, whom Sarah thought looked a lot like herself, surrounded by doodles and notes she'd made on the journey south. Hollywood was close, but she wasn't sure exactly where. Orange groves seemed to occupy most of the country at the moment and perfumed the air with a wonderful citrus smell. Fruit bins were stacked four high beside the station. More filled a wheezing flatbed truck crowned with a half-dozen Mexicans wearing battered straw sombreros, all of whom were staring at her intently.

She ignored them and opened her compact to check her face in the cracked mirror and reapply her lipstick. Sarah spied a man in a Stationmaster's uniform walking toward the ticket office and snapped it shut, "Excuse me sir."

The man smoothed his waxed mustache and tipped his blue cap, "At your service Miss."

"I'm trying to get to Hollywood… where the motion pictures are made."

"That's over the hill," he pointed to a low mountain range in the west mottled into tired greens and burnt browns by the ever-present sun, "shoulda gone on to Los Angeles. Take the Red Car trolley to Cahuenga, then all the way through the pass to Highland... and be sure and see Babylon down on Sunset Boulevard."

"Say what?"

"You know, from *Intolerance*. Still there and bigger than life swear to God. I seen Saint Mark's and Westminster Abby over in England in the War, but this is bigger. 'Course it's all wood and plaster and such, and it's fallin' apart, but sure is somethin' just the same sittin' in the middle of a field out on Sunset 'till the cows come home." The man checked his watch, snapped it shut, and placed it in his pocket, "You fixin' to work in the flickers?"

"I, I'd like that I suppose."

"You got the looks. Met Olive Thomas and the Gish sisters in Toluca Lake with Charlie Chaplin and Jack Pickford and they don't got nothin' on you Miss, if you don't mind me sayin' so. You look like 'em to be honest, 'cept for the shorter hair."

"Why thank you."

"No bother, it's true, but keep your eye out for flim-flam types and scoundrels over there. Place is fulla crooks. Mr. Griffith is makin' another big one at that new United Artists with Chaplin and Doug Fairbanks. I hear tell they need a whole buncha extras and they're always on the lookout for pretty ladies like you." He grinned, "You'd be perfect. Betcha get a job as soon as you show up."

"Do you think so?"

The Stationmaster nodded, "Sure do. Oh, the name's Carl Jones." He tipped his hat again and presented a hand.

She shook it, "Sarah Mae McCallum, from Victoria, in British Columbia."

"That's quite a piece to travel alone. Gotta say they grow 'em nice up there," he grinned, "you got quite a grip for a young lady if you don't mind my sayin' so. Well, gotta be gettin' back to work. Remember me when you're in the flickers Miss McCallum."

"Oh thank you, Mr. Jones. The red trolley eh?"

"Yep, there's one now." Carl pointed to a bright red coach coming down Lankershim, put fingers to his lips, and let out a shrill whistle. The trolley operator rang the bell, pulled a lever, and the big car rolled to a halt as he pulled the brake and rang the bell again. "Got a lady needs to get to Hollywood, Jake! There you go Miss McCallum." He escorted her to the trolley as electric cables buzzed and snapped overhead, holding his arm out at the step.

"Thank you kindly, Mr. Jones." Sarah gave him the radiant smile that had served her well since childhood, squeezed her tattered suitcase, and stepped aboard.

* * *

The next stop was at a dirt road with a red and gold hand-painted sign proclaiming **UNIVERSAL CITY**. Two chimps in purple diapers and bright red collars jumped from a wagon parked alongside as the trolley rolled to a stop and the shiny chains attached to them jingled. One stared at Sarah and his lips stretched in an impossibly wide grin. The other squatted and yanked at his bulging diaper. They made more faces as a man tugged on their leashes and led them up the road into the hills.

When the trolley reached Cahuenga Boulevard, she stepped off with her transfer at a little restaurant next to a battered adobe hotel that looked like it had been there since the Spanish days. Sarah went in, ordered a ham sandwich and orange juice for twenty cents, and stepped into the ladies room. She'd tied the suitcase shut with two scarves and had to unknot them to get her hairbrush. By the time she stepped out, the food was on the table. She sat down with a sigh and lifted an incredibly large glass of orange juice to her lips. "Oh," she blinked, took another sip, and then a gulp, "My...""Don't drink much orange juice?"A handsome hazel-eyed fellow at the next table ran a hand across sandy pomaded hair as he gave her a charming grin. He wore a crisp white shirt and bow tie, and had hung his coat and straw hat by the door. He reminded Sarah of Wallace Reid the actor or an older version of Jim the miner's son, who had been her first and only love for a brief time when she'd worked on her father's claim in the Klondike. Not that many hadn't tried since.

"Not often. It's rather dear where I'm from, and this glass is *huge*. I've just arrived from Vancouver actually."

"Canada? Quite a journey for a young lady your age. Are you visiting relatives?"

"Well, no, not exactly."

"Not traveling alone I hope. A lady such as yourself should have a chaperone on such an excursion at the very least."

"I have cooked in logging camps, worked with mining crews, herded cattle, dealt with wild animals, and can handle my own affairs, sir, but actually I am here to try my hand at motion pictures."

He ran manicured nails across the blond trace of mustache and held her gaze, "Mr. Griffith is looking for performers even as we speak."

"So I have heard, and perhaps I shall seek employment with him."

"Well, then, you must be born under a lucky star my friend. I am with Mr. Griffith myself, and can say without reservation that you would fill a part in our new motion picture *Broken Blossoms*. Why, just today he was telling me--"

Sarah leaned back in the red leather booth, "You're telling me that you're with United Artists?"

"Indeed, I am Warren Griffith, second cousin of Mr. David Wark Griffith from his ancestral home in Kentucky to be exact. Why just last night I was having dinner at Nat Goodwin's on the Santa Monica Pier with Miss Pickford and Mr. Fairbanks when--"

"Mary Pickford and Douglas Fairbanks... are you serious?"

Warren grinned and ran fingers across his lip as if twirling a nonexistent mustache, "It's a fact, Madame."

"Oh my word," Sarah put a hand to her own mouth, which she realized was hanging open, as Warren was staring at it, "Oh, pardon my manners, Mr. Griffith, my name is Sarah McCallum. But you're... you're serious?"

His hand slid across the table until his fingers barely touched the tips of hers and he winked, "Completely. Of course I'll have to make sure you're up to it. Do you have any acting experience?"

She nodded vigorously and took a breath. "I performed in plays at my girls' school in Vancouver, had the lead in a Robert Service pageant in Dawson City, and did a bit of vaudeville at the Strand in Seattle for Mr. Alexander Pantages. He has plans to build a theater here in fact, and promised me employment, but I shan't wait. Do you--"

"Wonderful. Where are you staying?"

"I'm not staying anywhere at the moment. I was planning to find accommodations this afternoon."

Warren blinked. "Then you're in luck again. We have several bungalows reserved for actors and actresses that you may be able to stay in free of charge, depending of course if you're hired, which I don't see much problem with at all, but of course I shall have to give you a screen test."

"A screen test?"

He nodded, "Shouldn't be any problem. Allow me to pay for your meal and we'll be on our way to your new career."

"Er, thank you, Mr. Griffith, but how do I know that you're on the up-and-up?"

Warren held out a creamy white gold-embossed card between two fingers with the name **Warren Griffith, Vice President in charge of Production.** Below it were the words **United Artists Motion Picture Corporation.**

Sarah turned the card over in her hand and returned a tentative smile.

"We discover our stars in the strangest places, Sarah. Olive Thomas was working a millinery counter in New York when she was discovered by the New Yorker magazine and then Ziegfeld you know. And Marion Davis--"

"And I shall meet your cousin, Mr. D. W. Griffith?"

"This very afternoon if he's back from location and the stars are in alignment."

Sarah fell silent as she waited for Warren to do something that would say *run*. He gave her that charming grin again and winked.

She swallowed, "I've just met you, sir, but I would be glad to take your card and arrive by appointment." She rose from the table.

He tipped an imaginary hat, "Sarah your reticence is perfectly understandable. You do appear to be what we're looking for, but I must tell you that we have quite a crop of young ladies arriving daily with similar aspirations. I do hope you find decent accommodations in the interim. I shall be out of the office for the next four days however, as I'm accompanying Roscoe Arbuckle and his lovely wife Minta to San Francisco this evening on the train. Please be careful and do not seek lodging in the vicinity of Selma Street, and avoid the rooming houses on Hawthorn entirely. You're obviously a well-raised girl and there are some rather bad apples there. I should hate to see you come to no good end while seeking gainful employment."

Sarah took one step toward the door before she turned and sat back down, "Very well, Mr. Griffith, I think I shall trust you."

* * *

After she'd finished the oversized sandwich she could hardly swallow from excitement, Warren led her to a scuffed Model T with a folded cloth top parked between the café and the old adobe hotel. A red-haired woman in a Mexican shawl eyed her as he helped her in. The woman lit a cigar, took a belt from a pewter flask, and smirked.

"Is something the matter, Miss McCallum?"

"Oh no, I just haven't seen a woman smoking a cigar, Mr. Griffith, and drinking in the middle of the day since Gastown in Vancouver."

He chuckled, "Where they service the sailors no doubt. We've got all kinds here too, Miss McCallum."

Warren walked to the front of the car, inserted the crank, and the engine roared to life on the first turn. He gave her a look of triumph, slapped dust from his hands, and jumped behind the wheel as she stood beside the car trying to reign in her smile. He stood up in the seat, took out a rag, wiped a bug from the flat glass windscreen, sat back down, and patted the leather seat beside him. Things were moving so quickly she could hardly believe it and the chance of making money before her meager savings were exhausted was a blessing. Sarah grinned at the oak-covered hillsides bathed in Southern California's golden afternoon light as a gust of wind billowed her skirt against the side of the dusty car. She smoothed it and stepped in.

Warren gripped a black billiard ball atop the gear shift as he tore his gaze from her legs to her face, "I live right up Lankershim in the hills and can arrange a screen test before we get to Hollywood," He said over the pop of the engine.

"Eh?"

"I'll write the report and have it ready when we get to the studio. It's not the usual procedure, but that way I can get it past two levels of useless hirelings who'll come between you and the real bosses. I have a camera, Klieg lights and makeup for that matter, and a typewriter complete with stationary and the proper letterhead. That way I'll show Miss Pickford or Mr. Griffith the report and we'll have you in a bungalow before nightfall. If it's Mary, her word is as good as any of the partners by the way, and Mr. Fairbanks, Mr. Griffith, or Mr. Chaplin will fall all over themselves when they meet you I'm sure. My word is wholly credible as to your abilities, and Miss Pickford is very supportive of aspiring actresses such as yourself. We've even got maid service and a swimming pool. Have you a bathing suit, Miss McCallum?"

"Er, no, I don't. Oh my. Is it far?"

"We'll get you one and it's not far in the least. I must say you are one lucky girl, although I should admonish you to keep your distance from Mr. Chaplin. He's got rather wandering hands as they say."

Sarah stared at Warren's oiled hair glistening in the sunlight, gave him a tentative smile, and nodded.

He put the car in gear and turned left in the opposite direction of Hollywood. Sarah hung onto the door as the engine rattled, watching traffic as he wound amongst cars, skirted the occasional horse, and passed a big truck full of vegetables. She slapped dust from her dress as they drove along a road called Ventura that skirted the hills and inhaled a scent she'd noticed ever since Redding. "What are those trees with the long leaves, Mr. Griffith?"

"Eucalyptus from Australia. It grows like a weed here."

"Are those what they make the poultices and cold rubs from?"

"There you have it. The damn Spanish Flu certainly sold a lot of that," he laughed, "there's a silver lining to everything I suppose. One might say money grows on trees around here." He turned between rows of sycamores, where the gravel trace of Lankershim crossed Ventura and wandered into chaparral slopes. "You'll be at the head of the line for a part that's opening up."

"What part?"

"Theda Bara is going on an extended sabbatical back East in order to correct some habits she's acquired and D.W. is planning to cast a vamp for the new studio to see if we can get a piece of the action. We're utterly without someone like that, and there's a lot of potential," he laughed, "the ol' stickler is going to let me direct one, and I couldn't help but notice that you have wonderful legs if you don't mind me saying so."

She smoothed her skirt again, "I played girls' hockey in Dawson City and Prince George, Mr. Griffith, as well as the girls' baseball team in Victoria, and herded cattle from horses in the Fraser River country as well. It's all good for the tone as they say."

He down-shifted with a howl from the gears. "You'd be marvelous in costume."

"You're not kidding?"

"Not at all, although you may need a dark wig. D.W. prefers brunettes for that type of role. He says blond isn't evil enough. Too virginal you know," His gaze was like the heat of a Klieg light beating against the side of her face, "How old are you, Miss McCallum?"

She stared ahead, "Um, eighteen."

Warren let out his breath and nodded.

* * *

They drove past sun-blistered ranch houses amid fine new homes of stucco and stone and came to a steep drive wandering up the slope to their left. On the right was a cream-walled mansion with a red tile roof that resembled a Moorish palace. Warren stopped the car and finally got it into first gear after three attempts to engage the flywheel with the clutch. "Hang on!"

She gripped the handle on the dash as they bumped up a narrow road between oaks to arrive at a rather rundown stone house surrounded by overgrown cactus gardens. The original road to the place was lined with the spiky alien shapes of huge century plants, and had long ago become a gully in winter rains. A broken retaining wall on the hill had mosaics of trees with bright fruits and colorful birds in their branches that were half-covered with the pale vines and blue trumpet blossoms of morning glories. A skinny Irish setter barked twice from where he was chained in the shade of a weeping willow, and a cloud of dust rose beneath his wagging tail.

"Hey, Duke," Warren stopped the car, turned off the wheezing engine, and came around to help her out, "It may not look like much, but it's free courtesy of the studio." He took her arm and she stepped down.

"It's... huge, Mr. Griffith."

"Part of an old Californio family's estate from the days of land grants, from the King of Spain and such. All this country hereabouts belonged to them. Not much to speak of for heating costs here. Care for a drink?"

"Oh no, Mr. Griffith, I don't drink. Besides, I heard the Volstead Act was ratified yesterday for the implementation of the prohibition of alcoholic beverages in the United States, and I don't want to be arrested or sent home. But didn't you say you had a motion picture camera?"

He gave her an unreadable look that morphed into another smile, "Around here we say to hell with the Eighteenth Amendment, doll, and we have until twelve a.m. January the seventeenth to drink up anyway."

"That's my birthday."

"Congratulations, and of course I have a camera, two of them as I said before, from the Triangle Studios in fact. After the influenza killed off most of their help, their equipment was spread amongst the three principals, one of whom is Mr. David Griffith, but enough of that. This way, Miss McCallum," He escorted her to the porch, "Watch your step please." Sarah lifted her skirts and stepped up. The gray boards creaked as she put the heel of a tall brown boot to them and he opened the door.

Inside was a living room with a stone fireplace surmounted by a dark wood mantle and two couches with Mexican blankets draped over them that flanked a low table with a green magnum of scotch upon it. Dark beams were overhead with an iron chandelier in a sheath of cobwebs. The place was dim and smelled like it needed a thorough cleaning, and Sarah's lip curled reflexively.

"Sorry for the mess," Warren stepped from the sunken living room up two stone steps and disappeared in a dim hallway, "Be back in a minute."

"What are you . .?"

"Getting the camera," he shouted from the back of the house, "for your screen test!"

"Shouldn't we do that outside for the light?"

"Of course." His voice echoed from the hall, "Make yourself at home, I won't be a minute."

Sarah glanced about. A big kitchen was in back done in red and yellow tile. She stepped in, ran a finger through dust across the tile counter, and examined a dirty six-burner double-oven Royal Charter Oak stove with an ash-choked wood box. Unkempt foliage filled the view beyond the grimy windows. Sounds came from the back of the house as Warren fumbled with something. Sarah rubbed her arms and turned toward the door. "I'm going to wait outside."

As she passed the hall Warren had disappeared into, a hand shot out and closed around her arm in a grip that made her catch her breath. *"Mr. Griffith!"*

A foul-smelling rag slapped across her face, and for an instant she thought of her lipstick smearing before she tried to tear it away. It burned her nose. Warren grabbed her wrist and wrenched her fingers away from her mouth, twisting her arm behind her back as her sinuses exploded with an acrid sting that hurt her eyes. The hand with the rag pressed tighter as he bent her head back, until she was staring at the dark beams with an iron chandelier like a wagon wheel in the night sky. She brought a heel down hard on the instep of Warren's shoe, ground with all her might, and tore the rag away from her face.

"Ow, bitch!" Something crashed into her temple and a flash of white devoured the dark circle of iron overhead.

II.

A pungent herb smell assaulted her nose. The sounds of crickets echoed in her ears. The insects' song rolled in and out like the tide along the beach where she'd grown up: in and out of focus. She was lying on warm sand on a summer night staring at stars. The stars were bright but fuzzy.

No!

Sarah blinked eyes that hurt and fought the weight shrouding her like a cloak. She wanted to sink back into sleep, to dream of running free in the woods with a friend she'd run to in times of doubt in her fantasies since she could remember. She could almost see those beautiful eyes…

No!

Rough wood beneath her scraped her shoulders. The herb smell was sharp and tonic. Underneath it was another smell like old death. The crickets roared in her head like fiddles played with knives and needles. Her throat ached. Her head hurt. Her arms and legs were spread in a very uncomfortable position and she tried to sit up.

"Ow!"

Sarah tugged at the ropes binding her wrists and ankles. She tried to make sense of her surroundings. The hillside above her glinted in moonlight as if shrouded in ice, and she fought to blink it into focus. No… it was mosaics, mosaics glimmering on a broken stone wall. A vision of a cemetery erupted, with her sister's polished red cedar coffin in a shaft of sun breaking through wet clouds. A pale face watched her from between the tombstones, whose eyes flashed blood.

Think! Remember!

A breeze danced across her stomach. It tickled her breasts. Her nipples hurt. She shook her head, and pain stabbed the back of it. She was raw between her legs. Sarah licked dry lips, smelled blood, and fought a sudden scream welling up beneath her ribs.

I've been raped!

Footsteps echoed downhill. She turned her face toward a dark stone house with yellow lights glowing in its windows. Warren... *Warren* was inside! The sound of a phonograph needle being placed on a record made a sharp shriek that preceded a torrent of sound, and *Alexander's Rag Time Band* began to play.

She rocked her hips. The cheeks of her butt broke a sticky film of blood.

I've been raped!

She jerked in her bindings, her head hit the board beneath her, and a white flash erupted in the back of her eyes. *I've been raped!* Sarah bit her lip and fought the urge to say it again and again like some dark chant drawing her into darkness. Getting free was all there was in the whole world, all that *mattered.* Self-pity was an indulgence she could ill afford.

She closed her eyes, and was back under blueberry bushes on Vancouver Island with black flies and mosquitoes hovering in a cloud around her. Night was falling. She could hear something big moving in the forest. Sarah had wandered away from the logging camp while her mother nursed her baby sister Angeline and her father worked to down a cedar from one end of a misery whip saw that was wider than the tent the family occupied. She was four years old and lost. She rested her chin on her knees and clutched a stick as darkness cloaked the world. She became tinier as night swallowed her. The sounds were a bear, and it was coming closer.

The Lady appeared when the bear was a few feet away, and with the most beautiful voice Sarah had ever heard, shooed him back into the forest like an errant puppy. Sarah spent the night in her arms with the only illumination the soft glow of the Lady's eyes. In the morning Sarah awoke alone.

She shook her head and tried to focus on the stars. The saving presence of the Lady was a childhood fantasy that couldn't help her now. She had to concentrate. Sarah closed her eyes.

Seven years later she'd fallen from a tree, broken her arm, and had to walk an hour to the logging camp. Sarah and a big cougar were both surprised when they met. She'd screamed bloody murder and used her good arm to throw rocks as she chased him into a salmonberry thicket with a cedar branch. A laugh rumbled her chest at the memory of that mountain lion as he crashed through the undergrowth emitting little grunts of fear. She thought she'd heard an answering laugh from somewhere nearby and imagined she'd pleased the Lady. No one would come for her here, and most assuredly not an imaginary protector of her childhood. She was on her own.

A sound so soft she would have missed it if her senses weren't straining for anything at all made her glance up. The pale shape of a huge owl hovered above her for a moment overhead, and its eyes flashed golden and green before it disappeared on silent wings.

Something moved. She froze. A dog snuffled, and its claws clicked on the boards. A wet nose investigated her leg, and a tongue licked tentatively. Duke's cold nose wandered up her thigh until he loomed over her with moonlight glistening in his coat. He licked at the blood, and Sarah trembled as words of protest balled in her throat. It *hurt.* She stared at the stars, bit her lip, and concentrated on breathing, "Duke," she hissed, "Duke, come here, honey!" Her fingers stretched toward the dog until the rope around her wrist dug into her. If she could get him to chew at the rope, she might get a hand free.

Duke looked up, snorted, and returned to her crotch.

"Dammit," her head fell to the boards, "please... *please* God, get me out of here!"

Silence greeted her entreaty. Sarah rocked her head from side to side and scanned the hillside for what she did not know. The flash of a pale figure made her blink, and she had a sensation like lips brushing her forehead. Sarah gasped and glanced around.

Duke sneezed on her stomach. It tickled. Sarah concentrated on the dog. She made kissing sounds, motioned with the fingers of her right hand, and held it as high as the rope allowed, "Chew on this!" Duke sniffed her hand. He began to lick her face. Her blood was on his breath. "Please, doggie." Her fingers wrapped in the long hair of Duke's right front leg and he made a little growl of protest, "The rope, please!"

The dog's eyes flashed green and he nipped at the rope with his teeth. He worried the knot for a brief moment and gave it a single jerk. His eyes flashed red before he yanked free from her grip and was gone.

"Oh thank you!"

The End of a Perfect Day, a popular song about the Hollywood Hotel, began to play in the house. Sarah craned her neck to scan the porch as the thick Victrola record skipped and hissed. She returned to her bindings. The knot had loosened slightly. She twisted her wrist and squeezed her right hand. She tried to spit on it, but her mouth was as dry as sand. Her eyes stung horribly. The house lights made halos.

The rope around her wrist had moved down to her hand. It felt like it was crushing the bones. Sarah ground her teeth, squeezed her eyes shut, and tried to make her hand even smaller as she tugged and twisted.

Her hand came free.

She stifled a shout, flexed it, rolled toward the rope holding her left hand, and tugged at the knot. She got a loop loose, worked the rope out slowly, and slid it off her other wrist. She sat up, making little tearing sounds as dry blood yielded its grip on her skin. She scooted down to get slack in the ropes around her ankles, leaned far to the left, then to the right, pulled loose the knots, and was free.

Sarah wobbled to her feet and put fingers between her legs. She winced as the crickets grew louder. The only way she knew out of here was around the house and down the drive. She scanned the hillside for another route and stepped off the platform onto cactus spines.

"Ah!" She sat on the rough boards, "Shit!" She grabbed the sole of her right foot and pulled a spine out of the ball, then another from the fold of her big toe. Stinging tears welled in her eyes and her vision blurred again. She wiped at them with a bloody hand, "Please God... *please* get me out of here!" She swallowed, "Please *Lady!* I know you're there. I haven't forgotten!"

Footsteps echoed on the porch. Her breath caught in her throat.

"You take the high road an' I'll take the low road, and I'll be a whorin' afore ya!" Warren's silhouette tottered against the moonlit yard as he waved a large bottle and stumbled off the porch onto the gravel drive. There was the sound of a zipper, and he peed an arc that sparkled as it splattered cactus. Sarah went flat on the boards and tried to make herself small as he glanced uphill. "Yo-ho! Time for another go around, my lovely?" His voice dropped, "Time for another screen test, my little broken flower? Ha!" He staggered up the hill through cactus and overgrown flowerbeds with his boots crunching gravel, "Good evening, my little Canadian cherry blossom. The boss sure loved you. You are gonna fill the till before this one's over. Ha!"

She lay still as death, listening to Warren climb the path until his head rose from between her breasts and grew out of her stomach like a gremlin in a bad fairy tale. Warren knelt at her feet, licked his lips, and chortled, "Yum." His sour breath rolled over her in a damp cloud of scotch and tobacco. A drop of spittle landed in her navel as he dropped his pants. The heel of a boot scraped her thigh. Sarah held her breath, watching through half-closed eyes as his penis nodded at her. Warren wobbled over her with his hand pressing hard on her thigh as he put the bottle down on her left.

Sarah seized his scrotum in her right hand and squeezed with all she had. Warren let out a strangled gasp. Her left hand wrapped around the neck of the bottle, and she swung at his head as he clawed at the hand crushing his balls.

His howl was cut short as the bottle greeted his temple with a resounding *thunk*. The thick glass didn't break and she swung again. It bounced off his head and he rolled to the right. Sarah straddled his chest with both hands around the neck of the heavy half-full magnum and raised it over her head as scotch splashed her shoulders and soaked her hair. Warren made a gargling sound silenced by the bottle breaking with a crash across his nose to spray a glistening fan in the night, and whiskey stung her eyes. Sarah sprang off him and stumbled backward rubbing her eyes. She teetered on the edge of the platform afraid of stepping onto the cactus, yet terrified he was going to come at her while she stood there naked and half-blind.

Violent trembling shook the boards beneath her feet as she got an eye open. Warren lay with his head tilted back. His face was black with blood in the moonlight. He stared at the sky, vibrating like a chicken she'd seen with its neck broken. She rubbed the other eye, knelt to the boards, picked up a thick shard of the bottle, and edged closer with the glass in her hand. She put a foot on his stomach and pushed.

A gurgling erupted from Warren's chest as blood bubbled from his smashed nose like a glistening cluster of grapes. Sarah pushed again and more bubbles came, but not as many. Warren's head rocked to the side as his tongue flopped out of his mouth like a dead dog's.

"You foul creature!"

An owl hooted from the trees as she flung the glass into the cactus and knelt to yank off his boots.

* * *

She threw open the door of the house, seized a fireplace poker from beside the hearth, and held it before her as she stalked from room to room ready to split the skull of anyone who appeared. A back bedroom had a big camera and two Klieg lights. There was a cluttered darkroom behind it. After ascertaining there was no one there, she retreated. The house was empty. She locked the doors, wandered in a circle beneath the rusting chandelier, and froze at the sounds of moaning until she realized it was herself. She slaked a terrible thirst with water in the kitchen and headed to the bathroom.

It took forever to bathe. Her limbs kept breaking into spasms and she dropped things. A part of her seemed to be far away from it all, listening to the sounds coming from her with detachment. She jumped at the sound of Duke on the porch and her head felt full of cotton. She followed the exploration of her fingers with a jet from a hose she screwed onto the brass spout of the tub. She rocked on her knees in the dirty tub, watching pink water flow down the drain. She washed her hair, scrubbed her skin with coconut soap, and gazed into red, puffy eyes in the fogged mirror. She found gauze, tape, and Mercurochrome in the medicine cabinet and bandaged her foot. She went into the kitchen with a towel wrapped around her body, another around her head, and the iron poker in her hand ready to swing at anything that moved. There were two cans of Campbell's Tomato Soup in a cupboard and she put them in a saucepan.

A telephone box was on the wall. Sarah ate staring at it as the sky began to lighten. Duke whined on the porch. She found a waxed paper package of greasy bacon in the ice box and gave him some. It was about time for an iceman or milkman to make his rounds. She listened for the sound of someone in the driveway. She glanced at the telephone again, stood up, and shook her head.

She found her suitcase amongst a pile of women's things in a back bedroom. Warren had done a thorough job of pawing through them, the beast. She put on her beige blouse and skirt, slipped her feet into her high lace-up boots, and pulled her red velvet hat over damp blond hair. She went to the bedroom with the two Kliegs and a big camera on a wooden tripod. On the camera's wooden shell was a brass plaque with **Keystone Studios** etched on it. She moved around the two Kliegs toward a bed covered by a silk comforter with a disconcertingly large spot of blood on it and shivered. The Kliegs almost touched the ceiling and were aimed at the bed.

There was a stack of film cans on a dresser. She picked one up. **Danielle, 8/12/19** was hand-printed on the paper label in thick black letters. She picked up another. **Christine, 9/13/19** was on it. She picked up a third, and **Sarah, 10/29/19** stared back at her.

"Sonofabitch!"

She squeezed the can until it buckled, threw it on the floor, and picked it up again. It was going to burn.

The den was festooned with trophy head mounts of animals with an ancient rifle above a stone fireplace. A large revolver lay on the table next to a leather easy chair. She put down the poker, snatched up the gun, and opened the action. It was a loaded Colt Army .45, just like her father's. Sarah had learned to use one by the age of ten in the North's endless summer days full of grizzly bears and wished she'd had a bigger one even then. She clutched the can to her breast and squeezed the thick butt of the pistol in her other hand with a sigh.

She went to Warren's bedroom, opened the nightstand, and gasped. A large roll of bills was nestled amongst women's scarves, expensive French sheep gut condoms, and a little chrome-plated Colt automatic. She put down the film can, picked up the money, glanced down the hall at the telephone, and bit her lip. A pair of women's khaki jodhpur riding pants hung in the closet, and Sarah took off her skirt and put them on. She tucked them into the tops of her dress boots and walked into the yard.

Sarah climbed between cactus and morning glory as dawn's first light illuminated the tops of trees. Mourning doves cooed from the branches of chaparral oak and eucalyptus, and the tannic smell of their leaves filled the cool air. A red tail hawk called. Squirrels chattered on their quest for acorns.

Sarah gazed up the hill at a half-buried stone wall with the remnants of a mosaic of a woman in blue robes with red eyes that was half-covered by vines. She stepped off the path and approached it. A third of it was gone and the woman's lower half was obscured by the dirt of the hillside, but the woman's eyes were definitely red. That seemed odd for some Mexican saint. The woman had wings of chipped yellow glass that spread out behind her and a bird that might have been an owl perched on her shoulder. Sarah returned to the well.

Warren lay where she'd left him, on weathered gray boards covering a low circular wall molded into the side of the hill. As she neared, a crow cawed and burst from the bushes to flap up the canyon with red dripping from its beak. Warren's right eye was gone from the socket.

The planks beneath him had separated during their struggle to reveal a dark void from which a stench wafted up on the cool air. She moved a board away, and the shaft of an old well appeared from which the smell of death came.

Something tickled her spine, "Danielle and Christine." She lifted a board and slid it to the edge of the well, raised another, and piled it atop that. Sarah stepped over Warren, put her back against the ancient stone wall with her heels against his chest, and shoved. Warren's head flopped into the void as if he were inspecting it before his shoulders took a dive and drew his legs after him. His bare buttocks glowed like twin pale moons in the waxing day for a moment, and he fell into darkness to land with a thud.

Sarah turned the planks over so the blood was on the underside, put them back in place, and spread the dusty ochre soil across them. She wiped her hands and walked back to the house.

III.

Sarah found a can of Hills Brothers Coffee, made some cow-boy-style in a blackened pot on the old stove, and settled the grounds with cold water. She sat on the porch in a peeling rocking chair with the gun in her lap and closed her eyes. Mourning doves cooed and warbled in the branches overhead like voices from a more peaceful world. Whatever Warren had given her, she felt like she weighed a thousand pounds. Sarah closed her eyes and imagined the Lady from her childhood watching her. She saw an owl with golden eyes and its wings stretching across the stars. She lifted an arm. It fell back on the chair. No milkman or iceman had appeared. Perhaps the house was too isolated to expect a visit. She knew she should be far away... but where? She couldn't think. The thought she might be pregnant grew a knot in her stomach. What could she do? Would the police in Los Angeles help? Would they arrest her? Might she be charged with murder? Would she bear some bastard child of that man? Would they send her to jail? Send her home? Sarah had no home to go to.

The smells of the chaparral hills strengthened as the sun touched them. She rocked as doves cooed, unrolled the money, and began to count it. There was eight hundred fifty-seven dollars in American currency, along with the three Canadian twenties and twenty-seven American dollars she'd had in her purse. It was enough to rent a house for a year with money to spare.

Warren's dusty Model T squatted in the driveway. She stared at it and yawned as the day grew brighter. She poured another cup of coffee to fill the void inside her, and the thick evaporated milk from a little can swirled in its darkness like a wisp of smoke from a cloudy future.

Someone might know Warren's car, although every Model T looked exactly the same except for whether it was a truck or a sedan. She certainly wasn't going to hoof it. Driving was easy. She'd run countless trips on the logging roads of Vancouver Island from the age of thirteen and certainly wouldn't make such an awful racket shifting as Warren had. Hell... the sonofabitch *owed* her that car.

As she sat rocking and listening to the cooing of doves, an odd peace came over her. She'd been drugged, raped, and had killed a man with her bare hands, or at least with a bottle. His money was in her hand. His pistol was in her lap. His car sat under a weeping willow with her savior Duke under it in the shade. Sarah smiled at the dog and shrugged sore shoulders. It must have been the shock and drugs that had made her think his eyes had changed color like that. She felt strange, as if part of her were removed from her mortal quandary watching her, awaiting a decision.

She dug teeth in her lip and tallied her losses. Having her mom die when she was four years old was worse than this. Her brother Paul dying at a faraway place called the Somme to be buried in some unmarked muddy grave in France was worse. Watching her father and sister grow pale as ghosts and vomit blood as they succumbed to the influenza was much worse. Angeline, who she'd held as a baby, had died in her arms. Now there was only Sarah to worry about, and here she was in a late October that felt like summer, healthy and with more money than she'd ever seen. She poured another cup of coffee and spit out the grounds. There's always something between life and perfection, but the coffee still tasted good. She took another gulp out of principle.

There were jerry cans of petrol in the shed and she filled the tank of the car, unwound the contents of the **Sarah** film into a pile on the gravel driveway, and splashed gas on it. She struck an Ohio Blue Tip match on the thigh of the jodhpurs and tossed it. An orange billow of flame erupted as the brown film stock withered and danced like snakes from the maw of Hell. When there was nothing left but a black spot on the gravel, she went back in the house.

A dark alligator leather suitcase with a big strap and brass buckle sat amongst a dozen others in a loft. She took it down and put her clothes in it. It wasn't a quarter full, but she'd fill it handily when she reached a decent clothier. A sack of Purina Farm Chow sat in the kitchen, and she took a heavy glass bottle of milk with an inch of cream atop it from the ice box and poured some onto the dry food in Duke's bowl. Sarah poured herself a glass and rubbed the dog behind the ears as he buried his face in the food. She scratched the base of his wagging tail. "You saved me, fellow."

Duke's tail beat faster. He looked up with the normal brown eyes of a dog.

"Well anyway, thank you."

She took the little automatic and slid it into her lead-beaded purse and hid the big .45 under the cushions of the couch. The suitcase went in the boot of the car. She put on her pigskin gloves and took the crank from its clip on the fender. Sarah yanked and tugged, but the engine wouldn't turn over. She put a rock under the front tire, checked to see that it was out of gear, and tried again. The crank bucked in her hands as the engine roared to life, almost hitting her in the face. She fell on the drive cursing, got up, dusted off, and climbed in.

When she reached the road, she examined the cream-walled Moorish castle across the way with wrought iron bars over its windows and a red tile roof. An Oriental man in a straw coolie hat clipped rose bushes in the yard, and he looked up and smiled. Sarah waved back as the house disappeared in the trees. A skinny grey fox with a squirrel in its mouth darted across the dirt road and dashed up the trunk of a leaning chaparral oak.

At a bend, she came upon a canary yellow roadster that was half off the road and nosed into the bushes. A pretty young woman in a straw sun bonnet stood beside it. Her fair hair was molded into spiral curls that bounced across a yellow sun dress over legs shod in sandals with leather straps spiraling to her knees. Sarah double-clutched the car, down shifted, and rolled to a stop, "Hello... um, do you need assistance?"

"Oh yes!" The girl nodded vigorously. Her startling violet eyes were wide with relief as she opened the passenger door, sprang onto the frayed leather seat, and gave Sarah a damp hug, "You're a godsend, sister! Ran the fuckin' car off the road I was so mad! Third Locomobile I've wrecked this year, goddamn it! The... the... *bastard!*" She made a loud sigh, "Serves me right, for trusting *any* man!"

Sarah swallowed at the language spewing from the girl's lips and fought the inexplicable smile beginning to twist her own, "Having a bit of trouble, eh?"

"I should say! Just because one tipples a bit and likes to try out a few things doesn't mean she's fair game for a man's friends! The... the *cad!*" She turned as the car lurched into motion, put a hand on the dash, the other to her breast, and absently ran a fingertip over a bruise on her neck that looked like it had been made by a mouth, "Oh, excuse me toots, I'm Olive, Olive Thomas."

"Um, ah, I'm Sarah McCallum."

"Nice to meet ya sister, I'm going all the way to Hollywood if you don't mind. I'll gladly have Mr. Selznick pay you for the trouble and buy you petrol should you need any. Oh... that bastard!"

The fog in Sarah's head began to part, "You *are*... you're Olive Thomas from the motion pictures, and Ziegfeld, and Harpers, and Vogue!"

Olive batted long lashes, "Yeppers, hon."

"I saw you in *The Follies Girl,* oh, and *Prudence on Broadway* at the Orpheum in Vancouver. You were wonderful! And *Madcap Madge,* but your hair looked so much darker."

"Thanks toots, it's the film stock. Those were Triangle flickers. I loved makin' *Madcap Madge,* got to mess with a couple fellas who thought they were the cat's meow on that one." She made a loud sigh, "Triangle's just a memory now. The influenza killed all the stars 'cept me and Alma Rubens, and she's into that heroin now. Makes for awful boring conversation what with her head droopin' all over the place," Olive shook hers, "she's done with the flickers and can't even get a look now. Oh well, I'm with Selznick nowadays. We just got *The Glorious Lady* in the can. They even wrote a song for me they're playin' all over the place. You hear it yet? I'll take you to see the movie if you want and I can get you a record for your Victrola. Ever been to a movie premier? It's the cat's meow. I'm readin' the script for my next one right now, called *Out Yonder.*"

"Oh my word... a motion picture premier?"

"Sure, toots. You got an accent. You're a Canuck huh?" Olive gave her an appraising look, "Bet half these randy fellas 'round here are just rarin' to jump your bones, not to mention some of the gals. Have you met some of the girls here?" She ran a manicured hand along Sarah's jodhpurs, "Jeez, you got legs up to *here.* So, whatdya do, you a dancer?"

Sarah squeezed the big wooden wheel and negotiated a turn, "I've... just arrived, actually."

"Well, if you want a job, Mr. Selznick will fall out of his chair to give you a screen test. Damn, you're built like a dancer. Wish I had legs like that." She winked an eye the color of lilacs, and the dusting of freckles over the bridge of her nose quivered, "Just don't bend over to pick anything up while you're in them offices. Bastards are all the same. Sometimes I wish I were like those Gish girls and could be happy with dames," she made a loud sigh, "give this girl the ol' stiff one, in spite of the trouble it comes with," Olive smirked, "it's the sonsabitches they're hung on most of the time. Did you know the rich Roman women had boy slaves just for fun, eunuchs that were proud-cut like a horse? They could still get it up, but nothin' came out I guess so no damn babies." She giggled, "Cute boy slaves with no blowback. Now... that'd be convenient, huh?"

The echo of cruel laughter exploded in Sarah's skull accompanied by a painful flash of light. She ground her teeth, kept her eyes on the road, and tried to retract from the chafing seam of the jodhpurs between her legs reminding her of her situation. She had no idea where she was going.

"Jack's okay most of the time. That's my husband, Jack Pickford. You know, who played Tom Sawyer? Mary's little brother? He can handle his morphine but he's no good on coke. It makes him brag too fuckin' much. This time he really went too far and tried to pass me off to one of his friends like I was some goddamn present." She snorted, "Hell, I'm makin' more dough than he is now, so maybe I'll give *him* to "ol Marie Dressler. She'd break his back. I mean I've been with some of his friends, toots, but that's *my* decision. The bastard! God knows what kind of mouth some damn fella's got when he's drinkin' with his chums. You've got to watch your image 'round here what with Chaplin knockin' up that fifteen-year-old and everybody sleepin' with half the extras in town. I ain't no goddamn extra!" She groaned, "Them scandal muckers workin' for Hearst would love to jump on any of us, and the goddamn Temperance Movement's screwin' things up to high heavens."

Olive put a sandaled foot on the dash and scratched a bruise on her knee, "Jesus, can you believe they actually *passed* the Eighteenth Amendment? Can you believe the states *ratified* it? Shit, I mean *Prohibition?* Now the goddamn Volstead Act's passed and it's really gonna happen. First they went for the heroin and coke with the Harrison

Act, now they go for the booze, and then they come for *us!*" She scowled at the treetops, "Jesus fuckin' Christ, Hollywood may not survive the goddamn Twenties! I'll have to move to some island!" She put a ring-covered hand on Sarah's arm, exposing a purple bruise on the inside of her elbow where the frilly sleeve of her sun dress ended, "Sorry, I'm probably shockin' your shoes off. I'm talkin' like you're one of Mabel's gang and we don't even know each other, but you just look so... so like you belong here, Sarah, with them ridin' pants and no makeup and all. I like it: a tough guy dame. It shows independence. You're cute like that. Do you ride horses?"

"I herded cattle in the Fraser River country."

"Wherever the hell that is. I dressed like that when I made *Toton* and it was a hoot. Did you say you just arrived?"

"Er, yes."

Olive made another stage sigh, "I need a turn at the steam baths and a massage. What do you say to a steam and a rub-down?"

"Eh?"

"It's fun. After a hard night, you just can't beat it and you look like you've had one too. Your eyes are red as beets, toots. You been doin' nose candy? Hope he was worth the ride. Don't worry, it's on me. Just wait 'til the boys see you after I've got you all spruced up," she ran purple-nailed fingers down Sarah's leg again, "gotta get you a costume for Halloween," Olive put a hand to her forehead and produced another groan, "and I'm still recovering from my birthday last week!"

She went on nonstop as they reached Cahuenga and paralleled double trolley tracks through the pass to Hollywood. Olive pointed out the occasional home on the hillside that belonged to some actor or director, and those of several people that she described as of "independent means." "Means they don't have to work while doin' their damndest to screw ya. Full time job, toots."

Sarah did her best to concentrate on driving as the fog in her head began to lift. She imagined Warren's face staring at the moon with bubbles billowing from his nostrils. The moon divided and became the pale cheeks of his butt as he disappeared into a hole in the ground. She felt like someone was looking over her shoulder, glanced behind her, and rubbed her eyes.

When they approached Hollywood Boulevard with its clang of trolleys and honk of horns, Olive fell silent. She watched Sarah, who was biting her lip and wondering which way to turn. "Right," Olive pointed and Sarah turned, "How old are you?"

"Um, eighteen."

"Bet you're not with a complexion like that. I got in the dancin' biz younger than that back East. Hell, I screwed Florenz Ziegfeld when I was sixteen on the roof of the New Amsterdam Theater while a thousand people stood in line down on the street waiting to see *me*. I just turned twenty and feel like an old maid sometimes."

"Well, ah, not a maid."

Olive shrieked, "Hell no! If you got it, use it toots. I got a big 'ol place on Wilshire, a flat in New York, a lease on a country place on Long Island, and that place up Lankershim where you found me. I got invites to every party anybody who's anybody throws around here, an income that's almost obscene, and I'm married to Jack Pickford. Kinda, anyway," her cheeks bulged, "things could be worse." Olive pointed left and they turned again, "We'll have us a nice steam, a cold dip, and a massage. They've got these Swedish girls who really get the kinks out. Watch out for Sonya; she'll do more than that if you give her the eye. We'll have one of the girls do our hair too. I wish my maid Blanche was there. She's the best. Then we'll eat at this place where all the waiters look like Greek gods and we'll go over to Gower and I'll show you around the studio and introduce you to Alan Crosland. He's directing my next flicker. I got my brothers Jim and Billy jobs with no trouble there, and you're a hell of a lot better lookin' than they are. I got a big director from Paramount sleeping on the couch where you picked me up for that matter. So... how's that sound?"

"Um, I--"

"Good. Here we are." Olive pointed to a beige bungalow under the shade of sycamores, and Sarah pulled up behind a limousine parked at the curb and killed the engine. A wrought iron fence surrounded a small garden in the yard with marble nudes and an artificial brook that bubbled into a pond full of giant goldfish under the shade of magnolia trees with huge, waxy white blossoms. A well-dressed woman with hair freshly curled emerged from the front door as it was opened by a tall middle-aged black man in a gray uniform, and a white poodle in a sparkling collar pulled her toward the gate as her heels clattered on the pink flagstones. The black man in the uniform dashed forward to open it for her.

Olive waved, and the woman blew her a kiss as a chauffeur opened the door of the limo. "That's Louella Parsons from New York. She's giving me good press right now, but I'll tell you 'bout that bitch sometime. I wouldn't trust her as far as I could throw her," Olive made a face, "she scares even that sonofabitch Zukor with her fuckin' forked tongue. That's what I mean about watching yourself around the press. She'll probably say she saw me ridin' in some dented ol' Model T in the papers tomorrow and make out I ain't got a pot to piss in," she shrugged, "oh well," Olive stepped down from the car, put two fingers to her lips, and let out a shrill whistle that made Sarah jump, "Hey George, help this lady with her bag!"

The black man pasted a semblance of a grin across his face as he strode to their car, tipped a gray version of a conductor's cap, and bowed, "Yes Miss Thomas, I mean Pickford."

They're both okay, but how 'bout just Ollie, George?"

George displayed a nicer smile, "Certainly, Ollie."

"Here ya go." Olive produced a damp role of bills from between her breasts, peeled one free, and handed it to George.

"Thank you ma'am."

"Cut it out. It's Ollie, honey."

"Yassum."

"George, cut it out!" Olive burst into laughter. She stood on tiptoe and kissed George on his mahogany cheek to Sarah's wide-eyed stare. His last grin was best.

* * *

Once inside, Olive checked the big suitcase with a snooty woman behind a pink travertine counter who reminded Sarah of a particularly unpleasant schoolmarm in Victoria and led her through a door into an anteroom festooned with couches, tables, and vases of yellow roses where women were having tea, and beyond that to a room full of polished wooden lockers. Olive opened one, put her straw sun hat on top of it, and yanked her dress off over her head to reveal a silk brassiere, garter belt, and silk stockings. Sarah's eyes widened at her lack of proper underwear. Olive unwound the straps of her sandals and put them in the locker, unhooked the stockings, slid the garter belt down to her knees, and stepped out of it. "Get naked honey. Towels are over there."

Sarah glanced around the room and swallowed.

"Come on, toots."

Sarah took off her too-warm clothes and glanced at the damp spot in the crotch of the jodhpurs as she stuffed them in a locker. She examined the bruises on her arms and legs, the scuff marks around her wrists and ankles, and hugged herself. Olive had a bemused look as Sarah hung her clothes in the locker and stuffed her lead-beaded purse heavy with Warren's automatic and money under the riding pants. Is it... is it safe in here?"

"Oh yeah don't worry. Boy, sweetheart, you must have some rough friends." She gave a dismissive look at Sarah's mismatched clothes, "We have gotta go shopping after this. Them clothes don't cut the mustard around here. Got any money?"

"Yes, some, I--"

"Don't worry I do. I can get stuff for free anyway. There's

places that fall all over themselves here to get on the studio's checkbook by having you wear their clothes. All the real stars get 'em free just to be seen in their stuff. Oh, and always say no if somebody asks you if you have money around here by the way. It's jake to never tell a fella you got any loot. With your looks you can always make the boys buy it."

"Jake?"

"Yeah, that's like great, ya know? Let's get wet."

After showering, they headed to the steam room with their hair turbaned in towels past a pink marble pool with several middle-aged women clustered at the shallow end. A tall young blonde who was totally nude stood like a gilded statue at the far end before she dove in and swam across the glittering marble bottom with her long, tan body undulating in clear water. She came up with a splash at the near end and swept golden hair across muscular shoulders. Sarah stared. The woman stared back, eyed Sarah's bruises, flashed perfect teeth, and winked.

Olive opened a door at the far end and a cloud of steam poured out. Sarah followed her in and sat on a cedar bench. She could hardly see, but they seemed to have the place to themselves. "My word, that woman's stark naked and as tan as a man who digs ditches!"

"That's Sonya, one of the sun worshipers. Doug Fairbanks does it all the time. You'll meet him. He's gonna be my brother-in-law as soon as Mary gets loose of Owen, that's her husband. They all lay out naked by some pool all day 'til they're brown as uncle George out there. It sure makes her hair blond."

"She's--"

"Beautiful?"

"Well yes," Sarah eyed her pale legs, "In a rather unfeminine sort of way, I suppose."

"It ages the skin, but I'd try it if I weren't under contract. Even with all the lotions they got, I just freckle. Shanty Irish ya know. Name's really Duffy. Sonya's strong as hell too," Olive chuckled. "She'll crack your back like an oyster if you let her."

"That's the masseuse?"

"Yep," Olive giggled, "and she was givin' you the eye toots."

Olive ran water into an earthenware bowl from a faucet at the end of the bench. "Gets too hot you can pour some of this on you."

"All right," Sarah gazed around the steam-filled room, took a breath, and tried to relax. She closed her eyes and began to drift off, until a sudden sharp sting awoke her and she jerked erect, "Ow."

"Whatsamatter?"

"I'm... sore," Sarah's shoulders slumped, and she put fingers between her legs.

"Musta been a stallion."

The sound of steam hissing from jackets at the back of the room grew shrill in her ears. Sarah stood up.

"Honey, what's wrong?"

Sarah's voice balled in her throat when she tried to speak but choked on something she didn't want to hear.

Olive put hands on her shoulders, "Hey... some bastard force himself on you?"

Sarah's breath came out as a wheeze, and she nodded.

"Lay down hon, just relax. Let me see."

Sarah clutched the towel to her breasts and lay down. Olive's hands parted her knees, but Sarah choked back a sob and slapped her hand away, "No! Please!"

Olive made an exasperated sigh, "Honey, it's all right for Chrisake, let me see."

Sarah burst into tears, "For God's sake... *no!*"

Olive put soft lips to her ear, "I'm your friend, Sarah."

Sarah moaned, closed her eyes, and parted her legs.

"Jesus Christ! The fuckin' pieceashit! You're red as a lobster! Damn! Listen toots, it happened to me when I started at Ziegfeld with a stagehand. Happened at a party in Laurel Canyon when I first got here too, but that bastard got his comeuppance let me tell ya. I can't even talk about it but nowadays I got fellas who can square-up with some sonofabitch pronto, even coppers who'll toss him off the cliffs at Pacific Palisades for a few bucks and a bottle. We'll get the filthy lug! What's the bastard's name?"

Sarah lay with her privates being examined by a film star, blinking at tendrils of steam and fighting the fuzziness in her head with all her might. None of this seemed real. She hadn't the slightest idea what to say.

Olive probed with a finger, "That hurt?"

"Ow," Sarah's breath whistled between her teeth as she balled a fist and fought the impulse to knock Olive across the room, *"yes!"*

"Sorry."

Sarah rocked on the wet cedar bench and stared at the droplets forming on the cedar ceiling, "I can't believe you did that!"

Olive patted Sarah's forehead, "Said I'm sorry toots. So what's his name? I got friends. Nobody's gonna hurt you when you're with me. If it's one of my neighbors, I gotta know right now."

"He's dead." Sarah's voice was flat in the steam-filled room, as if coming from someone far away.

"Huh?"

"I--"

"Sarah, you... you put it *to* the lug?"

It hadn't been but hours and she might well be putting her neck in a noose in a country full of strangers. Sarah bit her lip, wiped her face, and nodded, "I had no choice, Olive, he--"

"You did?" Olive squealed, "You *did?* You goddamn fuckin' Amazon... you *did!"*

Sarah sat up and tucked the towel between her legs, "I--"

Wet kisses rained across Sarah's cheeks and mouth as Olive put hands on Sarah's shoulders with a smile as big as the California sun, "Goddamn, I *love* you! You're *amazing!* Where did you do it? What's his name? Was he big? How did you do it? Did you bury him all by yourself, or is he just layin' about somewhere stinkin' things up like the dirty dog he is? Oh... *wow!*"

"I... shhhhh!"

Olive burst into giggling, "You have got to tell me everything! I won't tell a soul but this is just too good! It's fuckin' *great!* Oh Sarah... we were *meant* to meet like this!"

IV.

The story of her first day in Los Angeles came out accompanied by frequent bouts of sobbing and copious hugs from Olive, who listened open-mouthed to her tale. She caressed Sarah's trembling back, urged her to go on when she sputtered to a stop, and put fingertips to Sarah's bruises as if they were the stigmata of Christ himself. Olive whispered encouragement over and over when Sarah sputtered to a halt until she began again. Sarah's tears came in a flood, merging with the sweat and steam pouring down her cheeks.

Sarah returned Olive's kisses between bits of memory that surfaced in a rush and spilled out of her mouth as they rose into her mind from where they seethed beneath the surface. She could hear Warren's laughter and imagined she was lying at the bottom of a dark well. She saw the real well in her memory and shuddered. She heard other men's voices and wrinkled her nose as she smelled a sharp odor like paint and the cloying stench of death. The memory of a stabbing light beating against her eyelids and the looming silhouette of someone or something huge and horrible arose, and her voice cracked, "I cannot *bear* to think I might be pregnant!"

"Sarah hon, don't worry. There's a Gypsy lady with stuff for it. We can go to her bungalow right now if you want."

"What stuff?"

"Couple a' potions, one tastes like crap and the other she puts up you with a turkey baster. I know girls who've been knocked up four or five times in this town and never missed a casting call. Hell, there's--"

"No!" Sarah ground her teeth and stared into steam. Duke looming over her in moonlight flashed across her vision. His eyes flashed green, then as red as the sun melting into the sea... and somehow it calmed her.

"Well, chances are you aren't anyway. Is it your time of month hon when you're fertile? You know--"

"I... no, I don't think so."

"Well anyway, there's a doctor the studios use who can fix it once and for all if you are, no muss no fuss, and nobody knows the better. I'll pay for it, so let's not be so dreary about it okay?" Olive hugged her, "And if you got a dose, he can fix that too." Her fingers wrapped around Sarah's and she kissed her cheek, "Come on hon."

"Come on where?"

"I'm gettin' you something to wear. Shopping always helps at times like these, toots."

They showered, had their hair and nails done, and headed for a store.

* * *

"That sonofabitch ain't named Griffith," Olive held a beaded satin slip that passed for a dress to Sarah's shoulders, "He's a fuckin' cameraman for Mack Sennett named Kloss, or was, anyway, who tries to get into all the big parties and grab girls fresh off the farm like 'bout a thousand other lugs 'round here. Mabel Normand knocked two of his teeth out at a bash in Pacific Palisades when she caught him crawlin' all over her gal-pal Clarine. Those two are... never mind. Olive squeezed Sarah's hand again, "And no offence about farms toots."

"We didn't have a farm."

"Anyway nobody'll miss him. He's an obnoxious little shit from somewhere in the Midwest without any local connections, from fuckin' North Dakota or something." She placed a matching cloche satin hat that came down over the ears on Sarah's head, stood back, and nodded her approval, "This is the new fashion 'round here. It's called a flapper and it's the cat's meow at parties. The fellas can't see your eyes when you're talkin' to somebody else and that's pretty handy toots. Lotsa girls are cutting their hair to go with it. Your hair's pretty short already. Didn't know they were up on fashion in Canada like that. Bet it'll catch on. How about let's go search that house after lunch? That's the old Thompson place. Colonel Thompson got it way back when from some old Spanish family that was down and out, and they say his wife's ghost haunts it. She died back in the nineties or something, and he died before the War and left it to some relatives back East who never even came to see it far as I know. The flu may have got 'em for all I know. Oh, good golly, *Halloween!* What a place for a séance! There's a Spiritualist bunch that would love to have one up there. You ever read Conan Doyle? Houdini's back in town too. I saw him at the Orpheum and he's gonna be at the party I'm takin' you to tomorrow night. Sarah... didn't you say that Warren had films of other girls?"

Sarah sank between the racks of dresses, "That's... what it looked like to me. The film cans had girl's names on them. I only read a couple but I saw a projector and a screen for watching them in the den," She swallowed, "I certainly wasn't in the mood."

"Well... *I'll* watch. You said he had Klieg lights? They cost a bundle. That's why your eyes are all red. They can burn them something awful, so you musta been awake enough for that to happen so maybe you'll remember something. I've had to take two days off at a time to recover. It makes your makeup run like hell too. Rather work outdoors anytime. That's why they make movies here." Olive's upper lip curled as she stared out the window on Hollywood

Boulevard, "Musta loved watchin' himself on film, hurtin' girls."
Eyes the color of lilacs flashed with malice, "Believe me toots, that
sick sonofabitch ain't the only one. He musta stole those lights
from a studio, which means somebody helped him move 'em sure
as shootin'. They're heavier than hell, so he's gotta have accomplices
too. Boy...wait 'til Bee hears this one!"

"Bee? Olive, you can't be telling people, they might--"

"It's jake, toots. That's my friend Beverly Davis. You'll meet
her." She grinned, "Those Kliegs will fetch a pretty penny," Olive put fingers to her lips, "we'll need a couple big fellas and a
truck." She rubbed her chin, "You said that there's really dead
bodies down that well?"

The stench of death rose into her nostrils, and Sarah tottered
on her feet, "I, yes, yes there are."

"Eee-whew, *God!* Sarah, if you went to the right coppers,
it might actually help your career if you're interested in breakin'
into pictures. I'd invest in it, and maybe we could get Tom
Ince and who knows who else, maybe even this German guy
who makes really scary stuff. You know, just like a Mary Pickford flicker with a little gore: the innocent girl from the North
Woods, abducted and--"

"No, I really truly do not want to do that."

"Oh I know, gettin' raped and all. Listen hon, it's happened
to me and I'm doin' great. You'd be surprised how many girls
around here--"

"I--" Sarah avoided Olive's eyes and stared out the window,
"I couldn't bear to have my family hear that. They'd die."

"Well, yeah, I suppose it's still rather Victorian in Victoria."

"You have no idea," Sarah stared out the windows at Hollywood Boulevard, "I didn't intend to start out like this."

"Start out? Sarah, were you . . ?"

"No, but I've only been with one, well... with two fellows before."

"Hell of a Hollywood debut." Olive hugged her, "Listen, we should get you a good one so as you're not in a bad way about things. I've got a guy in mind. He's Italian, handsome as the Devil, and toots, I can say from personal experience--"

Sarah fought an urge to bolt for the door, "No, I don't think I'm ready for that."

"I understand. Things come in time." Olive gave her another hug and squeezed Sarah's bottom through the thin satin dress, "Anyway you deserve that dastard's money and whatever else we find up there. I'll help you make up for it so help me God, but we can't go to the cops. My friend Bee's got connections who can find out whoever was workin' with Warren," Olive kissed her cheek, "I think you're amazing and I don't want to see you leave here because of one crazy sonofabitch. Bad things happen to good people, it's a fact, but I'm going to introduce you to the *right* people and show you how a girl gets to the top around here."

Sarah's gaze wandered to an organ grinder on Hollywood Boulevard with his monkey perched on the shoulder of a well-dressed man. The monkey defecated down the back of his tweed jacket as the man handed the organ grinder a penny. The organ grinder smiled broadly as he glanced over the man's shoulder at Sarah and she found a little laugh welling up in her throat. She rubbed her eyes, "All right."

* * *

Olive took her to a restaurant with stained-glass flowers in the windows, where they were immediately escorted to a high-backed booth sheathed in green velvet. The smooth-cheeked waiter winked and hastened to bring a bottle of champagne in a pewter ice bucket. "Get it while the gettting's good; Prohibition's coming, darlings." He popped the cork accompanied by giggling from Olive, poured an inch into two champagne flutes, and stood waiting for her approval.

Olive winked back and lifted her glass to Sarah, "Try it hon, this is the good stuff. Better try it before January anyway. We'll all be drinkin' in somebody's basement or something."

Sarah sipped from her glass and made a face.

"S'good," Olive said, and held hers out for more.

"Could I have some water please?"

The waiter gave her an amused grin and brought two glasses with ice cubes. He filled them from a crystal pitcher as Sarah stared in fascination at the perfectly square pieces of ice. Making it must cost a fortune in this climate.

"We'll have the terrapin and orange sauce, Maurice darling, just a light lunch."

Maurice nodded, bowed, tucked the menus under a white-shirted arm, and left the table.

"So Sarah, how did he torture you?"

"Wh…what?"

"You know, like hurt you and stuff? I saw the marks. Can't you remember anything at all? Bill Taylor's chauffeur collects that bondage stuff and I've heard tell he likes for girls to do it to him too. Hear he's been a customer at some of the places that specialize in that kinda stuff. Such things do exist here." Olive scowled, "Eew, I wouldn't let that creepy sonofabitch Ed tie me up for all the tea in China! He collects all kinds of whips and shackles, although Bill's place in Westlake is clean as a pin. Been there lotsa times and some of the best dames in the business spend the night there. Bill's the guy Jack wanted me to give it up for last night: Mr. William Desmond Taylor the Director."

Olive's conversation had left Sarah totally lost. She shook her head, "I don't know what he did. I mean, I know he *did* but I can't recall much. It's just in pieces. I still feel in quite an odd way from whatever it was he gave me, although that steam certainly helped. My head is still rather tipsy, but like you said you saw the marks, and I hurt all over."

"How could a man enjoy that? Jesus Christ, good fuckin' riddance! I really wanta see the place though. It's s'posed to be haunted and sounds like the Devil's Lair in a picture I almost made with Tom Ince at Triangle. We could write a script, and we could let people know there really *was* stuff goin' on up there. That way we could get Hearst to give us all kinds of free press. I bet that bitch Hedda Hopper would even bite. Lon Chaney could play Warren… and," Olive grabbed her arm, "and you could play yourself!"

Sarah recoiled, "I really don't want to do that!" She swallowed a lump in her throat and stared across the room at the profile of a fair-haired man who was sharing a rack of lamb with a beautiful young woman less than half his age, "Is… is that John Barrymore?"

Olive glanced over her shoulder, "Yep, with another plucked flower looks like," She grinned, "or she's about to be. We'll go today then. Lots of parties tomorrow and you'll have more fellas after you than folks who hate the Blacksocks in Chicago with them gams of yours believe you me. I gotta get you on this before every good-lookin' boy around here is on *you*. They're all gonna try and take you away, so stick with me toots. You make me feel a whole lot better about my own little problems with Mr. Jack Pickford. It puts it all in perspective."

"If I'm going to be here at all, I'd like to find somewhere to live that's safe before any parties, and a job."

"Hon, the way you get a job here is *going* to parties, and with your looks, don't worry, and you're staying with me so we're all set."

Maurice approached with two domed silver platters. Sarah ran a hand over her face and gazed into Olive's deep blue eyes with the loveliest shade of lavender she'd ever seen, brimming with apparent kindness from under a cloche satin hat that perfectly matched their shade. For an instant they reminded her of that other woman she wasn't sure existed except in her imagination.

The artist Howard Christie had captured Olive's eyes beautifully in a painting. A poster of the painting had hung in the foyer of Pantages' theater in Seattle. Now those eyes were in front of her waiting for a response. Sarah sighed, shifted in the booth, and felt for any pain between her legs. She glanced down at the slinky slip she was wearing that passed for a dress here, fondled the dangling rope of pearls around her neck, and watched Maurice staring at a young man in the next booth as he served him wine with a smile on his pale too-handsome face. Sarah let out her breath, "Things are moving much too fast, I don't--"

"It's the Twentieth Century doll."

* * *

On the way back Olive bought gasoline at the Standard Oil station on Highland. When the young man washing the windshield, airing the tires, and checking the oil finished, he doffed his cap and asked for an autograph. Olive laughingly obliged and he cranked the engine with a grin before they headed over Cahuenga. As they pulled away, she lit a cigarette at the end of an ivory holder, took two puffs, and it blew off the end.

Sarah spun around, "I hope that doesn't start a fire!"

"Pshaw, watch the road!"

A wagon full of vegetables was in the middle of the narrow ribbon of white concrete. "Sonofabitch!" Sarah honked the horn, down-shifted, and jerked the wheel to the right.

Olive exploded in laughter, "That's more like it toots, thought you were some kinda Canadian schoolmarm there for a while."

"I worked for my father at a gold mine in the Klondike, cooked at logging camps, and herded cattle on a ranch with cowboys for that matter. I was around some rough characters at all of them and can swear like the worst of them have I cause or opportunity. I simply don't wish to speak so crudely while in better company. It's hardly proper."

"Yeah, well, that's nice. Sure glad they can't actually hear me when we're filmin'. Tol' Buster Keaton to shove it up his ass with the nicest little girl smile on my face a couple 'a weeks ago. He was doin' a stand-in on the set and played one of his goddamn practical jokes on me. He laughed like hell when I said it. I *love* that guy. On the screen it says I'm asking where my daddy's gone. Daddy-schmaddy, any lip reader could tell you that's a buncha hooey. His pal Fatty Roscoe Arbuckle chased me all around the goddamn studio that morning just wantin' my attention like a big fat kid. I mean, he's a dear, but I was awful hungover and felt like shootin' him at the time. Had a mind to make something out of it with Minta, that's his wife." She made a face, "He's kinda a sweaty pig, although he's still a damn sight cleaner than Charlie Chaplin. If people could smell him through the film, he'd be done pronto. You heard that talk 'bout sound comin' to the flickers?" She laughed, "It'd be 'Cut, cut, cut, Ollie!'" Olive reached between her breasts, pulled out the roll of bills, and held them between her legs out of the wind, "Stop at that old hotel where the Redline meets the Greenline, wouldya?"

"Why?"

"I wanta buy something."

Sarah's heart rose in her throat as the café where she'd met Warren came into view. She pulled up by the hotel on the opposite side from the café and squeezed the wheel until her knuckles went white.

"Whatsamatter?"

"I... that café's where I met Warren."

"Oh don't worry, hon, Fords all look the same."

"But what about the license plate?"

"Nobody pays attention," Olive stepped out of the car, caught her skirt in the door, and almost went down face-first, "Damn!" She yanked, ripping the hem, "Shit!"

Sarah giggled nervously.

Olive glanced over her shoulder and grinned, "Be right back." She stepped into a side entrance and disappeared up the red-tiled stairs.

Sarah sat with her arm on the door of the car. The sun was hot and the metal was almost too warm even at the end of October. The engine idled with an occasional pop from the exhaust. She ran a hand across the polished oaken wheel and glanced around for the redheaded woman in the Mexican shawl who'd seen her with Warren, but the only other person was a skinny man in a pinstripe suit and straw hat smoking a cigarette. He winked as soon as she looked at him, tipped the hat, and Sarah averted her face. Olive was right. The flapper hat was perfect for avoiding eye contact.

Olive reappeared skipping like a schoolgirl holding a flat metal object that looked like a liquor flask in her hand. She climbed in the car, "Home, James!"

Sarah double-clutched, fought the car into reverse, and backed against the hillside. She did the same to get it into first gear, and they pulled out onto Cahuenga.

"You drive good, Sarah."

"It's not that hard."

"Tell that to my first three flivvers. Love them Locomobiles but I sure am hard on 'em. Have to have the bodies custom made too, so fixin' 'em takes forever. Hit a kid in March on Gower, and the studio had to shell out to his mom." Olive shook her head, "Feel pretty crappy 'bout that. I sent him a new bike for Easter and paid for a trip to the Santa Monica Pier with his folks. Jack's driving is worse, though. Oh well, I got a limousine anyway."

When they turned up the gravel track of Lankershim into the hills, Olive had her pull over at a shady spot under sycamore trees. Sarah slowed, put the car in neutral, and yanked the brake as Olive took out the flat tin case and jerked the top off. Five small tubes were inside along with the brass top of what looked like a small plunger. She pulled out the plunger. It turned out to be the top of a metal and glass syringe, and she yanked out a tube with her teeth. Olive had a look on her face like a stroked cat as she put the needle of the syringe into the gray rubber stopper at the top of a tube with a tiny hole in it and drew half the liquid into the body of the syringe. She yanked off the elastic strap holding one of her silk stockings with a snap and handed the end to Sarah. Doves cooed in the sycamore branches overhead.

"Kill the engine," Sarah obliged, "and hold this will ya?"

Sarah gingerly took the end of the strap.

"No, tighter," Olive flexed her thin left arm several times, wrapped the elastic below her small bicep, and held the other end in her mouth, "Tightp!" she grunted through gritted teeth.

Olive put the needle to the edge of the purple spot on her inner arm and pierced the skin as Sarah ground her teeth and tried to avert her eyes, but she found herself staring as Olive drew blood into the syringe, where it swirled in a crimson spiral as it mixed with the amber liquid. Olive pressed down with her right thumb, the mixture disappeared in her arm, and she released the strap from her mouth with a snap, an "Ahhhhh," and she slumped on the seat, "Thanks a bunch, sister."

Sarah squeezed the polished eight ball Warren had mounted on the gear shift and stared at the road. She closed her eyes and listened to the hiss and tick of the engine, unsure of where she'd be when she opened them.

"Let's go, toots."

Sarah got out and cranked the engine. Olive slumped against the door like a wilted flower. Sarah put the crank back in its clip, got in, and put the car in gear.

Olive lay in the dappled shade with her right arm dangling over the door frame, staring into the branches above, "I love doves."

"What?"

"The mourning doves. Don't you?"

Sarah glanced up and nodded, "They are lovely. Even this morning when I was all alone and didn't know what was to become of me, I found peace in them. I just wanted to drift off into the treetops and away, perhaps even be them. It was as if all my earthly troubles were as nothing in the greater scheme of things. We come and go like dust in the wind, but the forest, the doves, and the trees live on. I miss the wilderness where I spent so much time. It makes me realize how small we truly are, Olive. So many others I've loved have already died before me and suffered so much more. My sister--"

"That's beautiful Sarah. You're so wise, wise beyond your years. It's all fate you know: kismet, karma... all that stuff. Did you know there's a Swami from India who says I'm to die young?"

"No. That's horrible, Olive."

"You can call me Ollie. He was just being honest. That's why people pay him I guess. I was really mad when he said it, but I thought about it and it's all right. I accept it like everything else. I've lived enough for a hundred lifetimes anyway, but there's so many rotten lugs around here I'd like to put in their places you wouldn't believe it. You're so brave, Sarah, you killed some black-hearted thug all by yourself for *real,* and you're younger than me. Olive leaned across the rattling gear shift and kissed her cheek, "I love you."

Sarah didn't know what to say, so she said nothing at all.

V.

As they neared Olive's Moorish palace in the hills, Sarah stared up the winding drive across from it that led to Warren's abode and the well of dead girls. A tiny gray deer stood in the rutted road to that musty house of horrors. It bounded off at the last moment into the brush. Sarah squeezed her eyes shut for a moment and almost missed turning into the drive for the beautiful home on her right.

They drove between flowers and knockoff Greek statues, passed a painted bronze Negro groom in a red coat and green jockey cap with a brass hitch ring in his hand, and up a pink flagstone driveway. Within the open door of the sprawling garage perched a glistening black Rolls Royce Phaeton limousine on tall whitewall tires. A blue dust-cloaked Packard touring car sat before another door. Olive's yellow Locomobile roadster squatted forlornly before a third door beside a pink stone retaining wall with its right front fender crumpled and two flat tires. Two Great Danes let out low-throated bellows and stood at attention like small gray horses, their whip-tails wagging.

"You two... don't you know your momma!" Olive stepped out and canted sideways toward the dogs in the warm breeze as they strained at their chains, and saliva spattered the flagstones, "Oh, you darlings!" She scratched them behind the ears, and the dogs shoved her back and forth on the pathway like a paper doll with their huge heads reaching her breasts, "Well, somebody got my car outta the bushes anyway. Musta been Lupita called the garage, unless Jack got his skinny ass up for a change. Come on Sarah, could be some sonsabitches here you can put in their places."

Sarah stared at the cavernous entry of the house, grabbed her gun-heavy purse, and stepped down from the car to hesitantly follow Olive to a dark wooden door with a little window in it that had a miniature balcony and curtains at head height. Olive tilted a potted cactus from amongst a plethora of strange succulent plants along the walk, produced a key, opened the door, and waved Sarah inside.

They trod mosaic tiles under a high-roofed atrium of whitewashed plaster and pink marble that was open to a second story that had balconies and arches on either side decorated in arabesques of stone. The place smelled of spices and incense, pipe tobacco, oranges, and a sweetish smell Sarah couldn't place.

"Miss Thomas, we worry!" A pretty middle-aged Mexican woman said as she appeared in a colorful cotton dress and a beige apron, wiping her hands on a towel.

"Hi Lupita, glad somebody did. This is my new best friend Sarah."

The woman's eyes widened. She continued to examine Olive before turning to Sarah, "So nice to meet you, Miss--"

"Sarah Mae McCallum, from Victoria, in British Columbia."

"Oh, so far. You like lemonade?"

"That would be lovely, thank you."

"Si, I be back." Lupita curtsied and disappeared toward what must have been the kitchen.

"Come on," Olive grabbed Sarah's hand and led her to a sunken living room where three large couches surrounded a low table covered with ashtrays, whiskey bottles, a thin brass pipe with a red tassel dangling from it on an ivory stand and a pink stoneware lamp in the shape of a nude woman holding up a crystal globe. The table squatted on colorful throw rugs across a red tile floor before a massive stone fireplace with its mantle bedecked with statuettes, a small globe, a crystal-domed clock and other knickknacks all watched over by an ancient musket over the fireplace. It reminded Sarah of the house up the hill, but newer, nicer, and illuminated by skylights through which sunlight fell between the rough dark-stained beams. She returned her gaze to the room, and with a start, realized that two of the couches were occupied by dozing men.

"Here's Jack," Olive stabbed a finger at a fair-haired man with an arm over his eyes and his mouth open who was snoring softly. The other couch was occupied by a tall man with a serape over his face. His long bare feet were crossed and dangled over the shiny wooden armrest. Two polished riding boots sat on the floor beside him. "That's Bill, the big poobah from Famous Players-Lasky at Paramount who's makin' features. Don't look so great today huh? Raving about Huckleberry Finn and raftin' down the Mississippi last night 'til I thought my ears were gonna fall off. That's his next flicker and it's all he's talkin' about. He directed Jack in *Tom Sawyer* a couple years ago. It was the same thing then; you couldn't shut him up."

"I saw that... that's William Desmond Taylor?"

"Uh-huh. Don't touch opium or morphine like dear 'ol Jack, just swills his Scotch like there's no tomorrow, and now they're even gonna ban that," Olive smirked. "Acts like it makes him better than the rest of us. His dad was some kind of military so-and-so in the British army and he's supposed to be a war hero himself, least that's what he says. Everybody 'round here's got some big fat story," she put a finger to her lips, "don't wake 'em. They killed enough they'll stay down for a while hopefully."

"I hope he didn't hear you," Sarah muttered.

Lupita reappeared with a crystal pitcher and two glasses on a silver tray. She glanced at the table and scowled, "You say don' disturb them so I no cleanup this mess," her voice dropped to a whisper, "you like your lemonade outside?"

"Just so, Lupita." Olive motioned for Sarah to follow.

They walked out on a flagstone patio to sit under a huge green umbrella at a pink marble table flanked by tall brass torches. The porch was surrounded by vines and flowers with fruiting citrus and pomegranate trees behind them, but Sarah only had eyes for a flat expanse of crystal blue beyond it that was surmounted by a pink stone rim. "Oh dear, is that a swimming pool?"

"Yep. Pretty jake, huh?"

"My god, I've--"

"I got bathing suits. Golly Sarah, you look like you swallowed the whole hog."

"How does it get so... *blue?*"

"They use chlorine to kill the algae. There's a guy who comes every other day just to take care of it, and to skim the leaves and stuff. Same thing the Italian fella I was tellin' you about did at our place on Wilshire. Eew-wee, I loved watchin' him take his shirt off! He looked like a fuckin' Roman God! One day I couldn't stand it anymore, so I just walked out of the shower buck naked and threw his handsome Guinea butt on the divan," she burst into laughter and hiccupped once, "he didn't even speak English... hell, he didn't even know I was a movie star, but that boy was *something!* Ow!"

"It looks like the sky on a summer day, like... like turquoise. I can't believe how blue it is."

"So let's take a dip toots."

* * *

There was a pool at the gymnasium in Victoria, several in Vancouver, and even two in Dawson City, but Sarah had never seen one outdoors like this. The water was a cool caress that purled around her flesh as she stretched into long laps and new birds sang in the trees. She felt herself relax as she inhaled the scent of azaleas and oranges, and her head began to clear. The nightmare of awakening tied up in darkness had at last begun to loosen its grip in the comforting water under the bright blue sky.

They dried their hair on towels, put on puffy silk robes, and got made-up in Olive's grand bathroom before mirrors ablaze with bulbs in rose petal sconces made of mother of pearl. Sarah was relieved to see the swelling around her eyes had abated. She looked nearly normal, the swim had broken the spell of Warren, and she was beginning to feel human again. Olive insisted on applying Sarah's makeup, and upon finishing a half-hour later, the two of them looked ready for anything the finest destinations in Los Angeles could throw at them. Sometime during the process, Sarah heard herself laugh.

They were deciding what to wear and drinking Italian coffee that Lupita brought on a silver service when Olive put her cup down, "Hey, let's put on pants and go up to the Thompson place."

"What?" Sarah blinked as she followed Olive back to the room and watched her take a large flashlight out of a drawer, "Ollie, I really--"

Olive opened a cabinet of bird's eye maple and inspected a dozen pairs of tailored women's riding pants on a mahogany rack. "I saw that gun in your purse. If you're worried, bring it. Can you shoot?"

"Yes, it's an automatic and I'm more used to a revolver, but my father had an American .45 automatic from the War we practiced with at the claim. They all work the same, more or less."

"Got me an ivory-handled break-top .38 scrimshawed by this handsome Boston whaler fella in New England," Olive took it out of a drawer, "I shoot it with Jack and Bill out back. We rent this place 'cause there's room for things like that... and private parties of course. Bet there's some good stuff up there, and that little bastard Warren sure don't need it if you put him away like you said you did."

"I... did... but what if he's got friends?"

"So? If they're just local people, we're girls, and I'm a movie star, remember?" Olive grinned, "I could probably get somebody to haul those Klieg lights out for an autograph."

"And if they're not?"

"Then you and me are probably gonna get in a dustup sister." Olive made a trilling laugh and rolled her eyes, "It'll be front page stuff if we have to shoot some bad guys."

A wave of vertigo roiled through Sarah, and she put her palms against the cabinet to steady herself. Olive's eyes widened, "I'm sorry Ollie, it's just that going up there--"

"Cripes doll, you're really tellin' the truth, aren't you?"

Sarah nodded.

"Then we'll beat it if there's even a mean dog."

They padded out past the living room. Jack was still sprawled on the couch, but Bill Taylor and his Packard were gone.

* * *

The house seemed just as she'd left it. Duke stood wagging his tail beneath a weeping willow that rustled in a warm southeast breeze. He whined at the approach of the car, barked once out of duty, and wagged his tail again. Sarah had released him that morning, but he obviously had nowhere to go. "Duke!" She embraced the dog, who licked her face and smeared her makeup as she scratched him all over, "I've got to do something for this dog! He saved me. I can't just leave him here without anyone to care for him."

"Ugh, he needs a bath. You're gonna smell like a barn, hon."

Sarah took the automatic from her purse, pulled back the slide, dropped it on a bright brass cartridge in the chamber, and thumbed on the safety as Olive stared in fascination. Sarah gazed at the mute house, heard *Alexander's Rag Time Band* playing in her mind, and let out her breath, "Well, let's go inside."

Olive's lip curled at the smell of the place as they checked the rooms. There was a darkroom at the back of the bedroom past the awful mattress with two smaller cameras beside it, another broken Klieg light, bottles of chemicals, photographic paper, and wires strung across the ceiling for hanging pictures. Three new cans of film sat on a shelf.

Olive wandered about the bedroom yanking open drawers. When she reached the dresser behind one of the lights, she gasped, "Look!" She began pawing through a pile of leather straps, "Manacles! Handcuffs! And look at this!" She held up a round red rubber ball enclosed in a leather implement. It looked like the pouch of a slingshot.

"Whatever in the world is it?"

"It's for putting in your mouth so you can't talk, like this:" Olive held it up, opened her mouth, held the ends to either side of her face, and pretended to be gagging. "You fasten it behind somebody's neck with this clip while they're trussed up like a hog before you have your way with 'em and they can't holler."

Sarah put a hand to her mouth, "Oh my God!"

"I saw a box at Bill's house that had one of these and some handcuffs covered in mink."

"Oh no. Oh my God."

"Told you that you can't ever tell with guys. Makes me want to stick to girls sometimes."

Sarah leaned against the wall. Her head was spinning again. "This is disgusting! How in the world can you live around things that are so *vile?*"

"You ain't kiddin' hon but there's all kinds in the world. Some of 'em bankroll flickers. Welcome to Hollywood. You'll find that out around here. I guess you already have. So where's the films with girls' names?" Olive went back to yanking drawers, "Bet somebody'll give us a grand apiece for those one-reelers if they're what I think they are. 'Course if there's bigwigs or movie stars in 'em, it's a whole 'nother ball game. We could be on to something big."

"I left them on the bed."

"Huh?"

A chill shot up Sarah's spine and the gun flew out of her purse, "I left them right here!"

Olive's violet eyes were as wide as saucers, "Oh shit... they've *been* here!"

They made for the door and bounced off each other as they arrived at the same time. Olive fought with her lead-beaded purse for possession of her Smith and Wesson as Sarah dashed into the den and lifted the cushions on the couch. The .45 was gone. "Someone took the pistol that I hid!" she blurted, and her voice rose two octaves, "maybe they're still here!"

"Cripes!" Olive was behind her, pressing against her back with a hand around Sarah's waist, "Let's get outta here!"

They bolted into the yard and reached the car panting. Sarah held up a hand, "Wait," she pointed at the ground, "whoever it was must be gone. Those are new tire tracks that are wider than the Ford's," she waved Warren's chrome pistol at the trees, "maybe we should call the police after all."

Olive wiped her forehead. She rubbed her eyes, turned to the house, glanced back at Sarah and shrugged, "We'll call them after we've cleaned out any good stuff that's left. It's what the studios always do with things like this. Whoever took that film musta been in on it with Warren for sure, but some dead bodies ought to do it for the coppers when we've got whatever's good," Olive gave her a trembling smile, "kinda like a haunted house with a treasure hunt thrown in huh? It's spooky as hell, but we could find something really jake and I can have people take care of this for us without the cops... anyway we got guns."

"I *do not* want to go back in there Olive! I don't want to see this place ever again!" Sarah shivered, "Bill Taylor actually buys that stuff?"

"Uh-huh, he says it's to keep it out of the hands of bad people like Warren, though of course he didn't *say* Warren," Olive fondled her .38, "I've seen weirder stuff. Halloween's tomorrow and all the crazies come out, so we want to be done here today. Come on Sarah, let's finish searching."

Sarah reluctantly followed her back to the bedroom. Olive began pulling things out of the dresser drawers where she'd left off. "Bet you anything he's got a safe somewhere. Oh look, here's a girl's purse... and here's a locket," she pulled a thin gold chain out of a pile of women's under things and snapped open a heart-shaped locket, "look." She handed it to Sarah.

Inside was a tiny picture of a pretty blonde girl cheek-to-cheek with a handsome young man in uniform. Etched on the other side of the locket was the inscription **Together Forever, Christine and James.** Sarah snapped it shut as the smell of death awoke in her memory and she tried to blink it away. "She was pretty."

"Looks like you, toots."

"That was the name on one of the film cans. I... I think she's in the well."

There was a leather portfolio of photographs under more girls' clothes in a drawer that whoever had cleaned out the films had missed. In it were pictures of girls tied up with the implements on the dresser. Their faces were strangely slack as from booze or drugs, and one looked dead. Olive leafed through them without comment as her fair complexion grew whiter. She put them in a box with the other things, put them in the car, and grabbed the flashlight.

* * *

They climbed past broken retaining walls and overgrown terraces toward the old well with Duke wending his way underfoot. Sarah clutched the automatic as doves cooed in the treetops. She glanced up the hill for the mosaic of the woman in blue robes with ruby eyes but couldn't see it. When they reached the low crescent of stone that marked the well, she stopped.

"That's it?"

"Yes."

"Eu-wee, creepy! Lon Chaney could do a flicker here for sure."

"All right, let's go."

"Oh no, I wanta look."

"You're kidding."

"Nope, help me move the boards."

Sarah shuffled to the opposite side of the well and wiped her sweating palms on her pants. She grabbed the end of a plank, and Olive put down the flashlight and grabbed the other. "Ready?"

Olive nodded.

They lifted the board and slid it to the stone lip of the well. Sarah was about to say *enough* when Olive let go, and it tipped to twist out of Sarah's hands with a kiss of splinters and slid six feet downhill in a cloud of dust. "Ow!" Sarah wiped her hands on her pants, Damn!"

"Sorry."

From the darkness below, the smell of death rose on a billow of cool air. Sarah began to gag and backed against the wall on the hillside into morning glory vines. She swiped at a bee as her eyes darted down the path. When she glanced back, Olive had the flashlight on and was leaning over the dark void with a hand on the rim of the well. Sarah blinked, expecting a shriek of horror, a gasp of revulsion... *something,* but Olive just stared. Sarah let out her breath and joined her to lean over the well.

Twenty feet below, Warren lay sprawled buttocks-up over a jumble of decaying corpses and bones that were covered with a thick coating of quicklime. Sarah squeezed her eyes shut and stepped back. She sat on the boards of the well, put her head between her knees, and began to heave.

"Wow," Olive wrapped a damp arm around Sarah's shoulders, "halfway thought you were fulla malarkey."

VI.

When they got back to the house, Jack was gone. "Mister Pickford, he go with his sister Mary and Mr. Fairbanks to town," Lupita announced, "Mary's husband Owen call here from New York. I tell him she with Jack, and no see Mr. Fairbanks and I have Diego take the tires to town for fix. He put two more on your car but the fender she all ugly."

"Thanks Lupita, you're a godsend," Olive turned to Sarah, "you missed meeting Douglas Fairbanks and Mary Pickford, but you'll meet 'em at a party or something."

Sarah rubbed her nose. The smell of death tickled it as she pressed her back against the atrium's smooth pink wall. It had to be her imagination, but it was there. Duke's eyes flashed green in her mind again, then red. She blinked and imagined stepping onto the next train north and using the money in her purse to start a nice little restaurant, even going back to work for Alexander Pantages at one of his theaters. Pantages was planning a bigger one on Hollywood Boulevard and she could transfer when it opened. Her uncle's leering face rose into her exhausted mind. She felt his calloused hands. She felt Pantages' arm around her shoulders with a hand sliding toward her derriere and let the thoughts of returning to Vancouver or Seattle die.

"Let's leave this stuff in the garage and take the Ford back up there."

"What?"

"Sarah honey, you can't just keep the fliver. We'll leave it up at the Thompson place and wipe it down. Haven't you heard of fingerprints?"

"Yes, actually, I didn't think of that though."

"You will around here toots; tons of investigating goes on. Somebody's always doin' somethin' to somebody and somebody's always gettin' the private gumshoes on their trail. It's a goddamn industry. When somebody famous dies while they're up to somethin' funny, the studios send in their own to cleanup before they call the cops, then they bring in the ones they can pay off. Seen coppers retire at thirty. That D.A. Woolwine's rich off it. Watched 'em cleanup after a fella hanged himself when the lead went to another swell who weren't just his rival, but his ex-boyfriend. He was cryin' like a baby at Mabel Normand's the night before and I wish I'd done something 'bout it, but boys like that are always goin' on a cryin' jag, so how can you know? Anyway, I learned a lot watchin' how the studios put things jake again."

"Well, it's hardly your fault."

They took the instruments of bondage, photos, and mementos of dead girls into the garage and put them on a shelf. Olive opened a window for light, took the little flask out of her purse, removed the half-full tube, and winked, "Time for an eye opener, toots."

"What is that stuff?"

"Cocaine solution. Ever read *The Seven Percent Solution* by Arthur Conan Doyle?"

"About Sherlock Holmes?"

"Yep, ol' Sherlock used it every day. That Harrison Act's the pits. Nobody here believes in it. This stuff's been gettin' a bum rap just 'cause some amateurs don't know how to use it like Sigmund Freud does. Know who he is?"

"Yes Ollie, he's a fellow in Europe who--"

"I read him. He's kinda tedious with his goin' on and on about how dreams are all sex and mommy-daddy stuff, but he's right about cocaine. He uses it to cure heroin addiction. I wish Alma Rubens had tried it. She might still be in the flickers. These new laws are a crock. Conan Doyle's a Spiritualist and cocaine's how he gets his inspiration for his books. Sherlock Holmes used a seven percent solution of cocaine to concentrate his mind and solve crimes."

"I, I suppose. Is that a seven percent solution?"

"It's fifty; you just use less."

"Oh."

"I need a little clarity after all this excitement, what with murders and you poppin' up and all. Besides I'm still a bit exhausted after last night. You oughta try it, Sarah, it'll wake you up from that hangover or whatever Warren gave you," Olive gave her the exaggerated look of concern Sarah had seen her make in the movies, "you're barely on your feet, toots."

"No… thank you."

"Well then, hold this would ya?"

Sarah was so tired she could hardly pay attention as she held Olive's elastic garter around her ankle this time and watched her place the needle against her skin as Olive chose a spot on her foot, "Gotta give my arms a rest." Sarah watched the solution disappear into a vein above the ball of Olive's foot and it reminded her of stepping on cactus spines. Her head spun and she fought nausea.

Olive glanced up as she slid the needle out, "Whatsamatter?"

Sarah swallowed the lump in her throat and stared at a cluster of red flowers glowing in the sun resembling the heads of birds. She fought the urge to bolt. There was nowhere to run to. She'd come all this way and here she was in the company of a genuine movie star in little more than a day, but none of this had she expected. "It, it's been just too much. I'm very tired and I don't feel so well."

"Sure you don't want some? It'll pick ya right up toots. Honest Injun."

Sarah shook her head, "No, really, thank you."

Olive closed her eyes and took a slow breath, "'Cuse me, this stuff comes on strong," she sneezed and scratched her nose, "sure wonder who took that film though, could be plenty of people. Bet somebody's..."

"What?"

"Huh?" Olive gave her a vacant grin, "Forgot what I was gonna say."

* * *

Sarah drove the Ford back to Warren's and Olive followed in her dented yellow Locomobile. As soon as they arrived, Olive began furiously wiping the Ford with a rag.

Duke sniffed at Sarah's leg and whined. "I have got to take this dog."

Olive glanced over her shoulder and made a face, "Jeez, I'll have Diego give him a bath," she shook her head, "I got to drive my poor car to our place on Wilshire. Just you watch hon, *Variety* will have a story 'bout me wreckin' another one day after tomorrow," she scowled, "no avoiding it. Wish there was a way to get home without goin' smack-dab across goddamn Hollywood Boulevard with everybody and their fuckin' uncle watchin'." A smile blossomed on her face that immediately transformed her into the innocent ingénue she portrayed in films, "Hey, there *is!* There's a shortcut over the mountains but I've never used it. It's pretty wild up there."

"No roving bands of Indians I hope."

"Nope, but they say there's hermits and crazies and such. Heard about a failed actor with a long beard who shoots at people, but that's probably a buncha hooey," Olive grinned, "we better get goin'. It's getting late."

* * *

Lupita made them a snack of ladyfinger sandwiches, caviar, brie, capers, crackers, and red wine. An overwhelming hunger seized Sarah as she watched her put down the heaping enameled tray. She loved the sandwiches with cream cheese, cucumber, and capers. Sarah spread the brie on crackers, tried the caviar, sipped the wine, and asked for lemonade. Olive downed three glasses of wine but hardly touched the food.

Lupita packed more food in a picnic hamper and placed it in the tiny trunk of the Locomobile after Sarah stuffed the black leather suitcase in. They changed into cotton summer dresses and put on straw sun hats with ribbons tied under their chins, and Olive handed Sarah a pair of goggles for the dust. Then they squeezed into the open two-seat roadster in a warm afternoon breeze, drove down the rutted road, and turned left along Ventura Boulevard toward Laurel Canyon. All eyes on the board sidewalks were upon them as they approached a junction with a trolley stop and a few stores, where they turned left into the hills with the breeze at their backs.

"That wind is so warm for this time of year."

"It's called Santa Ana. It comes up in the fall out of the desert and fans lots of fires. Got stuck on Mt. Loew once all night when a fire went right across the tram line. Boy that turned into a party. Love that Mabel Normand. She tap-danced on the tables and the boys were all howlin' like a buncha dogs. Hope we make it over before dark though."

"How far is it?"

"I'm not sure." Olive sped up as they passed the last cluster of buildings and rumbled up a lane shaded by tall eucalyptus with a string of pops rattling from the exhaust. She almost ran into the back of a wagon being pulled by two mules and scattered chickens from a nearby home under ancient mossy oaks full of mistletoe. They bounced over a narrow ditch and laughed when they landed with a thump. Sarah gripped the leather-wrapped handle on the maple wood dash and fumbled with her goggles as the road narrowed and became a switchback. Olive stopped the car and fought it into first gear.

The sky was darkening quickly in the east. Across the orchards and fields of the San Fernando Valley, the mountains were brown with dust blowing from the desert beyond and a canyon appeared to be full of smoke. They bumped up a forested gulch and, as the shadows of evening fell, some kind of animal darted across the road and a hiss erupted from the radiator.

"Crappers," Olive exploded, "I hope it don't boil over!"

"Did you check the water?"

"Hell no, that's the servants' job... or at least Jack's."

"He didn't look in shape to."

"Actually he loves tinkering with cars and likes to race 'em with Wally Reid, but lately he's been rather consumed with other things like morphine." The radiator let out a gasp and belched steam in a cloud that fogged the little windshield and dampened their faces. "Oh shit, oh damn oh shit!"

"Try and make it to the top Ollie; we can let it cool there!"

Olive stepped on the gas at Sarah's suggestion, and the car lurched forward with a pop from the exhaust. Sarah held on to the handle on the dash as a warm mist enveloped them and Olive moaned, "Shit... I don't want to be stuck out here!"

Up ahead the high roof of an open cab truck appeared beneath the branches of oaks. Olive shrieked and jerked the wheel to the right at the last moment. The tires wobbled on the edge of the road as the car trembled and coughed. Sarah stared into a gulch filled with the shadows of evening and produced a shriek of her own as the truck barreled by on the inside of the road within inches, accompanied by a bellow from the driver. The car slowed, hissing like a scalded cat as they made it to the junction at the top and the engine died. They rolled to a stop. Olive yanked the hand brake and got out of the car, staggered to a pink boulder, and sat down with a sob as the engine whistled through the radiator cap. Sarah stumbled out of the car to sit beside her as Olive sniffled, and a tear rolled down her cheek.

"It's all right, Ollie, we can find someone's place and get water while the engine cools."

"I don't want to be stuck up here at night. There's *crazies* in Laurel Canyon!" She clutched Sarah's arm, "Do you have your pistol?"

Sarah nodded.

"Oh good," Olive glanced left and right on the narrow road and shivered, "I hope somebody comes along soon. It's gettin' chilly."

"Somebody nice anyway," Sarah put an arm around Olive's shoulders. A mockingbird called, squirrels chattered in the dusk over possession of the day's last acorn, and cicadas buzzed in the treetops. Sarah noticed the same sharp herb scent from the vegetation as the hillside above Warren's and glanced around, "What's that smell?"

"Huh?"

"The spicy smell."

"Oh, yerba santa, those plants with shiny leaves. Indian tea. Heard it gave you a good jolt when I got here and made a big pot of it," Olive made a face, "but I only got the trots."

Sarah chuckled.

Olive stroked her hair and yawned.

* * *

She was perched above the river of her childhood that ran thousands of miles without a single bridge to wind amongst nameless mountains to a distant sea. The songs of wolves thrilled her nerves and her back arched as if a lightning bolt had struck her. She saw a white figure crossing the ridge top that turned before disappearing in the dark spruce forest, and her eyes flashed red. Sarah knew she had spoken but couldn't make out the words. She had to know the words--

She gasped at a sharp prick, opened her eyes, and grabbed the inside of her elbow. A full moon spread its blue phosphorescence across the world and crickets sang in the night sounding like knives and needles again. She glanced around with a jolt of panic and yanked at the garter wrapped around her bicep. It came off with a snap. Sarah rubbed her wrists and checked to make sure she wasn't bound. A cluster of lights in the valley from which she'd come went in and out of focus. She blinked and rubbed her eyes.

"Whoops," Olive's laughter echoed like a brass bell, "Sure woke ya up there!"

The world spun around her as Sarah sat on a boulder with cool night air caressing her flesh. She felt naked and checked again to make sure she was clothed. She shivered and ran trembling hands down her thighs.

"You were fast asleep toots. This nice old fella came by with a wagon and went back to his place for water. He's got one arm from the Spanish War. I told him I could get him a job as a wounded soldier in one of Mr. Selznick's pictures and gave him an autograph. Then I waited 'til the engine cooled so it wouldn't crack and put the water in, but when I went to wake you up, you were like a dead person, so I gave ya a little taste of the ol' eye opener. Hope you don't mind. You like it?"

"I... *God!*"

Olive placed a ring-covered hand on Sarah's arm, "Feel better toots?"

Sarah staggered off the boulder, bent over, and put hands on her knees. Her heart was roaring in her chest and she was wide awake. A half-remembered memory of cruel laughter erupted in her ears with a vision of bringing the heavy bottle down on Warren's face in the moonlight. She felt angry. She felt strong. She wanted to kill Warren again and again, until he sank into that awful well forever, never to rise in her dreams. She squeezed her eyes shut and saw huge green eyes staring back that slowly morphed to red. A rush ran like ginger ale under her scalp, and she gasped and clutched at her hair, "What... what have you done to me?"

Olive held her hands out to her sides palms up. Moonlight glimmered in the ringlets of her hair and pale dress, and her skin was blue ivory. She looked like a fairy. "Oh Sarah, it wasn't to hurt you. It's good isn't it?"

Sarah balled her fists, "God... I can't *believe* you *did* that... Olive!"

Olive wrung her hands, stared at the ground, and made a little sob. Her next one was drowned out by the hoot of an owl, so she began to cry.

Sarah shivered and stared at the owl as it left a glowing trail across the stars. She let out her breath, "Oh, damn..." She tried to hug Olive, but found herself sweeping her off the ground in her arms instead. She heard soft laughter in the distance. Olive pressed a cheek against Sarah's and hiccupped. Sarah shivered again at a feeling like cold fingers up her spine... yet she felt wonderful. Olive didn't seem to weigh anything at all, and she continued to hold her off the ground. "Christ! Oh damn, it's all right Ollie, it's done anyway."

"Sarah, I don't want to lose you as a friend," Olive's breath bounced in her ear, "really I don't. One doesn't have many true friends here. Sometimes I hate this life. Hollywood's the loneliest place in the world in spite of all the glamour. So was working at Ziegfeld. Men have been acting like they were my friends but treating me like shit as long as I can remember, and you made one of the worst pay the price for it. You're the bravest person I ever met Sarah and I just wanted to make things better for you. You deserve some fun after all that you've been through," Olive gasped as Sarah let her go, and her feet touched the ground, "So... don't you like it?"

Sarah ground her teeth and stared at the moon as the world spun. Olive was a pale wraith with moonlight glistening in her violet eyes. They looked transparent, and Sarah thought she could see the blood behind them. Sarah rubbed her own eyes, squeezed them shut, and a ghostly white disk hovered in the back of them. When she finally spoke, her words sounded like someone else's to her, "It's all right, I guess."

"Oh good. We're gonna find a party then."

VII.

Lorelei stood under the stars inhaling the smell of death. After all these years, she still had to steel herself to accept what came to her in this moment: the echoes of terror, pleading, and cries like a seething knot of Hell crammed into the narrow shaft. This well of souls that no other could know. She bit her lip as, with the power of her birthright, she unwound the knots of the past to follow each life back along her mortal path to save what she could. It was a holy thing and a salvage operation as she collected the souls within her until she felt she would burst. *Madness...* could someone who was the last of her kind be called mad? She sighed. This was her place in the world until a daughter was born to take up her burden. *My poor child.* Had her mother felt the same? Lorelei doubted it. Her mother had returned to killing each time the burden became too heavy.

Sometimes I envy you.

Her mind wandered to her own death in the future. Lorelei had no doubt it would be violent and shook the thought off. Tonight was not easy. Her burden had grown over her two hundred and forty years, not lessened. Sometimes now she forgot compassion for those whose struggles were so much less, for whom simple luck had spared them as they fumbled their way among the pits and traps of mortal passions. There was just so much one could do. She had no living relatives. Her kind had been eliminated from the rest of the world, and even an inkling of such as she in others she'd touched could result in their stoning and burning in so many places on Earth. So many girls and women were suffering for who she was without even knowing her. She'd resolved not to be killing villains in Hollywood on impulse. She must use her lovers in secret and do her best not to meddle with the chaos and violence of the lives around her. She's started a tong war in San Francisco that only an earthquake made men forget, and with the advent of motion pictures, she was leery of exposure. Her need of men for sustenance and her ongoing problems with daylight didn't help either.

She'd followed Sarah's journey since she'd found her huddled under bushes amongst the cedars while Lorelei was crossing Vancouver Island from a quiet cove where she'd had a ship drop her with plans to meet a lover who was returning from the Klondike. She'd felt the girl child alone in the night like a beacon upon windswept rocks, and like all she'd touched, had left something of herself in the girl. Lorelei smiled. Sarah had acquitted herself well here, although Lorelei had to give her just a tiny bit of help with the dog. Not killing Warren herself had been a struggle as she'd watched from the hillside.

Would I have let her die?

She gazed at the sky and steeled herself as she finished absorbing what she could salvage of the murdered girls' lives. She swallowed as if finishing a meal, sighed, and decided to head over the hill to Hollywood. There was a young fellow making quite a stir amongst powerful young women, and she was in need of another lover.

* * *

The Locomobile's big yellow headlights illuminated but a few feet before them as they drove down the Hollywood side of Laurel Canyon. The road made endless turns, and Olive's breakneck driving had become slow and careful. Sarah squeezed the leather-wrapped handle on the dash as she parried like a fencer the cocaine's assault on her brain, searching frantically for the person she had known as herself amongst the strange feelings boiling up inside her. She shifted on the seat and gulped the warm night air.

"Tell me about your home, Sarah."

"What? I, um, I'm sorry Ollie, my head is fairly spinning. I'm from Victoria on Vancouver Island. It's a beautiful town. The Queen built things there and the parks are marvelous. There are flower gardens in the summer that smell so lovely too. I miss the Provincial buildings downtown with their green bronze roofs... and the gardens, and the simple decency of people, and I so miss the bakeries."

"The bakeries?"

"Yes, I used to go with my mum to the park and we'd stop at a bakery for a treat. She died giving birth to my little sister when I was four. It's one of the only things I remember of her. They had the most marvelous creampuffs and the baker always kept a tray of little ones for his favorite children. Mister MacNaughton--he had these wonderful red muttonchop sideburns--and his nose would get so red when he was drinking. We children used to laugh and laugh when we saw him like that, but he was our favorite person downtown. I dreamed of those creampuffs when I was truly hungry, like when I had to hoof it out of Sulfur Creek with my dad in a fall snow. That's in the Yukon, in the Klondike. I cooked in a mining camp there when I was thirteen."

"How old are you really?"

"Seventeen."

Olive nodded, "Thought so. I struck out young too, from Charleroi, that's near Pittsburgh, from a too-big shanty-poor Irish coal minin' family where the only future for a pretty girl is to marry and start breedin' like a damn dog 'til she's wore out like an old pair'a boots by thirty. Either that, or go to work in the shirtwaist factories in some city or be a whore. I married at fifteen to get the hell outta there and ran away from the guy in New York but kept the name Thomas 'cause an Irish name like Duffy don't cut the mustard with folks in showbiz. I got with Ziegfeld after I won a contest to be painted by Christie for the cover of the New Yorker magazine. That was my break. I was workin' a clothing counter and fending off the goddamn pesterin' manager 'til then," Olive laughed, "boy, I took off lickity-split."

"I had one of Christie's paintings of you in Vancouver. I took it from the foyer of the Strand Theater in Seattle," Sarah ran a hand across her face, "Mr. Pantages let me when they changed venues," she giggled, "I had to fend him off too. I never saw such beautiful eyes as in that picture, but you're even better in person."

"Thanks, toots. I got a good shake when it came to peepers, huh? Harrison Fisher did paintings of me too. So what does your dad do now?"

"I didn't tell you the truth. He died in the influenza last winter, along with my little sister."

"Oh," Olive squeezed her hand, "I'm sorry doll."

"My uncle took the house in Victoria. He says it's for safe-keeping, but I know better. He runs beer and whiskey for the saloons in Vancouver." Sarah scowled, "He came home drunk one night and I fought him off, and I took the money in the cookie jar and left when he fell asleep. I've got nothing to go back to either... at least 'til the lug's dead, and then I'll probably have to petition a court to have anything at all."

"Neither do I, sister, neither do I."

They passed big new homes built at the mouths of gulches that were surrounded by high iron fences surmounted by polished spear points. Olive pointed to one on the left built into the side of a hill with a yard full of Greek statues and arches crawling with the vines of bougainvillea, enclosed by a stone fence shrouded in oleander. "That's Houdini's place. Looks like a castle."

"Perhaps he can make those awful corpses disappear for Halloween. That would be handy eh?"

Olive burst into laughter, "Tol' ya some coke would lighten you up."

They drove through the sun-bleached remnants of a ranch to a cluster of clapboard apartments, where Crescent Heights met a wide gravel road with a sign that said **Sunset Boulevard.** Olive stopped to let a trolley go by and sighed loudly as she put her head against the wheel, "Whew, we made it! I need a shower, a change of clothes, and a refresher!"

Sarah put a foot on the dash. The idea of more cocaine was almost tempting, but the needle wasn't. It had definitely changed her mood anyway, and being on the other side of a mountain from that horrid old house and death-filled well helped too, "Some sleep's in order for me. I'm nearly dead, Ollie."

Olive tossed a ringlet of hair from her eyes, "You're right. Tomorrow's the big parties. I suppose we could head for my place on Wilshire, but I'd like to stop at Bee's first. You can sleep in a big ol' bed there with silk sheets if you want."

"That sounds wonderful. You mentioned her before. Who is she?"

"Beverly Davis, the dame who can fix anything. Her places are the cat's meow when you want to get away. She's got a huge wardrobe of extra clothes just like the studios, and we can freshen up and change for our return so if Jack has company, I'll not be in this dusty old dress."

"Is it close?"

"Closer than Wilshire. You'll love her place on South Bellmore, Sarah. She has a great big swimming pool, tennis courts, a bar, a restaurant with room service, card rooms, and every room is different be it Turkish, Persian, Parisian, Victorian... you name it toots. The bathrooms are all done in black marble with full-length mirrors and they have these electric heaters in the walls to warm your bum. She's got outfits for every kind of occasion too, and I've got credit there."

"It's a hotel?"

"Kinda. It's a bagnio actually."

Sarah blinked, "Why on earth would you have credit at a whorehouse?"

Olive chuckled, "So many do sister. Actually some of her girls are the most fun to be around, and one can meet a lover there in privacy for the fee of the room with great service provided. There's something to be said for silk sheets, champagne, candle-light, and a discreet staff. She's even got enclosed parking through a private garage so nobody sees your flivver. A husband comes in through one door to visit a paramour, his wife enters through an-other to see some young stallion, and they'll never even know the other's there... and the drivers have their own lounge with a Vic-trola and refreshments. Bee has her girls serve them. The chauf-feurs sure like that," she giggled, "sometimes they drop a month's pay while they're killin' time. Bee covers all the bases toots."

Sarah shook her head as she tried to imagine it. After ev-erything else, it didn't sound half-bad. "Well, that's one way to do it, eh?"

* * *

They drove between palms along a wide boulevard. Sarah craned her neck to gaze at the strange thin trees reaching into a darkling sky strewn with stars until Olive slowed at a gatehouse. A man in a uni-form leaned out and scowled at the torn fender. He began to speak but recognized Olive and tipped his hat, "G'evenin', Miss Thomas."

"Hey Walt, what's cookin'?"

The man did something inside the gatehouse and, to Sar-ah's amazement, the wrought iron gate began to move of its own accord. They drove up a broad circular driveway between hedges toward a sprawling two-story edifice with a tile roof in which every window was alight. "Place is busy. Boy, the fellas sure gonna be wonderin' who the hell you are, Miss Sarah Mae," Olive squeezed her leg. "Stay close, hon. Fresh meat is always the sweetest."

A tide of exhaustion darkened with dread made Sarah's limbs feel leaden, and she squeezed her eyes shut against the glare, "I'm trusting you, Ollie. I don't have the slightest idea where I'll be laying my head tonight."

"Poor baby," Olive kissed her cheek, "I promise I won't let any of those big bad lugs getcha. You deserve some peace and quiet after all you've gone through." She squeezed Sarah's thigh, "Watch out for the dames too."

They neared a garage, and the door opened miraculously at their approach and closed behind them. Lights went on overhead, Olive turned off the engine, and they got out slapping dust off their skirts.

A door opened at the top of golden travertine steps and a Negro maid bowed, "Miss Davis says welcome, Miss Thomas."

"Thanks Tillie. We really gotta freshen up."

"Please follow me."

They were led down a hall and up a flight of carpeted stairs past windows looking down on a big room furnished with Persian carpets and oaken tables, on which couples were dining. Tillie opened another door and curtsied, "You care for some champagne, Miss Thomas?"

Olive sighed as she untied her sun hat and scratched her head, "That'd be lovely. Mumms Cordon Rouge Tillie, and I need to see something appropriate for the evening in both our sizes. Not too frilly, casual yet tasteful. Did Blanche pick something out for me?"

"I'll ask, ma'am."

They entered the room and Tillie shut the door behind them.

"All right hon, how 'bout a shower?"

Sarah answered with a resounding sigh, "That would be marvelous."

The room had French doors onto a balcony that gave a view of brightly lit tennis courts below, where attractive men and women wearing khaki shorts were knocking balls over the nets in the warm night air. Olive closed the shutters and pointed past the canopied bed to the bathroom, "Come on toots, I'll wash your hair."

The washroom's furnishings were indeed black marble with swirls of white around golden faucets. "Just toss that old hat and dress on the floor. They ain't worth keepin'."

"What?"

"Sarah... it's only clothes."

Sarah untied the ribbon under her chin, took off the dusty straw hat, and pulled the dress over her head, but clutched it to her breast, "What shall become of the dress?"

"They'll clean it and give it to some poor girl somewhere. Bee's got her own charity. She says never give to the organized ones 'cause they're all crooks, and if you're a madam you'll never get credit anyway. Last Christmas she turned the lights back on in a hundred homes out by Signal Hill and had her girls bring food baskets. This one ol' man broke down and cried and called my pal Dolores an angel from Heaven," Olive giggled, "she's more used to men callin' her a devil. You should have seen her face. She cried too. Anyway, don't worry, it'll go to good use."

"That's nice of Bee."

"She's one of the truest friends I've got. You can learn a hell of a lot from a madam, toots."

They showered and took turns washing each other's hair. By the time they emerged turbaned in towels, another maid had wheeled in a selection of dresses on a rack. A bottle of Mumms sat in an ice bucket on a pewter stand with two crystal champagne flutes on the mahogany table.

Olive aimed the bottle at the ceiling, popped the cork with a giggle, and filled the glasses before she clinked her glass against Sarah's. The crystal rang like a bell. Sarah watched it splash on the thick Persian carpet, blinked, and took a sip. It didn't taste so bad this time.

VIII.

Waves of rain slashed across the cedar shake roof and sang in rivulets down the drainpipes. Angeline's arm tightened around her waist. Her breath caressed Sarah's throat. Sarah yawned, stretched, and stroked her sister's face. She was safe in bed again. Safe under the eaves of the big house their father had built with earnings from the sale of his claims in the Klondike. She listened to the familiar sounds of rain and her brother Paul stoking the stove downstairs. Sarah squeezed Angeline's hand. Her fingers traced a ring with a huge stone on it.

She blinked and forced herself out of the sleep shrouding her like a leaded blanket. The sound of water wasn't rain. It was coming from a bathroom.

Sarah opened her eyes and gazed at herself stretched naked across a mirrored ceiling on purple satin sheets beside a girl who certainly wasn't Angeline. She rolled over and blinked at an elfin face with ringlets of honey-colored hair draped across it.

Olive brushed it away and opened eyes the color of the sheets. "Mornin', toots."

Sarah sat up and rubbed her own, "I... where--"

"You were out like a light after two glasses of champagne, so I had Tillie undress you and tuck you in. Armand said you looked like an angel on the bed." Olive giggled, "It took some moxie to keep that pretty boy off you."

"Wha... *who?*"

"I figured you wouldn't appreciate it."

A huge yawn split Sarah's mouth. She stared at herself on the ceiling. Sleep was wonderful, and she wanted to go back. She wanted to turn the water off in the bathroom, which was now quite irritating, and wanted nothing whatsoever to do with Armand, whoever he was. The idea of someone standing over her naked form made her shiver, and she drew the sheet under her chin, "My head hurts."

"Here," Olive kissed her cheek, bounced off the bed, and grabbed a bottle of Bayer's Aspirin from the nightstand, "I'll ring for some orange juice and coffee," she yawned, "I want a mimosa."

"What's that?"

"Orange juice and champagne."

Sarah put hands to her face, "Dear God, can you please turn off that faucet?"

Olive responded with a chuckle, "You sure were sleepin' like the dead. Bet somebody coulda shot off a gun in here and you wouldn't a' heard it."

Sarah rubbed her eyes hard and cracked her neck, "Is it any wonder?"

"You've had a rough couple'a days toots. Want breakfast?"

"Yes, please."

"I had Blanche driven over this morning to do our hair and Bee's got somebody who does nails. Halloween parties you know." Olive arose with blotches that looked like fingers across the pale skin of her buttocks, stumbled into the bathroom, and turned off the faucet.

A maid appeared with a cart containing a silver service for coffee, a large pitcher of orange juice, and a bottle of champagne in an ice bucket. Sarah helped herself to the coffee as Olive poured champagne and orange juice in a tumbler with ice and shook it. After downing two cups of coffee and a glass of orange juice, Sarah stumbled into the black marble bathroom, twisted the still-drip-ping faucet over the sink tighter, and sat on the toilet.

"Eek!"

"Whatsamatter?"

"There's no *seat* on the toilet! Only a bunch of little faucets!"

"That's a bidet," Olive sashayed in, squatted over the strange bowl, turned a knob, and water began to hiss as a stream bathed her privates, "it's for washing our little treasures, Sarah. Jeez, you musta seen it last night. Nice thing to have after a night with Armand. I used it already, but this is how it's done."

Sarah sat on the proper toilet beside her and yawned, examining the tiny flecks glittering in the polished black stone like stars in the sky above the hillside when she'd awoken. She glanced at the bidet and shook her head, "I wish I'd had that yesterday."

* * *

They went down to the patio after Olive's servant Blanche, who was a young good-looking black woman with iron-straightened hair, had put Olive's flaxen ringlets back into curlers, and did their makeup. They sat in short satin dresses, cloche flapper hats, and dark sunglasses at a marble-topped table beside a blue pool under cocos plumosis palms and magnolias with waxy, impossibly huge flowers trembling overhead in the warm breeze. A handsome young man with glistening blond hair brought them gold-embossed menus and bowed. Young women and a few men in shirt-sleeves lounged beside the pool on divans or read newspapers at tables. All were attractive, and most were downright beautiful.

"Are all these girls, you know... are they..?"

"Not all. Some are just like us, here for the privacy or to have a little fling." Olive nudged her, "Look how that guy's watching you from the balcony. I think he's with Universal, but some of these pretty boys are actually on call for the servicing of society women who desire an assignation. This is a full-service *call house,* toots. It's got more telephone lines than the New York Stock Exchange I bet. You can't tell the movie stars from the denizens of the half world here." She giggled, "Ain't much difference anyway."

"Golly."

"There's Bee." Olive waved at a tall woman standing at a sliding glass door onto a ballroom with crystal chandeliers and an ebony grand piano. The woman smiled and absently fiddled with her long brown hair worn in a braid over a tailored beige suit. She had startling green eyes and a high forehead and looked to be in her late twenties as she glided toward them. "Bee," Olive sprang up and hugged her, "this is my best friend Sarah. She's from Canada and just--"

"Sarah," Beverly Davis appraised her, seeming to find something she approved of in the time it took Sarah to respond.

Sarah arose and shook a ring-covered hand. Beverly held hers as she leaned to brush Sarah's lips with her own. "Our pilgrim. Someone told me you'd be arriving and I gather you had quite an ordeal."

"Um, how . . ?"

Beverly smiled, "And you're going to break into the flickers for fame and fortune, no matter what?"

"I, that was my intent, but I've had somewhat of a nightmare instead. I've been with Olive since then and it sounds as if she's told you. She said you're the one to trust with such things, but you'll excuse me if I'd rather not talk about it at length. Right now all I can do is go with what may in her company, as she was kind enough to take me into her keeping... but I'd still like to work in motion pictures, yes."

"With your looks, you can get somewhere, and I'm sure you'll keep your eyes open now. Things can only go up from where you came in, toots. They already have, obviously," Beverly sat down and the waiter hastened to pour her a cup of coffee. She poured cream from the silver service and yawned, "Where in Canada?"

"Victoria."

"Lovely town. I've had girls from there and their manners are a plus. The culture reminds me of my mentor in San Francisco. Ever heard of Jessie Hayman?"

"Er, no."

"You wouldn't have I suppose," Beverly watched two of her girls kiss and slide into the water giggling, "she's the greatest madam this continent's ever seen in my book. I ran away from a convent and started with her at fourteen on Ellis Street before the earthquake and fire, and stuck by her afterward in the chaos. She set me up with my own house on Davis Street at sixteen with the bankroll from one of her clients... and a bit of motivation from someone whom I can't explain as you might think me mad, even if you've had your own truck with her." Beverly gazed into the distance and sighed, "That's where I took the name Davis. I took the first name Beverly from the neighborhood hereabouts. I was Violet Adair for my first couple of years in San Francisco. My lover and sister in spirit Suzanne from those days is as close as anyone on earth even now," Beverly grinned. "She's busy producing a raft of daughters that are going to rule the world by her reckoning," Beverly's emerald eyes appraised Sarah from her feet to her face, "I'd say sixteen's not too far from your age. You're well-raised I can see."

Sarah shifted in her chair, "That's um, an amazing story, Miss Davis."

"I don't usually talk about such things, but from what Ollie's told me, you're a survivor who can put a villain in his place," she winked, "and you've got yourself a pistol, I believe." Beverly reached across the table and took her hand, "If you need someone to talk to, please try me. Don't worry, I could tell you tales from my own coming-up that would freeze your blood I assure you. You had the worst possible experience upon arriving here but have acquitted yourself remarkably well it seems, and you have

the seal of approval from a far more experienced soul than myself."
She flashed the whitest teeth Sarah had ever seen, "I admire a girl
with guts. Ollie was completely right to recommend not going
to the police by the way. They're a varied bunch and you certainly
don't want to talk to the wrong ones, and the Sheriffs are another
bunch entirely. They could even be Warren's friends, or co-con-
spirators for that matter."

Sarah focused on a huge white bloom on one of the magnolia
trees and swallowed a lump in her throat.

Beverly squeezed Sarah's hand. She winked at Olive, "Take
care of her kid."

"Oh I will, Bee."

A ripple amongst the guests announced the arrival of a fair-
haired man on the terrace. Although he was shorter than she'd
imagined, Sarah again recognized his profile and gasped. Beverly
glanced over her shoulder as he made his way to their table.

"Violet, er... I mean Bee! You're ravishing this morning."

"Anything in skirts, Johnny, how are you?"

"Tip-tops! How else could I be after a night at your resort?
And Ollie, my you're a sight! I loved your last flicker by the
way. The half-breed pickpocket of Paris! I l so loved it when you
dressed as a boy. You were quite convincing, and yet strangely
attractive... and who is this lovely sprite gracing your company?"

"This is Sarah, from Victoria in British Columbia."

"A profound pleasure," John took Sarah's hand and pressed
his lips to it.

"Mr. Barrymore, I... I'm--"

"Ravishing, lovely... sunlight glistening on a drop of dew
and the answer to my prayers, perhaps?"

Sarah giggled, having completely forgotten the horrors of
her first day for a moment.

John Barrymore squeezed her hand and released it with
what seemed the most profound regret. He turned to Beverly, and

in the most resonant stage voice, said, "Once again your hospitality was without equal Bee. Tell Diana how I appreciate her efforts whenever she awakes and that I shall cleave to her memory as I go through the day. I'm afraid it shall all be but a pale shadow after the pleasure of her company."

"Didn't you use those exact words when I was fifteen?"

John smiled, "And I meant them from the heart, Violet! Oops, there I go again. I'll always think of you as Violet. You were Jessie's best girl."

Beverly laughed, "I think you said that to Leah too."

"Well…"

Beverly arose, gave John a lingering kiss, and they parted smiling. She turned to Olive, "He's a character. Coming to the party tonight?"

"Count on it Bee. I've got to get home to Wilshire though and see what Jack's about."

"You'll probably end up at Mary's party then."

"I doubt it. Doug hates too much drinking when he's not with close friends and he's an absolute tyrant about *other* things, and Mary's having problems with Owen. The divorce isn't finalized you know. Mabel said that while Owen was raving drunk over at Buster's place, he said he was going to shoot Dougie. I don't want a scene if he shows up at the house," she scowled, "I'd rather not be there at all."

Beverly shrugged, "Have you a costume?"

"A studio full; I plan to take Sarah with me today to get outfitted."Beverly yawned, "Can't wait, then."

Sarah tore her eyes away from the pool, "How do you manage here Miss Davis? I mean with all this high-class clientele, and the… you know, the authorities?"

Beverly tapped crimson nails on the marble tabletop, "Doll, half the authorities are customers, and the rest are either rich old money or Jew boys from the studios trying to outspend them.

Heads would roll in City Hall were anything but good service to come from the coppers in regard to us. There'd be a new District Attorney damn quick for that matter. That D.A. Woolwine knows which side his bread's buttered on I assure you, and I've got a troupe of private dicks who patrol the grounds too. I've got women who know their husbands are clients who ask me for everything from styling tips to where I get my cooks." She chuckled, "I loan my housekeepers to the Mayor's wife for that matter and my gardeners do his yard. Besides, after the war and the flu, people want to have a good time. The Twenties will be roaring like a lion, just you wait and see. We're planning a New Year's party that shall dwarf all others, the last one before Prohibition. Studio heads will be making deals beside that pool and in our rooms, fighting over petty grudges and who gets the best girls, whining like the little boys they are, and puking in the hedges come morning." Beverly's green eyes sparkled, "You can count on it." She produced a small pendant from somewhere and slid it across the marble tabletop, "You might keep this."

"I, thank you." Sarah picked it up. The image of a nude woman in a tall headdress who had the wings and feet of a predatory bird was carved upon the blue stone. She was flanked by large owls, and her talons were fixed in the backs of two reposing lions. Her hands held strange symbols. When Sarah turned it over, there were chicken scratch markings on the back and it appeared to be very old. "Whatever in the world is it?"

"It's lapis lazuli."

"I don't mean the stone, I mean the person... if that's who she is."

"Her name is Lilith."

"Who?"

"The first wife of Adam. The one who wouldn't accept his God."

"What?" Sarah weighed the stone in her palm, "What is the language on the back?"

"Ancient cuneiform, from Mesopotamia."

"What does it say?"

Beverly smiled, "Your guess is as good as mine. It was given to me by someone for protection and I'm passing it on to you."

"I... thank you."

"Wear it."

Sarah slipped the thin gold chain around her neck and fastened the little clip behind it. The cool stone hung between and just above her breasts and felt good. She took a breath as she tried to regain their conversation, "But with Prohibition coming, what shall you do?"

"Raise the price of drinks doll. By the way, I hear you've got family in the liquor trade."

Sarah glanced at Olive, who shrugged, "I told her the way you get a job here is by going to parties Bee. Work's enough when you're at it. Hell, the parties are work too."

Beverly chuckled, "Listen to Ollie toots."

Olive grabbed Beverly's hand, "Excuse us Sarah, I've got something I have to speak to Bee about in private for a moment."

"Of course,"

Olive and Beverly glided to the other side of the pool and began a hushed conversation as Sarah's gaze wandered to a young man with an amazing body and immaculate hair who was standing on the diving board at the far end. He stepped to the end of the board and, with perfect form, clove the water in a dive that sent him the length underwater. He popped up at her end with a splash, swept back his hair and winked at her.

Is he a movie star, a guest... a prostitute... or a gigolo?

Olive and Beverly finished their conversation, returned to the table, and gave Sarah identical smiles as breakfast was served.

IX.

Beverly arranged to have Olive's Locomobile fixed at a garage and loaned Olive a limousine, and the chauffeur transferred the black leather suitcase to the trunk bolted to the back of the big black car. Rich burl wood paneling glowed in the sunshine as he opened the door of the boxy cab and they stepped in. The car smelled of leather, perfume, and aromatic pipe tobacco. Sarah stretched out on the red leather seat, took off her shoes, and wiggled her toes. Olive poured herself a scotch from a little bar built into the car's interior, and Sarah yawned. "What kind of car is this?"

"A Rolls Royce Phaeton Deluxe, a brand-new nineteen-twenty model. There ain't another in California yet I bet."

"I'm more used to Model T's... and wagons and horses."

"So, what do you think of Bee's?"

"It's a lot to take in. I'm still thinking about that bidet, actually."

Olive's cheeks bulged. Sarah felt her face reddening before they burst into laughter. "Good to hear ya laugh, toots. You're not still mad about that little shot I gave you, are you?"

"Actually I haven't thought about it at all. I'm too taken with what's going on right now I suppose. It's all so strange and new."

"You thinkin' 'bout what happened up there at Warren's?"

Sarah stared out the window, "Yes, of course." She'd been striving to remember anything about what Warren had done to her before she'd awoken on the hill, but it was either the chaos of dreams or a dark void. Something would come in time. It had to. Some people might simply strive to forget, but for her the feeling she must *know* grew stronger each passing moment. She would watch every step and not trust a soul here until they were vetted by her own measures. There must be somebody in authority here that she could trust if she were going to stay. She sorely missed the presence of the Mounties and the sense of security they'd given her since her earliest memories. She missed their courtesy and their red coats, and she had to find a way to make a living here rather than being in Olive's tow.

"I can't believe how brave you are. Bee thinks so too. She's pretty taken with you and she sees lots of girls who show up here--believe you me. She says somebody else does too, even if I don't know how the hell somebody would yet." Olive grinned, "Let's find costumes that are real scary at the studio. We'll have makeup turn us into witches or old hags or something, with--"

"I don't want to be a hag."

"How 'bout vamps, then? They're like witches, but young trollops, whose lusts are unquenchable?"

"Sounds like you."

Olive shrieked with delight, "Well you've gotta be something. We'll be vamp sisters then. You'll love it."

"All right," Sarah stared out the smoked glass windows at a crew of Mexicans overseen by a fat white foreman planting young palm trees along the road, "I like Bee."

"Everybody does. She don't take lip from nobody, and every rich fella wants her."

"Does she take on customers herself?"

"No, not like her girls anyway. A fella's gotta court her for a helluva long time to get any just like any society lady... except he knows there's treasure at the end of the rainbow without havin' to get hitched and register in the society pages, but he'd better bring back some diamonds from Paris or rubies from India while he's at it, and maybe a health certificate to boot. Then if she don't like him, she just takes the loot and passes him off to one of her girls if he'll settle for that, or the lug's on his way. 'Course she started real young to get where she is now. She runs things like a big business, just like the studios with lots of rich investors too. Bee's sellin' something that never goes out of style, toots."

Sarah shook her head, "It's all so different. I thought the vaudeville circuit in Seattle was wild, but this... I mean, there were girls who were offering themselves for, uh, sale, of course, but nothing like here where it seems they're almost respectable. Morality seems turned upside down here, yet every one of your friends seems so rich and happy."

"They're linin' up to be here hon. Look at the flickers playin' in every Podunk town in America. The movies are like a church where people can go to at night and eat popcorn. It's like that in Canada too, right?" Olive checked herself in her compact mirror and ran a finger around her lips, "We're goin' to Belmore tonight. Jack can come or go hang. He's got an invite from Bill to a shindig at Paramount anyway and--"

"Bill Taylor? That fellow gives me the heebie-jeebies."

"Bill? He was sound asleep when you saw him. Oh I know, the bondage thing. He's actually a nice fella and quite the director. Did you see *Tom Sawyer?* He's a real good guy to know when you're lookin' to break into the flickers. He's runnin' Famous Players Lasky at Paramount with Adolph Zukor and is churnin' out hits to beat the band. He's got Mabel Normand, Mary Miles Minter, and a host of other dames at his beck and call too... as long as they ain't more than half his age anyway. Fella's quite the Romeo."

"I would say Lothario, Ollie, but I'd love to meet Mabel Normand. She's taken more chances than any girl in her pictures: hanging from cliffs, flying aeroplanes, but what about all that horrid stuff that Bill has?"

"That's pretty jake in some circles. I've never actually seen him use it. Bee's got a closet full too, for them that prefers such and all."

"Dear God, she doesn't seem the type."

"She's not. It's a service like the milkman every morning. You think that every milkman drinks milk?"

"No."

"She says customers are like a herd of cattle, but cattle got to be milked, if you want the cream," Olive smirked, "There's plenty money in them thar crazies."

"I don't think I'll ever drink milk again."

* * *

They crossed Hollywood Boulevard past bungalows, studio lots with tents, ramshackle hotels, dilapidated stables, and a car dealership with a row of gleaming Pierce Arrows of several colors. Windmills from recently supplanted farms stood amongst the houses and were now pumping water to a profusion of fruit and ornamental trees in yards tended by Japanese gardeners in wide straw hats. To the west ,wooden oil derricks loomed on Signal Hill against the glimmer of the Pacific Ocean.

Olive cranked down the glass partition separating them from the driver, "Hey Dougie!"

"Yes, ma'am?"

"Take a right on Sunset. I gotta show my friend Babylon." The man nodded, made a wide right turn, and Olive cranked the glass up. "You gotta see this place. I climbed the stairs in back when I was drunk-as-a-skunk one time and almost fell off. They got it fenced now, but I can get in."

The road wound past saloons, bungalows, and farmhouses until they slowed beneath a structure that blocked the sun. Sarah glimpsed a sweep of broad steps beyond a fence on her left that was flanked by strange hawk-headed figures with wings.

"Stop here!" Olive shouted. She was out before Douglas could open her door, kicking a tumbleweed out of the way with her high black boots, "Come on!" She took out a hat pin, fumbled with a padlock on a plank gate, and in moments had it open. Douglas helped her shove the gate wide, and the car pulled through and stopped.

They stood below huge fake pillars sheathed in crumbling plaster rising a hundred feet above them that were surmounted by gigantic cream-colored elephants squatting on their haunches with trunks curled and tusks jutting from their faces. The one above Sarah had a tusk missing. A twisted sheath of chicken wire dangled across its rotund belly where it had fallen away. Beyond was a gigantic painted wall made to look like lapis-blue stone that was now pocked with holes revealing trusses and scaffolding within. The abandoned movie set was bigger than any building she'd seen in any city, and Sarah stood beneath its looming eminence, speechless.

"Well?"

"My God... and to think this was all made for a motion picture!"

"Sixteen reels of film, and now it ain't worth shit." Olive waved a hand, "That's the Great Gate of Imgur-Bel over there." She led Sarah through a jumble of lions, griffins, fierce-eyed statues with curled beards wearing strange pleated hairstyles, more elephants, soaring columns, and piles of disintegrating grey, pink, white, and blue fake stones. They passed through a door under one of the porticos and stood at the base of a very tall edifice of scaffolding and framework where a set of narrow stairs zigzagged all the way to the top. "Let's climb, toots."

"God no, that thing looks dangerous."

"Come on, Sarah, you're the frontier girl. Think Mabel Normand would be chicken? We go up here all the time. I'll show you where Belshazzar rescued the dame in the flicker. Got a little surprise at the top, and it has the best view of Los Angeles." Olive lifted her skirt and began to climb, "Short skirts are jake. I hope they get shorter."

Sarah followed her up the rickety stairs holding a handrail that was none too steady. Olive took more breaks than Sarah needed, and they came out on top of the great blue wall with Sarah in the lead.

Olive plopped down on a board balanced across two rusty buckets, breathing heavily and wiping her forehead. "Whew!"

Sarah gazed out over Hollywood, tracing the gravel track of Sunset threading its way along the base of the hills toward the ocean. Below them, the surface of Silver Lake Reservoir reflected a blue sky. To the right were the slopes of the Santa Monica Mountains with a few new homes on their heights and canyons full of chaparral oak, eucalyptus, and the occasional row of planted palms. The creamy white walls of a Moorish palace crowned a ridge top. A Tudor manor graced another, surrounded by an emerald lawn. "My, this was worth it."

"See?" Olive fiddled with a little cotton bag and proceeded to roll a cigarette.

"I didn't know you rolled your own."

"Just these toots," Olive struck a big blue tip match on the rough boards, lit the misshapen product of her labors, sucked hungrily, and puffed it into a burn, "Try some."

"I don't smoke."

"This is different," she let out a funnel of smoke from her lungs and refilled them immediately, "and this is the place for it. It makes you feel even higher." She waved the crooked cigarette at Sarah, "Come on."

Sarah took the cigarette and sniffed it. The acrid smoke stung her eyes and she flinched.

"Not in your *eyes* toots… in your *lungs.*"

"What is it?"

"Reefer, Mary Jane, wacky weed. The dingies smoke it when they're playin' ragtime and jazz, and the hick farmers and greasers grow it in the Valley for two bits a bag. You can buy a whole bunch for next to nothin', and it's legal too. It won't hurt ya."

Sarah gingerly took the crooked cylinder with a run on one side. A smoldering seed fell out of the end with a pop, and Olive grabbed the reefer out of her hand and licked it just below the spot that was burning unevenly. She handed it back to Sarah and pointed at it with her chin as a gout of smoke oozed from her nose.

Sarah put it to her lips and inhaled. A cloud welled up under her ribs, expanded rapidly, and exploded out in a fit of coughing.

Olive laughed, "No, real slow, like this." She took a long, slow drag and thrust her chest out.

When they finished, Sarah was dizzy from what seemed a lack of oxygen. She blinked and gazed at the ocean that was beaten gold under the sun. The rise of Signal Hill crowned with oil derricks loomed like a cluster of castles against the horizon. Downtown Los Angeles sat dwarfed in the center of a huge plain strewn with scattered clusters of buildings amidst dark oak trees, farms, and fields of golden poppies. The world had a saffron sheen that was broken only by the meandering Los Angeles River with its fringe of trees. "It's... beautiful." She stood up, swayed on her feet, and put a hand on the low retaining wall and the plaster cracked beneath her fingers. Sarah stepped away from the edge with her head spinning.

Olive kissed her cheek, "Think you can get down?"

* * *

They pulled into the drive of a two-story mansion on Wilshire, the chauffeur opened the door, and the girls stepped out giggling before a Victorian/Greek Revival edifice with green awnings. Sarah reached out to touch a lumpy pomegranate hanging from a branch and inhaled the sweet scent of azalea blossoms. She closed her eyes for a moment and felt the sun on her skin.

Blanche appeared in the doorway. "Mr. Pickford ain't home Miss Thomas, he gone with that Mr. Wally Reid over to the Hollywood Hotel to see some fella name Valentino and said for you to meet him in room two-sixty-five."

"Humph. He can catch us at the party."

Blanche's teeth flashed, "He said you'd say that. He wanta know what party you be goin' to."

"Tell him the one with the pretty girls," Olive grinned. "Come on Sarah, let's get in and out of here before those boring lugs get back." She led her through the atrium into a richly appointed parlor that had a polar bear rug and paintings of castles, and up a flight of green travertine stairs. "Gotta get some stuff for tonight."

The master bedroom had a huge mahogany door, high ceilings, and walls covered with gilded fleur de lis. Olive went to a tall bookcase, yanked on a volume of Rimbaud, and the shelf slid away to reveal the door of a safe.

Sarah giggled, "A secret door in a bookcase. It's like a scene I saw with John Barrymore in Doctor Jekyll and Mister Hyde." "Pretty jake huh?" Olive spun the dial on the safe and tugged at the brass handle with a grunt. The door opened to reveal shelves stacked with papers and jewelry boxes. She opened a little door at the top, reached in, and produced a stack of bills held together with a paper band. She slid some twenties out of the packet without breaking the wrapper and thumbed through them.

"Why do you need so much money?"

"Party favors. I got to sneak into the Hollywood Hotel to see somebody without Jack and Wally spotting us, so I'm sending you instead. You know what Jack looks like, but he's never seen you."

"Me?"

Olive nodded, "Uh-huh."

"I... all right, I guess. Is that the Hotel Hollywood that we drove by?"

"Yeah but everybody calls it the Hollywood Hotel. Then we'll go to the studio for costumes and makeup." Olive gave her a stage snarl, made her fingers into claws, and giggled, "We're gonna look awful tonight."

X.

The limo stopped at Hollywood and Highland in front of the Hotel Hollywood, a three-storey cream-colored building with gold-striped awnings, a façade like a Spanish mission, and a porch running on three sides surrounded by broad lawns and well-tended gardens. The intersection was crowded, and the car sat idling at the curb as a line of trucks unloaded fresh produce for the hotel's kitchen in the alley out back. Olive pressed two twenties into Sarah's hand, and Douglas opened the door. "I saw Wally's Packard on the other side. Go to the first door in the alley and up the back stairs to room three-twelve on the right, knock, and when a fella wearing eyeliner answers, tell him you're Ollie's friend come for the goods."

"What... whatever is going on?"

"It's a regular thing toots."

"What's the fellow's name?"

"Hughie... and *don't* let him get you to smoke anything while you're there, right?"

"I, um... certainly."

Sarah stepped out and walked between neatly trimmed hedges around a marble fountain with coins strewn across a blue tile bottom. She skirted a porch with lounge chairs under striped awnings where people were smoking cigars and drinking, though it wasn't yet noon. She found the first door at the back of the building, mounted the steps, and tried the knob. It was locked.

Sarah stood at the top of the steps, glanced up and down the alley, and raised a hand to knock.

The door opened on an aquiline-featured fellow with slicked-back dark hair who was dressed in a pin-striped shirt, suspenders, jodhpurs, a shiny straw gaucho hat, and riding boots. His dark eyes stared unfocused beyond her for a moment before they landed on the blue stone pendant hanging from her neck. Sarah caught the most pleasant scent surrounding him that wasn't of perfume or cologne, and she imagined he'd just come from the bed of the most beautiful woman in the world.

At the sight of Sarah, his dark eyes widened and his handsome face split a smile, "You are going in?"

"Yes, er--"

"Please, Madame," he bowed sharply at the waist and waved her in with a flourish, "you are staying here?"

"I, um, a friend is."

"He is a fortunate fellow indeed. Oh," a flash of chagrin crossed his unblemished features as he took her hand and kissed the back of it. Sarah felt a thrill as his lips brushed her skin and squeezed the money in her other hand. "My apologies, the name is Rudolfo... or Rudolph, if you prefer, Miss . . ?"

"Sarah, Sarah McCallum. You look so familiar. What, may I ask, is your whole name?"

He chuckled. "Rodolfo Alfonso Raffaello Pierre Filibert Guglielmi di Vanentina d'Antonguolla, but as I said, you may call me Rudolf."

Sarah swallowed, "How old were you before you could say that?"

She felt the heat of his grin on her face. "Four, my Mama drilled me."

"Well, it's wonderful to meet you Rudolph."

"I am racing my horse against Mr. Fairbanks this afternoon on the Hollywood Boulevard," he winked, "would you care to witness my triumph?"

"I, er, I really don't have time at the moment... best of luck though."

He gave her a flash of disappointment, "Then you must let me accompany you soon to see my new motion picture, *The Delicious Little Devil,* with Mae Murray at least. It is playing at the La Paloma not far from here," The clang of a streetcar made him wince. Rudolfo stared down the alley and tipped his hat, "I am afraid I must depart before I am paralyzed by regret at the decision I have made as to my own future," Rudolfo tottered for a moment on his feet, squeezed his eyes shut, and opened them, "and I must dine at once on the food of my own country. My body demands it, as she has--" he blinked and seemed to lose his balance for a moment as he held her hand in both of his own and warmth radiated up her arm. "You light up my day like the first rays of dawn, my dear Sarah. Perhaps if I am so blessed we shall meet again."

Sarah fought the overwhelming urge to kiss him, "It's... been a pleasure."

Rudolfo gazed up at the third floor with a look of profound regret, bowed, and disappeared down the alley as Sarah stood holding the door with her right hand balled in a fist grasping the last vestige of his warmth.

* * *

The operator opened the gilded cage of the elevator as laughter echoed down the hall of the third floor. Two young women staggered out of a room at the end with a bottle of champagne. They spotted Sarah and burst into giggles. She smiled back as she approached the door of 312. She thought she could smell the subtle scent she'd smelled on Rudolfo coming from 313 across the way, stopped, and examined the door as something fluttered in her stomach. She let out her breath, knocked on 312, and waited for a response.

The door flew open. Sarah stared at the most effeminate man she had ever seen, who was wearing a lavender silk kimono with eyeliner around reddened pale eyes that seemed to examine her with utter contempt, "Well?!"

"I, um… are you Hughie?"

"Who wants to know?"

"I'm Olive's friend, Sarah."

"Ollie?"

"Yes, Ollie, she sent me for--"

"Darling, come in!" Hughie yanked her into the room and slammed the door behind her.

The walls were obscured by tapestries and gauzy silks that made the place seem like the inside of a tent. In the exact middle of the room was a bed covered in red silk surrounded by carved Chinese camphorwood boxes, two carved stools, and a tall brass hookah. Sarah sensed someone peeking from behind the curtains to her left, but when she turned, there was only the rustling of drapes. The place smelled of incense, musk, and a cloying sweetish aroma that was nearly sickening. Under it all was the need of a thorough cleaning.

Without warning, the undigested smell of death roiled up from somewhere in her memory and Sarah fought an urge to bolt and run. She measured the distance to the door.

"Ollie sent you to pick up for the party?"

"I guess so. I mean… yes."

Hughie shot her a sideways look, like a snake about to strike, "Well, she *did…* or she *didn't.*"

"She did."

"All right then. Care for a couple toots?" Hughie folded his legs on the bed in the middle of the floor, took a black ball from one of the carved boxes, and sliced off a few flakes. He placed them in the bowl of the hookah and lit the pile with a long match.

"I, um, I was supposed to pick up and get downstairs. Ollie's waiting in the limo. Her husband Jack's here with Mister Reid. She doesn't want to be seen, eh?"

"A little reacharound while the dog's at play?"

"Say what?"

"I understand, darling. Here you go." Hughie opened another box and took out a package of yellow waxed paper the size of a candy bar that was tied with red ribbon. He tossed it to her, and she handed him the bills she'd crushed to a damp mass. "Ta-ta!" Hughie dismissed her with a wave.

A huge black man wearing silk pantaloons and a turban with a glass ruby in the middle appeared from behind the curtain and opened the door. Sarah hurried past the door of 313, and something seemed to leap out at her in the air of the hall as she rushed down to the street.

* * *

She got in the limo and handed Olive the package. Olive peeled the yellow waxed paper back with a grin to expose the dark lozenge that looked like a piece of tar and sniffed, "S'good. Hughie always has the best."

"Is that opium?"

Olive nodded and slipped it in her lead beaded purse, "Yeah, but we're not a bunch of depraved coolies around here. Hughie's a bit strange but he's harmless. This stuff's always at the best parties, and if you expect to be taken seriously, you've got to bring your own once in a while and not mooch off the other guests. What goes around comes around you know and if we get sleepy, I've got coke," she grinned. "We had this game of strip poker at Buster Keaton's I kept winning couple'a weeks ago. Everybody was smokin' 'O' and couldn't concentrate." She giggled, "The fellas were *so* mad. 'Ollie, when are you gonna lose some of those clothes like the rest of us?' While they were smokin' away, I was stayin' awake with the ol' eye opener that I was doin' in the bathroom. I won the pot and made Buster get down to his undies before I let him go. 'Course I coulda took him to a room." She chuckled, "Made him think I was gonna, too, but I was just show-in' them guys a girl can win the game and leave with the money *and* the goods. Boy, was he disappointed."

"I don't think I'll play that game."

"No need. The parties at Belmore are never like that. Bee's houses have much more propriety. They're an actual business, and she wouldn't let something like that go on in the parlor if you held a gun to her head. It all happens in the suites. You'll never find a spot on the glassware or a stain on the sheets either, ever."

"That's nice."

Olive threw her arms out and yawned, "Let's go to the beach to eat and have a drink." She cranked down the glass partition to the front of the cab and ran a hand glittering with rings across Douglas' shoulder, "Hey Dougie, let's go to Venice." Olive rolled up the window.

They headed down another broad boulevard past markets and warehouses alongside busy railroad tracks. Sarah cranked down the window, caught the smell of the sea, and inhaled deep-ly. When she turned around, Olive had pressed some opium into a thin brass pipe and held it out to her. "No, none for me thanks."

"You sure Sarah? It's fun."

"I'm sure."

Olive shrugged, "Put up the window." She lit the pipe with a match, sucked loudly, and blew out a thick white cloud with the same cloyingly sweet smell Sarah had noticed at the house on Lank-ershim and Hughie's room. Olive took another puff and put it out.

Sarah rolled the window down to clear the air, let out the breath she'd been holding, and took another big draught of the sea breeze as they paralleled train tracks toward the ocean. Build-ings with fantastical spires in bright colors appeared like some-thing from a painting where railroad tracks crossed a canal on a bridge toward the docks of Santa Monica. They approached another bridge arching over the green canal water decorated in plasterwork arabesques. She spotted a gondola with several well-dressed people seated under parasols being polled by a gondolier in a striped shirt and straw hat and caught a snippet of song in Italian. "My word…"

"You gotta see the pirate ship they got at the Pier. I met Jack at Nat Goodwin's resort here. I go to the Pavilion all the time to dance and there's so many places to party you can't keep track of 'em."

They drove between Italianate façades and crowds of tourists with vendors selling cold drinks and snacks, and the limo slowed beside a miniature locomotive complete with a coal car. People were stepping out of the seats in the low cars behind it as others waited in line to board.

"Here!" Olive barked.

Douglas stopped the limo suddenly, evoking the blast of a horn.

"Fuck you!" Olive shouted out the window. She laughed and yanked Sarah out of the Rolls.

"I can't park here Miss Thomas; I have to find a spot."

"Whatever, Dougie," Olive skipped toward a man in a conductor's uniform next to a booth that had a long line of people waiting at it, "Two for the train, Charlie."

The conductor turned, saw who was speaking, doffed his cap, and eyed Sarah, "Miss Thomas, why certainly."

Olive pressed a bill into his hand, "Keep the change, toots."

The conductor approached a couple with a small boy in the first car and whispered something. The woman scowled from underneath her flowered bonnet, but the man nodded as he stared at Olive with his mouth agape. The man tipped his straw hat, and the little family got out and moved to the seats behind. The conductor held out a hand, and Olive and Sarah boarded the little train.

When the train was full, a whistle sounded and they jerked forward. Sarah took off her satin cloche hat to let the breeze cool her scalp as Olive leaned back in the seat and stared into space.

They headed along a canal toward the amusement pier past a plethora of attractions. The rattle of a roller coaster and barking of vendors filled the air. A young man in a straw hat tried mightily to interest passersby in the girls dancing within a garishly painted edifice behind him as he pointed to paintings on bed sheets hanging on either side of the entrance.

"That's where Dolores worked when we met."

"Dolores?"

"Yep. That's the Race Through the Clouds coaster. I almost lost my lunch the first time I rode it. Boy... *that* would have made *Variety* let me tell ya: Olive Thomas the movie star pukes on the hoi polloi!"

"How will Douglas find us in this crowd?"

"Don't worry, he'll be waiting at the station when we're done, or drive around if we get off somewhere. He'll just drop my name and ask the bulls for help."

"Oh."

Olive craned her neck as they rounded a turn and began to wave frantically, "Hey there's Bill!"

A tall graying man in a pinstriped shirt and tweed vest was walking from the amusement pier with an arm around the shoulders of a petite, very pretty blonde who could have been his daughter, with his other hand holding a tweed coat draped over his shoulder. On spying them, Bill stopped, took his arm from around the girl, and then put it back with slow deliberation. The girl saw Olive and gave a little wave.

"And that's Mary Minter. Guess the ol' bag ain't around to chaperone. Wonder how he snuck her away?"

"Mary Miles Minter, the actress?"

"Yep, looks like a baby huh?"

"I, yes, she certainly does."

"She's just a few months younger than you are actually," Olive snickered, "The horny ol' buck couldn't stay away from her if you held a gun to his head. Come on," Olive stuck fingers in her mouth, let out a shrill whistle that made Sarah jump, and yelled at the engineer to stop the train.

The engineer turned with a scowl but when he saw who commanded, him he rang the bell. The train rattled to a stop before crossing a canal on another bridge. Olive lifted her skirts and piled out of the train with Sarah behind her. She stopped next to the couple they'd displaced and pressed a silver dollar in their son's hand. "Thanks, young Master. You can have the front seat now, and make 'em take you on the Race Through the Clouds."

The boy's eyes were as big as the coin, "Thank you Miss Thomas!"

His father tipped his hat as his mother looked away.

Olive greeted Bill with a hug. Mary eyed Sarah with a tentative smile on her child's face. Her cheeks were rosy from the sun, with the creamy texture of adolescence shaded by the broad straw hat. Mary's golden curls and bright blue eyes added to the impression she was very young indeed.

"Oh Mary... I can't *believe* that deal with Paramount!" Olive gushed, "good God, girl, Jack's sister is looking over her shoulder even as I speak I swear."

Mary gazed down at the pavement, "Thank you Ollie. How are you?"

"Just ducky, toots, oh, this is Sarah," Olive seized Sarah's hand and dragged her forward, "she's from Canada and is destined for great things herself."

Bill grinned, "Canada eh? I served in the Canadian Army in the War. Couldn't wait around for the States to get in when English and Irish boys were dying don't you know?" Bill towered over the three young women, seeming to draw sustenance from their company like a plant drawing water from its roots, "Well, seeing as we're all together, how about lunch on me?"

Mary jumped with a little shriek, Olive put hands to her ears, and Sarah blinked as half a dozen girls screamed at the tops of their lungs from the interior of an amusement with **The Cave** painted over the door. They appeared from the cavernous entry to form a giggling knot on the promenade before they dashed into the entrance of the **Plunge Bathhouse.**

"Yeah, I'm starving!" Olive shouted over the cacophony coming from **The Cave.**

"Well," Bill pointed toward a building on the corner with a triangular sign proclaiming **Mecca Buffet,** "Would the Mecca do?"

"Guess it'll have to." Olive nudged Sarah and winked.

They followed Bill and Mary into the busy interior. People were lined up taking trays to select food from a long counter, and a noisy couple stepped between them and began grabbing cups and plates as Bill and Mary moved down the line up ahead.

Olive leaned into Sarah and cupped a hand to her ear, "Bill can't be seen drinkin' with Mary," she whispered, "bet he's dyin' for a scotch."

"What's going on?"

"They're lovers, Sarah, not that yours truly has the right to criticize. I was doin' Florenz Ziegfeld when I was younger than that, but her mom hates Bill with a passion. She signed a contract with Paramount for one-point-three mill for nine features and Mom's in charge of the loot 'cause she's a minor."

"My God, that's--"

"Shhhh!"

They found a padded booth against the back wall with every eye in the place upon them. Sarah glanced about at the people whispering and chattering at the sight of three major celebrities. A handsome young man in a pinstriped suit and a straw hat was ignoring Olive and Mary and staring fixedly at Sarah. She winked at him and he broke a smile. Sarah grinned.

"I mean really, congratulations on the contract, Mary," Olive resumed, "we're all wondering what you'll do next with baited breath."

Mary glanced at the banana split she'd construct-ed, picked off a sliver of almond, and put it in her mouth. "Thank you Ollie. It's getting awfully hard to go anywhere in public though."

"That big hat's gotta help. You need some dark glasses toots," Olive gave her an impish grin. "Wouldn't it be jake if you two got together... I mean married?"

Mary's face lit up.

Bill's shoulder twitched as he squeezed Mary's leg under the table and gave Olive a gray-eyed look of disdain, "Ollie, we--"

Mary's gaze was like a puppy petted into bliss, and Sarah found herself grinning at the unfettered joy radiating from her. It was the same smile Angeline had when some wonderful surprise had come into their lives. One that Sarah supposed she'd had her-self once upon a time. It made her want things to actually be that way, though she knew it was impossible, and that Bill was a cad for making Mary believe in him. "Well I'm new here, but I have to say that I do still believe in true love, for what it's worth."

Mary's smile spread to encompass Sarah and grew to take in the world.

Bill's Adam's apple bounced as he ran a long-fingered hand across a patrician nose, "Well, we--"

"Miss Thomas." A policeman was at their table with his blue hat in hand.

"What?"

"Your chauffeur says you disappeared off the train. He came to the station and asked us to find you."

Olive winked at Sarah, "See? I tol' ya."

* * *

The limo pulled up to a gate in Culver City at an arched entry proclaiming **Selznick Pictures**, and Sarah felt a thrill ripple up her spine.

The man in the guard shack spotted Olive as she rolled down the window and grinned, "Been wonderin' where you been, Miss Thomas. Folks been saying you gone and skedaddled over to Paramount after that dustup with Miss Normand."

"Don't believe a hundredth of what you hear Patrick and a tenth of what you see. I've got a goddamn contract and I love it here. Besides, I love Mabel like a sister."

"Yes ma'am, glad to hear it." Patrick saluted and pulled a switch that rolled back the iron gate.

Olive had Douglas wait in the car as she led Sarah past what looked like open corrals with white sheets draped over them to diffuse the light and down an alley between whitewashed buildings with red numbers painted on big doors. She stopped at number twelve and twisted the iron handle. Hinges creaked as she pulled it open and reached for the light switch. The big room was filled with racks upon racks of costumes, and Sarah followed her between the rows as Olive put a finger to her lips with her brow tight in concentration.

"Here they are!" Olive dove between walls of fabric to stop at a rack full of black clothing, "Salome, the Queen of Sheba, vamps and tramps, the Wicked Witch... they're all here. We're gonna be perfect!" Olive held a black cape to Sarah's shoulders, "Hum, you'll need a black wig and some white makeup and eyeliner. Olive pulled another costume off the rack, "Let's get to makeup."

* * *

Two white-faced wraiths appeared an hour later in the studio cafeteria. No one paid them the least attention as they took trays and got in line. Sarah felt as if she was in some skewed fairy tale and adjusted her black wig. Olive's face was similarly framed in black hair, with black eyeliner around her violet-blue eyes. They sat at a long table with half a dozen other people and Sarah tried to still her nerves. She didn't recognize a soul from the movies, although they all obviously worked here.

"I love Halloween. It's my favorite holiday since the flu, even more than Christmas."

Sarah put down a spoonful of canned pears before it got to her mouth, "Why?"

"After seeing all those people die, I kinda like a holiday where the dead get their day, to play and all. They got the Day of the Dead in Mexico. We were down in Baja when they had that. They sell candy skeletons and skulls and stuff and go out to the graveyards singing and yammerin' away in their lingo drinkin' beer and tequila. I got one big belly ache from that stuff, let me tell ya. Not the liquor, the damn candy. It's got enough sugar for a year. Ever have tequila? Anyway if you believe in the Devil, you'd have to ask his permission to see most of the folks I've known since Ziegfeld days. Not to mention one goddamn fuckin' uncle in good 'ol Charleroi P.A."

"You too?"

"Triangle Pictures felt like home to me when I came out from New York, and then *boom;* the whole kit and caboodle collapsed with the Spanish flu. Cut a swath through the actors and help with people pukin' blood and dyin' like it was the Black Plague or something. Sure cut down on the hanky-panky for a while let me tell ya. Then Griffith, Ince, and Sennett fell out and went their separate ways, and I had to decide who I was gonna go with. I got with Myron Selznick here and we been cranking 'em out with money comin' in faster than ever. I'm his number one star now. That Jew boy's got a head on his shoulders let me tell ya, but just the same, one sometimes wonders why one's been spared and others haven't."

Sarah ate her pears and nodded.

A middle-aged man with a narrow face and thinning dark hair walked into the room, saw Olive, and waved. He came over, examined Sarah, smiled perfunctorily, and began speaking without an introduction, "Ollie, sweetheart, ready for New Orleans?"

"You bet Alan, right after New York."

"I'm sending you the script tomorrow. Wilshire?"

"Yes, but tomorrow I'm sleeping off tonight. How 'bout the next day?"

Alan gave her a thin smile, "All right kid. You're both rather horrible looking by the way."

"Thank you. Oh, Sarah McCallum, this is Alan Crosland. He's directing *Glorious Youth* in New Orleans in January." She grinned, "Cajun food and a big 'ol budget," she gave Alan a sideways glance, "but he'd better line up the refreshments after Prohibition hits if he wants to keep his crew."

"I wouldn't worry about that, darling. Storyville is a hoot. I'll probably have to get you an armed guard if you want to go there."

Sarah glanced from one to the other and smiled, "How nice to be outdoors and filming in January."

Alan nodded, "We're changing the title to *Youthful Folly,* Ollie," he turned to Sarah, "and where might you be from, Sarah?"

"Victoria, in British Columbia."

"Lovely town, I had the pleasure of attending a wedding there once. The gardens are fabulous. I see those beautiful blue eyes Sarah, but what color is your hair actually?"

Sarah drew the wig back on her blond hair.

"Ah, I'd love to see you with that corpse color scrubbed off. Perhaps at the pool party at Doug Fairbanks' place on Sunday?"

"Yeah, Alan, she's jake in a bathing suit you can bet."

"I've just been in town a couple of days Mr. Crosland."

"You've done well then. How did you two meet?"

Olive shrugged, "We're both orphans of the storm I suppose."

Sarah nodded.

XI.

Olive produced a tiny green vial from a crevice in the limo's burlwood furnishings and held it in front of Sarah's face. "Care for a sniff?"

Sarah leaned against the big leather seat and drew her knees up under her chin, "Is that cocaine?"

"Yep. Been layin' off the nose for a week now. It was starting to bleed and drip something awful, but Mabel showed me how you got to rinse it out with warm water every time. We can do that at Belmore," Olive pulled the cork stopper, stuck a miniature silver spoon no bigger than a toothpick into the vial, and lifted a little pile of powder to her pretty nose.

Sarah gazed out the window and scowled.

"You really oughta try this. Oh come on, don't tell me you didn't like that shot, Sarah. It got you right out of your funk in a jiffy hon, you lit right up. This is way milder anyway. Everybody does it. You've got to loosen up, toots."

Sarah tapped her foot on the floorboards and continued staring out the window. "I'm letting everyone I ever knew down acting like this. I came here at some expense and far greater risk than I'd ever dreamed of to find honest work, and so far all I'm doing with you is running around to strange parties... and this. This isn't me. How can I ever look at myself in the mirror again? I mean I don't want to offend you, and I like you dearly, and things are wonderful here in a way, but these drugs are scaring me half to death Ollie," Sarah had a look of genuine misery. "What's to become of me?"

"Hon," Olive put her hand on Sarah's, "you're not letting 'em down. They're gone, so how does your family know? Do you believe in communication with the dead? It's Halloween so maybe you can ask them yourself tonight. There's Spiritualists coming to Belmore for a séance, and believe me they like this stuff too. They say it puts 'em in closer touch with the departed."

Sarah dug teeth in her lip, brushed hair away from her face, and grabbed the vial and spoon with a scowl. She threw some into one nostril and put a hand to her nose trying not to sneeze as seltzer water hissed in her brain.

Olive giggled and squeezed her shoulder, "Do the other side or you'll be lopsided all evening." She rummaged in her gauzy black gown and produced another vial the light pooled in like a dark red ruby.

Sarah rubbed her nose, "What's that?"

"Fake blood, I had Charles the makeup man whip it up. Here," Olive opened the vial, stuck a little camel hair brush in it, and wrapped fingers around Sarah's chin, "You'll be dripping blood from your mouth like a real vampire."

Angeline's death-white face crashed across Sarah's vision on a rising tide of cocaine. Blood ran from her quivering lips and smeared her chin where Sarah had touched it. Sticky blood coated Sarah's fingers and hollow coughs wracked her sister's chest. She was holding Angeline's clammy flesh again as her little sister trembled in a chill wind striving to blow her off that precipice on which she teetered. Sarah clung to her with all her might as Angeline's head drooped back in a cascade of blond hair like the head of a doll. An abyss opened beneath them, and she fell where Sarah couldn't follow.

"*No!*" Sarah grabbed Olive's wrist.

"Ow! Hey!"

Sarah clutched Olive's thin arm for a moment, staring into her startled violet eyes. She let go and burst into tears, "Oh God, I'm sorry!" Sarah sobbed and squeezed Olive, who was trying to hold the brush away, "I, I saw my sister when she died of the influenza like she were right here... right *now,* right with me!" Sarah put hands to her face as her lower lip quivered and a squeal of anguish rattled it, "I'm so sorry!" she gazed at her makeup-whitened hands and fought another sob, "I think I'm losing my mind!"

Olive rubbed her wrist and swallowed, "Damn you're strong. It *was* a bloody damn flu, wasn't it?"

Sarah nodded vigorously and fought to swallow a huge lump in her throat, "Yes... our Doctor Woodsworth called it 'hemorrhagic.'"

"Damn straight hon. I saw people die from it too, lots. But it's Halloween, and don't that make blood all the more appropriate? I mean we're alive, toots, and wouldn't your little sister want to have fun on Halloween? Think of her as one of the guests at the séance. Maybe that'll make things better or something."

Sarah examined the face *Photoplay* and *Vogue* praised as childlike and angelic that was close enough to touch. She'd hung a photo of a painting of Olive by Harrison Fisher cut from the pages of *Vogue* on the wall of her tiny room in Vancouver after her uncle had taken the house in Victoria even before she knew who she was. *Olive Thomas.* Even in the dead white makeup and black eyeliner with fake blood dripping at the corners of her mouth, Olive was beautiful.

Olive blinked long lashes and wiped a tear from Sarah's cheek with a fingertip. She licked her finger, smoothed Sarah's makeup where it had a streak, and kissed her. Her lilac eyes glowed, "You really need some blood Sarah, come on."

* * *

Belmore had cars bumper-to-bumper along the wide circular drive and the street beyond the gate. Since they were in one of Beverly's limos, they had a spot in the garage. Douglas helped them from the car while remarking on the quality of their costumes, and Olive tipped him again.

They entered through a parlor all in gold having a table set in the middle with a punchbowl surrounded by ladyfinger sandwiches. Young women in evening finery, witches' hats, gilded masks that covered all but their eyes, and cat whiskers painted on smooth cheeks examined them as they passed. There were so many beautiful women here that Sarah began to wonder if her dreams of being in pictures were no more than that. These girls were all worthy of far more than a look, yet most were probably whores… or call girls, or whatever they preferred to be called while engaged in trading their bodies for some form of financial success.

Olive led her through the crowd by the hand nodding and smiling as it parted for them, and Sarah held on tightly as the cocaine made her blood seem to surge from one end of her body to the next. Her skin felt flushed, and she badly wanted to check herself in a mirror.

They arrived in the Persian Room, done in crimson wallpaper with geometric patterns and shimmering golden tapestries flowing down between high windows. A glowing chandelier of sparkling crystal dangled six feet down from the high ceiling. The carpet was thick, crimson, and full of intricate patterns from the distant Zagros Mountains. Another rush ran through her. Sarah stared at a piece of watermelon ground into the rug and tried to get her bearings.

"There's Bee," Olive waved at Beverly, who was standing with two white-bearded gentlemen in tuxes, one with a monocle and ebony cane, and the other in a blue Admiral's uniform.

Beverly smiled, excused herself from their company, and people parted at her approach. She locked eyes with Sarah and brushed her cheek with the whisper of a kiss, "Back so soon, my dear." Her finger touched the blue pendant between Sarah's breasts, "I'm glad to see you've kept this."

"In all honesty I've no better place to go, Miss Davis."

Beverly made a little laugh and raised an eighteen-button evening glove to her lips, "Honesty's a wonderful thing between the right people, as is lying at times. A girl with your looks and moxie must have learned that by now. You seem so fresh I can't get over it," Beverly turned to Olive and kissed her cheek in turn, "I think you've found your complement in her, your doppelganger." She grinned, "I wonder what kind of equilibrium two girls such as you might arrive at? Should be interesting, Ollie."

Before Sarah could ask what *doppelganger* meant, Beverly led them into the big ballroom she'd glimpsed from the patio that morning. It had a band equipped with brass and woodwinds, whose members were taking a break at the long buffet table at the moment. An open bar against the windows was doing a landslide business pouring drinks as magnums of scotch, bourbon, gin, and schnapps emptied into glasses. Ice cubes rattled and champagne bottles popped, launching corks amongst the streamers of orange and black draped from the high ceiling.

Olive inserted herself into the crowd around the bar that parted for her as it had for Beverly and returned with two brimming champagne flutes. She shoved one at Sarah, who grabbed it before it spilled on her dress. "A toast, toots!"

Sarah stood holding the glass, staring at the bubbles crawling up its sides, "For what?"

"To us, hell... to surviving. You coulda died your first night here and now you're on top of the world. I don't know... how about to you gettin' a good one tonight to make up for that go-round with Warren?"

"Please don't talk about that." Sarah downed the glass in one toss and burped.

Olive put fingers to her lips, "Sorry," she chuckled, "you sure finished that one quick."

Sarah felt little bubbles percolating in her stomach and accepted another glass off a tray from a girl in a French maid's uniform cut to the thighs.

* * *

When the band resumed, a man stood on the platform and sang a song written for Olive for her new film *The Glorious Lady*. It was called *The More I see of Somebody Else, the More I Think About You*. Every man in the room wanted to take turns dancing with Olive, and she tried to oblige as it was performed three times more. When the fourth time ended, Olive wiped sweat from her brow, held another gentleman away for a moment, and clapped her hands, "Something faster!" The band stuck up a faster tempo, and Olive spun into his grateful arms.

Someone took Sarah's hand, and she tossed the black cape on a chair and joined him. She'd done a bit of ballroom and had been in a vaudeville troupe for two months in Seattle, but this was an overheated room full of beautiful people and skirling horns where the women danced with her as much as the men. Sarah closed her eyes and was tossed spinning from the hands of a tall, dark gentleman she'd surely seen in some picture into the arms of another who caught her as she fell. Her wig fell to the polished boards, to be snatched up by someone who placed it back on her head at an angle. She gasped as a beautiful woman with black hair, green eyes, and the whitest skin she'd ever seen kissed her. Sarah stared into her eyes as time seemed to stop dead, inhaling her sweet breath before the woman sent her spinning amongst the crowd. Sarah looked back for her, but she was gone. She stood stock still in the middle of the rippling crowd. Ice formed in her spine as she searched for the woman. She gripped the lapis pendant between her breasts. It felt hot.

Strong arms enfolded her. She was holding the man she'd almost run into behind the Hollywood Hotel. He wore a gaucho's hat, a red silk scarf with a shimmering silver shirt, and incredibly tight black leather pants. A Cheshire grin spread Rudolfo's face as they stared into each other's eyes from inches away. The band began a tango, and she partnered with the handsome Italian for two dances. People clapped amid shouts of 'Bravo!' All the chaos of the last two days seemed to have led to this: a dance in a ballroom amongst streamers and music and laughter where she was free and floating as if on clouds. She was the one who gave the first kiss. Rudolfo answered with a second.

When Rudolfo bent her backward in the grand finale, she noticed a stocky man in a black cape watching her, whose face was painted in a death's head grin with eye sockets darkened to skull-like pits. He flashed yellow teeth as Rudolfo lifted her to her feet. She glanced back, but the man too was gone. Sarah searched the crowd as Rudolfo made to kiss her again, but she put a palm to his chest and pushed him away.

Rudolfo's face fell, "Dear lady... I have offended you?"

"No, I--" another ripple of fear shot up her spine, "I'm sorry... I... excuse me!"

She dashed off the dance floor, nearly tripping on her long black dress as she dodged another couple who were kissing in an alcove, passed through the blood-lit Persian Room, and glanced around. There had to be somewhere she could be, somewhere she could hide. She saw Tillie and ran to her. "Is Beverly here?"

"She's with guests in the front parlor. Is there something wrong ma'am?"

"Could you find her, please?" Tillie brought her to Beverly, who excused herself from her company the instant she saw Sarah's face. Beverly gave her a hug, "Do you need to be alone, love?"

"Oh yes." Tears rolled down Sarah's cheeks, and she swiped at them angrily.

"You're safe here. Tillie, take her to the Gold Room next to mine and let not a soul disturb her unless she wishes."

"Olive will--"

"We'll let Ollie know, doll. Go get some rest. Ring the bell should you need anything and don't worry about some trifle. You're safe here."

"Oh thank you so much, Miss Davis."

"Just Bee," Bee kissed her on the mouth and ran a finger across her smeared makeup, "You should wash your face. You look like a sad mime."

Sarah nodded, began to laugh, and started to cry again.

* * *

She awoke with makeup smeared across a silken pillowcase. She was still wrapped in the black witch's shawl, threw it off, and sat up with a groan. A pitcher of water stood beside the bed. She filled the glass beside it to staunch a throat so dry it felt as if it were going to bleed. There was no sound of a band, no raucous banter in the hall, not even moans of real or feigned passion from the adjoining rooms.

She made her way to the bathroom and stared at the parody of a witch in the mirror before she scrubbed the awful makeup off with a golden washcloth. A high-pitched shriek came from somewhere below, muffled by the heavy oaken floorboards. It sounded like Olive. Sarah stared at herself for a moment in a black silk slip and skirt and went to the door.

The hall was dim with only small lights in sconces near the ceiling as she padded on the gold carpet with feet in fraying silk stockings toward the stairs. A stern female voice came from one of the parlors admonishing someone to remain silent, followed by a sudden banging of furniture and a collective gasp. Sarah approached the room. The door was open a crack, and she peered in.

Bee, Olive, John Barrymore, Buster Keaton, Douglas Fairbanks, and a middle-aged woman sat in a room lit only by candlelight around a round teak table that had an inlaid pentagram of ivory in its center. The woman who had commanded silence held up pale ring-covered hands, and they bowed their heads. "Speak, Charlotte! Roam the ether no longer, but return to council the living!"

There was a loud knock from beneath the table, and those sitting in the circle gasped.

Sarah felt her mouth tighten in a smirk. She'd seen this stuff when she'd worked for Pantages in Seattle and had been offered a job as a "witness" by a guy whom she wouldn't trust handing her a glass of water for fear of what he'd put in it. She sighed and returned to the refuge of the Gold Room.

* * *

Lorelei grinned at the look on Madame Hari's face as Lorelei raised the table a few inches off the floor, which certainly wasn't in the program, and the wire for the little lead knocker snapped. The expression of Madame Hari, whose actual name was Gladys Drumph, was priceless.

Beverly chuckled. Olive shrieked. Buster Keaton bent down and glanced under the table, "There's a little knocker there... but how in hell did..." He sat up with his trademark blank look and shook his head.

"Well!" John Barrymore said.

Douglas Fairbanks pushed away from the still-rising table and pulled at a pencil-thin mustache, "It's as stable as a goddamn freight car! How the hell did you do that?"

Madame Hari opened her mouth to reply but only swallowed.

"I will not rest until my killer is hung!" A melodious female voice came from above them in the room, and all eyes rose to the darkened lamp in the middle of the ceiling without noticing Beverly's bulging cheeks. *"He lives a life of luxury amongst you as I roam the Netherworld without rest!"* A ragged wail seemed to come from the floorboards, the candles went out, and the table dropped with a thud on the rug.

"Ow! Goddamnit!" Douglas shouted in the dark.

"Shit!" Olive's nails scraped the wall as she lunged for the light switch.

The light came on to illuminate a panting Olive with her hand on the doorknob, Douglas Fairbanks holding the toe of his boot, Buster Keaton examining the underside of the table again, and John Barrymore with a glass of sherry he'd snatched from the table as it rose. He finished it and smoothed his hair.

Beverly rose, "Well, Madame, I'd say your fee is well deserved."

"I... thank you," Madame Hari muttered. Her face was pale.

"Damn, Charlotte didn't tell us *who* the bastard is!" John muttered, "He could be dining in the parlor this moment for all we know."

Olive wiped her forehead, "Cripes, don't make me any more nervous!"

"I get the knocker gimmick, but how did you raise the table?" Buster asked.

Douglas had removed his left boot and was examining his big toe, "What about that goddamn voice? What the hell was that?"

Beverly chuckled, "You mean who, don't you?"

"It must have been Charlotte LeBlanc," John Barrymore said, "wasn't it?"

"Perhaps," Beverly said, "I believe you knew her to some degree, John."

John shivered and shrugged to hide it.

"Perhaps it is she who comes to you as a succubus in the night; you might ask her yourself."

John stared at the drapes, "I do say Bee, please stop."

XII.

Golden light filled the drapes and a robin sang in a magnolia tree amongst gigantic white blossoms. An iridescent green hummingbird hovered for a moment at her window and disappeared in a twinkling.

It's the first of November!

Sarah stretched across saffron sheets, yawned, and gazed at herself in the mirrored ceiling. She ran her hands down her stomach and between her legs. Nothing hurt. She stretched again as the room rotated around her. The girl in the mirror was every bit as well-formed as any of those girls at the party... or any of those movie stars for that matter. Better than most actually. Mary Minter was downright pudgy in comparison and she was getting a million-three.

A Million-Three! How much is that? She could retain a barrister and buy back the house from her uncle, and start a hotel in Victoria, or Vancouver, or buy a boat, or perhaps even some claims on Bonanza Creek or Eldorado, and own a hostelry in Dawson City. Even Olive was thicker in the waist for her size, much thicker than in the first films Sarah had seen her in. Her fingers wandered down her stomach again, and Rudolfo's impossibly handsome face came into her mind with a look of disappointment. Sarah sighed.

A vision of Warren's face in the moonlight erupted with bubbles oozing from his mouth, to flicker for the briefest moment before it subsided. She heard a woman's familiar distant laughter and let out her breath. Much too much had happened. She simply wasn't going to think about it today. Being alone in the wonderful room with a button to push for service was a gift she owed Bee for in spades. Sarah couldn't begin to tell her how much it meant to her right now, but she would try.

She yawned again and considered her situation. Rudolfo would have been wonderfully convenient at a place like Belmore. After all that was the purpose of this place. She sat up and swore at the inkling of a headache.

There was a knock on the door, "Miss Sarah?"

"Yes?"

"Miss Olive is here to see you."

"One moment!" Sarah sprang up, snatched a gold satin robe from the closet, and tottered to the door rubbing her eyes.

As soon as Sarah turned the knob, Olive burst in and wrapped her arms around her to smother her in kisses as the door was shut by the maid, "Oh Sarah! So was I right? How was he?"

"I... how was who?"

"Rudolph! Didn't you . . ?"

"No, Olive!"

Olive's mouth fell open, "What? You *didn't?* God, what a handsome devil. I saw a maid coming from the room he was in with the sheets and they had some blood on them. I was afraid things got a little rough or it was your time of... I, Sarah, he's the number one new fella in Hollywood, and you... you *didn't?"*

Sarah stalked to the drapes and tore them open on the day, "Christ! Are you forgetting exactly what I have been through? How cruelly I've been *used?* I very well could be in an asylum for God's sake, babbling like a child had I been of weaker stuff!" Sarah produced a loud snort that left a bemused expression on her face, "I mean... my God!"

Olive stared at the floor and somehow produced a quick tear at the corner of her eye, "I'm so sorry hon. Anyway you won't believe what happened at the séance. We've all been waiting for you to come down so we could ask you about Rudolfo and tell you about last night, and have breakfast together. Guess I got a little ahead of things, but when he saw you here, he changed his plans to leave and paid Bee extra."

"Paid her?"

"Honey, everybody who has an assignation in the suites of Belmore pays for the privilege. It's for the service and privacy. I mean think about it, somebody's got to keep this joint up," Olive's cheeks bulged, "seein' as I don't work here, I ain't exempt either, toots." Olive patted Sarah on the back, ran her hand down the hollow of it, and squeezed her butt hard, "Well, mine was just ducky anyway after that really spooky séance."

Sarah rubbed her eyes, "Then Bee must have refunded him his money unless he was with someone else. She was there when I asked." She shook her head, "I didn't ask. She was just there when I needed her. *Paid?*"

Olive nodded, "And you could have had Valentino and you let him go!"

"Exactly who is he anyway? He wanted to take me to one of his motion pictures when I ran into him at the Hollywood Hotel."

"Guess you'll have to find out from some of the girls who've been with him. Damn, I wish I'd known. There went a hell of an opportunity sister. Wonder where he traipsed off to? I didn't see him again after you monopolized him on the dance floor for half the night and I thought he was with you. We all did."

Sarah ran hands through her hair, "I've got to get cleaned up. What have you been up to?"

"Oh, I got a good scare, and then I had mine, sister."

"What, er, what was he like?"

"Great, both of 'em. Dolores is a way better kisser though."

* * *

They had breakfast on the patio. Sarah had three glasses of orange juice, four cups of coffee, two croissants slathered in butter and jelly, and eggs benedict with the whites fluffy as whipped cream. She stretched her legs in the sun in a yellow summer dress that had appeared in the closet while she was bathing and pushed the sunglasses that had appeared on the dressing table back up her nose with a fingertip.

Olive yawned, "That was one scary séance. Even Madame Hari was scared. Buster thinks it's all a fancy ploy and wants Houdini to investigate, but everybody else thinks it was probably real. Wish Houdini was there."

"What happened?"

"Madame Hari called on the spirit of Charlotte, this girl we all knew who was in the flickers a bit and worked for Bee too. Some dastard gutted her like a fish and left her at the gate by the film set of Babylon."

Sarah stiffened, "My God, there are too many things like that around here. I'm glad I didn't go."

"So what do you want to know about Valentino?" Olive changed the subject, "I doubt he'll be around again if you just tossed him off like that. Them Guinea boys got a lot of pride, and he's gotta be embarrassed."

"I don't know. He certainly acted as if we might yet meet at a later date."

"Yeah toots, I bet he wants to, but he's gettin' married next week."

"He is?"

"Yep, some dame named Acker. Probably won't last. Marriages come and go here like snow in July." Olive shook her head, "Boy, Sarah, are you *sure* that you've only been with two--"

"I told you I've had boyfriends, but only one who actually got... you know, in."

"Valentino sure would beat Warren huh?"

"Olive!"

"Sorry."

Sarah put her chin in her palm and stirred cream into her fifth cup of coffee as Olive sat next to her in a big straw sun hat watching a young man across the pool like a little girl on an endless vacation. She supposed Olive couldn't imagine all that she had gone through, any more than she could remember exactly what had happened herself. Even though she said she'd been raped, it seemed none of it was quite real to Olive, as if it all were an endless motion picture that just needed editing in the final cut. She knew Olive wanted to help in her way. Sarah tried to imagine what Olive had done with a man and another woman while she'd been curled up in a ball all alone under satin covers upstairs. She glanced at Olive's lips as they caressed her glass of mimosa. Kissing Olive wouldn't be hard to do.

"You missed Houdini. He got out of one of Bee's copper pal's cuffs right here on the patio. He had a row with the Spiritualists before the séance and left early though. Says they're all phonies and he can prove it. It was a really good séance anyway. Even Madame Hari was scared. The table rose in the air, and there was Charlotte's voice from out of nowhere. It sounded kinda different from what I remember, but I guess being dead can change things. You should have come. Anyway we should go to Houdini's house this weekend in Laurel Canyon for a get-together so you can meet him."

"When does someone actually work around here?"

"Flickers are like men and sex: lots and sweat and action, and then *poof!* All done!"

Sarah found a laugh welling up and put a finger to her lips, "Rudolfo certainly can kiss I must say."

"Boy, did you miss out on that one. Toots, I wasn't gonna say it, but I hear tell he's got the biggest--"

"Oh stop."

"I mean it. My girlfriend Dolores says it's like skyrockets and stuff, and she's been around toots. Says he knows how to use it," Olive sighed, "love to give him a try before Monday."

"Is that when he's getting married?"

She nodded, "Girls keep kissin' but men usually don't. Most sonsabitches just get up and wander into the bathroom, then come out lookin' at their watches mumblin' 'bout somewhere they gotta be, but them Guinea boys are romantic as hell. It makes me want to catch up with that pool guy again. Wish I could remember his name."

"Speaking of marriage, where's your husband?"

"Probably passed out between two trollops at one of Bee's other places. Hell, he could be here for all I know. Remember what I told you about this place?"

"She has more than one?"

"One on Redfern and another I've never been to. She's got Swiss bank accounts and rich backers who know it takes a madam to bring home the bacon. She's looking at opening a fourth place I hear."

Sarah closed her eyes and let sun beat on their lids, inhaled, and smelled sex. "Perhaps you'll have to introduce me to your Gypsy lady if I stay here."

"The studio doctor, more like," Olive studied Sarah sitting there with her eyes closed, "Sarah, I want to go get that stuff up at the Thompson place."

Sarah opened her eyes, "What?"

"Bee may know who those girls are in the pictures. Maybe some of them worked for her, or at least she knows who they worked for, and I can sell a lot of that stuff including the bondage crap. Remember that I said they take care of all kinds of customers around here?"

Sarah's upper lip curled, "I thought I was beginning to understand a few things, but I can't understand that."

"Bee knows people who can take care of this without any fuss, and I really want to make sure whoever it is helped Warren kill those girls is caught Sarah, and you do too. Bee and the studios know bosses in the police who'll have their boys set it straight and on the quiet if we have something clear-cut to hand them, along with a little financial incentive of course."

"You mean bribes?"

Olive split a warm baguette, spread butter and marmalade on it, took a bite, and nodded.

"I don't want to go back up there. I want to get a job and never think about it again."

"Bor-ing. Sarah, maybe it's true that it's not all it's cracked up to be makin' flickers, but it sure beats some damn job. It's the parties and the people, who you *know*. I've broke my back rehearsing, even directing, and sometimes I think it's just 'cause it feels so good when you stop and have a wrap party. You get some great idea, and by the time you can do something with it, all these other people got to put in their two cents and it's never the same, and the makeup and the Kliegs are pure torture. They're hot as Hell and awful. Isn't it more exciting to be here? There's already a couple big producers from the party wondering who you are, and you've got one actor on the way up who just might want you in a shoot he's in 'cause his big ol' ego can't take rejection and he's gotta try again maybe, so take it easy, and things will come."

"I can't have sex with everyone."

Olive pursed her lips, "Ain't it a shame?"

Against her will, Sarah chuckled.

Soft hands touched her shoulders and massaged her neck. "How are you feeling dear?" Beverly lilted, "Get some rest?"

"Um, hello Bee. Thank you so much for the room."

"That fellow Valentino is getting quite a reputation around here, but it seems he found one he couldn't catch. No need to go all red-faced about it, love."

Olive was watching Sarah with a little girl grin on her face.

"Do I owe you money, Bee?"

Sarah's companions burst into laughter.

"No, and I'm grateful you're not angry at me for that matter. We arrange things here in a very eclectic manner. People are the most unpredictable product imaginable, and when I saw your condition last night, I simply had to adjust. I'm not a heartless person and we don't practice white slavery," Beverly sat on her left, "and in spite of her banter, Ollie's rather protective of you too, you know." It was Olive's turn to blush. "You're always welcome here Sarah. Now, Ollie has some things she wants to say amongst the three of us I believe."

Olive nodded, lit a cigarette on the end of an ivory holder, and squinted through the smoke, "We were discussing Warren. It may be a secret, Sarah, but Bee's the best keeper of secrets in Hollywood. Gotta be. This is way too important for the two of us. We can't deal with it by ourselves, and Bee knows people who can fix things like I said."

Beverly studied Sarah, "You're keeping a remarkably even keel after that event at Warren's, and I want to apologize again for last night. You never know with girls around here. We keep track of any eventuality and try and make it pay the bills is all."

"Um, that's all right… and thank you again for the room. I hear you had quite a séance. Sorry I missed it."

Beverly stared at the red tile rooftops and pursed her lips, "Scared the bejesus out of Madame Hari. Her little knocker trick couldn't match what was in store."

"You knew?"

"In a way, Sarah," she smiled, "you remind me of myself in Frisco before the earthquake and fire. I landed there at fourteen determined to have a go and never go back to my family. Spent a year working with Jessie Hayman on Ellis Street before the earthquake came. It was like the whole world was bleeding and burning, what with looters, toughs from the Barbary Coast and Chinatown running rampant, and the Army shooting men down like dogs in the street. There was a fellow hung from a lamppost right in front of Jessie's house, but it wasn't a year later I was running my own house at the age of sixteen on Davis Street thanks to my mentor… and someone else I don't need to mention who thinks rather highly of you and may reveal things in her own good time. That's when I took the name Davis. It all came from what Jessie saw in me in those days--"

"Someone else? Who would have been in San Francisco who knew me? I was three years old in Victoria at the time of the earthquake."

Beverly smiled, "You've had someone in your corner ever since a night in the woods, Sarah. Adversity breeds either strength or weakness, or at least it brings it out in a trice. You've shown strength in your trial by fire so far. Sometimes it takes years to see that in a girl, and even then she may fold when the chips are down."

"So far?" Sarah blinked, began to speak, and stared at mourning doves on the phone lines beyond Belmore's walls. She sighed, "Well, thank you, but I'm not that kind of girl, and I'm not ready for any more trials."

"Don't be offended. That's not the point. I speak more to the point than most women because I don't have the time to natter about mundane things while hubby's pretending to run the world. I get more women like that in the afternoons while the man of the house thinks they're playing bridge than you can believe by the way. We've got boys and girls who work the afternoon shift for society ladies. Several are putting themselves through a university that way," Beverly yawned. "Rich women need their recreation too you know, and discretion is not just an art but an absolute in such circumstances." She leaned back in her chair and took a sip of coffee, "Think how *that* would shatter the pride of those movers and shakers. Never had a man yet who could stand a truly strong woman, although there's one or two that I'd like to snatch off his perch for a college try." She sighed, "They respect you in their way when you're as rich as they are and you have the connections they need, but they'd never marry a whore, or at least stay loyal to one no matter what claptrap they spout in the throes of passion. And after they're done, all women are whores anyway."

"Damn straight," Olive interjected.

Sarah inhaled, "I hope not, Bee."

"Bee has fellas who can go up there to Warren's packin' heaters in case there's trouble."

"I can use a gun Ollie; I killed a grizzly bear when I was fourteen."

Beverly stood up, "All right then, how about the three of us go?"

XIII.

They got into a big grey Packard for the journey to Cahuenga Pass and pulled out of the circular drive onto a street full of cars of every color. Cobra and eagle hood ornaments glistened on custom bodies as American and European chassis passed by on tall whitewall tires with red and gilded spokes. Immaculately attired women walked dogs with bejeweled collars on the ochre sidewalks before sprawling mansions swathed in bougainvillea, oleander, narcissus and morning glories along broad streets beneath the towering palms.

Driving through Hollywood to Highland, they passed neighborhoods of clapboard bungalows and beige plaster courts full of lean young men and girls congregating for a new gold rush offered to some with a pretty face. It was as if the Great War, the Influenza, and the winters of the North were a dream from which Sarah had awoken to endless sunshine, yet night here hid an evil for which she didn't even have a name. But she deserved to succeed, and there was bad everywhere. "I just might learn to live here."

Olive yawned, "You've been from the pit to the pinnacle already toots. Reminds me of a flicker I did."

"I still haven't met your husband, except while he was sleeping."

"Ain't no great shakes awake. 'Course he gets plenty of work 'cause of his sister and *Tom Sawyer* was a hit. Mary takes care of Jack and Lottie like they're her kids. He calls her the Queen when he isn't calling her the Czarina or something worse. They're Canadians like you."

"Eh?"

"The Pickfords are from Toronto, shanty Irish from some hardscrabble past just like you and me toots. They're really named Smith, but I guess it was too common like Duffy or McCallum. Maybe you should call yourself Sarah Taylor, or something."

Sarah shook her head, "But I heard he was in the American Navy."

"He got drafted under the Allied Draft Agreement and spent most of his time sipping brandy with some officers on a cruiser in San Francisco Bay, teaching flying' out in the Valley, and procuring girls for the brass," Olive laughed, "I wouldn't fly with him if you held a gun to my head. Mabel Normand's way better flying an aeroplane but they don't let folks know 'cause she's a girl. She did all her own flying in *A Dash Through the Clouds*. Did you see it?"

Sarah nodded.

"Jack got a dishonorable discharge for smuggling girls onto a battleship, but the studio fixed it. He got a nice lieutenant's uniform out of it. He wanted to wear it in a picture, but the blue comes out black on film. They have to make them dark grey, so it didn't work. He wears it to parties though."

Beverly nodded and down-shifted, "They do love their uniforms."

They turned left on Highland toward the San Fernando Valley up Cahuenga Pass and passed the little café where she'd met Warren. Sarah glanced at dirt roads winding into the hills on either side. Were more secret horrors like Warren's hidden in those canyons? More bodies? Her hand slid to her purse and stroked the gun. Her eyes felt heavy and she considered doing some of Olive's cocaine for a moment. Beverly wouldn't be pleased. Beverly didn't seem to have many bad habits at all, beyond selling other people's bodies to select buyers. Sarah liked her and was grateful for the refuge her bagnio had become. She wasn't going to disappoint Beverly by displaying a taste for drugs. At the moment the thought made her stomach jump and churn. She stared at the passing traffic, ground her teeth, and resolved to never do it again.

Beverly turned the Packard into a farmer's market where fruit was piled on tables under a straw roof and wreathes of chilies hung from twine. "Let's get some cider."

"Yeah," Olive seconded, "I'm thirsty! Do they have the hard stuff?"

People shopping at the stand immediately spotted Olive, and an adolescent girl asked for an autograph. While Olive was busy, Beverly waved to an elderly Mexican with a thick white mustache beyond the plank counter. She picked up a dark fruit from a pile, ran her thumb across it, and selected several more, "Muy bien Joaquin, I'll take these and some cold cider for my compadres."

"Si, Miss Davis," Joaquin made haste to provide her with a paper bag as a boy opened a dripping ice box in the shade of the awning and handed her a milk bottle filled with golden apple cider. Beverly put a few more fruit in the bag.

"What are those?"

"Avocados, Sarah."

"Never seen one."

"Then you're in for a treat. We'll have Lupita make us guacamole for lunch." Beverly added a big paper bag with dark stains full of fresh corn chips, a Mason jar full of maroon sauce with green things in it, and several dry chilies to her purchases.

When they got back in the car, Olive took a long drink from the bottle and passed it to Sarah. The car hit a pothole just as Sarah put the bottle to her lips, and it splashed down the neck of her dress. "Shit," she yanked a handkerchief out of her purse, "yuk!" Her companions laughed.

Olive pointed at the adobe hotel ahead, "Stop there wouldya?"

"Not on my time, love.""Bee…"

"I'd fire a girl for that."

"Bee, I am *not* one of your girls!"

"No, you're one of my clients as well as one of my friends, and in spite of my better judgment, I care about you. You've got to watch it Ollie. How many cars have you wrecked? What about that kid you hit in March? Can he walk yet?"

"Yes," Olive snapped, "I sent him a bike and he's riding it… and I bought his dad a Ford."

"Good, but I don't want you all loopy if we're going someplace that could be dangerous, and I'll be damned if I let you handle a gun after using that stuff."

Olive assumed a look of misery that would do a mime proud. Sarah chuckled. Olive gave her a hurt look and let out an extended sigh, "I suppose you're right." She gave the adobe hotel a mournful glance when they rolled by, and a red-haired woman stood in the doorway, cigar in hand.

* * *

When they reached Olive's Moorish castle near the end of Lankershim, a limo was parked in the garage. The Great Danes let out a deep bay before almost knocking Olive down, and the sound of Duke barking from the back yard echoed over the roof.

Beverly stopped the car, cracked her neck, and stepped onto the pink flagstones, "Where are the pictures?"

"In there," Olive skipped toward the shade of the garage, having dropped her act over passing the hotel, "I bet you know some of them Bee!"

"Perhaps," Beverly took off her pigskin gloves and beat the dust out of them, and Sarah walked around the Rolls Royce to join Olive at the shelves in the back of the garage.

"Here," Olive waved the package of photographs.

"Miss Thomas, you have company?"

"Hi Lupita, just a couple friends. Bee bought all this stuff. Can you make us some guacamole?"

"Si," Lupita gathered the groceries and took them in the house.

Olive waited until Lupita was out of sight and began taking pictures out of the leather binder.

Beverly held up a hand, "Wait until we sit down."

Olive handed them to Beverly, and they walked through the house to the patio in back. Duke came barreling across the veranda making little squeals of pleasure, and Sarah fell to her knees, scratched him behind the ears, and dug her fingers into the hair of his chest. He smelled clean and his coat glistened. His tongue flicked across her nose. She sat back on her heals wiping her face with the back of a hand and laughed as a vision of his eyes changing colors came to her.

When they were seated, Lupita appeared with three cold Dos XX's beers, put down three chilled glasses, and returned to the kitchen. Sarah stared at the bottle in front of her as Olive and Beverly poured theirs.

"Whatsamatter?"

"People don't drink it chilled where I'm from. Then again I've never really drunk it at all but for a wee taste. Didn't like it much."

"Warm beer's crazy. I remember poor folks drinking it like that in Pennsylvania. Hated it." Olive poured beer in Sarah's glass until the pale brown head began to run down the sides, "This was brewed for the Twentieth Century, that's what the two X's mean." She held her glass up in a toast, "Salud!"

Beverly had spread the pictures out on the tabletop and was holding one up in the sun, "I know her: Danielle."

Sarah shivered as a warm breeze turned to ice, "That was one of the names on the film reels!"

"She worked at my place on Redfern. I'm surprised she used the same name, but if she was going on a call with a customer who knew her from my place, it makes sense. He cut her," Beverly put the picture down on the table and pointed a purple nail at a long dark line from the girl's navel that ran down between her legs. Olive jumped up and came around to see. Sarah leaned forward clutching her beer as Beverly threw the photo down, "Bastard!"

Beverly swept up the pictures and dropped them in her flowered lead beaded purse when Lupita brought the food. Lupita put a big bowl filled with chips down and a smaller one with mounds of green stuff flecked with brown and red. Sarah watched the others take a chip and scoop it up. She did the same and did it again. She wasn't used to spicy food, but this was excellent. "That's quite good." She took another drink of her ice cold beer. She liked that too.

"How handy are you with that gun, Sarah?"

"I'd rather have a revolver to tell the truth. I've shot an automatic but not this one. They're rather complicated and I don't really trust them. I'm quite proficient with a revolver however. I find them more accurate also."

"Ollie, give her your gun."

"Whoa," Olive shook her head. "Hang on a minute." She went in the house and returned with a big Colt double-action military piece, a huge thing with a wooden handle that had a lanyard ring in the bottom of it.

Sarah took the heavy gun, opened the action, and spun the cylinder as Olive put a box of ammunition on the table. The gun was well-oiled and the action clicked like a well-tuned machine. "This shall do, I suppose. My dad had one just like it and I finished off a bear with one. It certainly will stop the biggest man."

"All right," Beverly produced an engraved Smith and Wesson .38 from her purse, "just like a bunch of gangsters on their way to a dust-up."

"Hope there's no spooks up there."

"Halloween's over, Ollie."

"Yeah, but the ghosts ain't."

Sarah scooped more guacamole with a chip and began to wash it down with the amber beer but to her amazement the bottle was empty. She blinked, "Did you know Danielle well, Bee?"

Beverly gazed at the citrus trees over the pool and up at the hills beyond, "She was rather emotional. Moved her from Belmore to Redfern due to some clashes with another favorite girl of mine, but I finally had to let her go. Women lovers are like that sometimes."

XIV.

A tiny gray deer stood in the rutted drive of the old Thompson place. Her antenna-like ears flicked as the car approached, and she bounded into the brush at the last moment on delicate legs with a black and white flash of tail. Duke let out a bark and stood with his front paws pressing into Sarah's thigh. She wiped a drop of his saliva away and shifted his weight on her leg.

Warren's Ford was where they'd left it. Sarah spun the cylinder on the heavy revolver as Beverly pulled up next to the dusty Model T and killed the engine. Duke jumped over the doorframe to land with a grunt in the yard and sprang onto the porch.

Sarah stepped out of the car, "He'll let us know if anyone's here."

Duke followed his nose across the porch, sneezed, and returned to the yard. Olive tapped her flashlight against her leg.

"Well?" Beverly asked.

Sarah stepped onto the porch with the big gun in hand and tried the doorknob, "It's locked."

"Did you..." Olive began.

"No, I didn't have a key."

"Somebody's been here." Olive sidled behind Beverly, holding the flashlight like a gun. Beverly had her pistol out. "Let's not stand out here. We should check for an entry."

Sarah nodded and began to walk around the house to the right. Beverly and Olive went to the left. Sarah came to a living room window and peeked over the sill into the dim interior. She continued around and boosted herself up on the stones of the wall to peer into the kitchen. When she reached a back patio half-engulfed by morning glory vines, she stepped through a tangle of dead vegetation to the kitchen door and tried it. The pitted brass knob turned with a groan of protest, and she opened the door breaking cobwebs. She stepped into the kitchen with the revolver pointed at the interior door as she crossed the kitchen to the living room and jumped at a grating noise from the other side of the house.

"Hold my foot!" Beverly hissed.

Sarah put a hand to her breast and walked down the hall where Beverly and Olive were attempting to climb in a bedroom window, "Hello."

"Eek!" came out of Olive's mouth as Beverly's .38 spun to point at the bedroom and at Sarah.

"Hey," Sarah ducked behind the doorframe, "it's me!"

"Give us a hand, then."

Sarah entered the bedroom and yanked Beverly up over the sill with a grunt. Beverly put her pistol down on a dresser and slapped at her skirt as Olive stood outside staring up at the window.

"Go around to the front door Ollie; I'll let you in."

Olive nodded.

When they were all together, Sarah led them to the master bedroom.

"This guy had his own darkroom Bee," Olive began, "he had Klieg lights and movie cameras and--" she nearly ran into Sarah in the doorway, leaned around for a view, and gasped.

An empty bed frame sat in the middle of the room. The big dresser was open and empty as was the closet. The dim light through a dirty window made it look all the more forlorn.

Sarah flipped the switch for the overhead light a couple of times but it didn't work. "Cleaned out."

Beverly glanced around the empty room, "Somebody needed a crew, if there were two Kliegs and motion picture cameras."

"And a mattress and box springs." The vision of a blood-stained comforter across the bed arose and a knot appeared in Sarah's gut. She put a hand to her mouth and rocked on her feet.

Beverly shrugged, "Saved us the trouble."

"I *wanted* that stuff! Shit! I've directed a couple flickers. I've got screenplays and know the biz as good as any damn fella and I could--"

"What about the bodies?"

Olive shrugged, "I don't suppose they wanted those."

"Show me."

* * *

They climbed up the hillside as doves and mockingbirds called from the trees. When they reached the old well, a fresh layer of dirt atop the boards greeted them.

Sarah scanned the hillside for the mosaic of the woman in blue robes but couldn't find it. She tapped the big Colt against her leg, "They've been here too."

Olive's previous curiosity was lacking and she hung back on the trail.

Beverly's expression was unreadable. She sighed, "Well, let's look."

With a scowl Olive moved to the opposite end of a board, Beverly moved to help her, and Sarah took the other end. The layer of dirt made it all the heavier as they fought the board toward the edge of the well until there was a gap wide enough for the flashlight.

Beverly took it out of Olive's hand, turned it on, leaned over the hole, and glanced down, "Take a look." She handed the flashlight to Sarah.

Sarah played the yellow beam around the shaft as it danced on a fresh layer of dirt six feet down. Fresh dirt clung to the well's stone sides, where it had landed during filling. Warren and the girls were at least a dozen feet beneath it, if they were there at all. "Golly, that's a lot of dirt."

Beverly brushed off a board, lifted her skirt, and sat down on the lip of the well. "Somebody made sure there's no evidence anyway."

"But somebody can just dig them up, Bee."

Sarah stared into the well, "What if they're not there, Ollie?"

"Sarah's right. Whoever did this brought a crew. That means it's somebody with the connections and backup to set things jake for themselves... so we've got to think about ourselves."

They sat on the lip of the old well as a mockingbird trilled overhead. Duke crisscrossed the hill, following his nose.

Beverly rubbed a scar on her throat, "I think it's all for the better if we forget this little incident for now. I'll keep my ears peeled as to who and what might be at play. Ollie, you and I must make sure Sarah's always safe with one of us."

"Okay, Bee."

Sarah smacked the pistol down on the boards with a bang that made the others jump, "Just because someone cleaned up this place and filled in this old well doesn't mean they set it *straight*, Bee! There are dead bodies down there, or at least there *were*. Girls who came from somewhere seeking a new life, with families and loves, perhaps even children, who have been cruelly *murdered!* Christ, Bee, you said Danielle was your lover. As far as we know, we're sitting above her butchered corpse this very moment! You saw the photos and I saw her name on one of the film cans. How can you let such a thing go unpunished?"

Beverly put a hand to her lips and gazed at her until Sarah blinked, then let out her breath, "I'd say that you've already punished one such scoundrel, love."

"But he wasn't alone, Bee!"

Sarah stared into Beverly's green eyes and noticed the scar on her throat for the first time. It looked as if someone had tried to cut it. She shivered. Who *were* these people she was calling her friends? How could they live here when their own friends were literally swept under a pile of dirt and just go on as if everything were normal?

"Sarah's right Bee, it's jake to put those lugs in their places. We can't call the coppers though 'cause some of them could be in the pocket of whoever the fuck did this. For all we know it's somebody we see every day. They're workin' in the flickers that's for sure, and they must have money too. That's scary."

Sarah studied the expressions of her companions and for the first time felt utterly equal. They were all lost as to where the threat was and all facing the unknown. "This gun's too big. I want a little revolver like you two have that I can put in my purse. I don't like that automatic."

Olive made a nervous giggle as the sound of a vehicle coming up the drive ended their conversation. "Oh shit." She dug for her pistol.

"My car's sitting right there, so I suggest we walk back down as fast as we can, smile, and keep the guns hidden. Be ready to use them however."

"Oh... cripes!"

Sarah took Olive's hand, "I won't let anything happen to you, come on."

They hurried down the path through cactus and morning glories in time to see the tall cab of a truck bouncing up the driveway with a white box mounted on the back following a maroon four-door convertible. The truck ground to a halt behind Beverly's Packard, blocking it in. The stocky driver of the big maroon car dressed in a chauffeur's uniform stepped out and opened the rear door for a taller figure. "Hallo," a tenor voice echoed across the yard, "Mr. Schmitz! Anybody home?"

Beverly put her hand on Sarah's, "That's Bill Taylor. Put that thing away."

"Where?"

Beverly snatched the big .45 out of Sarah's hand and jammed it in her purse as Sarah fought the urge to snatch it back. Olive put her gun away, and Sarah let the others walk ahead as they approached the yard.

Bill Taylor stood in shirtsleeves with hands on his hips beside the purple car. He wore khaki pants held up by leather suspenders that were tucked into the same tall riding boots Sarah had seen beside the couch at Olive's place. In that stance without the distraction of Mary Minter, he reminded her of a British officer with his strong nose, erect posture, and pale eyes that looked used to command. Sarah blinked as she realized he *was* one of the British officers she'd seen in films. Two short, dark-mustached men in rough clothing with flat tweed caps stood behind him, obviously being from **Tomasio Moving** as the hand-painted sign on their truck proclaimed.

"Olive, Bee... and Sarah! What a surprise. Didn't know you knew Warren. Where is the fellow? I'm here for the Kliegs that he got from Triangle. They came from Keystone and Mack wants them back to square-up with me. I got a load of stuff at a cracking price when he was short on cash the other night in a card game at Harry's, and I told him I'd fetch the Kliegs myself to make him better about me besting him."

"Warren--" Olive began, but Beverly grabbed Olive's wrist and twisted her arm. "Ow!"

"Sarah was just getting her dog," Beverly said, "he's run over here again for a handout. We were surprised no one was home ourselves. Here Duke," she clapped her hands and Duke cocked his head, "new car, Bill?"

"A McFarlan, had it custom built and took delivery today."

"Lovely."

"Thank you," Bill nodded, "and he even left his dog. Well, looks like he's better tended with you Sarah. Never saw his coat so shiny. By the way forgive my inattention; William Desmond Taylor at your service. Never did get your full name I'm afraid."

"Sarah Mae McCallum, Mr. Taylor, from Victoria in British Columbia."

"That's right, a Canuck! Love the country! I fought as a Canadian in the War, and you have a perfectly lovely Irish name to boot."

Sarah felt her cheeks warming and found herself curtsying.

"She's not one of my girls Bill, she's Olive's dear friend and quite proper."

"I've gathered as we've had lunch already, but didn't you say that you were looking for work in film, Sarah?"

"Ah, yes sir."

"Excellent. My god, what a beauty you are if you don't mind my belaboring the obvious. You have a complexion that's perfect for the camera. Have you any experience?"

"Yes, ah, I did some vaudeville with the Pantages Circuit in Seattle, as well as Vancouver."

Olive nodded vigorously and squeezed Sarah's hand.

"Lovely, we must look into it. Well, I must have these gentlemen move those lights. Hear there's some darkroom equipment here also Mr. Schmitz has had forever. That's his Ford right there. I wonder where he's got to?"

XV.

After Bill discovered the house was empty, he dismissed the movers and followed the ladies to Olive's place. "Damndest thing, fellow took the makings of a small studio but absconded without even his Ford. There must be a posse hot on his trail, as they say in the Westerns."

Bill's handsome young chauffeur stood behind him leaning against the stucco wall beside the patio. Lupita brought drinks for them all, and Bill motioned for him to sit with them at the table, "This is Ed, by the way."

Ed nodded, exchanged glances with Beverly, and shook Sarah's hand with a smirk. Sarah's skin crawled away from his palm. She fought to maintain the smile on her face. She'd heard women say men undressed them with their eyes, and Ed actually made her feel that way.

Bill held up his glass, "Salud."

Sarah stared at the greenish liquid as she brought the crystal goblet to her lips. It smelled salty, somewhat bitter and of lime, and the rim of the glass was crusted with salt. She let out her breath, took a sip, and grimaced.

Olive chuckled, "Takes some gettin' used to."

"Whatever in the world is it?"

"It's made with tequila, from Mexico."

Sarah wiped her mouth, "Oh."

Beverly sipped hers, "William, did you know Warren well?"

"I met the fellow on a shoot. Wholly adequate as a camera operator but I didn't exchange much but the usual courtesies. He worked for Mack and D. W. most of the time. Why, and don't you mean do I know him well?"

Ed stared across the pool into the hills seemingly ignoring them, but Sarah noticed tension in the muscles of his thick legs under his slacks. They twitched as he exchanged grins with Bill. He caught Sarah's glance and gave her another patently lecherous grin. Sarah looked away and cocked the flapper hat to avert her eyes.

"Yes of course Bill, however I think of him in the past tense as obviously he's gone. Will you report the theft to the police?"

"Perhaps, but unless he gave it to some Bolsheviks or they're on some ranch in the desert, the studios will catch whoever's trying to use it in this town. For all I know he's sold it to my own company and I'll be squaring-up with Zukor at another card game, double or nothing. Nothing to get in a snit about anyway. You never know how things work out. Mack will throw me some business to make-up, or let me use one of his contract players for the trouble I'm sure."

"That's why Bill's so successful around here," Olive said, "he doesn't play grudges or make enemies easily."

Beverly nodded, "Perhaps that's why so many of our young female stars seem to prize his company to such a degree."

Ed made a sharp noise that became a stage sneeze. Bill shot him a passing glare, and Ed excused himself from the table.

Beverly made a loud sigh, "Ah... those young ones."

Olive giggled.

Sarah glanced from one woman to the other wishing she had some cold water. They all seemed to be drinking twenty-four hours a day and it was much too early for her. "What will you do when Prohibition comes? I don't see Hollywood going dry I must say."

"Just another way to make money, love. When the saloons are down, the call houses shall flourish."

"Call houses?"

"Tol' you Sarah, that's what madams call their houses. When somebody calls on the telephone, they have whoever they're looking for ready at the house, or off to the location that they're *called* to. Remember?"

Sarah stared at her toes, "Oh right."

"Bugger it all! What a silly sack of shit to ban Scotch! It's the damn *dope* that's the problem! And you are aware that I have made a few enemies on that account Ollie, as I am four-square against it. Bee, I'm sure you're making preparations for the inevitable, but I shall sorely miss being able to stop for a beverage wherever and whenever I care to." Bill turned to Sarah, "You're a Canadian. Thank God your people have sense. I joined the Canadian army while the Americans were sitting on their damn hands. I wasn't going to wait for them to take it to Jerry when British boys were dying by the bushel. My father retired a Major in an Irish regiment and I couldn't let the family honor go hang. He took three bullets in the Boer War."

Olive yawned, "We know Bill. Sarah's brother died at the Somme."

"Oh," Bill put a long-fingered hand across Sarah's and squeezed, "God bless him, and I grieve your loss lass. So many have lost a loved one in that god-awful war it's a damn shame. Now with this damn prohibition, the Canadians shall enjoy more freedom than we here in the States. What the hell did we *fight* for? The krauts wouldn't have taken a man's bottle I assure you." Bill grinned, "Can you envision a German without his beer? No schnapps? You could make a pretty penny with family in Canada Sarah, what with a few relatives shipping that fine blended whiskey and good beer to these parts."

"Tisk," Beverly laughed, "they have liquor laws there too and are moving in a similar direction I believe. Sarah' s but a young thing Bill, not a gangster."

"Oh right, of course."

"Actually my uncle supplies saloons in Vancouver."

Watch it Sarah, Bill considers young flowers fully grown and quite ready to bloom. One from the liquor business might be too much for him." Beverly put a hand on Bill's, "Of course I started in business myself at fourteen and don't regret it. That's a couple of years less than your dear Miss 'M,' and I'm doing quite well thank you."

"Please, Bee…"

"I find your blush appealing, William."

"You would, you she-wolf."

Sarah joined the laughter a moment late.

Olive rose, "Excuse me, but I've got to use the ladies' room." Her eyes caught Sarah's and darted toward the house.

Sarah stood, "Me too."

Bill nodded, "Always a group project with the ladies."

When they were upstairs in Olive's bathroom, she turned on the lights in rose petal sconces around her makeup mirror, checked her face, and squeezed Sarah's bottom, "Boy, Bill's awful touchy 'bout Mary."

"I guess so, but it looks as if he'd better be."

"Yeah, everybody knows they're lovers and Bill's scared stiff her mom will blow the whistle and ruin him. Mrs. Shelby would do it too. Mary's her meal ticket, she banks everything she makes, and sister, she's a fuckin' goldmine!" Olive shrugged, "Bill's a sweet sort actually. He's forty-five and is rather guilty 'bout the thing, which is more than I can say for the rest of the lugs here-abouts buzzin' 'round the youngsters. He bends over backwards to help my friend Mabel too, although folks like Hughie Faye sure don't like him. Hell, they hate him 'cause he's so against dope. Bill paid for all Mabel's treatment back East when she got over-board with the cocaine," Olive scowled, "and it should have been Mack Sennett with what he put her through."

Sarah stared at Olive in the mirror and shook her head, "I had the impression that he had all these horrible bondage things, and he was terrible and strange. Then we meet him at the beach, and he seems absolutely decent and rather shy. Now you're telling me he's a fine fellow, whom I admit he does seem at first glance. But, does he do such awful things with young Mary? I simply can't imagine that."

"Never seen him actually use that stuff. His chauffeur Ed is the one who picks it up, not Bill."

Sarah shivered, "That guy gives me the heebie-jeebies. But didn't Bill want to have sex with you and you stormed out of the house, because your... your own *husband* suggested it?"

"Yeah, but that's pretty much the way it goes 'round here. I was a bit touchy after a rough night, but unless he's a pansy, what would one expect? He treats Mary like a lady anyway, and keeps her and Mabel at arm's length when they're near each other. Bill walks on eggs for the sake of peace when he's makin' a flicker with any of 'em actually. He's a pretty skookum guy compared to most here."

"He's still with Mabel Normand too?"

"Uh-huh, he's got a bit of a thing with her too. Mack Sennett don't know it 'cause he's too took up with Mae Busch."

Sarah let out her breath, "God, I can't keep track."

Olive giggled.

"I suspected Bill of somehow being in with Warren in regard to that horrible place, and I thought, I thought that you were of the same opinion somehow in spite of what you said."

"Told ya, Sarah, Bill's all right. He's got somethin' else goin' I don't even want to talk about but it sure ain't killin' girls. This murder stuff's got you all upset for good reason but it was just an awful random thing. Something you already took care of better than any other girl could," Olive yawned, "I been a tad jittery myself." She opened the makeup table, pulled out containers of rouge, lipstick and brushes, and lifted a false bottom in the drawer, "I been dyin' for something all day what with Bee ridin' me like that. She wouldn't even let me stop at the hotel on Cahuenga for some." Olive grinned, "Now it's time for a pick-me-up." She took out another flask that held tubes and a syringe, and plopped down on the stool before the mirror with an approving glance at her reflection, "Hold the elastic, wouldya?"

Sarah took the end of the garter strap and watched the needle pierce Olive's skin. Blood swirled up into the glass tube and mixed with the amber liquid before it disappeared back into her arm. Sarah fought dizziness, swallowed, and released the elastic with a snap when Olive said to. Olive leaned against the wall with a sigh and yawned.

"Doesn't that stuff make you all jumpy?"

"Huh?"

"You're yawning."

"It's all what you're used to. You could use one too, Sarah."

Olive's eyes were focused somewhere behind Sarah's, as if she were looking right through them at the back of her head. Olive tottered on the seat and slipped a hand around Sarah's thigh for balance. Her fingers brushed between Sarah's legs as they came away.

"Oh damn," Sarah leaned against the makeup table and flexed her arm, stared at the inside of it, and let out her breath, "does it hurt?"

"Just a little prick; I'll be gentle." Olive slipped the needle into a fresh tube and filled the syringe halfway, pointed it toward the ceiling, and squirted some out the tip.

"Aren't you wasting it?"

"Got to get the air out. You can't put air in your veins or it could kill ya."

"Maybe it's not such a good idea after all."

"Pshaw, you and me are gonna do somethin' special. You deserve it."

"What?"

"You'll see," Olive wrapped the garter strap around Sarah's arm and handed one end to her, "Put it in your teeth, remember? You should see how to do this yourself."

Sarah inhaled, nodded, gripped the strap in her mouth, and grabbed the other end with her right hand. The prick of the needle made her jump. "Ow!"

"Stay the fuck still!"

A shiver ran up Sarah's spine and she closed her eyes and fought nausea as she felt her blood being sucked out of the vein. Suddenly a flood coursed up the inside of her arm, reached her shoulder, charged into her heart, and percolated up her neck to explode in her head with cold white fire. A great cool hand seemed to push her down as Sarah began to slide off the table.

"Whoa!" Olive's hands were on her shoulders holding her up on the stool. Sarah's eyes fluttered, and she began to tip. Olive lifted her with a grunt as she began to fall and tried to slide her onto the bed. Sarah felt her legs helping for a moment before she went limp across the satin comforter. "Wow Sarah, maybe that was a little bit much."

"Uhhhh?"

Olive's lips brushed her forehead, "It's okay hon."

Sarah nodded and took a long, slow breath. If she could just concentrate on breathing, things should be okay.

Olive unbuttoned Sarah's blouse, "Got to get out of this and get some air."

Sarah nodded. The cool air was good on her skin. Olive pulled her boots off and Sarah lifted her leg to help her. She felt her skirt slide down around her knees. It was heavy around her foot, and she kicked it free. Olive's smooth fingers were dancing across her stomach and her nails tickled. Sarah giggled and concentrated on breathing. Breathing was important. Olive's soft lips found her own to help her, and Sarah sucked the breath from them. They tasted sweet. Olive's tongue tickled the inside of her mouth, and Sarah giggled around it. Olive giggled too. Her laughter echoed inside Sarah and ran rings around her skull. She saw Olive in the painting from **Vogue** with her lavender eyes huge and her lips red as cherries holding a bouquet of flowers. Sarah sneezed.

Olive's mouth left her own to tickle her throat before it glided across a nipple. Her tongue flicked across it, her lips fastened on it and sucked. Sarah felt it stiffen until it was as big as the room. She was tottering on the swaying blue walls of Babylon, gazing out toward a billion golden poppies rippling in the sun in slow waves that tickled like a million tongues. The tongue grew larger until it found its true target between her legs, traveling around the lips to settle on the rosebud at their crest.

Sarah gasped and arched her back on the satin comforter as her head dug into the silken pillow. She wrapped hands in the ringlets of Olive's hair as saliva ran down her thighs to pool around the cheeks of her butt. "Goddamn!"

Olive's giggle was muffled but the meaning was clear.

XVI.

The moon was a spotlight beating against her eyes. Sarah rolled over to see Olive stretched out on the sheets beside her, pale as the wraith she'd seen above Laurel Canyon when she'd awoken from that first shot of cocaine. An owl hooted, seeming as close as the girl beside her. She glanced at the window, sat up, and rubbed her eyes.

She slipped off the satin sheets, wiggled her toes in the thick carpet, yawned, and something flashed in the back of her eyes from the motion. Sarah fought vertigo for a moment. When it passed she arose and went to the window.

The world was a luminous wonderland in the moonlight. Her eyes skipped over the foliage and faux Greek statures in the yard to follow the stone pillars of the garden fence until they landed on something perched upon the last one. It was the owl. Its huge eyes blinked with a flash of green and morphed to blood red in an instant. It spread huge wings, flapped once, and flew across the road and up the hill toward the old Thompson place. Sarah fought the urge to follow, sighed, dressed in dry jeans and a man's shirt, and stepped out the door.

* * *

The pale broken walls holding up terraces that must have once held spectacular gardens reminded her of the ruins from ancient

times she'd seen pictures of in history books and seemed far older than the Spanish colonial days when they'd been built. She
followed the path to the well, and where she'd seen the mosaic
of a woman in blue robes, stepped off it and headed directly up
the hill.

Something made her look up as she climbed. The owl was
there on silent wings above her. Its eyes flashed golden, filling
Sarah with a rush of satisfaction that had no reason she could com-
prehend as it glided on over the hill. She continued toward the
broken wall, where ten thousand bits of glass in the shape of a
woman had waited for perhaps centuries... perhaps forever.

When she reached the mosaic, she knelt and ran her palms
over it. Sarah sat with her back against it looking out over the
scattered lights of the San Fernando Valley. A sensation of soft
wings enfolding her grew, and she closed her eyes to make the
feeling last. She opened them on distant mountains aglow under
the moon. The Milky Way arched above, and far to the north she
thought she saw what she'd missed so much: the aurora in a flash
of green. After an hour she arose, went back to the house, and slid
into bed beside Olive.

* * *

A shaft of light drove her dream of Angeline over the horizon. Sarah squeezed Olive's leg between her own and played with a strand
of golden hair in sunlight slanting through the blinds. The silhouette of a pomegranate tree quivered against the lavender silk
curtains in the window and the ticking of the clock in the sunken
living room echoed through the house. Dust motes danced over
her head. She yawned.

She rolled on her back, ran hands through her hair, and
stared at the polished beams overhead. Her muscles were sore, her
mouth tasted foul, and she had to pee. She rolled off the bed and
tottered toward the bathroom. There was an ivory-colored can of

Elkins Tooth Powder beside a boar bristle toothbrush in a paper wrapper, and she proceeded to scrub her teeth as she sat on the toilet peeing buckets.

The sound of a car came from the driveway. Sarah imagined her favorite teacher Miss Fitzgerald from her girl's school in Victoria walking in to find her like this. Miss Fitzgerald's pale diamond of a face framed by graying braids stared back, with her dark eyes big as saucers. Would she consider Sarah a hophead dope fiend, a whore, a *lesbian?*

Miss Fitzgerald had always seemed somewhat that way and favored Sarah with lots of touching Sarah responded to politely. The other girls had treated her like a bumpkin from the Territories when she'd arrived in Victoria from the Yukon, but Miss Fitzgerald had kept her after school to assist with grading papers. She always kissed her on the cheek goodnight and one night switched to the lips.

Olive was a fantastic kisser. Sarah supposed she'd had a lot of practice and sighed. She wanted to take a shower and make plans for the day. She rinsed her mouth in the sink and turned on the water over the tub.

"Sarah?"

"Um?" Sarah imagined Olive on the sheets with her fair body aglow in the sun as she stretched across them, waiting, "Ollie?"

"My husband's here."

Sarah put her face under the hot water of the shower, gasped, and reached for the shampoo. The word *husband* grated like the rough boards on her bare shoulders when she'd awoken to far different circumstances but days ago. There went another go-round with Olive anyway. "Oh?"

"That's his car out there. He's with his sister."

Sarah swallowed, "Mary?"

"No, Lottie. I can't believe she's even awake at this time of day. It's Sunday morning and she's always sleeping off a drunk about now. Something's up."

"What does that mean?"

A storm of giggling echoed off the tile walls as Olive pulled back the curtain and stepped in the tub. Her hands found Sarah's butt, squeezed, and she kissed her under the water, making gargling sounds as it ran into her mouth, "That they'd better damn well wait toots."

* * *

"We're going to church." Olive announced.

Sarah searched for sugar amongst the gaggle of silver vessels on the table, found it, stirred some in her coffee, and yawned.

"Yes," Jack said, "there's a noon service we can't miss. It's important."

"I... really don't have anything to wear."

"I've got stuff that'll fit you in a closet Sarah. Lotsa closets in this place."

"What kind of church?"

Olive shrugged, "Episcopal, Methodist, Catholic, Jewish, maybe an Indian medicine man or a Swami from India throwin' flowers in the sea at Pacific Palisades while he's squeezin' the tush of some girl with daisies in her hair. They're all the same 'round here."

Sarah put a hand to her mouth.

"We're going to join Mr. Hearst at the Cathedral," Jack said, "it's All Saints Weekend."

"William Randolph Hearst?"

Jack nodded. He was a handsome man of twenty-three dressed in a fine tweed suit this Sunday morning with a white carnation in the lapel. His morphine habituation gave him a somewhat waxy pallor however. "He'll be there with Marion Davis and she's promised me a part in her new picture at Cosmopolitan, the studio he's built for her. He'll do anything she tells him to you know."

Olive nodded, "Must love that kootch."

Lottie sprawled on a couch in the living room, glaring from dark eyes ringed from endless nights of partying. She tossed back long dark hair and snarled, "You coulda let me *know* Bill Taylor was here for Chrisake! I've got scripts for another serial that will out-draw *The Diamond from the Sky* I swear! Goddamn it!"

There was silence from her brother and sister-in-law. Sarah poured herself more coffee.

Olive snorted, "Mr. Moneybags. He's married and here he's bringin' his mistress on his arm gussied up like a fuckin' princess to a big ol' Mass. Damn… you have gotta *love* this town!"

Sarah examined the colorful bits of peppers in her eggs. She took another bite and washed it down with a big gulp of orange juice. Thank God for orange juice, the sacramental wine of her Hollywood communion. "Holy Mary Mother of God, bless me for I have sinned."

Olive snorted and orange juice came out her nose, "Ow! Ow!" She put hands to a red face and bent over the tablecloth until her forehead touched it.

"I clean that up!" Lupita said from the kitchen.

Sarah howled.

"You two seem rather in a good mood this morning."

"Yes, dear," Olive's voice was hoarse. "I was growing dyspeptic worrying for your welfare over Halloween, but now am fully renewed by your mere presence Sunday morning."

"That fucking coke is making you crazy, Miss America's Sweetheart."

"That fuckin' morphine makes you look like a goddamn corpse, Tom Sawyer."

Jack arose, bowed, fell to one knee, and kissed Olive's hand before they embraced in a well-performed kiss for their audience of two. Jack grinned, sat back in his chair, and straightened his tie.

"Come on kiddo," Olive motioned to Sarah. "Let's get changed."

* * *

Olive had clothes hanging in every closet of the house, most brand new, and still sheathed in the paper wrappers from the stores where they'd come from. She took Sarah to a closet in an empty bedroom where all the clothes seemed to be Sarah's size.

"Why do you have my size?"

"For Dolores, she's Spanish and likes lots of color, but there's some stuff that will work for Sundays here too."

"Dolores?"

"Got her a job with Carl Laemmle at Universal, but she scooted over to Belmore after a couple'a months. Says the clients are more honest and the money's steady. Remember? I was with her when you were almost with that Valentino guy."

"Oh, yes."

Olive stood on tiptoe and kissed her, "I'm sure glad you picked me up the other day. It's karma. This is all just going swimmingly don't you think?"

Sarah held Olive's waist before her fingers traced the curve of her cheek and Olive's violet eyes glowed. Sarah studied the lines around them and felt... no, she *knew* Olive was older than she claimed. She gave her a peck on the mouth, "I feel rather strange though, going to church today."

"Kinda screwy huh?"

Sarah nodded.

"You'll get used to it. It's all what people want to see, not who you really are, but if you can make the money to live like you *really* are..." Olive gave a gigantic shrug, "so the hell *what?*" She took a proper white Sunday-go-to-Church dress from its hanger and laid it against Sarah's shoulders, "I've got the perfect hat for this."

* * *

Jack pulled the black Rolls Phaeton from the garage, filled the tank from a jerry can, and they piled in for the trip downtown. Lottie had her hair up with enough makeup to somewhat hide the circles under her eyes. Jack kept the pale countenance of a ghost. Olive sniffed cocaine. Sarah turned it down. She had a terrible urge to put on pants, boots, and run off into the hills to get lost in these strange new mountains for a day to just be alone. She wanted to sit on the highest peak around gazing at whatever the distances revealed. She closed her eyes and heard the cry of an eagle. She heard Angeline's laughter as they dashed amongst red-barked cedars rising all the way to damp heaven on Vancouver Island and smelt the green forest floor as their heels threw up moss.

Cruel laughter broke her reverie. A blinding glare seemed to burn her closed eyes, yet she heard a distant voice that soothed her fear, that of a woman. She heard the distant chanting of a Catholic priest and smelled the incense. Sarah shivered. Perhaps she was going crazy.

They drove down Cahuenga past people in their Sunday best. Sarah recognized Rolls-Royces now, but she was at a loss identifying many vehicles. Some had gilded eagles for hood ornaments, winged women holding torches, or snarling lions. She recognized the 'A' of a Pierce Arrow and the hissing from a White Steamer, then a Stanley that was much louder as it left a trail of water on the road. A red two-seater beep-beeped as it tore around them on the two-lane white concrete road. "That's a Stutz, a Bearcat." Olive said when asked. She pointed at another limo she said was an electric German Siemens. Sarah recognized a bright gold Locomobile roadster weaving between the equestrians and horse-drawn wagons. She lifted her eyes from the parade of motorized wealth, stared into the sun-baked hills, and sighed.

Olive squeezed her hand, "Whatcha thinkin'?"

"I was thinking about getting out of this dress and going on a hike. There's a dome in the Klondike, which is what we call mountains there, that's right above Dawson City. Midnight Dome. You can see up and down the valley of the Yukon and up the Klondike River. I've been on much higher mountains but that dome is special to me. The world seems so vast and endless along that river. It makes one's mortal endeavors seem so small. I suppose it's my mind seeking some repose or whatever after the last few days."

Olive bit her lip and played with a freshly curled ringlet of hair, "Sounds fun. I get pretty sick of playin' the simp ingénue in the flickers myself, not to mention dealin' with all the randy lugs that bankroll it. Got to dress like a boy in *Toton the Apache* for a few reels last year with Selznick. I was a crooked little pickpocket in Paris, half-Apache, and crazy as hell. Did you see it? I wore a suit and tie, and a hat with suspenders and boots, even a fake mustache. It was fun 'cept the crotch in those things chafed the fuckin' bejesus outta me."

Sarah laughed, "No, but I'd sure like to."

"I'd like tryin' one of those flickers like Mabel Normand's. She's somethin' when she's tied to a railroad track or when she goes off a cliff, isn't she?"

Lottie leaned through the open partition separating the driver's compartment from the back and eyed Sarah with either curiosity or malice, Sarah couldn't tell which, "Ollie, could you let me have some of that coke?"

Jack wore a flat grey motoring cap and goggles that he certainly didn't need for dust in the enclosed vehicle, and glanced over his shoulder looking like an automaton Sarah had seen in some futuristic German film at Pantages' Strand Theater in Seattle.

Olive nodded, "Sure Lottie, come on."

Lottie scooted through the partition from the front like a snake, gathered up her skirts on the seat across from them, and smiled.

Olive pulled the shiny case with cocaine and a syringe from her purse. She checked her supply and scowled, "Jack, stop at the hotel!"

Jack's grumble came from the front of the Rolls and they

pulled into the yard of the adobe. Olive got out and Jack killed the engine. Sarah stayed inside the car and cranked down a window with an eye out for the red-haired woman.

"Got to use the water closet," Lottie announced, stepped out, and walked into the café.

A blue Packard police car pulled up between the hotel and the café. Another followed.

Jack rubbed his chin, "Damn." He took off the goggles and lifted his cap to smooth his hair.

"What's the matter?"

"Lottie's got a problem with coppers. Not a bone of subtlety in that girl. Actually she's got a problem with just about everyone. No one's been able to handle her since Bill Taylor directed her in *The Diamond from the Sky*. I don't know how he did it for twenty episodes to be honest. She's got a bit of a problem with Mary being so successful too, and has been known to throw a tantrum on the set, but Bill Taylor has the patience of Job." Jack tapped a cigarette on the burlwood dash before he stepped out, lit it with one foot on the running board, and struck a pose.

Sarah leaned back in the big leather seat and studied her feet in high-heeled patent leather shoes. They felt cramped. Her feet were sore already.

Lottie came back, glanced into the car, and scowled, "Them goddamn coppers are in the hotel."

Jack crushed out his cigarette and flicked it into the road, "Drat."

The red-haired woman in a Mexican shawl appeared from the stairwell and glanced their way. Sarah sunk down in her seat as the woman hurried toward the back of the building. There was the crunching of leaves as the woman climbed the hill. Sarah saw her catch her shawl in some branches, yank on it, swear, and stumble out of sight behind some bushes. "What in the world?"

Olive barreled down the stairs, "Yipes! Let's get outta here!"

Jack jumped back in the Rolls, twisted the electric starter, and the big engine rattled to life as Olive opened the door and Sarah grabbed her hand to pull her in. Before they made the road, a policeman appeared in front of them, held up his hand, and the whistle in his mouth gave a piercing blast. Jack stopped the car, and the policeman approached the window and leaned in to inspect the driver.

Jack tipped his cap, "Good day, officer."

"Good day, sir."

Olive straightened her Sunday bonnet, cranked down the rear window, and gave the cop a million-dollar smile, "Is there a problem officer?" she lilted. Sarah found herself wishing that movies had sound to capture her voice.

The cop doffed his hat, "Miss Thomas!"

"Hello. What seems to be the trouble?"

"Buncha dope fiends headin' to the hoosegow, ma'am. You'll excuse me, but do you folks have business here?"

"I had to use the water closet," Lottie snapped, "of all the God--"

"Ah-hem," Olive squeezed Lottie's hand and gave the cop an apologetic look, "we should certainly be on our way then."

"I'd not come near this place today if I were you. God knows what a buncha hopheads might do around the likes of a fine little lady like you." The cop turned from Olive, smiled at Sarah, and doffed his hat again.

Olive blew him a kiss as they pulled out onto Cahuenga before she took off the bonnet, scratched her head, and sighed, "Pull over somewhere before we get to church. Now I *really* need a boost."

There was the roar of an engine and tires squealing on gravel followed by the howl of a police siren. Olive, Lottie, and Sarah all tried to peer out the tiny rear window as a lavender Rolls accelerated around them, causing a tan Pierce Arrow coming from the other direction to go off the other side of the road and bounce in the ditch. Jack swore, jerked the wheel to the right, and the tires dropped into the ditch on their side of the road. The car tipped hard, the three women screamed, a tire popped with a bang, and the car skidded and bounced along the bottom of the ditch before they came to rest at a forty-five degree angle as the lavender Rolls disappeared toward Hollywood with the blue police Packard in pursuit.

"Goddamn it!" Jack roared.

Sarah separated herself from Olive, who was sprawled against the right door. Lottie was pressed against the window in front of them, holding her nose, from which a stream of blood ran. Sarah slid up the rear seat, opened the left-hand door, pushed with a grunt, climbed out, and pulled Olive and then Lottie out onto the sloping side of the ditch.

Lottie wiped her nose on her Sunday dress and stared at the blood on her hands. Olive blinked violet eyes and smoothed her skirts. Jack pulled himself out of the front seat with the goggles around his chin and his motoring cap at a crazy angle, slapped his pants, and gave Sarah a vacant stare.

"That was Mabel Normand, the action Queen," Olive grinned, "when she's got that party powder up her nose, ain't no stoppin' her."

XVII.

Lottie and Jack flagged the first taxi to come by so she could change her bloody dress at her apartment and get to the church. In spite of Jack's pleading, Olive refused to go with him. Olive and Sarah went into the little café where Sarah had met Warren to wait for a cab they called from the café's phone, planning to return to the house on Lankershim. The place was crowded with people having late Sunday breakfast, but two men stood and offered them their table instantly. Olive gave them her autograph. One of them winked at Sarah as they paid their bill, and they left beaming.

"So what are we gonna do today?"

Sarah rubbed her eyes and tried to focus on the menu, "That does it. I am going to get out of this dress and go for a hike."

"Where?"

"Up in the hills of course."

"Why?"

"Because I want to."

Olive caught Sarah's leg between hers under the table and squeezed.

"I'm still going to take a walk."

Olive pouted.

"You can come with me. It's good for you. I think Bee's right about some things by the way."

"What?"

"That you should watch yourself with the--" Sarah paused as the waitress approached with a pot of coffee, "you know."

"Nice to know you care."

"Of course I do. That's a silly thing to say."

Sarah ordered an omelet, coffee, and orange juice. Olive ordered French toast with whipped cream and strawberries and a cup of hot cocoa.

"You liked it too Sarah."

Sarah felt a warming in her cheeks before she let out her breath and spoke, "All right I suppose, but not all of the time. I still feel rather out of sorts from last night and my body's saying I need exercise. It will do you good too, Ollie. You need to get out in the fresh air and stretch your legs once in a while."

"Hope I didn't make you feel bad, doin' that with me."

"Not *that,* the cocaine, Ollie."

"You sure you're not feelin' guilty 'bout what we did? I mean I can understand that. Lotsa girls do. "

Sarah leaned back in the red leather booth and stared in her coffee cup. How did she feel? Miss Fitzgerald's stern face popped into her mind, wide-eyed in shock. Sarah snorted and put her hand over the stupid grin spreading her own as she tried to swallow a mouthful of eggs.

Olive's cheeks bulged. She ran a finger across the back of Sarah's hand, "I want to do it again."

"I gathered that."

"Well?"

"Well, all right."

Olive nibbled a drooling strawberry off her fork and winked.

"But I still want to take a hike. It's like summer in the North here. I want to clear my mind... and no coke."

"Fine then."

* * *

When the taxi dropped them back at the house, Olive declared that western wear was just the thing for a hike. They donned jeans and boots with colorful checkered shirts, Stetson hats, and neckerchiefs for their sojourn into the hills. Lupita made them a lunch, packed it in a khaki knapsack, and placed it alongside a colorful blanket-sheathed canteen with ice cubes in the water.

Sarah had never "dressed" for hiking before, at least not like this, and chuckled as Olive examined herself in the mirror, "You look like Mabel Normand in *Mickey*... or even Tom Mix in western."

Olive responded with a kiss, and her lavender eyes scanned Sarah's, "Should we take a gun?"

"Not a bad idea. Do you have a revolver that's smaller than that big old Colt?"

"You can carry mine if you want," Olive reached into a drawer and handed Sarah her engraved top-break Smith and Wesson with scrimshawed ivory grips, "I bet you're better with it anyway."

Sarah stuck the pistol in a back pocket of her jeans, pulled it out, and tried it again. "It catches on my pants. Do you have a holster?"

Olive rummaged in another drawer and produced a fancy tooled holster that Sarah put the gun in. She undid the turquoise-studded buckle on the wide tooled leather belt, slipped it on, and adjusted it at her waist.

They walked past the road to the old Thompson place and followed the dirt trace of Lankershim into the hills. There was another property on the way up, a rambling sun-bleached ranch house and barn with sheds, and a Model T truck on blocks. Tired yellow poppies dotted a meadow in the first days of November as horses stood with their tails methodically swatting flies. A rooster crowed.

The road ended in a washout, where they climbed around a pile of rocks and logs into the shade of trees. The now-familiar smells of the chaparral hills mixed with new scents for which Sarah had no name. Cicadas buzzed like electric wires in trees, and mockingbirds shrieked as they continued up the gulch until the remnants of road disappeared.

Olive groaned, "Ain't this far enough?"

Sarah shook her head.

The vegetation grew thick along the creek, so they headed up a hillside covered with dry grass and Manzanita, where a covey of quail burst like a bomb from the blue-tinged leaves. "Eek!" Olive threw her hands up and almost fell backward on the slope. Sarah caught her and they laughed.

"This feels so much safer than Hollywood to me, Ollie."

"Shit, got something in my sock." Olive plopped down on a stone jutting from the hillside and yanked at the grass seeds covering her stockings, "Goddamn foxtails."

Sarah sat beside her and did the same as Olive took out a hand-rolled cigarette that was narrow at the ends and bulged in the middle. She struck a match on a rock, lit it, and handed it to Sarah.

Sarah let out a cloud to smoke, trying not to cough, "This looks like a worm that swallowed a marble."

"Wonder how cowboys roll 'em on horseback? Watched Bill Hart do that last summer while he was shootin' the breeze with Tom Ince just like it weren't nothing at all," Olive shook her head, "I can't even do good on a fuckin' table. Anyway you said no cocaine. This stuff's pretty mild, and legal too."

Sarah handed it back and stood up, "Let's find a place for a picnic."

They were sweating by the time they found shade. Sarah plopped down with a sigh on a patch of green grass beside a brook under the chaparral oaks. A woodpecker's tap-tap echoed from the trees, and the ever present mourning doves cooed.

Olive collapsed beside her with a groan, "Got my exercise for the goddamn year!"

"Pshaw, you should do it every day."

Across the San Fernando Valley, a belt of clouds lay low on the Santa Susana Mountains hiding their crests, and the sky seemed to hold its breath before a cool breeze began to waft up the canyon.

Olive sighed, "Oh, that's nice."

"Feels like rain."

"Naw, it don't rain this early, not 'till December I bet."

Sarah opened the knapsack, took out two neatly wrapped sandwich quarters in waxed paper with two oranges, and put them on a rough cotton towel Lupita had included. She shook the canteen and glanced at the brook, "This sure warmed up. That water looks good."

"Gotta be cooler than what's in the canteen."

Sarah nodded, got up, walked to the little stream, and balanced with her hands on the rocks as she put her mouth to the surface of the water and drank.

"How do you do that?"

"It's easy Ollie; you just need to use your arms. Haven't you ever been in the woods before?"

"Sure, when I was a kid in Charleroi outside Pittsburgh, and during picture shoots, but they always had caterers and such. I'd hate to have to... you know, to do my business out here."

"You mean shit?"

Olive laughed, "I climbed a mountain in the Catskills with my first husband and gave it up for him in a nice grassy field full of yellow and purple flowers on an old Mexican poncho just to get the hell outta Dodge... but he really wasn't the first anyway."

"My first was outside too. I rode with Jim up King Solomon's Dome from Hunker Creek while our fathers were in Dawson City. It was a sunny day, and so romantic, but the damn whitesocks started biting before we were done."

"Whitesocks?"

"They're these horrid little red flies with white feet, that bite like--"

The sound of a car made them glance up, and sunlight flashed on glass through the trees as a vehicle bounced on an unseen road above them.

Sarah stood, "Guess we're not so out in the woods after all."

"Guess not."

The vehicle came to a halt, and two doors opened and slammed shut. Sarah sat back down beside Olive, scanning the trees uphill.

Olive's arm went around her shoulders. Her lips brushed Sarah's ear, "Glad we got that gun, toots."

Sarah nodded.

The voices of men rose over the sound of the brook and faded in the purling of the stream. Sarah unwrapped a sandwich quarter and took a bite. It was corned beef and cheese, and she chewed as the men carried on an inaudible conversation screened by brush and trees. A snap of twigs accompanied the sound of something being dragged.

Sarah stood up, swept up the food, stuffed it in the knapsack, and motioned for Olive to follow. They moved under a low-hanging willow and squatted in the shade. A moist breeze wandered up the canyon, making the scent of the chaparral hills grow stronger. A faint whiff of death seemed to tease Sarah's nose, and she rubbed it.

"That's far enough goddamn it!" came a rough voice, "This bitch's coyote bait before anybody finds her, just like the other one."

Olive's eyes were as big as silver dollars.

Sarah un-holstered the gun and held it in both hands.

"All right," came the response, "damn... it looks like rain."

"Not in Southern California."

"Let's get back to the car. We sure don't want to be stuck on a fuckin' dirt road if it does."

"Hold your horses Mack, I gotta piss." The sound of some-one peeing seemed much too loud from where Sarah and Olive squatted under the branches of the willow.

"I--" Olive began.

Sarah's hand clamped on her mouth, "Shhhh!"

A buzzing exploded near her booted foot and Sarah glanced at a brownish-yellow pattern of diamonds in the litter of dark leaves. It looked like a rippling coil of rope. A lavender tongue flicked as the snake came into focus, and the rattle on its tail vi-brated in a blur.

"Eee!"

Sarah squeezed Olive's mouth hard and felt her teeth grind together under her fingers. She grabbed a stick with the other hand and flipped the snake away. The snake rattled and twisted through the air before landing ten feet downhill, making serpen-tine tracks in the leaves as it disappeared.

"Hear somethin'?"

"Shit yeah, a fuckin' rattlesnake. Let's get the hell outta here. I need a drink. That bitch already bit me and once is enough."

"I'm with you Mack."

The men scrambled uphill, cursing as they slipped and plodded along the creek. Doors slammed, an engine roared to life, wheels bumped on a dirt road, and for an instant a maroon car with a canvas roof was visible through the trees.

"What do you think they were doin'?"

"I suppose that we'll have to go see."

Olive grabbed Sarah's arm, "I don't want to!"

Sarah gave her a peck on the cheek, "We can't go without looking. Don't you think?"

"I don't want to... and what about snakes?"

"Come on. I'll take the stick." Sarah headed into the brush along the creek.

Olive moaned as she scrambled after her, "Look out for snakes!"

"I am!"

Fifty feet up Sarah spotted a pale glow amongst dead brown leaves. She rubbed her eyes, and the naked body of a girl came into focus. White ribs protruded from a pool beyond. The luminous mushroom of a skull loomed past that amongst the wet rocks with its empty sockets staring at her.

"Goddamn it!" Sarah's hands went to her mouth as the stick fell in the creek with a splash. The corpses were in the water from which she'd been drinking.

XVIII.

A rumble of thunder split the damp air as their heels skidded down the hill.

"Shit! It's gonna rain!"

Sarah glanced over her shoulder. Olive's face was a mask of misery. Sarah fought a laugh whose source she couldn't imagine, but it was swiftly replaced by a burning in her gut. She saw the corpses in the creek and belched. The taste of death was in her mouth. A tidal wave of nausea followed.

"I'm goin' back to Wilshire! Too much shit goin' on 'round here sister! Hey wait!" Olive plopped down on a damp rock and jerked off her boot, "My feet are killin' me!" She began straightening her bunched-up socks, yanking them up toward her knees with little grunts of effort.

Sarah sat beside her and did the same. She took off her hat and pulled her tangled hair away from her eyes. "This is absolutely awful! I don't want to come back here either. Los Angeles is simply horrible, Olive!" She stared up at the opaque sky and shuddered, "I have got to find a decent place to live!"

"Sarah... you can stay with me."

"Thank you Ollie, really, but I'd prefer a safe place of my own," Sarah brushed another wet strand of hair from her face. She wanted to go home but had none. She wanted to go to the police but couldn't trust them. She wanted *out*. "There has got to be a bungalow I can rent or something; I've got the money."

"Oh Sarah, thanks for not saying you're leaving. I'll make sure of it then. I know one on Alvarado where everyone in the court's from the studios and--" The sky trembled, cut loose with a roar, and a big drop landed in the middle of Sarah's forehead. Olive flinched as more drops hit her. She pulled the big Stetson hat down tight and groaned, "Let's get outta here."

The leaves around them clapped as a wave rippled across the hillside and it began to pour while they headed down the ravine. Churning brown water had appeared in the previously dry gulch they'd climbed but an hour earlier. Olive dislodged a rock that splashed into the rising torrent. A soaked bobcat sprang from the bushes and bounded uphill.

Sarah shouted over the roar of the water, "Who do you think those men were?"

"How the fuck should I know?"

"Doesn't Bill have a maroon car? It looked like his."

"Lots of 'em in Hollywood. Didn't you hear their voices? How coarse they were? Those were lowly thugs from the ass-end a' somewhere believe you me. It's *not* Bill Taylor, Sarah! Get that outta your head!"

Sarah swiped at the water dripping off her brow into her eyes, "They must be the ones who were with Warren anyway. This place is terrifying, Christ! I just wanted to take a hike in the hills. I went out last night while you were sleeping and was perfectly all right. Where I'm from people don't even lock their doors, and no one carries pistols in town for that matter. The Mounties wouldn't have it."

"Well, thank God you do! Oh shit!" Olive's boot had come off in the sucking brown mud at the bottom of a puddle, and she hung from a branch on the hillside balancing on one foot.

Sarah backtracked and tugged the boot from the mud. She pulled her own feet from the mud one at a time, shook out the water in the boot, and glanced up. Rain had plastered Olive's hair to her cheeks and water was running off her nose. Olive teetered on one foot and sneezed.

"We've got to get back to the house."

"You ain't kiddin' sister!" Olive squeezed Sarah's shoulder with a trembling hand and took an unsteady step out of the puddle. She pulled on the boot, emitting little grunts of misery, and began walking. Water in her boots squeaked and squished with each step, and her red-checkered shirt hung from her like a wet blanket. She looked like a soaked cat with her matted hair hanging from a thin frame as she tottered down the path wiping water from her eyes.

They came around a turn to be greeted by a deafening roar. Where the path had been but a short time before was a freshly cut chasm a dozen feet deep with brown water foaming at its bottom. Small tree trunks, leaves, and branches churned and ground against the banks. As they watched, another piece of the bank broke off and collapsed into the torrent.

"How can we cross that?"

"We can't Ollie; we've got to stay on this side and find a way across farther down."

"Oh, drat... Sarah?"

"Yes?"

"I'm glad you're with me."

"You wouldn't be here at all if I didn't force you. You'd be happily playing with your cocaine or something."

"And drinkin' mimosa."

"And dancing to the Victrola."

"And makin' love to you!"

Sarah inhaled, "Come on. Let's find a way out of here."

The water forced them back up the hillside. They fought their way through a tangle of branches and slippery leaves until once again Olive shrieked, and Sarah turned to see Olive sliding down a steep bank toward the foaming brown water. Sarah swore and went after her, dislodging a rock that almost hit Olive in the head, and they both bounced down the slope in the mud. Olive came to rest on a little knob up against the roots of a log with a howl, and Sarah stopped in a glissade of mud just before smashing Olive's face with the heel of her cowboy boot.

They huddled shaking. Olive's hat was gone and her face was plastered with brown goo. Her immaculate ringlets of honey-blond hair were random dark tangles around a pale face that was now as white as the corpse in the creek.

"You are never, *ever* getting me out here again!" The violet hue of Olive's eyes had darkened to a deathly purple. "You must be a magnet for dead bodies or something."

"What? For God's sake Ollie! They were here before *I* came! You just lived here in blessed ignorance and never even *knew* it!"

Olive blinked and wiped her nose, leaving a long brown streak across her cheek, "Think we're gonna die?"

"No, but we had best better get up off our bums if we're to not catch our deaths of cold."

Olive placed a cold-lipped kiss on Sarah's mouth, moaned, and struggled to her feet, "That Swami told me I was gonna die young," she gazed into the gray clouds and wiped her eyes, "if I did, I wonder if people would even remember me. I bet there'll be so many movies coming that nobody will even care."

"That's a strange thing to say."

"It's true, sister. What the fuck have I done that's worth remembering anyway? Really?"

* * *

They stumbled dripping out of the darkness onto the tile floor of the atrium, stripped off their soaked clothes, and ran pink and shivering to the shower upstairs like two half-born marsupials who were seeking a pouch. Sarah and Olive stood quaking under the hot water together as Lupita's shocked voice echoed through the house.

Jack knocked on the bathroom door, "Well. Thought you two were dead or something. We were about to call the Sheriff and round up a posse."

"We almost *drowned!* I've never been so wet in my entire life!"

"Ollie, are you coming back to Wilshire tonight?"

"Yes."

"Well, your Locomobile is fixed and in the garage there. Bee Davis had it delivered this afternoon. Not too suited for this rain though."

"Thank you."

"The Cadillac is at the shop and the limo is loaned to Mabel. I've borrowed Wally's Packard."

"Fine."

"Fine then, see you when you get out."

Olive put a trembling cheek between Sarah's breasts, and Sarah ran a hand through Olive's hair and down her neck. The hot water was salvation in and of itself and they lingered, rocking in each other's arms.

Lupita brought hot tea and they dressed for the trip to Wilshire. Olive pulled on her clothes with shaking hands and Sarah hugged her to calm her down. When Olive reached for the cocaine, she stopped her. "I don't want to even see that right now, Ollie. I've had enough. I can barely stand to look at it. Please don't use it."

Olive bit her lip and put it back in the bottom of the drawer, "Got to have a reefer though."

Sarah sighed.

Olive's hands were trembling, and she tore two of the little cigarettes apart trying to roll them. Sarah took the tray from her and rolled a perfect one.

"Where did you learn to do that?"

"Loggers had me roll their cigarettes for a penny a dozen when I cooked for them on Vancouver Island. I did the same for the mining crew on Sulfur Creek in the Klondike. I got a dime there. I raised it to a quarter and collected a lot of gold dust and nuggets. I was only ten when I learned."

"Thanks, lady."

"You're welcome."

Olive blew her nose.

* * *

Jack drove them in Wally's Packard to Hollywood. The Red Cars on the double trolley tracks through Cahuenga Pass were jammed with people fleeing the occurrence of rain. Cars, trucks, and wagons were stuck in a mudslide at the mouth of Brushy Canyon across the way. Olive sniffled and blew her nose until it was red. She moaned, "I've god to be at the studio to read da scrip for *Out Yonder* in da mornink!"

"I'll send Blanche to the pharmacy as soon as we get home."

"Da pharmacy's closed, Jack!"

"Then we'll have the doctor come to the house. The studio's got one on call. You ought to know that by now Ollie."

Olive nodded and blew her nose again.

Sarah stared at the wet streets in the yellow glare of headlights. The vacuum wipers hissed as Jack stepped on the gas, slashed at the sheen of rain on the windshield, and fell back limply when he slowed. Two girls stood on a corner huddled against the rain as streams of water ran from their vulcanized canvas slickers and soaked their satin skirts while they shared an umbrella. One of them bent down to look into their car as they stopped at the corner of Western to make the right toward Wilshire. She waved at Jack, spotted Olive and Sarah, gave them a disappointed stare, and stood up to check the next vehicle.

"Poor things, workin' on a nibgt like thiz."

Sarah stared at the whores and let out a sigh. She squeezed Olive's hand.

"They'll be in a warm bed before we are, sweetheart."

"Yeah, Jack, long enougph for some fella to finish opff... then back on da streedt," Olive blew her nose again, "gob anoder handkercheph?"

Sarah watched the girls recede through the tiny back window until they were illuminated by the headlights of a big car that stopped for them. It would be so easy for some fiend to lure them into his warm car, especially a nice one, and take them wherever he pleased. Just like the ones in the hills or rotting in the well. A now-familiar chill wandered up her spine. Sarah grimaced at the realization she was getting used to it.

She closed her eyes and was at the train station on Lankershim boarding a northbound one. She heard her sister Angeline's laugh and saw the gentle streets of Victoria with the green bronze roofs of its Empire buildings. She smelled the bakeries and tasted a tiny creampuff. She was hired on again by Alexander Pantages to work at the Strand in Seattle. She would even tolerate his advances and the cutting glances of his jealous wife Lois that he'd jilted violet-eyed Klondike Kate for. She drifted back to the Klondike and was climbing King Solomon's Dome under an aurora that lit up the universe in green, red, and deep purple -- twelve years old and full of confidence with a rifle slung over her shoulder with a solemn vow to never need boys at all.

She opened her eyes. Olive was staring at her.

* * *

When they reached the house, Sarah was shown to a guest bedroom and provided with silk pajamas by Blanche. Olive came into the room, gave her a sniffling hug, and staggered to the master bedroom she shared with Jack. Sarah put the pajamas on the bed and wandered down to the parlor.

Jack was smoking a pipe and reading the *Los Angeles Times.* Another man was sitting with his back to Sarah, gesturing with his hands as he spoke with his shiny blond hair shaking with the motion, "I've no *life,* Jack! None! I've got a racecar driver's license but will the studio let me *drive* one when I'm not on a set? Here I play the big hero in *Double Speed,* and I can't even get behind the fucking wheel of one in real life! It's a crock! Thank fucking god I've got someone around with the same bad habits anyway."

"Indeed, Wally." Jack looked up and saw Sarah.

Jack's companion glanced over his shoulder and blinked. He stood, took some sheet music off the mahogany grand piano, and put it over a syringe and squat brown bottle lying in a lacquered tray upon it.

Jack smiled, "Sarah, meet Wallace Reid."

Sarah examined the tall, handsome man who stood to greet her, the same man she'd been giddy over at the theater in Vancouver with her sister Angeline a thousand years ago. "Hello, Mr. Reid."

"Wally, just Wally,"

Jack took the pipe from his mouth and motioned to a chair, "Care for a brandy?"

Sarah sunk into the big silk-upholstered chair and nodded. The fire in the marble hearth and the sound of rain outside reminded her how much she'd missed them both. She might as well have a drink.

Jack sprang up and poured brandy into a snifter from a crystal decanter on the ebony grand piano, "I'd offer you a cigar but I doubt you'd want it. Cigarette?"

Sarah shook her head.

"Care for a chaser?"

She nodded again, and Jack called for Blanche, who brought three glasses of ice water on a pewter tray.

Jack raised his snifter in a toast, "Cheers."

"To our lovely guest."

Sarah brought the glass to her lips and inhaled the earthy, wooden bouquet. She took a sip and swallowed. It burned its way down but lit a pleasant fire in her stomach. She wiped her mouth and drank half the glass of water.

"So, how exactly did you two meet anyway? You just seem to have popped up while me and Bill were sleeping one off. Family in these parts?"

"No, not really, I was driving down the road past your place there above the Valley when I saw Olive with her car off in the bushes and offered her a ride."

"Driving? Didn't know you had a flivver."

"It was... a friend's."

"Oh I see. Well, she's damn lucky it wasn't some scoundrel or worse. Ollie's but a tiny thing, precocious and beautiful to a fault as I'm sure you've learned by now. She wasn't in any condition to be driving anyway."

Wally lifted his chin off his chest and nodded, "Girl's dangerous behind a wheel."

Sarah sighed, "No, she wasn't in any condition."

"Girl certainly can get in a snit when she's dabbling with the coke. Glad she didn't do something to make you toss her out again," Jack chuckled, "she would have been mad as a wet hen."

"I suppose you all were rather loopy at the time."

He grinned, "I'll give you that. So, what do you think of the way we live here? Seen more than most I'd wager, what with Ollie having you in tow."

Sarah stared at the amber liquid in the crystal snifter. She swirled it in her palm, red in its depths with the light of the fire. She examined handsome Jack in his quilted silk bathrobe with a smile you could paste on every movie poster she'd ever seen and glanced at his movie star guest, who was struggling to stay conscious a few moments longer. *Morphine.* Jack could be one of them, whoever they were. Handsome blond Wallace Reid could be one too. The ones who did those horrible things to girls and left them discarded and dead like spent packages of their drugs. A wet white skull glowed in a glade somewhere in the Hollywood Hills like a puffball mushroom springing from the damp recesses of her mind. She really didn't have any idea what they were up to... or *why*. "I wonder if any of it's worth it, actually."

Wally raised his head, "Did you come to try out for the flickers?"

Sarah blinked, "I thought so."

Jack gave her that Hollywood smile again, and Sarah felt the heavy bottle of scotch in her grip as she swung with all her might at Warren's staring eyes. She could feel it shatter in her hands, and the shock and thrill of it rippling through her body. Sarah swallowed and squeezed her fists until her knuckles went white. She wanted to rip Jack's head off but forced a reflection of his smile, bit her lip, and tried to focus on what he was saying.

"You're quite attractive, Sarah. Most picture stars are smaller women however. Ollie fits that mold as do my sisters Mary and Lottie, and the Gish girls, as well as a host of others like Mary Minter and Mabel Normand. You're rather tall and quite well-muscled for a girl. It's a type more suited to the chorus line and dancing. Your hair's rather short, too. There's plenty of work in dancing though. I could recommend you to some of the club owners I know."

"I'm going to look for a place to rent in the morning. Olive said there's a bungalow on Alvarado."

"Ollie's somewhat untutored in regard to such things, although she certainly means well. That place is rather dear if it's the one I suspect. I'd suggest something more temporary and fitting for your situation."

"What do you suggest?"

"You'd be doing quite well if you could get a room at the Hollywood Hotel. Everyone who's anyone will notice you there.

You're bound to catch their eye. I know someone planning to leave for new digs tomorrow, and he can hand off his room to you. I'll make a call to him and to the management as well. That's pretty much the way it works around here."

"Yep," Wally yawned, "that's the way it works."

XIX.

"Miss Sarah?"

"Um?"

"Miss Olive's keepin' to her bed, but she wishes to speak to you."

Sarah stepped out of the bathroom into brilliant sunshine spilling over the Santa Monica Mountains through the windows. The cooing of mourning doves came from three date-laden palms fighting for space with wooden oil derricks over the red tile roof across the street. She had on her red velour skirt along with a red silk blouse Olive had given her and glanced at herself in the mirror before stepping into the hall. Blanche opened the door to Olive's bedroom and shut it behind her.

Olive sat on a huge canopy bed enfolded in a silken bolster that had arms like an easy chair. Her nose and eyes were red, and a pot of tea and a cup were on a little teak table across her lap. She swiped at her nose and grinned, "Look like shit huh?"

"You certainly did come down with a cold."

"I'm sendink Jack to pick up the scrip from Alan. I can read it in bed," Olive's moist eyes flicked across Sarah's face, "Jack says you're gonna get a room."

"It seems proper. You've been wonderful, Ollie, but I don't want to impose."

"You'll never impose on me but it's probably a good idea. Jack's an odd duck with Wally and all huh? I'll miss you so much

Sarah. Call me the instink you get settled," Olive blew her nose and her big violet-blue eyes began to brim with tears. She shoved aside the little table, threw her arms out, and Sarah sat on the bed and hugged her. "He says he got you a room at the Hollywood Hotel."

"Yes, I'm going there now... and shopping for some clothes."

"Wish I could go with you."

"You've got to get well."

Olive dug her chin into Sarah's shoulder, "Sometimes I hate my life."

Sarah hesitated before asking, "Why?"

"It's just so much crap! Jack's friends drive me crazy, and whenever I meet somebody I really care about, I have to go back to work."

"Well, you are a motion picture star... and married."

"Yeah, I am," Olive wiped her face, grabbed another handkerchief from a pile of clean ones, blew her nose, and tossed it on the floor with the others, "Sure was a scary hike we took huh?"

Sarah nodded.

"I'll call the cops and tell them about the bodies up there and just hang up when they ask my name."

"That's a good idea."

"Wish the limo was fixed. I could have you driven to the hotel."

"That's all right; I'll take a taxi."

"Love you Sarah."

"Love you too Ollie."

Olive made a wet wheeze, hugged her, and they parted.

* * *

She decided to say goodbye to Blanche before the taxi came and found her sitting in the solarium at the back of the house with sunlight glistening in her ironed-straight hair. The Japanese gardener from the house on Lankershim was raking leaves and tattered blossoms out of the damp grass beyond the windows.

"Thank you for everything Blanche."

Blanche looked up in surprise from a book she was reading and began to rise.

"No, don't get up, I just wanted to thank you for being so nice."

"You're welcome, Miss Sarah. Ain't often somebody come lookin' for me jus' to say that roun' here."

"What are you reading?"

"Huckleberry Finn. Think that Mr. Taylor's gonna make it just like the book? Jack played Tom Sawyer for him a couple years ago, but it weren't like what I read that much."

"I doubt it. Perhaps when they get sound someday they'll be able to have more conversations without filling the screen up with words."

Blanche studied Sarah, "You're worried 'bout Miss Olive."

"I... yes."

"Let me tell you somethin'. That girl's already burned the candle at three ends when there ain't no more than two," Blanche shook her head and gazed out the window, "loving boys, Lord, loving girls... you'll 'cuse me, ma'am, but I ain't seen her so up about somebody much as you since that grip Nate had when she was makin' *Toton*." Blanche fell silent and watched the gardener push a wheelbarrow full of the rain's leavings across the pink flag-stones outside.

"Tell me about him."

"Ain't that much to tell Miss Sarah, jus' an honest cowboy from Oklahoma... 'ceptin' he was black."

Sarah's mouth fell open.

"I sees your feelin's, but he was better than most believe you me, an honest-to-god hero of the three hundred sixty-ninth in the Champagne-Marne over there in France who come back to the States just wonderin' how he stumbled into her world. He was always lookin' over his shoulder kinda unbelivin' it could be happenin', wonderin' if somebody gonna kill him at the drop of a hat. She come up with all kinda excuses jus' to disappear with him. I was always coverin' for her," Blanche grinned, "kinda like you, Miss Sarah." Her mouth grew thin, and her fingers danced across the book in her lap, "Please don't say nothin' 'bout that. I got four children and no man to feed 'em."

Sarah swallowed, nodded, and her fingers closed around the doorknob behind her.

"She's like a little girl Sarah, just... samplin' everything and everybody that sparks her fancy like they's candy or somethin'." Blanch put fingers to her lips and stared out the window, "It's like she knows she don't have that much time 'for it all runs out and she just has to eat up the whole wide world first."

Sarah caressed the door knob, "I've... got to be going."

"Guess so. Don't know if you even want to know, but you're the best thing in her life right now. Don't know if it'll make any difference in the long run, but it's been nice to have you 'round Miss Sarah. Keeps her from drivin' off a cliff anyway," she grinned, "or runnin' over somebody else with that goddamn Locomobile."

Sarah looked up from the floor, "Thank you Blanche, I'll never tell a soul about Nate either."

"That'd be wise, Miss Sarah."

* * *

The air was scrubbed clean by the rain with the green of the hills seemingly renewed overnight. Pink flower petals stripped by the downpour coated sidewalks, and gardeners were sweeping up the mess before sprawling new homes aglow in the sun. Sarah sat in the back of a big Siemens taxi holding the note Jack had given her with the name of the man who was leaving the Hollywood Hotel. Jack had called ahead that morning and all was arranged. It was all very convenient, and Sarah supposed Olive's obvious attraction to her had quite a bit to do with his aid in getting her out of the house. She knew now it wasn't the first time. "Whatever," she said to the ornate Spanish façade as they pulled up in front of the hotel.

"Ma'am?"

"Oh nothing, thank you."

The driver tipped his cap and stepped out to grab her suitcase from the trunk. He carried it across the lawn on the flagstone path and up the marble steps, where the door was opened by a bellhop who grabbed it. Sarah opened her lead beaded purse, paid the driver the dollar fare, and tipped him a quarter. She handed the bellhop another quarter as he placed her suitcase by the polished teak desk.

Several people were lounging on heavy Spanish-style chairs and couches under wrought iron chandeliers hanging from the polished oaken beams. All were eyeing the new arrival, as was a tall man with a pencil-thin mustache in a shiny black suit behind the desk who glanced at her clothes with a dour expression.

"Excuse me," she began.

"Madame, welcome to the Hotel Hollywood. Do you have a reservation?"

"I was looking to assume residency of a Mr. Jenks room, who is scheduled to depart today. Mr. Jack Pickford recommended me to you I believe."

"Ah, Miss McCallum, certainly. Mr. Jenks the astrologer has just left this morning. The staff is preparing the rooms as we speak and they shall be ready by noon at the latest. May we store your luggage in the interim?"

"Yes, thank you. Um, how much, how much is the... are the rooms?"

"For how long may I ask?"

"At least a month I suppose."

"The monthly rate is two-hundred dollars."

Sarah tried to hide her expression while she counted out the bills as a handsome couple glided past and eyed her curiously. She felt their stares and walked out onto Hollywood Boulevard as soon as she'd made arrangements to buy new clothes.

* * *

When she returned lugging her purchases, a bellhop took them up to her room and she handed him a quarter. The desk man gave her two keys to number 265 and the manager, who looked just like the man behind the desk except for a touch of gray at the temples, escorted her to the elevator. The operator opened the brass cage and the manager stepped in beside her. "So, Miss McCallum, is this your first time in Hollywood?"

"No, uh, well, I've been around for a few days that is. I've been staying with Miss Thomas and Mr. Pickford, but Olive's come down with an awful cold, and I wanted to have some room of my own as to not inconvenience them."

He ran a hand across his upper lip and tamped down his mustache, "My sympathies. She's one of our favorite people. People call her the most beautiful girl in Hollywood for good reason with those remarkable eyes. Pardon me, but are you of the McCallums of Boston?"

"No, er, of Victoria."

"Canada, I should love to see it one day. Well," the operator opened the cage of the elevator, and the manager gestured to the left, where he led her down a thick golden carpet to an antique Spanish door. He unlocked it and bowed.

There was a sitting room done in early Californian like most everywhere else she'd been. Fresh flowers were in vases on either side of a dark leather couch with a low table between it and two oaken chairs padded in dark leather. Beyond was a bedroom with a huge Spanish bedstead that looked like it had come from a real hacienda. To the left was a small kitchen done in colorful tile, and beyond that a tiled bathroom with a table and illuminated vanity mirror in its entryway.

"Is this to your satisfaction?"

"Oh, absolutely," she handed the manager a dollar; he bowed and shut the door. Her new clothes were hung in paper wrappers in the closet. Fancy toiletries were on the vanity table by the bathroom, and the hat and shoeboxes were on the bed. Sarah took off her cloche flapper hat, tossed it on a chair, swept the boxes out of the way, and bounced on the colorful blanket.

A room of her own!

* * *

Shouts and laughter awoke her to a streetlight that was much too bright through the window. She squeezed her eyes shut again, drew the curtains, and felt for the lamp in sudden darkness. People were running up and down the hall outside laughing and talking in high voices. It sounded like they'd been drinking.

She sighed and stretched on the silky sheets. No one was waiting for her, watching her, or trying to touch her. No frightening strangers were lurking with offers of fame. No faces were at the window. She yawned and grinned at the ceiling. *Wait…* someone *was* waiting on her. She was supposed to call Olive. Sarah found the note with the number and grabbed the receiver of the ivory and gilt telephone the hotel provided in the room.

The hotel operator answered, "Good evening, number?"

"Poplar eight-eight-nine-nine."

"Just a moment."

Sarah ran a hand across the leather of the couch and absently dug her index finger into the burn hole of a cigar while the operator connected. The phone rang at the other end four, then five times, "Mr. Pickford and Miss Thomas' residence."

"Hello Blanche, this is Sarah. Is Olive there?"

"Oh no Miss Sarah, she was feelin' better and drove her car over to a friend's. Hope she ain't goin' on another binge or somethin'. Mr. Pickford was in a tizzy she'd get in an accident, but left after shoutin' 'bout it for a while with Mister Reid. You want to leave a message?"

"Do you know where she went?"

"She said she was gonna see Bee."

"Oh thank you. Just let her know I called. Room two-sixty-five at the Holly... the Hotel Hollywood."

"I sure will Miss Sarah. You have a safe night now."

"Thank you Blanche, same to you."

* * *

She showered and got dressed in her new clothes: a smart beige skirt and blouse with puffy sleeves and a daringly low neckline that she'd found at a little shop a block away on Hawthorn. The sounds outside her room were exciting now that she had somewhere to retreat to with a door and a key. She checked her hair one last time, fluffed it a bit, and opened the door onto a crowd of men in white tuxes and women in gowns, cloche hats, and slinky satin dresses with dangling ropes of pearls. Sarah was nearly hit by a champagne bottle and stepped back into the room. When she glanced out again, a man was coming down the hall with a young woman in his arms, swinging her like a baby while singing in Italian. The lights glistened on his slicked-back hair as the woman's shoulder length auburn hair swung in time to his steps and her white wedding gown trailed behind them. His eyes met Sarah's and she froze. Rudolfo flashed her a grin before turning to a balding well wisher beside him.

"Mazel tov!" The man shouted, throwing arms around the bride and groom's necks.

Valentino waited for someone to unlock the door across the hall for him and carried his bride within. Shouts went up, drunks banged on the door and walls with a battery of suggestions, and the wedding party proceeded to the bar. After a moment's hesitation, Sarah shut the door behind her and joined them.

Downstairs, a raucous celebration was underway. She sat down at a table being cleaned by a waiter, who looked up with a smile as she slid into the booth. Three more girls appeared and filled it.

The one nearest her squeezed Sarah's knee, "Damn, don't you wish it was *you* up there?"

"He's a stallion, I hear," the brunette next to her said.

"Honey, all Italians--"

"That's a crock. I know a Guinea who ain't worth spit."

"Yeah, well, with your luck I ain't surprised toots."

The two pretty brunettes and the redhead beside Sarah chattered on as the waiter brought champagne without anyone asking. He popped the cork and poured four glasses.

The redhead lifted hers in a toast, "To Valentino... and what's-her-name."

"Jean, Jean Acker."

"Yeah."

They drank. Sarah actually liked it this time and held out her glass when the waiter refilled them. The redhead put her hand on Sarah's, "So what's your name sugar?"

"Sarah."

"Hi, I'm Jenny. This here's Helen, and this is Toodles."

"Fuck you Jen, it's Marny."

"Nice to meet you."

"So, you workin' the chorus line or the flickers?"

"Not yet, I'm a friend of Olive Thomas. Just down from Canada actually."

"Olive Thomas! Howdya meet her?"

"That's none of your biz, Jenny."

"Hey Marny, just askin'. Hear the girl's a spitfire. Tears up every party she goes to. That true Sarah?"

"Well, she's rather sweet, actually."

"Guess you'd know if you're friends," Jenny shrugged, "we were at a barbecue out at Inceville on the beach and got invited to the wedding. Who'd turn down free drinks and grub? I never had scallops before. By the way, they're hiring extras for a new shoot-em-up tomorrow."

"Where?"

Helen shook her head, "Boy, you are new. Up the coast past Santa Monica at a great big spread where Tom Ince makes all his Westerns. They got all the equipment in the world, and an ol' time frontier town saloons and all. Place is jake... and lotsa crazy parties."

Marny scowled, "'Cept when Dolores got--"

"Shhhh, can it, toots!" Jenny grinned, "It's a great place to meet people too. Got a job at the Starry Night dancin' the first time I went there. Some fella dressed up like an Injun turned out to be the owner of the club. Met a cop playin' a cowboy and he got me off the next time I had a run-in with Johnny Law too. Hell, he'd *better* have after the time I gave him. Handy fella to know toots. 'Course if you're already chums with the likes of Olive Thomas, you probably don't need the likes of us tellin' you what's what."

"I do want to meet people. I was sitting in Jack Pickford's den with him and Wally Reid last night, and to be honest, I couldn't stand them."

Jenny's eyes widened and she glanced at her friends, "Well... I guess."

"You said that they're hiring for a film tomorrow?"

"Yep, casting call's at noon. Wanta come?"

"Why yes, that should be fun."

"Okay. Hey, how did you end up at the wedding?"

"I'm staying at the hotel, but I know Rudolf."

"Jeez, him too?"

"Oh yes."

* * *

She stumbled up the stairs from the bar two hours later planning to meet the girls in the café at eight a.m. for breakfast.

The champagne had her lightheaded, but she'd burned plenty off dancing, and had half a dozen men's cards stuffed in a little pocket on the thigh of the new skirt. As she wobbled on the stairs, Sarah found herself wanting some of Olive's cocaine. She stopped, ground her teeth, and cast off the idea. When she reached her floor, she pulled the key from her purse, took off her shoes, and coasted down the gold-carpeted hall toward the refuge of her room with her toes exulting in the soft pile beneath them.

Rudolfo sat on the floor outside room 264 across the hall clad in a red and gold silk bathrobe staring morosely at the wall. His fingers were around the neck of an unopened green bottle of Mumms Champagne and his eyes were closed as his bare feet rocked to some internal beat. His hair had made a spot on the oaken wainscoting. As she approached, he looked up.

Sarah put a hand to her mouth, "Ah... hello, eh?"

"I am shamed before myself, and now before you Sarah, my beautiful Sarah."

"What in the world?"

"She *refuses* me!" Rudolfo tottered to his feet, took a breath, and struck a heroic stance against the bitter winds of pathos washing over him, "She refuses Valentino... on his *wedding night!*" He turned red-rimmed eyes to her, "May I come into your room to hide my shame? Do you have men's clothes perhaps?"

Sarah put fingers over a laugh threatening to erupt, "No men's clothes, Rudy. It's not Belmore you know, but you can come in."

"Grazi, grazi, sweet lady."

She unlocked the door and led the chastened Latin lover into her room. "This is so amazing, I mean here we are, and it's supposed to be your wedding night, and... what's *wrong* with that woman?" The laugh Sarah had been fighting won out, and she brought her hand back to her mouth.

Rudolfo shot her a look of misery, "She is a lesbian... a *lesbian!* What foolishness I have succumbed to, to wait for the conja... how do you say? The conj--"

"Conjugal."

"The conjugal bed, without ever tasting the fruits of love... the bitch!"

Sarah gasped for air and bit her tongue, "Oh, God."

"I see your laughter, your scorn, I am undone!" Rudolfo put the back of a hand to his forehead, struck another heroic stance, and stared at the drapes.

"Oh don't be silly. You're a movie star and you just got hitched to the wrong girl for what... a night?"

"I am a Catholic, and divorce is worse than--"

"Why, because it's public? What about that stuff you do at Bee's?"

Rudolfo shrugged, "As you say, dear lady, it is not public. No one would believe who I met there anyway."

"Who?"

"Someone who was there the night we danced. How can I say this? She is Bee's friend and lover, and... I cannot mention her to you or she might never appear for my bed again."

Sarah's mouth dropped open, "Is... she someone's rich wife?"

Rudolfo grinned, "Marriage has never been in her plans. She lives beyond our little schemes and mortal plans. She is not of our world, nor is she concerned with my problems at the moment." He shrugged, "Though in truth such talk must well make me seem mad."

"Who in the world are you talking about? Some film star?"

Rudolfo gazed out the windows with an expression Sarah couldn't read at all and sighed, "She gives more than she can possibly take... yet I give her my blood."

Sarah swallowed the lump in her throat, "Say what?"

"I cannot talk of it. I do not understand it but she brings the most wonderful women into my life. Like you, Sarah."

"I am utterly at a loss, Rudolfo."

"She knows you. She held you in her arms as a child and told me we would lie together."

Sarah shook her head, "That's not possible... then she's an old woman?"

Rudolfo chuckled, "Old age hasn't touched her beauty, only her heart perhaps. She says she held you in the night when you were lost in a forest."

Sarah glanced at the door of her room as her legs began to tremble. She closed her eyes for a moment, inhaled, and resolved to put his words out of her mind, "Well, anyway, you don't have to go back in there with that woman you married, if you don't want to."

"It is the shame of this night that leaves me destitute and without solace, for I am Catholic!"

"So what, Rudy? I'm Catholic too... kind of anyway." Sarah saw Olive saying the same thing about marriage in the first minutes they'd met and started giggling again. Her eyes roved over Rudolfo standing before her as he stared mournfully at the closed drapes. Sarah closed her eyes, saw those other eyes watching her, and heard an echo of lovely laughter soft as those imagined wings enfolding her on the hillside.

Take him, love.

Sarah blinked and glanced around for the source of that voice, but the hall was empty. She took a deep breath, came up behind Rudolfo, slid her hands across his muscular shoulders, and opened his bathrobe. "Think of all the girls going to picture shows who shall be thrilled beyond measure knowing your bride was crazy or foolish enough to not consummate the marriage on your wedding night. You can get it annulled, Rudolfo. Ollie has been waiting to get her hands on you for that matter," Sarah's hands continued around his waist. Her fingers explored down his hard belly and wrapped around a cock that leapt to attention in her palm, pulsing like a beating drum. Rudolfo sighed as she ran her tongue down the back of his neck. She felt a wry smile spreading her lips. She was in control and it was about time. She blew in his ear.

Rudolfo trembled as she nibbled the lobe, "Truly," he murmured, "you are an angel."

"If you say so..."

XX.

Sarah yawned, "I like this hotel."

"You could move into my rooms, my lovely friend," Rudolfo whispered, "you are my salvation in this wretched desert of Hollywood." He rose on an elbow with a smile, "We should make a motion picture together."

"Rudy, you're still married."

Valentino rolled over to stare at the ceiling, "You are right, sweet Sarah. Such foolishness is what caused my troubles in the first place... but we must be friends."

"There you go."

"I must call my tailor's and have them bring clean clothes."

"How about just getting back into your rooms?"

"But I must be dressed to go down and get another key. What would people think if I am locked out by my own bride?"

"Oh," Sarah yawned again and peeked out through the curtains as the roof of a green trolley rolled by accompanied by a snap of sparks from the overhead cables and the clang she'd been hearing all morning, "My word, what time is it?"

"Time has no meaning in your presence."

"I'm flattered but I have to meet someone at eight. I have to get cleaned up. I'll go down with a note from you that you need another key."

"But why would I need another key?"

"I don't know… your bride dropped it in the toilet, I suppose, while she was overcome with passion."

Rudolfo laughed, sat up, and cracked his neck. His skin smelled like her. She smelled like him. She stroked his manhood, which stirred immediately and leapt to attention. She kissed him and made a face, "Morning mouth."

"Eh?"

"That's what I call it anyway. Excuse me." Sarah jumped off the bed and headed for the bathroom.

* * *

She had a key for Rudy by seven-thirty and left him to deal with his bride at a quarter to eight. The way he'd said *lesbian* reared its head and echoed in her brain as she padded down the carpeted hall. What exactly was she supposed to be after her fling with Olive, some man-hating, unfeminine creature now? Some witch with a mole on her nose cackling over a caldron? Warren had given her reason enough to hate men if she thought all men were like *that*. They weren't, and she certainly didn't hate them all either. She shrugged hair out of her eyes and chuckled. A breakfast was in order.

She ordered coffee, croissants, poached eggs, and orange juice, then waited for her ride with growing doubts they'd show. At eight-fifteen Jenny bustled in, glanced around, and waved before she planted herself in the opposite chair, "Guess it's just us two Sarah; Helen and Marny couldn't drag themselves out of bed."

"How late were you?"

"Pretty darn late, toots."

"Um, time for some coffee?"

"Oh yes please." Jenny flicked purple-painted nails at the waiter, who was already on his way, and grabbed a croissant from Sarah's plate to tear off a bite with a flash of gold tooth, "Ain't much fun if we have to stand around all day. The good times are when the director takes one look at you and points a finger, 'That one!' and you walk right by everybody else to get the part," she grinned, "and if you miss, you can try and get near him at the barbecue afterward for the next time."

"What do they pay?"

"Starts at five bucks a day. It depends. I did a two-reeler a couple months ago for fifty," Jenny grimaced, "but that goddamn assistant director had the most awful breath."

Sarah rubbed her eyes, "Well, it's something."

"If you're keeping the likes of Olive Thomas for company, it must seem rather paltry."

"Have to start on my own somewhere, eh? That reminds me, I have to call her." A knot formed in her stomach, and Sarah put down her second croissant. Why hadn't Olive called?

"Don't take too long. I borrowed a bartender's Tin Lizzie and I don't want him to see it parked outside when I'm supposed to be gone. He might get the wrong idea."

Olive hadn't come home, but Blanche gave her the number for Belmore. When Sarah gave it to the operator, she could almost feel the woman's smirk on the other end of the line. The telephone was picked up after one ring.

"Davis residence," A woman's voice answered.

"Hello, I'm calling for Olive, Olive Thomas."

"I'm sorry. We don't have anyone here by that name. I suggest you try the Selznick Studios."

Sarah clutched the gilded receiver to her breast. What was the protocol for calling a bagnio? She had no idea. "Um, my name's Sarah McCallum. May I speak to Miss Davis?"

"One moment, I'll see if she's available."

There was a long wait as Sarah sat on a couch by the table with the ivory and gilt receiver to her ear, listening to the crackle of the line and faint sounds on the other end.

"Hello, Sarah?"

"Bee! I'm so glad to hear your voice. I was hoping Olive was there. Her maid said she went over there yesterday and she's been rather ill, and--"

"Yes she is. The little scamp thought she was going to have a party. I took one look at her and put her to bed with a thimble of laudanum, a gallon of orange juice, a menthol poultice on her chest, and a pile of hankies. She's sleeping at the moment, thank God."

Sarah ran a hand through her hair and sunk onto the couch, "Thank you Bee."

"Impulsive little thing isn't she?"

"I was worried."

"Girls can do that to extremes. It's why I don't keep one anymore. Take my advice and watch yourself that you don't fall into that one. Ollie told me about your time together by the way."

"She... did?"

"Sarah, do you remember what we said about secrets?"

"Yes."

"You're safe as long as your little friend only tells her stories to me. It's jake to have someone to trust in this town and I'm used to it. I've got a lot of girls who have no one else to trust in this whole part of the world," Beverly chuckled, "so what are you about today?"

"I'm going to some place called Inceville by the ocean, to see about a part in a motion picture."

There was another chuckle on the other end, "Watch out for cowboys and Indians then. Dolores got hauled off on the back of a horse by a rough fellow when she was an extra there this spring and had to fend him off with a hatpin. I hope to see you soon, Sarah. You're always welcome here. Any messages for our little friend?"

"Yes, just tell her to get well, and--"

"That you love her?"

"Just say hello Bee."

"All right, she'll appreciate your concern. We'll keep the girl until she's halfway sensible I suppose, although Prohibition will likely end sooner. 'Till she's well enough anyway. She brought a script to read in bed at least. She's got three pictures ready to film this spring and told me she really wants you to see her at work and not playing. She even cried a bit, Sarah. Your opinion of her is rather important I suppose."

"Thank you so much Bee."

"Don't mention it love."

Sarah bounced out of the hotel into a dented blue Model T and hopped in beside Jenny. A bellhop turned the crank and they started out for Inceville. They drove to Sunset and followed its winding trace along the base of the hills toward the ocean. The crumbling walls and towers of Babylon rose ahead over roofs and oil wells, grew closer, and finally loomed overhead with their pale stern statues and ancient monsters. Sarah stared into the face of some hawk-headed god holding a hatchet until she got tired of looking behind her.

They passed through small junctions that were fast being swallowed by the sprawl of Los Angeles at the bases of green canyons with heights topped by new mansions. Old clapboard stores stood surrounded by peeling outbuildings with expensive Rolls, Mercedes, Cadillac and Siemens limousines parked at wooden porches next to farm wagons, battered Ford Model N's, Model T pickups, and men in overalls. Servants of the newly rich did some shopping beside farmers who'd been here for generations and roosters crowed from chicken coops. The smells of orange, grapefruit, tangerine, and lemon mixed into an all-pervasive citrus smell that perfumed the air.

They reached the road along the beach from Santa Monica and hit the narrow concrete ribbon of Highway One. Sarah inhaled the smell of the sea, and a flood of memories arose like dawn over the mountains. Foundations were going in along a distant stretch of beach for something huge between them, and the march of the Santa Monica Pier with its Ferris wheel, pirate ship, and roller coaster aglow in the distance as busy crews swarmed over boards, beams, and iron rods poured into massive concrete forms that had been built out into the water for a big U-shaped structure.

Jenny stared for so long that Sarah was afraid she'd miss the next curve. "That's going to be Hearst's new beach house for his mistress Marion Davis," Jenny said wistfully. "What a god-awful playpen."

"My word."

"She started with Ziegfeld like your chum Olive. It gives a new meaning to beach house, that's for sure."

They left the pavement and drove where the road was hacked out of steep slopes over the ocean, winding down, across, and up canyons opening into the hills with the occasional rutted trace branching off. Monterey Cypress twisted and flattened by the constant sea breeze clung to shoulders of rock running into green water. A hillside was blackened by a recent fire, mud had washed down in the rains, and they had to slow to cross patches of it drying on the highway. Clusters of new bungalows gathered above secluded beaches, where people were swimming in November. Sarah caught a glimpse of one where the people appeared to be nude, but trees quickly obstructed her view.

Jenny left the highway at a wide canyon before crossing a one-lane wooden bridge and drove toward a sprawling cluster of buildings along a gully with pools of rainwater sparkling in the sun. Below them on the canyon bottom were the wooden palisade of a frontier fort and the false fronts of a Western town. Above those was a long, wide building constructed to provide a great deal of interior space with doors big enough to swallow a house. On posts beside the dirt road leading to the main street of the prop town was a whitewashed sign proclaiming **INCEVILLE**.

"Now I feel like I'm in the pictures."

A crowd of people stood in the gravel parking lot before the big shed of a studio emblazoned with a shield painted with the name **INCE**. Jenny pulled over and turned off the engine that wheezed and dieseled to a stop, and they got out.

A short man in a tweed cap, jacket and pants, brown spats and canvas leggings was walking up and down the line of hopeful extras with a clipboard, occasionally putting his pencil to his lips in concentration and making a mark. When he got to Jenny and Sarah, he stopped, "Back again Jen?"

Jenny nodded, "You betcha Jules, how 'bout another kissin' scene?"

The man grinned, put the pencil behind his ear, and slid his hand across her backside, "Jen you're a card... and who's this with you?"

"My friend Sarah."

He put a hand to his chin, "Rather tall. Can you ride a horse? Can't find a girl that can ride a horse worth spit around here."

"Yes sir. I worked two summers on a cattle ranch in the Fraser River Valley."

"Where might that be, Montana?"

"No sir, British Columbia."

"Really. Well, we've got a scene where an Indian grabs a girl by the hair," he glanced at Sarah's blonde shoulder-length tresses, "which in your case will be a wig. You've got to slip a hand up to the pommel at the same time and throw a leg over the saddle in front of the fellow while he pretends to lift you. It's rather quick, but you look a good deal more athletic than the rest of this bunch. Tried it yesterday with a man in a dress, but Mr. Ince didn't like the way it looked. Think you can handle that?"

"Yes, absolutely."

"We'll see. Pay's seven dollars and fifty cents a day if you work out. Maybe more if you're good. Don't get hurt. We don't pay for that."

"All right."

"What's your name?"

"Sarah McCallum."

He made a mark on his clipboard, "Sarah M. Go tell wardrobe you're the hostage, get your duds, and go talk to Mr. Hart."

"How 'bout me Jules?"

"Well Jen, I suppose we can use another barroom Jezebel. You can smoke a cigar and give Bill Hart the eye when he walks in before the shootout," Jules grinned, "I'll let you be the one to warn him before the bad guy shoots him in the back. You'll get a sentence on screen to boot and that's another fiver." He ran a hand across her behind again, "Over to wardrobe, toots!"

"Thanks!" Jenny gave him a peck on the cheek and headed into the building.

William S. Hart was famous for the Westerns Ince had cranked out since leaving Triangle for his own company, and Jenny said he was here from his new partnership with United Artists on a loan. He was a square-shouldered man dressed in a white cowboy hat, checkered shirt, neckerchief, a concho-studded gun belt, and wide tan chaps pinned with silver conchos and leather lanyards. He wore alligator skin boots, chewed tobacco, and looked a bit too much like Sarah's father. Mr. Hart politely greeted her like a gentleman and immediately began grilling her on her knowledge of horses. When satisfied she actually knew enough to try, he shook her hand and kissed the back of it, "We usually say break a leg kid, but don't."

Sarah inhaled and nodded.

"You okay?"

"What, oh yes, Mr. Hart. Thank you for your concern."

Sarah spent the next hour practicing leaping on a fat pinto horse ridden by a Mexican who called himself Guadeloupe dressed as an Indian. Guadeloupe was an excellent horseman, but didn't have either the reach or size to give her much help mounting at speed. He nearly tore her arm from her body the first time and almost went down himself. Sarah spent ten minutes on a folding camp stool cursing and rubbing her shoulder with an ice pack pressed to it wondering if her film career was over for the day or perhaps forever before she got up to try again.

The third try she got in front of him to the applause of Jules, but Guadeloupe began to fall off the back. He grabbed her hard around the waist and Sarah grabbed the reins. The horse stopped suddenly, put his head down, and nearly threw them both.

Jules muttered something and motioned for the cameras to get in place for the shot. Reflectors of polished metal were being set up behind them in the direction of the ocean, casting a glow that made her squint. The fourth time she got on again, but they wobbled like drunks to the laughter of the crew.

The fifth time Jules looked at his new platinum wristwatch, gave an exasperated glance in their direction, and walked over, "Do you think you can do this? Have you seen *Mickey?* Mabel Normand dresses as a boy, rides as a jockey, jumps off cliffs, swims the rapids, and hangs from a roof. Ever see her tied to a railroad track with a locomotive coming at her in *Barney Oldfield's Race for Life?* She had to duck down in a hole at the last minute or be killed. *That's* doing the job. Have you heard that line Sennett used to promote her: *'She rides like a centaur and swims like a fish with muscles as strong and springy as cold-rolled steel?'* That's the benchmark Mr. Ince wants to surpass, although I don't think we'll ever get a girl with that much moxie. We may have to get another man to play the girl after all... or perhaps a larger rider," Jules tapped the megaphone on his tweed pants, "I just can't get a woman to--"

"No, no, we *do* it!" Guadeloupe protested.

"Let's give it another go eh?" Sarah lifted the heavy skirts she was wearing and leapt off the horse in the dust, wobbled in tall-heeled boots that were much too tight, and walked to her mark as Guadeloupe rode back to his.

Jules returned to his post beside the cameraman, lifted the cone of the megaphone to his lips, and shouted, "Roll 'em!"

"Hai!" Guadeloupe dug his heels into the horse's flanks and the gelding sprang forward. Sarah threw her hands up like a woman in terror, turned to run alongside the horse, and slipped a hand along Guadeloupe's leg as he grabbed at the long wig that half-blinded her as he pretended to be lifting. Her hand found the pommel again, and she sprang for dear life up and over the neck of the horse. Guadeloupe's arm wrapped around her waist and he let out a "Hai ay hai!" as they both settled back and charged up the hill away from half a dozen extras dressed as townsmen waving rifles and firing blanks in a white cloud of smoke on a shouted cue from Jules .

"Cut! Bravo! Well done!"

They rode back downhill to the applause of the crew.

William S. Hart stood with arms crossed as Sarah slid off the horse and, as her feet hit the ground, he tipped his hat, "If you'll pardon my English ma'am, that was damn good ridin'."

"Why thank you Mr. Hart."

"You looked like a natural."

"What does Mabel Normand get for that kind of work anyway?"

"Ol' Goldfish's payin' her two thousand a week. She made six figures from *Mickey* with Sennett. 'Course Mary Pickford, Ollie Thomas, and Mary Minter are gettin' way more playin' little ingénues without any rough stuff, but it's a rare girl that can do this let me tell you. You're kind of ambitious. Isn't this your first day?"

"See you at the barbecue."

XXI.

A little man in shirtsleeves and a straw hat had been watching Sarah's performance from the hillside with binoculars. Thomas Ince had been keeping tabs on Jules and, while taking in the action, found himself impressed. He approached Sarah, doffed his hat, gave her an extra ten dollars, and offered her twenty dollars a day for more work like the horse trick. "I want to see what you can handle."

"It's a start," Sarah shook his hand before he changed his mind and almost yanked him off his feet.

Ince stepped back from the tall blonde but a wry smile spread his thin face, "Day after tomorrow then, be here at seven."

The barbecue started at six. Ince had a truck deliver ribs, frankfurters, and all the trimmings every day at that time. It was a cheap alternative to paying well, the crew loved it, and it had become a place for those hoping to get work to gather and catch a free meal.

From her walk, it appeared Jenny had come upon some liquor. She giggled as she wandered amongst the help looking for the most famous male face in the crowd. It being Inceville, there weren't many beyond Mr. Hart, who was nowhere to be seen. She drifted over to Sarah, who was negotiating a gristly pork rib while sitting on one of the logs lain in a semicircle around a concrete and stone barbecue that was built above the high tide line. "Pretty slick toots!" Jenny plopped down on the log beside her and shoved over the young grip who'd been doing his best to start a conversation with Sarah, "What's he payin'?"

"Twenty a day for trick work like that riding stunt."

"Gosh damn, that's great!"

A half-dozen cowboys and Indians were coming down the beach from a rocky promontory to the north, swinging heavy buckets. Guadeloupe saw Sarah, let out a whoop, shook his bucket, and stepped to the concrete table used for preparing food. He pulled out a big pink half-shell the size of his grinning face with dripping grey flesh hanging from one side. Guadeloupe slid the Bowie knife on his belt out of its sheath, levered the quivering mass from the shell onto the table, and began trimming and slicing it as he pounded the pieces with a little mallet while singing merrily in Spanish. A cowboy shoved more driftwood in the fire and slid a big fry pan on the bars of the barbecue. A blond dance hall girl poured flour into a bowl with a big puff of white that drifted away on the sea breeze. Guadeloupe dredged the disks of grey flesh in the flour and dropped them in the sizzling oil to shouts of approval from those around him.

"Ever have abalone toots?"

"Yes, we have it in British Columbia. I didn't know they were found this far south."

"Probably not for long the way these fellas go at it."

Sarah tore a tough strip from her rib and wiped her hands on a thin cloth napkin. It escaped her grasp and blew away in a gust of breeze to spiral up over the walls of the frontier town in the smoke of the barbecue and up Santa Ynez Canyon. Someone offered her a beer and she washed the last swallow of meat down. Someone lit a reefer. She turned it down. "I've got to find a cheaper place to stay. That hotel is much too dear."

"There's plenty of places, Sarah. Me, Marny, and Helen are renting a three bedroom bungalow on Pico for thirty bucks a month and Helen might be leaving. You could move in. I'll keep you posted."

"Thank you."

"So tell me 'bout Olive Thomas."

"What?"

Jenny gave her a knowing smile, "What's she like... really? We hear about all the parties and such, and her wild husband and friends. Jack Pickford had quite a rep himself before they met. Ever see that flicker with Mary Pickford's squeeze Doug Fairbanks where he plays that detective in *The Adventures of Coke Ennyday?* It's a hoot; it's a spoof on Sherlock Holmes about this coke-crazed detective. He may play all clean and on the up-and-up but he's soon to be her brother-in-law, and she's been seen at coke parties dancin' on tables, disappearin' with boys...the whole shebang. And Jack and his friend Wally Reid are downright notorious around here. They're half of a bunch called The Four Musketeers that go down and tear up Tijuana all the time. So is she as wild as they say? I know you say she's sweet and all, and that's the right thing for a friend to say, but people know things honey. I'm surprised you turned down that reefer, with friends like Olive."

"She has her vices I suppose. She's had a tough life."

"Ain't we all, sister?"

* * *

Sarah filled the tank of the Ford, bought Jenny cigarettes, and was dropped off at the hotel. Jenny promised to pick Sarah up the morning after next at six as they stopped with a pop of the clutch and a screech of tires in front of the Spanish façade proclaiming **Hotel Hollywood**. Sarah ran up the path and across the porch past people lounging under the awnings, hurrying through the lobby, intending to get to her room and clean up.

The manager smiled from behind his desk and held up a manicured hand, "Miss McCallum, greetings. I have several messages for you."

Sarah tucked her tangled hair under the rumpled satin flapper hat, and he handed her some creamy slips of paper with **Hotel Hollywood** emblazoned across the tops in golden ink. She thanked him and headed for the elevator.

There were three from Olive, one from Bee, and one from Bill Taylor about an opportunity at Paramount. She called Olive before she'd even taken off her coat. Blanche answered, but Olive came on the line so quickly Sarah could feel the receiver being yanked out of Blanche's hand, accompanied by a little gasp, "Sarah!"

"Hi Ollie!"

"Where have you been?"

"Didn't Bee tell you?"

"Said you'd found some work is all. God I miss you."

"It's only been a day, but you won't believe what I've been about. I've been out at Inceville making a Western with William S. Hart. They had me leaping on a horse with an Indian and riding off into the hills. Mr. Ince says I'm a natural for women's action roles and wants to have me do such things at twenty dollars a day. Think I could ask more? Perhaps you could mention it to him. My feet are rather sore from the boots they made me wear, but otherwise I'm just thrilled with my first day in the flickers."

Laughter rippled in the phone, "Oh...wow."

"What?"

"Nothing, it just seems so *like* you, but can't you get hurt like that?"

"I suppose, but they couldn't find a girl to do any of it, and the director Jules took one look at me, and--"

"Sarah you're so strong, no wonder that worm Warren didn't stand a fuckin' chance with you."

Sarah gripped the telephone as fragments of memory boiled out of the place Olive's words had touched to hover around her like a cloud. She could feel a dark tide rolling from the shadows of the hills, pooling in the rooms upstairs with Hughie Faye and his weird den of opium and gathering around her window like a boiling storm full of eyes and voices whose owners she couldn't ever see. She saw the skull in the creek, like a weird white egg ready to hatch in her nightmares. She heard, she *felt* Warren moaning in pleasure or pain, a deep, rough laughter, and a stabbing light that cut like a knife. She heard screams. *Were they her own?*

She stared at the blinds, aching to close away the world outside of a sudden yet paralyzed. Something in her reached out to those gentle white hands long ago in a dark forest. Hands far stronger than any she'd ever known. She remembered the sensation of soft wings enfolding her. Her hand went to her purse, and her fingers searched for a pistol that wasn't there.

"Sarah?"

"What?"

"Want to come over?"

"Yes!"

"I'll send the limo."

* * *

A limo was in the drive when she arrived. Douglas opened the car door and she stepped onto pink flagstones under a leafy pomegranate tree. Sarah ran her fingers across one of the knobby hard fruit hanging from a branch and stepped in as the front door was opened by Blanche. Sarah hugged her, "I missed you," and Blanche kissed her cheek.

Sarah wore one of the new outfits purchased on Hawthorn. It was a short lavender satin dress so popular in Hollywood, with a string of faux pearls and a matching satin flapper. She glanced at the other big black Rolls, hoping someone wasn't going to ruin Olive's plans. *Her* plans.

Olive appeared in the foyer, hugged her, gave her a peck on the cheek, wrapped fingers around Sarah's arm, and hissed in her ear, "Mary's here. We got to be on our best behavior."

Sarah fought to concentrate on what she was saying as Olive's breath tickled her cheek, "Ah, all right."

Jack appeared from the den sporting his best Hollywood smile as Sarah walked arm-in-arm into the parlor with Olive.

Olive's grip on her arm tightened, "Sarah McCallum, I want you to meet my sister, America's Sweetheart."

Mary Pickford was sitting in one of the gold upholstered chairs and rose as they entered. Her golden curls were just as in the color pictures in magazines and posters, though they seemed less full. Her child's face had a warm flush paintings hadn't matched and films hadn't yet aspired to. It was hard to believe she was Jack's older sister by four years. Mary was the eternal little girl: innocent in appearance yet resourceful as the world demanded. She was also the business brains of the Pickford siblings, the lover of Douglas Fairbanks, one of the Big Four at United Artists, and the undisputed female power player in all filmdom.

Sarah felt a flush come into her cheeks and she curtsied deeply.

"Oh, I love that. You're Canadian?"

"Yes, Miss Pickford."

Mary gave her a wonderful smile and crossed the room to give her a hug, "Don't be so nervous. That's not the hurly-burly Canadian cowgirl Ollie's been telling me about."

Sarah ran a hand over her face, as if she could change color by doing so.

"Is Sarah your real name?"

Sarah nodded.

"Few of us have one I'm afraid, except for Mabel Normand," Mary sighed, "one wonders what we've created of ourselves."

Sarah nodded again.

"Would you care for some tea?"

"Yes, thank you."

Jack gave Blanche a curt wave. She already was bringing the tray. Jack seemed a pale ghost around the golden warmth of Mary:

the brother whose whole world depended on her star quality and who only reflected her shine. Mary Pickford was the first person Sarah had met who seemed to live up to her legend just by being in the same room.

"Your hair is beautiful in person."

"Thank you. Of course there's a bit more of it in the flickers. George Westmore my makeup man is a wonder. He buys long blond hair and curls it on a stick, then brings dozens of these perfect long ringlets in a special case he has to any location we're filming, and pins it amongst the real ones so it looks perfect. Turns me into Little Miss Sunshine without the trouble of me having to redo it in the middle of a shoot. Costs fifty bucks a curl, too."

"He buys it at Big Suzy's French Whorehouse downtown," Jack interjected.

Mary frowned. She noticed the look on Sarah's face and chuckled, "That's true. Breaks my heart sometimes to think of some poor farm girl cutting it off for me, but I suppose they've had somewhat rougher duty." She glanced at a thin gold watch sparkling with diamonds on her wrist, "I've got to be going. We've wrapped our first United Artists feature and we're planning the cast party for *Pollyanna.* Jack and Ollie really must bring you along on Thursday."

"Sis, I was supposed to meet Wally and--"

Mary shot her brother an unreadable look, "If one doesn't drink or carouse to excess, there seems to be time for so many things. Well," she held out a hand, "you're a lovely girl. Ollie tells me that you've been jumping on horses for Tom Ince."

"Yes."

"I noticed those bruises on the insides of your calves. Rather rough, but I do admire it. Whatever it takes, eh? I worked with Ince in Cuba a few years ago," she chuckled, "what a fucking cheapskate."

Sarah burst into laughter and put fingers to her lips.

"I'm serious. You won't get rich off that guy, but you're on the right track. This business is chock full of little ingénue girls with curls and flowered bonnets. I ought to know. One more scampish little hoyden won't make more than a ripple, but a girl who can take a fall and come back swinging is rare. Mabel's done it with Sennett and now with Goldwyn, and she's as small as I am. You're quite the dish yourself, but far tougher looking to be honest. There's a feel about you, Sarah. I'll see what we can do for you at United Artists. Just watch out for Chaplin. He thinks anything in a skirt is there for his personal entertainment, so be warned. We Canadians have got to stick together, eh?"

"Thank you, Miss Pickford."

"Mary, just Mary, oh, you have got to come to the house I'm building with Douglas in Benedict Canyon. We're going to call it Pickfair," Mary sighed, "and here I am still married to Owen, and Douglas is on a train to probably give every dime he hasn't hidden somewhere to his wife Beth in some court back East this very moment. Means we've just got to work twice as hard to make it again... and all because of our unquenchable passion for one another." She glanced at the floor, "I suppose that our Hollywood ways are rather a shock for you Sarah."

"Not anymore, no."

"I'm just a little shanty Irish girl from Toronto trying to make it here amongst all these men, or at least stay on top now that I have, someone who always had to support a family before I could dare to have one of my own. Well, I'll see you again young lady." Mary kissed Sarah's cheek and floated out the door to her limo.

* * *

After Mary left, Jack poured himself a brandy and sat down in the chair she'd occupied. Sarah and Olive stared wistfully at each other. Jack rubbed the moustache he'd begun growing for his next part and sneered, "Have 'one of her own.' There's one thing the little Czarina won't pull off. Wish she could. She might stop being the policewoman with the rest of us and take it out on the brat. Fucking balderdash."

"Jack…"

"Oh come on, Ollie! You know damn well she had an abortion seven years ago so she could have her glorious career and be the so-called little girl all the world loves, and her wondrous Douglas, he's the 'teetotaler' who just bought out a whole goddamn saloon and hid the inventory away for Prohibition. Putting together a hell of a bar in the basement of that place they're building, you know that? How much fucking longer can she play a little girl, for god sakes? I can't even get cast except as some insipid do-gooder simply because I'm her fucking brother. I want to be a villain, damn it! I want to do some damage on screen and make the damn lumpen masses jump out of their seats like Lon Chaney! I'm *bored!* I've been acting since I was a kid too, but it's always Mary-Mary-Mary. She'll never have children now anyway. They ruined her fucking plumbing with that scoop job."

Sarah gasped.

"Got you with that one, eh Sarah?"

"Shut up Jack!"

"Well it's true, Ollie."

"And where would you be without her? I admire her more than anyone else in this whole damn town. She's not a fucking weakling who drowns her sorrow in anything but work. God, if we had one *tenth* the moxie, we'd be building our own Pickfair by now. And I'm speaking about myself too, you know. We're weak!"

"And what would we call it, my frolicsome little Ziegfeld girl? Picktom? Tompick? Oljack? Jack's Gin Soaked Olive on a Stick with a dash of cocaine?" A guttural laugh rippled Jacks lips, and his eyes wandered around the room and settled on the cabinet beside the bookcase.

"Fuck you, Jack," Olive seized Sarah's hand and dragged her toward the bedroom, "and don't disturb us."

Jack grunted. He already had the morphine out.

XXII.

Blanche brought breakfast in the morning and informed Olive that Jack had left for the Hollywood Athletic Club with Wally and planned to head for Tijuana with friends for the night.

"Hell with him." Olive squeezed Sarah's thigh between her own after Blanche left. She got up and spread marmalade on an English muffin while watching herself do it in the big mirror across the room.

"I'm rather bothered by all this bickering between you two. It puts me in an odd position, as I really seem to be the cause of it."

"We were spattin' like Kilkenny cats way before you came, toots. Jack's only good in bed when he's mad anyway. He used to be all the time, but that goddamn morphine's got his goat now. God, we did it once hangin' over the ocean under the Santa Monica Pier on a goddamn beam when we first met after dancin' and drinkin' champagne all night. Got so dizzy, and the waves were crashin' like crazy under us. That was the cat's meow," Olive sucked marmalade off a finger, returned to the bed, and lay down beside Sarah, "You musta caused some fights up there in Canada yourself. Lookers always do and anybody can see you're one. I had fellas fightin' over me way before I ever actually had one. So did you I bet. Married that way-older guy I knew I'd never stay with just to get the hell outta Charleroi, and he looked daggers at every young rake who gave me the eye let me tell ya. Had good reason for that matter. Jack's got all the showgirls he wants, and pals like Wally, but people always get jealous. He's gonna go down to Tijuana now with that 'Four Musketeers' bunch to drink himself stupid, if that's any more possible. I hope Lew Cody brings lotsa cash to grease the cops down there if they get in a fix. Shit, Sarah, it's gotta be the same where you're from too. I mean… jealousy and all."

"Of course, but remember I'd only gone all the way with one, um… three fellows… and never with a girl."

"Um. Bet that Acker dame Valentino married would be in a snit about you even though everybody knows she likes girls. It's pride. People are just like that," Olive grinned, "so is he really as good as they say?"

"I already told you. He was remarkable, although he spoke about some other woman."

"Eee! Tell me, anybody I know?"

"Somebody named Lorelei."

Olive shrugged, "Never heard of the dame." She giggled and put hands to her face, peeked out between her fingers, and grinned at the ceiling, "I have gotta try him now that he's not getting married. Jack's probably with some whore in Tijuana anyway." She rolled over and glanced at the clock, "Well, not yet. He's probably passed out in the back of somebody's car. Tonight, I bet. I hope he don't catch nothing." Olive cupped Sarah's right breast in her hand with a critical eye, as if she were examining a bolt of cloth on a store counter, "So come on, Sarah, didn't you have any other sweethearts?"

"I was giddy for the son of a whaling captain when quite young, as well as Jim, whose father had a claim next to ours on Sulfur Creek. I still dream about that trip up King Solomon's Dome. We couldn't get together while our fathers were around and only found the opportunity a couple of times more," Sarah scowled at the ceiling, "that September we were surprised by his father at the Grand Forks Hotel where we'd got a room. I still don't know how he found us, but any miner who saw us riding there would have remembered I suppose. My dad kept me stuck on the claim after that, so Jim went down to Dawson and bought some strumpet in Lousetown. More than one, actually."

"*Lousetown?*"

"It's on an island in the Klondike River. That's where the Mounties moved the Segregated District... the whore district, from Fourth Avenue after the Gold Rush petered out for the smaller miners and the big companies moved in. Anyway that ended it."

"*Lousetown!*" Olive let out a string of giggles, "They won't cool their heels forever, toots. Whoever said the way to a man's heart is through his stomach sure weren't me. Don't even like to cook. Sid Grauman is building a theater on Hollywood Boulevard with the loot he made up there called the Egyptian, and your Pantages guy wants to build one here too, right? Bill Taylor was up there. He spent a winter in a cabin with that poet guy, what's his name... Robert Service."

"Really? Bill Taylor was there? With Robert Service? I know all Robert Service's poems of the Gold Rush by heart. I had to recite them in a pageant."

"Yeah, what's that one about the fellas shootin' each other over the girl, the Lady known as Lou, and she gets the gold in the end?"

"The Shooting of Dan McGrew."

Olive nodded, "Small world, toots."

"I'll say."

Olive glanced at the half-read script beside the bed, picked it up, and put it back down, "I'm already late for a rehearsal at the studios. Wanta drive the Locomobile?"

"Certainly... do you think I could borrow it while you're there?"

"But Sarah, this is your chance to see how it's done. It's a six-reeler. Ince's brother Ralph's directing, and you can probably get a part just by telling him what you did at Inceville. I'll introduce you." Olive slid a leg over Sarah's thigh, "You don't want to watch me?"

"I spent all yesterday on a film set. I'll come back this evening I promise. I'd just like to do some thinking this morning and exploring, if you'll trust me with the car."

Olive's violet eyes widened and darted across her face. Sarah glanced at the fine lines around them that were usually hidden by makeup, just like the needle marks on her arms. Olive blinked long dark lashes, swallowed, and took a breath, "All right, it'll be a long day. Probably won't get off 'til eight or nine tonight. Where are you goin'?'"

"Is there a museum around here?"

"Sure, in Exposition Park. Are you going there?'

"Thinking about it but I suppose I just want to drive around. Maybe take a walk. It's all still new for me. I want to do some more exploring in the hills perhaps."

"Cripes, another hike? Sister I've had enough hikin' for a lifetime!" Olive yawned, "I smell you all over the place."

"It's both of us."

"Sarah?"

"Um?"

"Think I'm immature?"

"Well, you're impulsive I'd have to say that."

"You never, *ever* woulda done it with a woman if I weren't, toots."

"You're right." She squeezed Olive back.

"Damn, you're strong."

"You get a grip riding horses."

"I'll say."

* * *

She dropped Olive at Selznick Studios on Gower and turned the car toward Exposition Park. The thirty-eight horsepower Locomobile had far more power than a Model T, and she laughed as she sped around wagons and cars on the way.

It took an hour to get to the Los Angeles County Museum of History, Science and Art. It sat before a leafy park with fountains that had couples strolling, people walking dogs, and women pushing prams. The organ grinder she's seen on Hollywood Boulevard was there with his monkey, surrounded by a crowd of children. Sarah parked the Locomobile and stepped up the marble steps into cool shade under tall Corinthian columns into the rotunda.

The huge skeleton of a mammoth greeted her with its dozen feet of curving tusks. A vision of a tusk coming out of the frozen gravels of the Klondike flashed through her mind. Sarah stopped for a moment and gazed up at the skeleton in wonder. She'd seen mammoth bones since she was a kid but had never seen a whole skeleton assembled. Finally she turned her attention to a desk, behind which sat a prim woman.

"Excuse me."

"Yes?"

"Do you have someone here who is schooled in archaeology?"

The woman responded with a pleasant smile, "Of course. How might we help you? Did you wish to see the Egyptian collection?"

"Well, almost, I... I'd like to find someone who can identify something that I believe is from Mesopotamia."

"Oh I see. What?"

"This," Sarah lifted the blue stone pendant out of her blouse.

The woman shrugged, "Yes, I think so if he's in. One moment," she picked up a telephone and dialed. "Professor Knight, I have someone who has something from Mesopotamia she'd like to show you. No, it's not a dealer. Yes, yes, all right," she looked up, "he'll be here in a moment."

"Thank you."

Sarah sat on a hard wooden bench as the wait stretched an hour. Finally, a short gentleman with a balding head and grey muttonchop sideburns that had long gone out of style appeared in a wool coat and vest that looked much too hot for this climate even in the cool environs of the museum. He nodded from within a halo of smoke and took a burl wood pipe from his mouth, "I'm professor Knight. How may I help you?"

Sarah rose from the bench, "Thank you for your time, sir. My name is Sarah McCallum and I'd very much like to know something about this," she undid a button of her blouse and held up the amulet.

Professor Knight's eyes spent a moment looking past it at the hint of cleavage before he focused on the stone, "Ah, it looks like Inanna or Lilith, or some other goddess. It could be Sumerian, Akkadian or Babylonian. Does it have any writing on the back?"

"Yes, that's what I wanted to know about." Sarah turned the pendant over to show him the cuneiform scratches.

"Capital. It appears to be in good enough condition to be decipherable. Come to my office." He motioned for her to follow him and stalked off down the hall.

In his office, Professor Knight switched on a light attached to a big magnifying glass on a flexible arm over a green baize blotter he swept clean of papers and an ashtray before he sat down behind the desk, "Please have a seat." She sat across from him in a rickety chair, took off the pendant, and reluctantly handed it over. "Hum," he scratched a sideburn, "hum..."

"What is it?"

"It's Akkadian cuneiform I believe, or Sumerian. They're quite similar. It appears to say, 'Daughter of Light, Mother of Night, the... lapis,' I believe it says 'the lapis lazuli gates... that's the *blue* gates... of the City shall fall before you.'"

"Blue?"

"Yes, as in this lapis stone. The word is synonymous here. The gates of Babylon were covered in lapis lazuli you know. This could serve as either a protective incantation or a curse."

"Why a curse?"

"Goddesses and gods were always jockeying for dominance you know. Those girls didn't like losing their dominion to Babylonian patriarchs like Marduk, and of course the god of the Jews was an up and comer at the time who didn't like females getting in his way either. Same with the Greeks, who usually had their gods rape foreign goddesses wherever they encountered them, although that occasionally produced some bastard god who was an even greater problem." He grinned, "Quite an orgy of deities you might say. I'd say this was made for a woman, perhaps a Priestess of Inanna, or of Lilith herself. Quite curious, really."

"Who was Lilith?"

"A girl who didn't like some of the doings of male gods, or of men I suppose, at least that's what the Old Testament tells us. She's been shackled by quite a list of crimes in the Bible where she's mentioned at all. Most of it has been demoted to the apocrypha, those are the books outside the approved Bible. You might speak to a Rabbi who has studied such things I suppose. There's a synagogue hereabouts with a brilliant fellow who has taken the reigns," his tobacco-stained thumb rubbed the amulet, "this is a beautiful piece. Does it have any provenance?"

"What?"

"A history of where it was found, who found it and in what context?"

"No, not that I know of. It was a gift."

"Pity, it could be worth quite a bit if it did. Well," he smiled, "it's quite a conversation piece and still rather valuable, and now you have at least part of a story to go with it."

"Thank you so much for your help."

"Not at all. It's not every day a pretty young lady appears with the amulet of a goddess," he took the pipe from his mouth and squinted, "are you in the flickers?"

"Yes, I suppose I am. Here, please," she handed Professor Knight a five-dollar bill.

"I don't--"

"Please sir, you've been quite helpful."

The professor shrugged and took the bill.

* * *

Sarah was about to start the Locomobile when a man's manicured hand took the crank from her own. She spun around with a start.

"Sarah!" Rudolfo's teeth flashed, "What are you doing here?"

"I, I was visiting the museum. How are you?" She could smell that scent again that had to be of another woman, yet she found it wonderful at the same time.

"I am blessed! The marriage was annulled by the Bishop of Los Angeles when we swore the marriage was not consummated... there, see, I pronounced it correctly!" Rudolfo chuckled, "He only asked us one hundred times. I am not to announce it yet so as she can act as my wife in regard to some business. The studio gave her a check," he grinned, "and I gave something to the Church of course."

"Well, congratulations."

"What are you doing this moment?"

"I was going to, ah, Belmore."

He responded with a bemused grin, "I shall not ask why. As you said we should be friends, but please, let me accompany you to see my motion picture before you go. It is playing but a short walk away."

"I... oh, all right."

* * *

The Delicious Little Devil was playing at the Empress Theater a block away and a matinee was about to start with not much of a crowd. Rudolfo pulled his hat down over his eyes as he paid the girl in the ticket booth. It didn't work. The girl gasped as she recognized him and dropped the silver dollar he handed her before she could give him the ninety cents change.

"You may keep the rest, lovely one."

"I... I..." she stuttered.

"But please, lovely lady, do not speak of our presence to anyone."

"Oh... yes sir!" was followed by a shrill giggle.

The usher recognized him immediately and was convinced to allow them to sit in the closed balcony with another silver dollar and a promise of silence. They were seated squarely in the middle of the empty upper seats as a single organ player in the pit below began the accompaniment and the curtains parted on the credits.

"You are far more beautiful than Mae Murray, my leading lady," he whispered as her name came on the screen.

"Oh stop."

It was a standard plot of a poor working girl who pretended to be someone she wasn't to get a show job, met a handsome young man with an Irish name played by her Italian friend, was pursued by a villain that was eventually dispatched by him in a fight, and ended up in his arms wealthy and happy. Sarah spent most of the movie being kissed and kissing Rudolfo back.

"Look, look at her chin," Rudolfo's hot breath bounced in her ear and across her throat, "Yours is far more lovely. Like a fine sculpture. Sarah, we must make a motion picture together!" She was aware of the throbbing erection in his pants and found her hand upon it. He groaned, "You must come to my new apartment with me after the picture."

When the movie ended the usher allowed them to leave by a door onto an alley with their fingers entwined. He began to pull her in the opposite direction from her car, when Sarah detached herself from his damp fingers. "I have somewhere I need to be, Rudolfo."

His mouth fell open, "But…"

"We have time. I've got to speak to someone about something."

"What is his name?"

She put a hand to her mouth, "Beverly."

His flash of chagrin was priceless, "Oh, forgive me."

"We'll meet again. You know my room."

When that smile blossomed she almost changed her mind. "Then allow me to accompany you back to your car, at least."

"That's all right. I'll be fine." She grabbed him, locked lips, and pushed him away with her hands on his shoulders, "I've got to go!" She tried to not laugh at his mournful expression, and without looking back, started down an alley deep in shade while listening to the sound of his boot heels that eventually headed the other way.

A few feet from the sidewalk, a dirty coat went over her head and she was slammed against the wall of the theater. Sparks flashed in her eyes as her head hit the bricks.

Not again!

Sarah elbowed the assailant out of instinct and he hit her back hard through the coat. Her head bounced against the wall again and she felt herself sliding down it. Sarah tore at the coat, and her fingers wrapped around the stone pendant around her neck as she sunk to her knees, "Help!" her voice came muffled through the heavy coat.

The rough hands upon her were gone and there was the hollow sound of a body being thrown with great force against the brick wall across the alley as Sarah yanked the coat off her head.

The woman standing over her smiled and held out a white hand. Sarah took it, and was lifted to her feet.

Her eyes were so many colors. Sarah blinked and tried to focus on them. She gazed at the crumpled body across the alley in a spreading puddle of blood and back to those huge eyes set in a perfect white diamond of a face that was framed by glistening black hair falling to her waist.

The woman blinked as if the dim light of the alley was the glare of a Klieg light and sighed, "It's awfully hard to hide here, what with film, and telephones and cameras and such. I've been having Rudolph see you but it appears it almost got you killed." She gazed at the broken body beneath the far wall, and her lips curled in contempt, "They're like vermin. It simply never ends!"

"You're--"

"Your protector at times. It's my greatest weakness... not protecting you in particular but the habit. I suppose it's a maternal thing in a way. I was thinking Beverly could school you and I could stay out of sight. Of course I could have but this time you were going down for the count and I didn't feel like letting that scum ravish you. You've had enough roughing up since you arrived, and I believe you've got potential."

Sarah grasped the stone dangling from her throat, "My God, you're..."

"Whoever you care to call on as a figure of speech," the woman nodded at the amulet, "that's my mother's mother's mother, by the way." She put smooth fingers to Sarah's cheek, "I can make the swelling go down. Close your eyes."

Sarah did and felt something far stronger than the rush of cocaine she'd experienced with Olive. She was drifting on a warm river filled with a multitude of voices stretching in every direction yet flowing together like a symphony. She couldn't feel her feet and wondered how she could be standing. Time seemed to stop, and after an eternity she opened her eyes. The woman was gone. Sarah put fingers to her cheek. The swelling was gone too.

XXIII.

When she arrived at Belmore, the guard smiled and opened the gate without questioning. Beverly was on a divan on the patio sipping iced tea. Sarah sat down beside her and accepted a glass from an attentive butler. Bee ran a hand across Sarah's and patted her cheek, "Your face looks fine. Thought I'd see you again."

Sarah gazed across the blue pool at two girls giggling and whispering in the shallow end. One of them was Sonya, the masseuse. Sonya winked at Sarah and grabbed the slim brunette beside her underwater, who emoted a stretched-out, high-pitched stage shriek. Sarah flashed Sonya a smile, took a breath, and began, "You're the most honest person I've met here, Bee."

"Thank you. I hear you ran into Valentino again."

"How did you know that? Did he tell you?"

"No, I've got friends everywhere, or at least contacts. Friends are much rarer actually, but I have a true one who keeps track of things."

"They certainly are. I wish I had such a friend."

"You do."

Sarah swallowed, "You know..."

"She tells me at times. When I was younger than you, she saved a lot of girls during the earthquake. I was one."

"How can I find her again?"

"If she desires it, you will," Beverly yawned, "but you were coming here before that little incident after the theater."

"You know."

"Yes. Why did you come?"

"I'm... not sure. I know part of me wants to work in the flickers. I've got a director waiting at Inceville but part of me is ready to leave right now, and part of me wants to be with Ollie, but that shall never work out in the long run I'm certain, and a big part of me is going crazy wondering whoever it is who has done those horrible things to me and all those other girls, and part of me very much wants to go to the authorities but after all I've seen I certainly don't trust them, and you are the only person who makes me feel like I'm not mad after what just happened to me, and--"

"And part of you wants to work with me."

Sarah tossed hair from her eyes and leaned back on the divan. Sonya was staring at her from the far end of the pool. "I'm afraid that you've judged me wrongly, Bee."

Beverly put a bejeweled hand on her arm, "I don't mean what my girls do. You've got smarts and moxie. I'd say you're cut out for management."

"What?"

"You've passed the test of a woman who makes her way in our world. You killed a filthy user of girls who would have done it to others, Sarah. You've saved girls you will never know great pain and grief. Our mutual benefactor is justifiably proud of you. I ran away from a convent at fourteen and met a wonderful educated woman on the train north who brought me to Sacramento where I was coached, and then given to a man who stood at the helm of our golden state. One could say she was evil in that she used me for her own gain and sold me to him I suppose, but she was the first person who seemed to care for me since my mother put me in that convent when she took a new man. Isn't life strange? From there I went to San Francisco where my family came from and had the great fortune to meet Jessie Hayman as I said before. She wanted girls who spoke four languages at least, but my French and Latin did quite well and she made an exception. I took the name Violet Adair. I wasn't truly tested until things collapsed in the earthquake. I was only fifteen but had seen far more of the rough side of things by then. Jessie had a car and petrol in a garage across the street to escape in when the fire was coming toward Ellis Street from the south of town," Beverly smiled, "but the street was collapsed at both ends, gas was hissing in the basement, and the fire was crossing Market by then, so we set out on foot."

"Who did?"

"A tall red-haired madam, eight young ladies of comfort who were fluent in a dozen languages, an old Chinese cook, and a black maid named Belle who Jessie left most of her money to," she chuckled, "it was quite a week."

"What happened?"

"I killed a tough from the Barbary Coast that evening and three more in the next two days. We survived and spent a few nights with some Chinese singsong girls who'd been rescued by someone who knows you well. After the earthquake I was set up by an heir of Comstock money with a house of my own and became a madam at sixteen. The earthquake and fire were a formative experience I would not do over, but it was meant to be. I see you're at a similar place now, Sarah."

"I see Warren in my dreams."

"That's quite natural, but you see she who was in them first, Sarah. Focus upon her."

"How would you know that?"

Beverly shrugged, "She told me of course. Did you actually kill him with a magnum of scotch?"

"Yes, it was heavy but I can't remember it being so, just smashing it down on his face and his nose bubbling in the moonlight like..."

Beverly put her hands to her face trying to control laughter, steepled slender fingers tipped by purple nails before her lips, and fixed Sarah in a green-eyed gaze.

Sarah felt teeth in her lip, "I'm glad you find it amusing, and I am dying with curiosity about this person who knows me and has saved me once again, and if I couldn't hear from someone that she actually exists, I would most likely go mad. Perhaps I shall find it amusing eventually, but I still dread the mere idea I might become pregnant here or catch some dreadful disease."

"I've got a doctor who can see you. It's on me. You certainly deserve that and it can be remedied. Look at these girls. You wouldn't believe how many have had the same experience as far as rape is concerned."

Sarah watched Sonya emerge from the pool and stretch her perfect body on a towel placed on a divan for her by an attentive male servant.

"Sonya too, the cad kept her locked up for a week." Beverly yawned, "Didn't you say your uncle supplies saloons in Vancouver?"

"I, yes."

"With Prohibition coming I'm going to need a supplier I can count on. You're in a perfect position to do very well here."

"I want nothing whatsoever to do with my uncle."

"Love," Beverly's hand slid back to her own, "I understand, believe me, but the rest of your family is dead and the slate's wiped clean. You can invent a new you here and just use the bastard like he tried to use you to set yourself up. I've got people who can take over once you get the business running on that end and can keep you out of the dirty work. They can even take care of that lug of an uncle if that be your inclination. The remuneration would be considerable, I assure you." A smile began again in Beverly's green eyes before it crept to her mouth, "You don't have to tell me what he did. I can see it love. It's such a familiar story."

Sarah felt her face grow warm. Was she that transparent?

"You're the kind of girl I'm looking for in many ways it's true, although I don't know where you're going. Don't get me wrong. I should do everything I can to convince you, Sarah, and

you're smart and strong enough to know it. Right now you're ob-
sessed with finding out who else abducted you, although you can't
go slaying every sonofabitch in Hollywood," Beverly chuckled,
"there would be no one left, and of course you're in somewhat of a
way about Olive whether you admit it or not."

"I'm really not in such a way. I don't know how truly deep
her feelings are for me but it's something that just happened and
I don't feel bound by it. I could have been anyone who fits her
tastes and I know that. It was happenstance that it was me this
time. Honestly, Bee."

"Well then, when you get settled down a bit we should talk.
You and I would make a good team. You're not one to fall too
easily into somebody like Olive's little snares and that's all for
the better, and believe me Sarah, success is the ultimate revenge.
There's nothing else even close to it."

Something washed over Sarah in a wave. She closed her eyes
and squeezed the arm of the chair. *Is it imagination?* It was as if the
force of Beverly's will was closing around her like a cloak as she
stretched there on a divan like a cat in the sunshine. Sarah stared
into the branches of the magnolia tree overhead and tried to focus
on a huge waxy white blossom, "It's a shock to hear you say that,
and to find part of me completely agreeing with you is even more
of one. I suppose it's because I feel safer here than anywhere I've
been since arriving and I actually do want to believe it."

"But it feels natural, doesn't it?" Beverly grinned, "You never even asked her name."

"What . . ?"

"Lorelei, it's Lorelei, Sarah."

* * *

She found herself drifting toward Sunset focusing on the tall silhouette of Babylon in the distance that slowly grew closer until it
dwarfed all but the hills behind it. She entered its shadow, parked

under a eucalyptus on its east side and killed the engine. A mockingbird resumed its song and a trolley clanged in the distance.

She fondled the pistol's bulk in her purse and walked around to the gate to try Olive's hat pin trick on the lock. After several tries and bending the pin into several shapes, the lock gave up its hold on the shackle. She shoved the gate open enough to squeeze in and draped the chain back around it with the now open lock on the inside hidden by the links of the chain.

The rows of winged bulls with human heads and Semitic beards greeted her. Pale rearing elephants beyond them flanked a huge faux iron wooden gate now guarding nothing but the tumbleweeds and trash of Hollywood. She passed under the shadows of statues to the rickety stairs that led to the top of the wall and began to climb.

It was a long slog but the stairs were in shadow and she was hardly sweating or breathing hard when she made the top. Sarah sat down on the board between two buckets, gazed out over Hollywood, and took the tiny vial of cocaine she'd found in one of Olive's drawers out. She cupped her hands against the breeze but lost the first tiny spoonful to the wind and had to kneel below the edge of the wall to get the next one to her nose. She repeated the process, inhaled, and sat back down on the board wishing she'd brought some water.

Far below people were going about their lives, exchanging money, hurrying somewhere, eating, having sex, and trying to beat each other to whatever perceived reward awaited them. Someone was dying no doubt, and probably not just the elderly or sick but the young and the beautiful. Someone was committing murder somewhere, she was sure of it. The rush of the coke made the top of her head tingle. For a moment she wondered if she would make it back down as she perched on the tallest structure in the west of the Americas... a *movie prop*. She imagined girls like her scurrying from the farthest reaches of the earth toward this monument to unreality as she sat with her drugs and her thoughts. She closed her eyes and saw whores at a Halloween party, a flash of a white face, and corpses in a well. *Focus on her!*

What had brought her here? Who was this person who had been watching her, this Lorelei? She wanted to believe she was the one who had saved her long ago under the dark cedars from a bear, and again through a dog in the Hollywood Hills, a *dog,* and she had certainly saved her in that alley.

"Enough games, show me!"

The breeze buffeted her face with the distant voice of some woman singing, another performer in a dive along the gravel trace of the Sunset Strip, but her mysterious protector didn't appear.

"Forget it!" She stood up, hocked up the biggest ball of spit she could muster from a dry throat, leaned back, and spat it into space to watch it make a spiral curve toward the earth below.

* * *

Sarah drove to Hollywood Boulevard, turned on Highland, and headed through Cahuenga Pass. As she shifted, her hand slid into her purse and fondled Olive's break-top .38. She stopped at the fruit stand and bought some Mexican candy that looked like pure sugar glued together with molasses, a box of dates, figs and apricots, and a big milk bottle filled with fresh-squeezed orange juice. She took a bite of the candy and an overwhelming sweetness filled her mouth. She cut it with a big gulp of orange juice and stuffed the bottle between her legs as she shifted to get around a truck loaded with produce.

When she passed the adobe hotel, the red-haired woman was standing in a second story window. Sarah waved, eliciting a grin and a flash of sunlight on a flask as the woman raised it to her lips.

She turned up Lankershim under the branches of sycamore trees. A vision of Olive sprawled in the Model T with her arm dangling over the door in dappled shade flickered across Sarah's mind like a film reel. For a moment, she felt the revulsion she'd first known at Olive's self-imposed helplessness and the needle's bruises before it changed into overwhelming affection and protectiveness. A sob fought to well in her chest. She cursed. So many had to play little girls or vamps to survive here, and Olive had seen enough of that for a dozen lifetimes.

The girls in the well.

Sarah fondled the .38.

The girls in the creek.

Sprinklers were on in the yard of the Moorish palace, and she stopped on the driveway to watch sunlight dance in fans of water across the emerald lawns. The low voices of the Great Danes sounded as she killed the wheezing engine, followed by a high-pitched bark of greeting from Duke. The Japanese gardener was busy taking cuttings from stalks surmounted by budding and blooming flowers that looked like the red, purple, and orange heads of birds. He turned and bowed. Sarah blew him a kiss, and he grinned.

Duke leapt with an insistent whine into the passenger seat of the Locomobile and his tongue lapped her cheek. Sarah laughed. She ran fingers through the red hair of his chest as she held him away from the paper bag and its contents. "Make your eyes change colors," she whispered.

Duke's eyes remained doggy brown.

Lupita stood in the door wiping her hands on a towel, "Where Miss Olive?"

"Rehearsing at the studio."

"You like lunch?"

"No thank you Lupita; I've ruined my appetite I'm afraid. I wanted to change my clothes though."

"Plenty clothes here." Lupita went back in the house.

Sarah changed into jeans and a brown checkered flannel shirt, found tall thick socks that she held up with garters, and tugged on the same scuffed cowboy boots. She found a beige scarf amongst a plethora of colorful ones and put it on her head. Soft browns were far more useful for what she had in mind, as they blended with the chaparral hills. She found a holster for the pistol, slid one of the wide western belts through it, and fastened the big silver concho buckle over her navel.

She examined herself in the mirror. The scarf made her hair seem short indeed. She drew the gun and scowled at her reflection, "What the hell are you doing?" She stared at the girl in the glass, awaiting an answer. When none came, she walked out of the house.

Duke danced in pleasure with figure eights around her as they crossed the road and climbed the drive to the old stone house. His ears rose at some sound, and he bolted ahead. Sarah cursed under her breath, keeping her hand on the gun as she climbed the driveway.

Duke was sitting on the porch when she reached the house. Warren's Ford was gone. She tried the door, but someone had locked it. Sarah sat on the porch in the peeling rocking chair staring at the dark spot in the gravel drive where she'd burned the evidence of her degradation. Now that it was gone, she very much wanted to see it. It could tell her what she wanted, what she needed to know. Nothing remained of that dark time here but a maddening, incomplete jumble of memory that harried her sleep and roiled her dreams. She had to dig it out or it would always be there, disturbing her sleep and nagging her waking days. She had to find Lorelei. Lorelei could answer all her questions.

She rubbed her nose, and glanced up the hill at mosaics on a crumbling wall sparkling in the sun. She could make out the remnants of a bird with a long blue tail perched on the branches of a pomegranate tree on the crumbling ochre stones. Sarah sighed. She stepped off the porch and began to climb through a riot of blue and white morning glory flowers. She tapped the pistol against her leg. She looked for the mosaic woman in blue robes up the hill but couldn't see her. A bee in the trumpet of a flower buzzed loudly as she continued toward the old well, scanning the slope for its circular wall. The wall was gone.

"Damn!" She hurried the last few feet and arrived where the well had been. A smooth expanse of dirt greeted her. She knelt and dug with her hands until she felt one of the wall's stones, cursing at what it was doing to her nails. The stones had been piled in the pit of the well, and the boards were nowhere to be seen.

She stood and wiped her hands. It was as if none of it had ever happened, as if some dark force expected her to willingly forget, to go on oblivious to all the evil around her into this new life of drugs, parties, and bedding film stars of both sexes. She plopped down on the hillside with a groan. Duke sniffed her ear.

The sound of a car bumping up the road shook her from her musings. Duke ran back down the path as she stood and hurried down the hill. Duke's friendly bark echoed from below, followed by feminine laughter. Sarah stuffed the gun back in the holster.

A grey roadster sat in the yard, and a tiny woman in a beige dress with big dark eyes and masses of dark curls was on her knees hugging Duke. Sarah recognized her immediately.

Mabel Normand glanced up, blinked, and gave her a grin, "Hi!"

"Hello! Please don't mind the gun. I borrowed it from Olive Thomas… for protection."

"You're Sarah then."

"Yes, Miss Normand."

"Fuck that. Everybody calls me Mabel, 'least when they're not callin' me crazy."

Sarah laughed.

The driver's door of the roadster was open with a table unfolded from its inside that held an assortment of makeup containers, lipstick, and brushes, each in its own compartment. A three-legged stool was before it, and Mabel dusted off her skirt and sat on the stool while continuing to scratch Duke behind the ears.

"I've never seen that done with a car door."

"It was a present from Mack Sennett after I wrecked the Stutz. I was going to have this Mercer painted lavender like the Rolls, but he threw a fit and threatened to spit his damn tobacco juice on it every time he saw it. By the way, do you know what happened to Warren who was living here?"

Sarah shook her head.

"Guess it's back to Hughie Faye. He's rather strange but always comes through, although his prices are the pits. Looks rather like a snake charmer from Bombay, doesn't he?" Mabel gave her a conspiratorial grin, "Ollie's still using him, right?"

Sarah nodded.

The sound of another car coming up the drive made them turn. The big Isinglass headlight covers of Bill Taylor's maroon McFarlan flashed in the sun as it pulled up next to Mabel's Mercer and the engine growled to a stop. Bill was behind the wheel and sat for a moment staring at them. He ran a hand across a high forehead. His mouth was a thin line as he stepped out, glanced from Mabel to Sarah, and sighed, "Hello, Mabel, hello Sarah."

"Bill!" Mabel bounced over with the same manic energy she showed on screen and gave him a mean hug. Bill stared over the top of her head at Sarah before he smiled and bent to bestow a tender kiss upon Mabel's forehead, which only came to his chest.

"I thought I'd find you here. Where's Clarine?"

"Shopping, I came up to see about Mack's equipment."

"I wish I could believe that was all you were after," moisture glistened at the corners of his eyes, "you've got to stay off the dope Mabel! It almost killed you last time and you've just come back to start anew."

"I'm not using dearest, I swear."

Bill ran a hand through graying hair, "At least that scoundrel Warren's skedaddled out of here. No one's seen him for almost a week, and as you can see the house is empty. Perhaps what he's sown has come to be reaped. One can only hope, the despicable cad. If I'd known it was him selling you that poison, I would have wrung his worthless neck. One can only pray he meets his due. I just wish I knew who else you're getting it from. Was it Hughie Faye?" Bill held Mabel at arm's length with his hands on her shoulders and stared into her eyes, "You glorious, childish, unmanageable minx. After that sanatorium stint back East, I'd hoped you'd learned your lesson. You can't believe how I've worried!"

Mabel coughed and produced a pink monogrammed handkerchief she held to her mouth for a moment. When her hand came away, Sarah saw a spot of bloody phlegm. "I'm fine Bill, got to be going though. I'm practicing flying for the next picture."

Bill hugged her, "Do be careful. You've been in two crashes already."

Mabel made a hoarse laugh, "Third time's the charm toots."

* * *

Mabel loudly offered to meet Sarah at Olive's house, but as soon as Bill was heading down the drive, invited her to go flying instead.

"Up in a machine?"

"Yep, I've got a pilot's license and a Jenny right here in the Valley."

"Isn't that dangerous? I mean, Bill said that you'd crashed twice already."

"I was making pictures both times and was only the pilot once. Besides, all I had to do was climb out of a tree the first time and wade out of a pond the second. Ollie says you're tough as me seein' as you did a little trick ridin' for Tom Ince. You gonna be a scardy-cat now?"

"Well no, I suppose. How did you hear that?"

"Word travels fast around here. Did you see me win that horse race in *Mickey* and dive off that cliff?"

"I certainly did. It convinced me that I should come here if they were letting girls do such things. It was wonderful. I was--"

"Flew an aeroplane over Hollywood in *A Dash Through the Clouds* with the stick between my knees shootin' six guns. Now *that* was dangerous. They even had to say the pilot was doing the flyin' from the back seat just to get some theater owners to show it 'cause a woman isn't supposed to. Hell, he was the one filming. He got burning powder in his eyes from the blanks and was screamin' bloody murder. I told him if he dropped the camera and we had to land and do a whole 'nother take, I had a real bullet in my pocket and would drop his chicken-ass in a reservoir and say a bird hit him and he fell out. Fella sat up and did his job pronto."

Sarah laughed, "And that smokestack scene where you swooped down on the fellow climbing. It was thrilling. I have *so* wanted to meet you Mabel; you're the woman in Hollywood who's doing the things I'd like to do."

"Yeah, and you're a blonde. Griffith thinks all blondes are to be cast as *spirituelles,* that's his name for angels, while us dark-haired girls are to be voluptuous tramps men use like a doormat before they wither like a fuckin' plucked rose," Mabel waved her hands in disgust, "what a fuckin' lug! That, his obsession with the darkies, and his skinflint ways sent me from Biograph to Keystone. I stayed away from Triangle 'cause of him too. Can you imagine him directing me and Fatty like Mack did? He couldn't! Griffith doesn't have a funny bone in his body I swear. I'm a comedienne at heart when I'm not takin' a fall or tied to a railroad track. Even his stab at comedy looks serious, all the elements with none of the feeling if you ask me. He thinks every goddamn thing has to be a fuckin' morality play... another little *Intolerance.*"

"He certainly left quite a set there on Sunset. It must have cost a king's ransom."

Mabel shrugged, "He gets lots of backing but puts it all back in the next flicker. Babylon shows he leaves a pile of crap behind. He won't even let his girls get around us lowlifes who do comedy nowadays. The sonofabitch acts like I don't even exist! This whole Hollywood biz goes from one big fat ego to the next. Well, anyway, all those flickers with Fatty and Buster made me, but Keystone went away when Mack went to Triangle, and I had to deal with grumpy ol' Griffith again, so I left. Then Triangle pretty much got slaughtered by the flu, the assets are in court, Essanay's got half their help, and Mack's still trying to get back with me. We did okay with *Mickey* though. He built me a whole studio for that one. It all came back in spades, but you know when I was taking the cure, it was Bill Taylor who kept tabs and sent me flowers every day just because he cared, not goddamn Mr. Mack Sennett. And to think I almost married that shanty Irish bastard!" Mabel put a ring-covered hand on Sarah's arm, "No offence, I'm half Irish myself in spite of the French name. So are Mack and Bill Taylor," Mabel rubbed a scar on her hairline, "I'm working with Sam Goldfish now in Culver City. That Jew boy's a businessman with a plan. No bullshit."

"Goldfish? Who is he? Bill Hart mentioned him."

"It's Goldwyn now. He changed it from Goldfish. Guess it was too Jewish. Some of us still call him that."

"I see."

"So, are we goin' flyin'?"

"I've got to be back at Selznick Studios to get Olive by seven."

"Plenty of time, toots."

"Well, all right."

XXIV.

Mabel drove the Mercer down Lankershim past a big new sign for Universal City where the smell of fresh tar rose in the afternoon heat. As they neared the train station where Sarah had arrived, people were stepping down from the cars of a locomotive. She glimpsed a pretty redhead wearing too-warm clothes with a cardboard suitcase clutched to her breast, who looked lost amongst the long sheds and bins of citrus fruit crowding either side of the little station. Sarah inhaled the scent of oranges, blinked, and started to ask Mabel to pull over to give her a ride, but they were headed away from Hollywood. Sarah exhaled and held her tongue.

They drove down the main street of the little town of Lankershim into country with shacks and ranch houses passing orchards, eucalyptus windbreaks, and Mexican laborers. Fields full of hay stubble were dotted with bright golden poppies that had sprung to life from the rains. A huge dark condor rocked on a warm updraft over the meandering Los Angeles River.

After a long ride through more fields, Sarah spotted a rickety tower in the distance that was surmounted by a zigzag stairway. An enclosed box with windows at the top was painted in a red and white checkerboard pattern, and it had a balcony running around it. An orange wind sock hung limply from a pole on its roof. Three rows of biplanes and a single monoplane with guy wires radiating to the wings from a pole on its top were parked on the near side of the gravel strip. Four large structures with big doors on the far side of the airfield reminded Sarah of the studio building at Inceville. A shiny tri-motor biplane sat in the open bay of one.

Mabel pulled between two trucks and killed the engine, "Good day for flying: no wind."

Sarah felt the knot under her navel, nodded, and turned toward the drone of an engine. An aeroplane was approaching from the direction of the Santa Susana Mountains to the east, and a man came out of the tower onto the narrow porch and held up a checkered flag. The plane wobbled its wings in reply and came around in line with the airstrip with a clatter and pop from its engine. Its wheels touched down in a cloud of dust and it rolled toward them. Two men ran out from one of the buildings along the strip, shoved the tail around, and dragged the plane into the line of parked ones before the prop had spun to a stop.

Mabel cocked a finger, "Come on."

Sarah followed her to a long flat-roofed shed as the pilot of the newly landed aeroplane and its ground crew watched them with interest. Mabel led her into a narrow room with lockers, to one with **Normand, M.** on it. Mabel unlocked it with a tiny key, took out a leather flying jacket, two leather caps with chin straps, and two pairs of goggles. She handed a cap and a pair of goggles to Sarah and put on the jacket. It was embroidered on the back with a picture of a yellow biplane and bright crimson letters proclaiming *Mabel at the Stick.*

Sarah stood holding the goggles.

"Don't worry toots, it's as easy as driving."

"Maybe, Mabel, but you can't fall a thousand feet out of a car."

"Sure you can, on the coast highway. Besides, there's belts to hold us in sweetie."

"What if the engine fails?"

"Ever heard of parachutes?"

"Do you have them?"

"Nope!" Mabel made a high-pitched laugh and bounced out the door.

"Is there a W-C around here?"

"Behind the building!"

Sarah took a deep breath and followed.

* * *

The aeroplane was in the second row at the far end with its lacquered yellow canvas body stretched taut over a wood and metal frame. It was the exact same color as Olive's Locomobile. Mabel had the ground crew release the cables holding it to rings on stakes driven into the tarmac, and they wheeled it out onto the edge of the runway. She stepped up onto a thin sheet of metal on the wing next to the fuselage, struck a heroic pose for a moment, and got into the hole containing the front seat. Sarah put her foot in a little metal loop below the hole for the rear and stepped in to sit in a woven wicker seat that squeaked as she settled into it. There was a metal stick with a red leather grip in front of her. She put her legs around it and her foot hit a pedal.

"Don't touch the pedals! Leave that to me."

"All right."

A stocky man in a flat leather cap and glasses greeted Mabel. He walked to the propeller, and two men gathered around the tail of the craft. Mabel adjusted a valve for the fuel and pulled a lever that rattled as it was drawn back, "Let 'er rip!"

The man reached up, yanked down on the propeller, and leapt back as the engine coughed once. He tugged at his mustache and stepped in to try again as Mabel fiddled with something. The man yanked with a grunt and sprang away as the engine roared to life with a gasp of gas fumes that blew dust across the goggles Sarah had barely got on over the tight leather cap.

"Whee!" Mabel yelled over the whine of the engine. All three men held onto the tail, and the plane began to strain in their grip. The man in the tower waved a flag, the men released the tail, and the plane jerked forward and rolled down the strip. The engine grew louder as they gained speed, hurtling toward the far end of the field.

Sarah's stomach fought to stay behind as the wheels bounced once and they were airborne. The plane's shadow crossed the fence at the far end of the field and grew smaller as it danced across orange groves, emerald alfalfa fields, and the backs of Holstein cattle. Sarah's heart pounded hard in her chest, but a pleasant thrill tickled her spine as they rose over fields and farms. The mountains grew smaller. She knew she would see over their tops at any moment, and a shout of delight burst from her lips.

Mabel turned with a flash of teeth, "Pretty jake huh?" She banked left over farms of the San Fernando Valley, leveled off, looked over her shoulder at Sarah, and pointed out a tall smokestack in the distance, "There's the chimney!"

"What?"

Mabel gunned the engine and bore down on the grey smokestack with a think plume of smoke drifting from it that rose beside a four-story structure shrouded in ivy surrounded by a high brick fence. "This is where we filmed the scene in *A Dash Through the Clouds*; it's a Catholic boys' school. Hope the headmaster's watching!"

"What are you doing?"

The engine whined as Mabel opened the throttle. Wind screamed in Sarah's ears through the cap as Mabel assaulted the chimney in a tight turn that seemed as if they were going to fly right into it. Something in Sarah's body wanted to leap and run, but there was nothing around but air. The aeroplane seemed to hit a bump in the air, and her whole body tingled. She saw rivets in the rungs of the iron ladder on the side of the smokestack as they shot by.

Instead of heading toward Los Angeles, Mabel banked right and headed northeast toward the mountains at an artificial waterfall cascading down from a great pipe bringing water to the burgeoning city. She pulled back the stick, climbed, and followed the pipe into the mountains. "Owens Valley Aqueduct!" she shouted over the wind and noise of the engine.

Sarah nodded as she tried to take in the vistas spreading before her in every direction, "This is marvelous!"

"Pretty jake, huh?"

"Yes, it's wonderful!"

They flew over brushy canyons with the occasional ranch or dirt road until Mabel pointed at a cluster of jagged rocks in the distance, "That's where Bill Hart and Tom Mix make Westerns," she shouted, "Enrico Vasquez used to hide out there."

"Who?"

"A Mexican bandit!"

"Oh!"

Ahead was a pass with pine trees at its crest under a thin mantle of snow and a switchback road. A Model T truck struggled up the pass as a cloud of steam poured from its radiator, leaving a cloud of dust in its wake.

Sarah laughed, "This sure beats driving! I'd love to fly an aeroplane!"

"I can get you lessons. Hell I'll teach you, I--"

The engine coughed, the plane trembled, and Mabel turned to the controls. Sarah bit her lip and stared at the back of Mabel's head with a fringe of dark curls billowing around her leather flying cap as she tugged at something. The engine coughed again and the plane dropped, driving Sarah's stomach halfway up her throat.

"What's the matter?"

"Don't know! Feels like--"

The engine cut out completely, and they began a wobbly glide into a canyon. Sarah fought a scream welling in her chest as Mabel fought with the stick, trying to keep the plane level as she yanked out the throttle, choked the engine, and cursed. The engine caught again, and the prop began to spin from more than the wind with a loud pop from the exhaust.

"There's something wrong with the fuel!" Mabel's complexion was several shades whiter, "We gotta land!"

"Please do!"

They glided into a pink-walled canyon toward a dirt road, sending doves and quail up in clouds from along a creek winding between pink boulders. Mabel guided the Jenny between cliffs that grew higher by the instant. The wheels touched the rutted road, the plane bounced with a howl as the landing gear was knocked ajar, and the prop threw a stinging cloud of gravel in their faces. A crack appeared in the right lens of Sarah's goggles. The plane twisted, pivoted to the left on its one remaining wheel, and sunk prop-down in the edge of a marshy pond with a bellow of steam.

Sarah felt herself to see if she was in one piece and fumbled with her belt.

Mabel unbuckled hers and stood up in the front seat, "Well toots... that's three!"

XXV.

They were beside a road and, after some discussion, they decided to follow it in the direction Mabel said was the way out of the mountains. She pointed with authority, "Saugus is this way."

Sarah squinted into the sun-blistered ochre hills, "I borrowed Olive's car. She'll be worried sick when I don't return with it this evening."

"Don't sweat the small stuff toots. We're alive, ain't we?"

Sarah chuckled and kicked a pebble, "At least I've got the footwear for hiking."

Mabel examined her own feet with a frown. She took off her fancy leather coat and tossed it in the aeroplane. "Hope nobody takes that. Damn, I sure don't want to walk far in these shoes. Praise God for little favors anyway. I did a couple flickers 'round here and I remember these red rocks. This is Texas Canyon. There's a ranch that way where we can get a ride to Saugus and a telephone. Mack will send somebody. Hell, he'll probably come himself. He always does when I'm in a fix if I'm not on the other side of the country."

"That's good."

Buzzards circled overhead. The thin cry of a hawk came from somewhere in the hot blue sky. Yellowjackets buzzed over the carcass of something in the bushes accompanied by the too-familiar stench of death. They took off the hot leather caps and gave it a wide berth. They walked for half an hour and sat to rest in the shade of an ancient stunted oak as quail scurried away under the brush, too hot to fly.

Mabel swatted at a hovering wasp and moaned, "Sure could use a beer."

"A cold one, American style."

"Do they still drink it warm in Canada? Mack's from Canada and I've never seen him do that."

"Some do I suppose."

"Ugh."

"I didn't drink beer in Canada. Sure tastes good cold by a pool in Los Angeles with chips and guacamole though."

Mabel began to laugh but it became a cough, "I need water."

"There's water in some of those ponds. Do you think we can drink it?"

"Rather not. You know those stories about poison water holes."

"That would be dreadful."

"You're tellin' me sister."

"Then we must find civilization in all haste."

"Wish I was back filming *Mickey* and diving off a cliff into that nice cold river in upstate New York."

Sarah gazed at Mabel. Her head was framed by a mass of dark curls that were plastered to her neck with sweat. "How did you find the courage for that?"

"How did you jump on a horse over and over 'til they got the take for pin money?"

"Something to prove I suppose, and fear of failure."

"See? It just gets crazier the farther you go. Everybody in Hollywood is afraid people will get tired of them up there on the screen, so when the director says jump, they jump. It's easy to make even a coward jump off a cliff if you've got a worse outcome waiting when you don't. You know, we oughta do a Keystone flicker together: *Mabel and Sarah, Lost in the Wild.* 'Course Keystone's not around anymore. Maybe we could pitch one to Essanay with Billy Bevan and Ben Turpin for the bad guys. 'Course, Mack would kill me for not doing it with him."

"That would be fun."

"And just out of the camera shot, there'd be a caterer with a table full of cold beer and soda," Mabel sighed, "the studios make sure you're taken care of."

"And cold orange juice."

"Ever have mimosa?"

"No, but Ollie loves it."

"You should try it. I love it too. Had a hell of a time at Buster Keaton's place in Laurel Canyon last summer drinkin' mimosa and doin' a little party powder with Ollie. This rich German who fled the Kaiser with a buncha loot proposed to her and she brushed him off like a fly. He gave her a pearl necklace and she gave it right back. Then he gave her a diamond ring. Ollie took his ring and threw it right off the porch like so much dirt."

"Really, with a diamond, eh?"

"With a whole *buncha* them. That ring could keep a poor family in the chips for a few years at least."

"What happened to it?"

"He stormed off, but the next day the gardener saw him crawling around on hands and knees in the leaves searching for it. Don't know if he found it. Maybe it's still there, or maybe some hobo had one helluva lucky day." Mabel wiped her brow and licked dry lips.

"Thank you for the ride by the way. It was still worth it. I want to fly again."

"Don't mind crash landing?"

"It shall make a great story I suppose, how I crashed in the desert with Mabel Normand in a Jenny, and how a handsome fellow came to our rescue on a palomino horse with a canteen of cold water, perhaps someone like Zorro. Wouldn't that be a good plot for a motion picture?"

"Wish it were now and it was beer. Then we could turn it into a comedy sketch and we could run from the banditos with Fatty."

Sarah gazed at Mabel's pale face in the shade. She was always living in a movie just like everybody else here, whether there were cameras around or not. Sarah chuckled, "I shouldn't care to share a horse with him."

Mabel began a laugh. It disintegrated into a hacking cough.

Sarah put a hand on her back and felt the spasms wracking her, "We've got to find some clean water Mabel."

They got up and came to where water trickled from a cleft in the pastel rocks forming a pool on the west side of the canyon in afternoon shade.

Mabel bent down, balanced herself on her hands just like Sarah did, drank deeply, and went into another fit of coughing that doubled her up. She pulled a silk handkerchief from her purse, wiped blood from her lips, and shook her head, "Can't walk in this goddamn heat. My head is spinning. I fear I'll faint if I go farther."

Sarah did the same to drink. It tasted like the best water she'd ever had. She sat up and wiped her mouth. Mabel was pale where the sun hadn't reddened her. Sarah put a hand to the clammy skin of Mabel's forehead and felt a deep scar at her hairline, "You're not well."

"Just a little cough, toots."

"We should rest here until it gets cooler. Perhaps that handsome vaquero on a palomino will show up."

Mabel nodded weakly and sat down in the shade with a groan.

Sarah leaned against a cool rock and gazed into the hot blue sky. The black wings of turkey vultures circled over something dead across the canyon as they rocked like kites in a hot updraft.

They sat for a while in silence. Doves returned to the trees above them, eyed the water greedily, and began a mournful cooing in the long afternoon. Tiny grasshoppers exploded like popcorn from the brush and Mabel began coughing again.

"Are you all right?"

Mabel put a hand to her mouth. The cords of her neck stood out as she fought a spasm wracking her. She took a rattling breath, rubbed her forehead, and made a wet sigh, "I've an awful headache. Spent three weeks in the hospital after that little bitch Mae Busch hit me with a vase four years ago and it comes back at times like this."

"What happened? Someone mentioned that when I was working for Ince."

"You can't trust 'em, they're all the same."

"Men... or women?"

Mabel began coughing again, regained control, and nodded without naming a gender, "Mack always said he wanted to marry me, and we set the date for the Fourth of July in nineteen-fifteen. God... I *believed* in him! Spent five grand on my trousseau at Madame Frances' dress shop goddamn him to hell! I *loved* that man! We were the greatest team too, and wrote scripts in a day. You've seen those flickers I did with Fatty haven't you?"

Sarah nodded, "Of course."

"I directed Chaplin in a few too, but he never gave me credit 'cause I was a girl and everybody had to think it was always Mack. *Men!* Anyway I found Mack in bed with that little bitch in a hotel room in Santa Monica on the night before our wedding! She was my bosom buddy too. We had a group called The Dirty Four. Those guys have all their buddies like the Four Musketeers, and we could talk dirty and get wild without somebody lookin' down their snooty noses at us and compare the men we'd been with, even swap 'em. You know, it's really easier for girls if you don't let 'em snow you with their noise. Maybe that's why men have to keep things the way they are, and if we do what they always have they call us sluts. We were one hard partying bunch, sister, but she knew about Mack and that he was the only one who really mattered in my whole goddamn life. Shit, she was like my goddamn sister. I told her everything that was going on! When I found them together, I was so mad I couldn't see straight," Mabel kicked at the hard mineral soil and scooted farther into the meager shade, "And then I made the stupid mistake of looking away after I told the little tramp I was gonna rip her damn eyes out and she up and brained me with a vase. I spent days... *weeks* in the hospital with a concussion. Had a high fever too. The movie rags said I was already dead and done for from an accident while filming."

"I read that. People were talking about it in Victoria."

Mabel sighed, "They said I got hit with a fuckin' shoe while I was doing a wedding scene. Kinda funny, huh? Like *hell!* Mack would come to the hospital with truckloads of flowers and sit next to my bed crying and begging forgiveness. Hell, he still needed me for his goddamn flickers. Me and Fatty *were* Keystone except for them silly cops and Chaplin, who he let go over petty cash after one fucking year. Charlie used to come crying to my trailer and tell me I was the only one who understood him. He thinks he's the cat's meow with women, but sister let me tell ya, I can't stand his B.O. Shit fire, he had a piece of banana stuck to his coat for *sixteen fucking days* once. The man's a cockney gutter snipe with a brain and I was too softhearted not to stick up for him every time he needed it, just like I always did for Roscoe. I'd probably do it again I'm such a sap. I was like a mother to all of 'em but that's another story. So after I recovered, me and Mack worked together again seeing as I was his headliner. He was so guilty he even opened the Mabel Normand Studios for me where we made *Mickey* and it was the biggest hit either of us ever had. Even spent a night or two with him after a year or so just 'cause he's a great roll in the hay, best I've had actually, but I'll never marry him so long as I live, so help me God."

"But then... why did you spend a night with him ever again?"

"Like I said toots, he's a damn good toss on the sheets. Besides, he's one of the only people who'll shut up about it, seeing as his career is up there for the public to see just like mine. People like us have things in common is all, and it's just... *convenient.* It's the way things happen 'round here. If you've been staying with Ollie, you must have noticed that by now."

"I suppose you're right. I did it with Valentino for somewhat the same reason I suppose, at least for him," Sarah laughed, "but it was convenient for me too. In fact it was my doing."

"Valentino?" Mabel rolled her dark eyes, "how was he?"

"Quite romantic actually, he was distraught over his bride locking him out of their room at the Hollywood Hotel but he certainly performed for me. It was quite enjoyable, although he was muttering about some woman in his sleep named Lorelei, who's a friend of Beverly's that I never actually met until the other..." Sarah blinked in the glare as she considered trying to explain that particular facet of her life. Without mentioning everything else, it wasn't worth trying. She chuckled, "They *are* little boys. I can see what you mean about being a mother to them."

"No... I mean, people talk about what he's got down there, you know... endowment-wise."

Sarah's cheeks bulged, "Oh. Well, from my limited experience I would definitely have to say huge."

"Damn, I heard that. My, Sarah, you really *have* seen the sights in a short time."

"Not all good I assure you," Sarah stared at the circling buzzards, "did Olive tell you about the dead girls?"

"Say what?"

Sarah bit her lip. Olive actually had kept the story to herself it seemed, except for Bee, "I was tricked by a fellow who said he was a vice president at United Artists on my very first day here, and abducted, and... and raped. He fully intended to kill me for that matter."

"Oh my word!" Mabel seized Sarah's hand and squeezed until her rings hurt her fingers, "Dear! I'm sorry! Jesus, whatever happened?"

"I killed him."

Mabel's mouth fell open. She stared at Sarah wide-eyed until a yellowjacket attempted to investigate the moist yawning cavity decorated with lipstick, and Mabel jerked away with a yelp and fluttering of hands.

"I got loose when he had me tied up and brained him with a magnum of scotch, several times actually, and it killed him. I met Olive that very same day. I wasn't at all sure what I was doing at the time or where I was bound, as I'd just escaped from his clutches as it were, and I was in an odd way also since he'd given me some type of drug. Olive, well, you know Ollie, she just kind of swept me up in her world, and for the last few days I've been trying to fit in and find work in the flickers. That was the reason I came here after all, but I'm going to find out who his friends and accomplices were believe you me. They're still out there Mabel, and they must be stopped. Bee Davis is looking into it this very minute."

Mabel stared with the same fascination Olive had at the spa upon confiding in her, "Who have you told, Sarah?"

"Just Ollie, and Bee… and now you."

"Well, Beverly Davis is the best person to. She's got more connections than the studios when it comes to the law, more dirt on them anyway, but why do you think he had friends, and what did you do with… with the body?"

"He had a camera and Kliegs set up in a bedroom where he filmed whatever he did to me as well as the other girls. There were films and pictures there of them but it all had disappeared afterward when me, Ollie, and Bee went back to investigate. That takes at least two more accomplices… and the well… the well where I put his body, it had the bones of other girls in it. It was all filled in when we went back… and me and Ollie were up in the hills a couple of days ago behind her house, and two men dumped the body of *another* girl from the road up there while we were sitting under a tree nearby, but they didn't see us… and there were at least three more bodies up there too, and--"

"My God," Mabel ran a hand across her face, "I bet that's what happened to that Johnston girl from Ziegfeld Mack was eyeing at Triangle. He was going to give her a big part and she just disappeared. I thought maybe it was me that scared her off 'cause I gave her a ration at a party the night before. She left her bungalow in Glendale with all her clothes and everything and left with Warren the cameraman to--"

"That's him!"

Mabel's dark eyes grew even larger, "Then he's been at it for three years at least!" Her mouth fell open again, "You... you killed *Warren?"*

Sarah swallowed, "It was him or me, believe you me Mabel. I cannot begin to tell you what he did to me." Sarah stared into the sun-blistered rocks across the canyon and made an attempt at swallowing. Her throat was too dry again. She sighed. It would be terribly helpful if she could actually *remember* what Warren had done, come what may.

"And to think of all the times I bought..." Mabel shook her head, "you win Sarah, you're the toughest."

"Eek," Sarah sprang up, almost knocking Mabel off the boulder, "a scorpion, oh horrid!"

Mabel added her shriek to Sarah's and leapt up to join her, clutching at Sarah's shirt. Sarah reached for a rock and brought it down on the creature with a resounding report accompanied by a crackling sound as the scorpion was crushed.

"I do *not* want to spend the night here!" Mabel wailed.

"Howdy, ladies."

A man astride a palomino horse had approached unheard during the short time their little drama had unfolded. He uncocked his six-gun after seeing all the screaming was about a bug and shoved it in a scuffed holster. He wore a battered grey Stetson hat over a permanent squint framed by a grey beard and showed a full set of tobacco-stained teeth in a smile as he dismounted,

"Howdy, Mabel."

"Ohmygod, *Flint!*" Mabel sprang across the intervening distance as if someone had taken half the frames out of a film reel and hugged him, then turned to Sarah with a smile as big as the hills, "Flint was my wrangler on a couple of my movies! He's a real cowboy and--"

"And what in hell are you doin' with an aeroplane in my cattle's waterhole if you don't mind me askin', Miss Normand?"

Mabel made a croaking laugh, "Just what it looks like Flint. Can you get us out of here please?"

"Yup."

XXVI.

It was past midnight when Flint's battered Model T pickup dropped them at the airfield. Mabel thanked Flint profusely and promised him work in another Western as she kissed his grizzled cheek. Sarah kissed his other while trying not to breathe the mixture of tobacco and whiskey his leathery skin exuded.

Mabel scratched her matted hair and groaned, "I'm just pooped! Now I'll have to get someone to salvage the aeroplane out there in the country and haul it in on a truck. Godamnit, with that story you told me about Warren and dead girls, I just can't deal with it at all at the moment," she made a stage sigh, stretched, and produced a movie smile, "time for a little pick-me-up," she opened the door panel of the Mercer where she kept her makeup, tugged at something, freed a small box, and began to fumble in it, "could you get the flashlight from the trunk hon?"

Sarah opened the trunk and rummaged amongst several changes of clothes until she found the big rubber-covered implement and switched it on. Mabel placed a carved Chinese camphorwood box with a mirror in its lid on the fold-out table and proceeded to lay out two thick lines of white powder across it. Sarah tottered in exhaustion, holding the light. She looked forward to the boost, even as part of her took a step back in the cricket-singing night with a terrible scowl of judgment. When her turn to snort the cocaine came, she bent down gratefully as Mabel held the light. Sarah inhaled half into one nostril and then the other with a deftness that would make Olive proud. She held her nose fighting a sneeze as the stuff made its way into her system and straightened up still holding it, "Can I drive?"

* * *

Sarah stepped away from the wheel of the Mercer at two in the morning at the house on Lankershim. Mabel hugged her and swore on her mother's grave she'd not tell a soul about Warren or the girls. "I'll do some investigating. We'll get to the bottom of this without the coppers, honey, and find the right people to put things jake. Trust Bee."

Sarah kissed her cheek and Mabel pulled out of the driveway as the dogs barked from the back yard. She banged on the big carved door with the little brass knocker. When a sleepy-eyed Lupita finally opened it, Sarah mumbled a greeting, stumbled past her to the telephone, grabbed it, stabbed the cradle of the receiver several times with a stiff finger, and gave Olive's number to the operator.

It rang twice and Olive picked it up, "Hello!" her voice was shrill in the earpiece.

"Oh Ollie, I'm so sorry. I went flying with Mabel Normand in an aeroplane and we crashed in some place called Texas Canyon way out in the desert, and this old cowboy named Flint something-or-other found us and we drove back in his truck, and he had a flat, and--"

"Sarah I was so worried! God... you *what?*"

"I went flying with Mabel Normand."

"Golly, and you crashed?"

"Yes, well, we had to land because the engine kept dying and then we were gliding, and then we were falling, and then the wheels broke and we went down in a creek in the middle of nowhere. God, it was so *hot!* I thought maybe we were going to die out there, but this old cowboy Flint found us and Mabel knew him from some flickers they did and--"

Olive's laughter filled the receiver, "Oh God, you are *so* lucky!" There was a little sob on the line, "I thought you'd just taken off, and... oh, I'm so stupid!"

"No you're not."

Olive sniffled into the phone, "Where are you?"

"At your house in the hills, Mabel dropped me here. I'm much too tired to drive back tonight. I have got to get some sleep."

"I can have the limo get you."

"That's silly. You'd have to wake Douglas and the Locomobile would still be here. Let me get some shuteye and come over in a few hours. I'll be fine, Ollie."

There was silence on the other end, "Guess so. I've got to be back at Selznick in the morning. I've got another block of work piled up and I can't do much else for a few days. Will you come?"

"Oh damn, I'm supposed to be at Inceville! I've only got a couple of hours to get ready. Can I use the car? I'll have to stay up somehow. Jesus... I've got to get cleaned up!"

"Of course. Sarah?"

"Yes?"

"I'm not really twenty."

"I'd guessed that Ollie."

"You did?"

"You've done too much for that age."

"Oh, so that's how you guessed?"

"Uh-hum."

There was a wet sigh amongst static on the other end, "I'm twenty-five. Does that make a difference?"

"Why in the world should it?"

"Okay... love you Sarah."

"Love you, Ollie."

"Did you like Mabel?"

"I sure did. She's a spitfire and so fearless. She makes me want to fly aeroplanes and jump off cliffs."

"Bill Taylor told me you were together. I thought maybe you and Mabel... oh, never mind."

"Oh my God, you thought we--"

"I said never mind."

An exhausted laugh bubbled up in Sarah's chest to be joined by Olive's on the other end, "God, me and Mabel Normand!"

"Wouldn't be the first time we had the same tastes, believe me. 'Course it was men but it just shows we think alike. Anyway I'll see you tonight. Please be careful at Inceville. You've had no sleep and it's rough work. There's something in the false bottom of the top drawer of the makeup table, if you want to stay awake."

"All right, love you Ollie."

"Love you so much Sarah."

* * *

She showered and wandered to the living room smelling of lavender and swathed in a satin bathrobe with a purple towel wrapped around her head. Moonlight poured through the skylights, bathing the room in a blue-white glow that pooled in the crystal globe cradled in the arms of the marble nude on the table. Sarah hadn't noticed how much it looked like Sonya before.

It would be nice to try some mimosa, but there wasn't champagne in the ice box. Sarah found herself at the bar taking a bottle of tequila from the shelf. She uncorked it, sniffed, and made a face. She corked it, then uncorked it again and took a swallow, "Eyow!" Sarah plopped on the couch wiping her mouth. The clock on the mantle chimed three times in its case with a tone only gold and the finest crystal could achieve. She got up and climbed the stairs to the bedroom.

The big bed where she'd first made love with Olive was perfectly made, its satin comforter luminous in moonlight falling through the windows. Sarah imagined Olive stretched across it as she sat at the makeup table and opened the top drawer, turned on the lamp with its mother of pearl visor, and lifted the bottom of the drawer up to inspect its contents. One of Olive's flasks greeted her. Sarah took it out and twisted off the top. All five tubes were full. She slid one out staring at the liquid within and tipped it to watch it slosh from one end to the other. Well... if it was good enough for Sherlock Holmes. A chuckle rippled her lips, "Elementary, my dear Watson."

Sarah took out the body of the syringe, screwed on the needle, inserted it into one of the tubes, and filled it halfway. She squirted a bit out the end of the needle like Olive had done and watched it spray a glistening arc in the yellow light of the lamp to soak into the carpet and disappear in a twinkle.

She found one of Olive's garters and wound it around her bicep. She flexed her arm and examined the muscle. Her arms were bigger than any of the pretty girls she'd met in Hollywood except perhaps Sonya, and she preferred they stay that way. She felt the flow of blood as her heart pounded. The vein in her arm vibrated to it. She remembered when she thought it was going to burst as she'd scrambled up a cliff to avoid a bear on the Fortymile River at the age of ten. Life had swelled in her like a great wave as she stood panting, clinging to lichen-stained rocks and screaming at the bear below, then at the whole wide world with mountains that were nameless and a river that ran who-knows-where. She missed the Klondike. She missed its vastness that made her feel part of everything, even when she'd been afraid. It was a good place to die if it came to that. Fear was good sometimes. Fear made you feel alive. Sarah chuckled. She could take Sonya in a fight.

What's Sonya like in a bed?

Sarah loved being strong. She loved the way Olive squealed like a little girl when she tossed her around. She loved the way Guadeloupe let her take over the horse as naturally as anything when she leapt up in front of him. She loved the way Rudolfo gasped in surprise when she seized him inside her, using him until she was in charge, the mistress of their mutual pleasure. Sarah tightened the garter and pumped her arm like she'd seen Olive do. She twisted it and held the loose end in her teeth. Her face was close to the inside of her elbow as she inserted the needle, and her breath rolled across the inside of her arm. She felt the prick but ignored it.

She ground her teeth when blood appeared as she raised the plunger as a ripe cherry plume swirling in amber liquid. She stared at her blood mixing with the liquid in the tube and slowly pushed the plunger back down with her thumb.

"Owph!"

She released the garter, dropped the syringe, and fell on the floor as a cold white wave charged through her body. Her heart bounced in her chest as if it were going to burst. She ran hands up her cheeks into her hair, holding the top of her skull so that it wouldn't explode from the fizzing rush boiling in her brain. She gasped and blinked as the moon outside the windows grew larger. It echoed in the back of her eyes when she squeezed them shut. An owl hooted in the trees. Its voice echoed in the halls of her veins. She thought she saw a white face in the window, or was it in the room? She gasped and glanced around. Was that woman watching her now... *Lorelei?* Why hadn't she come to their rescue in the desert if she was so damn powerful? It had to be the coke.

Sarah got on the bed, rolled across it, and put a hand between her legs. She sat up, concentrated on breathing, and clambered to her feet. She slipped her trembling limbs into clean clothes, jeans, and a flannel shirt. She took off the amulet hanging from a thin gold chain around her neck and put it on the dresser. She picked it back up and examined the woman on it with the high round breasts of eternal youth holding what looked like seashells and sticks in her hands as she perched naked upon the backs of contented lions with the talons of a predatory bird, flanked by great staring owls. "All right Lorelei... or Lilith... or whoever you are."

Sarah put it back on, Olive's Smith and Wesson came out of her purse. She broke it open, spun the cylinder, snapped it shut, and slipped out the front door without waking the dogs. Sarah stood in the moonlit drive for a while. She took a few deep breaths and headed to the hillside where a part of her was buried as surely as the corpses of girls.

* * *

She walked a luminous path through the inky shade of trees. She felt as if she were floating and spun in circles with the gun in her hand pointing at shadows. The owl hooted again. She broke into giggling, "What the hell am I doing?"

"*What you were meant to do.*"

"Who was that?" Sarah's grip on the gun tightened, "Who's there?"

Something burst from the nearby bushes with a crash and she almost fired. Three deer bounded away, shaking leaves and filling the air with the scent of crushed vegetation and their musk. "Fuck it." She inhaled the good wild smell of them and stuck her tongue out at the white flash of their rumps as they disappeared amongst the quivering branches.

Another noise made her freeze. She stood still, straining her ears until her head throbbed. Up ahead was a pounding, and then scraping followed by a loud thud. Sarah stepped into the deep shadow of an oak tree and broke open the action of the .38, running fingertips over the cartridges in the cylinder. She spun it, squeezed it shut with a click, and stood listening. She should run back to Olive's house and call someone: Bee, Olive, Bill Taylor, perhaps even the police... *anyone.*

Sarah closed her eyes. Her demons had returned in the dark and it was her fate to meet them. She was alone in this world, without family, without a single soul she could truly understand, but she was the maker of her own destiny. She grasped the amulet between her breasts and took a breath.

Two men's voices came from within the stone house, the same voices she'd heard with Olive up the creek as they chatted casually over the body of their victim. They were the voices she'd heard in the vaguely remembered nightmare she'd awoken from tied up on the hill. She stared at the moon. An owl left a phosphorescent trail against the stars, wobbling its wings like a Jenny coming in for a landing. Its eyes flashed golden, then red. She was *watching.* Sarah felt her face stretch in a grin.

A big convertible car stood before the porch with moonlight glowing on its pale canvas top and tall whitewall tires. It was Bill Taylor's McFarlan, and the ironbound trunk over the rear bumper was open.

"Jesus Christ, this thing is built like a fuckin' bank vault!" a deep voice barked from within the house.

"That's the idea, Mack."

"I don't fuckin' got all night, Ed."

"Yeah, what else you got to do that'll make you this kinda loot?"

"Yeah you're right. Rich lugs sure pay for a little kooze don't they? How didya keep Warren from gettin' into the safe?"

"Think I'm loco? He never had both keys."

"Yeah, and now we don't either. Wonder what he did with his?"

"Hell if I know. It weren't on his stinkin' corpse. He didn't have no clothes on in that fuckin' hole."

"I'd like to make the sonofabitch pay who made me crawl down that goddamn well. Whoever put it to the swell probably took it with 'em. Wonder what they got outta him first?"

"They said it was a girl, remember?"

"Shit... a goddamn dame did him in."

"Yeah, they said it's the one we left here. I seen her across the road with Olive Thomas wearing a flapper and drinkin' a margarita the other day. She didn't even look the worse for wear. From the looks a' him, I'd say she did a pretty good strip search."

The house echoed with rough laughter.

"Always thought he was a tough guy, and then he went and cashed in off some bitch from the boonies."

"He's still gettin' the last laugh on us, dyin' with that fuckin' key hid somewhere."

"Check up his ass?"

"Fuck you Mack."

There was a guttural laugh, "You think he emptied it before she greased him?"

"How? Think he was plannin' to get whacked? Anyway he didn't have both keys, remember?"

"Oh, yeah."

There was another flurry of pounding followed by a groan, "Goddamn it, we gotta cut the whole thing outta the concrete. There ain't no goddamn way around it."

"That'll take all fuckin' night."

"Better get movin' then."

"Damn!"

The pounding resumed with the sound of a tool chipping at cement. Sarah eased up onto the porch and picked up the rocking chair, moved it to the far end away from the door, and settled in it with a soft squeak. She sat with the gun in her lap and searched the trees for the owl. A night bird called she didn't recognize, and the owl answered. Something pale scurried across the yard and a silent form swept down to snag it in its talons. The creature gave out one high-pitched cry, and the owl disappeared with its prey in the night.

* * *

An hour later the men ceased their labors.

There was a groan, "All we gotta do now is move the fuckin' thing."

"I'm takin' a leak."

"Me too."

Sarah eased out of the chair and pressed her back to the wall in the shadows holding the pistol against her chest. The men came out on the porch and she trained the gun on them as they stood at the other end. A knot in her stomach formed, and Sarah dug her teeth in her lip. This was part of being alive, of being alone. She was like the owl in the trees. They were the rabbits and the owl was her Goddess, watching over her.

"The boss is gonna reward us big time," the smaller of the two said as twin arcs of urine sparkled in the night.

Sarah stood in silence clutching the gun staring at the stocky profile of the one who'd spoken. It was Ed Sands, Bill's chauffeur. The other man was huge with a neck that disappeared into sloping shoulders and thick trapezoid muscles, aptly fitting the deep voice and coarse language that spewed from him.

Ed finished pissing, yawned, and cracked his back, "Got a couple wannabes comin' to the new digs tomorrow, couple'a redheads. Tol' 'em it's a secret and they'll meet Wally Reid, maybe get a sports car ride to Venice."

"Ha... a sports car ride," his companion laughed, "just what the doctor ordered. The flickers draw dumb broads like mice to cheese and it ain't never gonna end. I'm damn glad we had to move, Ed. What a spot we got this time."

"We got to watch our step there Mack. We're in the middle of fuckin' Hollywood almost and they're lookin' for Sennett's equipment." He sighed, "Let's load up. I got to have the car back at Taylor's bungalow by seven. Peavey goes out to check it every morning like fuckin' clockwork."

"That goddamn pansy of a nigger's trouble. You oughta let me fix him so you can have more time with Taylor. Ain't nobody gonna look for a missing swish nigger anyway. How much did you get Taylor for while he was back East visiting that Normand dame?"

"Plenty, I wrote some checks from his desk on the Famous Players account. Sonofabitch hasn't even looked at it in a couple'a years and there's thousands there. Rich guys do dumb things like that all the time and the guy trusts me. I got some of his personal rolled cigarettes right here with real gold 'round the tips. Wanta smoke?" At the sound of a car bumping up the drive, Ed put the cigarette back in its silver case and snapped it shut, "Who the fuck is that?"

"Shit if I know. Shit, my gun's in the car."

A Rolls limo appeared in the dappled moonlight beneath the trees. Its tall tires made an arc around the rear of the McFarlan before it ground to a halt. There was the sound of the brake being pulled, and a tiny figure clad in shiny slacks, silk jacket and flapper hat glistening under the moon stepped down from behind the wheel.

"Sarah, hey Sarah, where are you!"

"Shit!" came out of both men's mouths, and they bolted toward Olive.

Sarah sprang across the porch as the rocking chair fell into the cactus with a crash, "Hey!" she screamed.

Ed spotted her standing at the end of the porch with the pistol pointed at him. He threw his hands in the air, "Wha--"

"Don't move! You're finished! Put your hands up where I can see them you sonsabitches!"

Ed had raised his hands, but Mack stepped behind him, blocking Sarah's view of Olive.

"Ollie! Get where I can *see* you!" Sarah waved the gun, "and move away from your friend, Ed!"

Ed dove off the porch. Sarah saw his head for an instant as he bounced to his feet and the gun went off with a loud *pop,* splintering a porch post where he'd been a split-second before. "Goddamn it!"

The big man sprang into the cactus garden, rolled in a cloud of dust with a howl, jumped up, and began barreling toward Olive, who let out a yelp and ran behind the Rolls. Sarah aimed at Mack's back, but Olive was right behind him. "Damn!" There was a scraping on the porch behind her and she spun around.

Ed head-butted Sarah in the stomach and she slammed against a window that burst in a cascade of glass. She raised a hand to protect her face as she fell and shoved the pistol barrel into Ed's side with the other. The knurled hammer clicked under her thumb as the back of her head hit the heavy oaken table.

XXVII.

"Three little piggies in the belly o' Babylon!" a voice echoed in her skull.

Sarah rocked her head to the sound. She was perched beside Olive on a high blue wall. Los Angeles stretched to the ocean below her, shimmering and golden with a billion poppies blooming among smoldering ruins. Across a jumble of ancient statues, a great gate between two crumbling towers gave out a grinding roar as it opened. Suddenly, the sun was gone. Cruel laughter erupted from the stygian darkness of the other side before bubbles of blood mushroomed out in the moonlight. Her head ached. The wall trembled.

A pale hand stroked her brow. Soft lips brushed her forehead. She grabbed at the blue pendant at her throat, reached out, and put an arm around Olive's shoulders. Olive's violet eyes were huge, brimming with fear. The green surface of the reservoir below them shuddered and shattered the moon's reflected face into a million fragments as the wall began to lean out over Hollywood, farther and farther. Olive screamed. Sarah grabbed her hand, grasping with her other at the fake blue stones that flaked to dust beneath her fingers.

* * *

The grating of metal across concrete felt like a rusty wire dragging through her brain. Sarah jerked from the sensation and yanked at the leather straps holding her hands and feet. She opened her eyes, put a cheek against the blue painted boards beneath her, and examined her surroundings. On a tripod above her looming like an angry bear was the same movie camera she'd seen in the house in the hills, with **Keystone Studios** etched across the brass plaque on its scuffed wooden shell.

A white rage erupted in her middle and curdled in her gut. She raged at her captors, at the world, at *herself.* Pure hatred exploded in a rush that made Olive's cocaine pale. She could break her bonds with the force of it and pulled with every ounce of her strength. The effort shook her chest and twisted her shoulders until she whimpered, but her bonds grew tighter.

Moaning came from her right. Sarah turned her head to see a dark-haired girl spread-eagled, tied to rings set in the blue painted planks. The whites of the girl's eyes glowed in the dim light around dark irises, and she blinked, "Are you Sarah?"

Sarah licked dry lips and nodded.

"I'm Dolores," Dolores' eyes flicked as she glanced over Sarah's shoulder and she motioned with a finely sculpted chin, "Ollie's behind you."

Sarah turned to her left to see Olive sprawled beside her similarly bound. Olive was very still and Sarah couldn't make out any breathing at all. "Jesus, where are we?"

"I don't know. Bee sent me on a call at the Hollywood Hotel for Wally Reid, but when I got to the room, somebody put a rag over my face, and--"

"These are the bastards who've been kidnapping and killing girls!"

"Shhhh! Not so loud!"

Sarah stared at the rough cut beams of the ceiling and glanced at Olive again, "Is she . . ?"

A key turned in the metal door. Sarah glanced at the terrified face of Dolores before they dropped their heads to the boards in feigned unconsciousness as the door ground over the concrete floor with the sound that had awoken her. Heavy footfalls approached. Sarah peered out of half-shut eyes at the huge silhouette standing above her. There was a click, a hiss, and a blinding light beat against her eyelids.

"This one's comin' 'round." The jowls of the big man called Mack were a blur through her nearly closed eyes against a ceiling of bare lumber and the hissing glare of the Klieg. Rough fingers stroked her crotch, and she trembled as blunt fingers began probing, "'Member me, sweetcakes?"

"We got customers, Mack."

The fingers withdrew.

There was a groan to her right as Dolores arched her back in the glare, fighting her bonds. Mack's hand was between her legs. In the harsh light, Sarah saw the marks of teeth in a vicious purple crescent on Dolores' left breast. Sarah rocked her head back to Olive. Her eyes were closed and she looked dead. Sarah stared at her, willing breath into her, searching Olive's chest for any movement. The grating of the door came again, and she tried to peer around Mack's bulk as someone entered the room.

"Got that nice young blonde in the middle, boss, the one who caused us all the grief. "Remember her?"

"The Canadian brat? Hell yes, good work. You boys--"

There was a long moment of silence, with only the hissing of the Klieg light.

"Whatsamatter?"

"You fucking idiots! Do you know who that *is?*"

"Yeah sure… what the hell else were we supposed to do? We had to scram outta there and they both knew me. We got the safe for you and you can have yourself a movie star, and… hey, not to worry boss. We'll hide all three where nobody's ever gonna find 'em. There's old mines in the desert where we can dynamite the tunnels shut after---"

"Jesus Christ! *Olive fucking Thomas!*"

"I don't--"

"Get them out of here, now! I'll have every inch of this set condemned tomorrow as an eyesore and down to bare dirt, and make Griffith pay for it if I have to jail him to do it! I'm leaving, and I don't want to ever see your fucking faces again! You'll get out of town tonight with these three, and just keep going if you've got any sense... and never come back!

"Whoa, what do we do with them?"

"You already told me what you're going to do with them. You'll just have to do it sooner. Dear God, they'll have every cop in the country searching for her with those goddamn nags Parsons and Hopper filling the papers with it every fucking day! Olive Thomas! Hearst will love it! I don't fucking believe this! Jesus Christ!"

"What about our money, Mister--"

"You're lucky to get out of here alive after this, you sonofabitch! I've got a hundred triggermen called cops that can come in here and leave nothing but stinking corpses, and I can fit your name with a collar that will never come off, Ed! You're worth more dead than standing here shooting off your fucking mouth! You don't have shit in the real world. Christ... you fucking idiot, she's a *Pickford!* Why didn't you just kidnap the fucking Queen of England while you were at it, you lowlife fool? I'm letting you go for past favors but don't push me, and turn off that god-awful light!"

The light went out, and the sound of grating came again as the door was yanked shut. There was a long pause accompanied by the shuffling of feet.

"Tol' ya, Ed, we shoulda buried this Thomas bitch up there in the well and everything woulda been jake. He never even woulda known. Now we got the shitty end of the stick just 'cause you wanted to bring the little broad along."

"Shut the fuck up and help me untie these whores."

"Do 'em now?"

"Just chloroform, we don't want a mess. Besides, I always wanted to fuck a movie star."

"Damn straight. We gotta get our money's worth."

"We ain't never gonna get that Mack, but I'm sure gonna take some out on this blond bitch who caused all this trouble in the first place. Shit, the goddamn bottle's empty."

"The little movie star was wigglin' too much. I had to give her a couple more doses. There's another bottle in the car."

"Okay I'll get it. You get 'em ready."

The door opened and closed again.

"Shit," Mack grumbled as he released the shackles on Olive's thin wrists with a key, lifted her like a rag doll in his arms, and rocked her like a baby in the light of a single yellow bulb, "well, gonna have me a movie star." He put her down and began tying her wrists and ankles behind her back with the leather straps as he hummed the tune to the Hollywood Hotel song, *The End of a Perfect Day*. When he finished, he went to Dolores on Sarah's right.

Dolores shrieked as Mack began to unshackle her, and a fleshy slap echoed in the low-ceilinged room. "Quiet down bitch, you're gettin' another dose soon as Ed gets back. Christ, what a goddamn racket you make. Fuckin' greasers never know when to shut up."

He left Dolores moaning on the boards and came to Sarah, who lay limp as he opened a cuff. His thick fingers squeezed her cheeks together until her teeth ground in her mouth, and he rocked her head back and forth as he stared through a cloud of foul breath, "Good girl. You be still now." He unfastened the binding and reached for a belt with his free hand with his other on her throat. Sarah fought the urge for every muscle in her body to tense as she lay helpless with Mack's fingers around her windpipe. He slid the thick leather belt under her and took his hand off her throat as he reached for the free end to draw it together.

Her knee came up hard in his face. It was like hitting a brick wall, but Mack grunted and loosened his grip. He grabbed at her, but Sarah coiled away from his hands like a snake to spring off the platform and roll across the plank floor to her feet with the thick belt in her hand.

Mack glared, wiped his bloody nose, cracked his knuckles, and grinned, "Where you gonna go now, sweet cheeks? Had ya before anyway, 'member yet? Bet it's just comin' back," he cackled, "betcha been sore all week. Wouldn't a got away from me up there, but I left that little squirrel Warren 'cause he thought he could take care'a business and wanted a little more. You cost us plenty, havin' to change locations and hide all this shit. Now we gotta blow town ta boot," his upper lip twitched over yellow teeth, "you and me are gonna have a real payback party if you don't behave. You put that belt down and be a good girl, and maybe I'll let ya go after we're done, and you can go home to momma on the next train."

In a moment that stretched forever, Sarah glanced at Dolores, whose terrified eyes were as big as saucers. Something began to vibrate in Sarah's middle, something that wanted to paralyze her, as if Dolores' fear was contagious, engulfing her to sap all the strength from her body and leave her a limp husk. She glanced at Olive, motionless on the platform, trussed for disposal, and thought of Olive talking about the Swami's prediction of an early death. Sarah put a hand to Olive's bare foot and squeezed. Olive moaned. Sarah jerked at the sight of the blue amulet lying on the boards beyond Olive. She snatched it off the table and put it on with a gasp of relief.

Outside an engine roared to life. Mack glanced at the door, and a flash of anger rippled his coarse features. "Motherfucker, where's *he* goin'?" He turned back to Sarah, snorted like a bull, and charged.

Sarah grabbed at a two-by-six beam across the low ceiling and swung over the platform to put it between them. As she did her foot knocked over the big movie camera, it hit the Klieg with a crash, and a reel of brown film burst open to unwind across the rough lumber floor as the Klieg and camera went down in a nimbus of breaking glass. Sarah landed on the other side of Dolores, who had one hand free and was yanking furiously at her bindings.

"Goddamn it, come 'ere, ya little whore!" Mack reversed direction and came at her from the other end of the room like a freight train. As he closed Sarah swung the heavy leather belt. The buckle caught on something, jerked Mack's head to the right, and came off his nose with a gout of blood. Mack howled and staggered into the wall holding his face. Bright red blood poured between his fingers, "My *eye!*"

"Help me!" Dolores screamed. She'd managed to get both hands free and was yanking at the straps holding her feet. Sarah sprang toward her and tried to pull the strap attached to Dolores' left foot loose. Glass cut her own feet as she yanked with a roar of effort. The leather belt tore free from the bolt and washer holding it to the platform. "Look out!" Dolores shouted.

Mack's bloody hands were reaching for her throat. Sarah lurched backward and rolled on top of Dolores, who was trying to unbuckle her other ankle. Dolores shrieked as Sarah scrambled across the blue painted boards and stumbled over Olive, who gasped. There was shouting outside, but Mack ignored it. His whole purpose was Sarah. He bared yellow teeth like an enraged bear with blood pouring from a left eye squeezed shut and his right fixed on her like a hawk on its prey.

Sarah landed on the floor, backed up and slipped in a puddle of blood into the wall, to slide sprawling on the floor, and in an instant Mack was over her. Sarah's fingers became claws like the talons of that naked goddess. Their only purpose was to tear Mack's other eye from its socket. As he lunged she rolled to his blind side, skittered upright and yanked open the heavy door.

Sunlight blinded her as she crossed a dirt yard and came out of the shadow of high walls. She could hear Mack behind her, panting and stomping as he barreled after. She glanced up at the stern visage of a rearing painted elephant with flaking tusks, sprang up a rickety stair, and grabbed at the swaying railing with her bare feet pounding as fast as her trembling legs could take her. The glass in the ball of her right foot left a trail of blood as Mack wheezed behind her with each step he took shaking the stairway.

A loud crash below made Sarah turn to see the maroon McFarlan plowing through the fence surrounding the abandoned movie set and fishtailing in a cloud of dust onto Sunset Boulevard. Mack stopped and leaned over the rail as two blue police Packards and a black Rolls limo pulled into the yard through the hole the McFarlan had made, to stop amongst the disintegrating plaster stones and statues. Mack glanced up at Sarah with his yellow teeth glowing in sunlight. He snarled and began climbing again.

Sarah flew up the stairs toward the broken crest of Babylon with her eyes darting about frantically for a weapon. She sat down on the sagging board across two buckets where she and Olive had gazed out over Hollywood, and pulled a splinter of glass from her foot. It came out with an arc of blood and she tossed it over the edge. She heard herself moan and cursed the sound of her voice. There wasn't time for that. She squeezed the stone between her breasts, her only item of apparel, and gazed into the hot sky, "Help me!" There was a two-by-four leaning against the lapis blue wall, and Sarah grabbed it and held it like a bat.

The structure creaked as Mack neared the top. She could hear footsteps behind him and shouting, but they were far below. At the end of the narrow catwalk along the top, a low door opened into a castle-like turret filled with trash, lumber, and chicken wire. Sarah stepped in and began to pick her way across the room toward a door at the far end. A nail pierced the big toe of her other foot and she yelped.

Mack's gasp was loud as he made the top of the stairs just as she reached the far door. Sarah pushed, but it held. She put her shoulder against it and shoved. Boards were nailed across the other side of it and it was solid as a rock.

Mack's sweating face glowed in sunshine as he filled the door of the room. She couldn't even swing the two-by-four in the space she'd trapped herself. Sarah gulped air and tried to still her pounding heart. The trembling in her spine threatened to seize her, to reduce her to whimpering prey before the onslaught of Mack's ferocity. He was the angry grizzly rearing its head on Sulfur Creek, popping his jaws at a fourteen-year old girl with a too-heavy rifle wobbling against her shoulder. Sarah cupped the base of the two-by-four in her hand, held it like a spear, and aimed for his throat.

Mack blinked his one good eye as he peered into the shadows of the room and stared at Sarah pressed against the far wall, "All right, wanta fight, bitch?" His blood-stained sneer of hatred filled her vision as he rushed at her and Sarah jabbed with the two-by-four. Mack slapped at it, but it caught a glancing blow across his already wounded eye. He screamed and stumbled back into the sunshine with his hands to his face, "Jesus Christ, I'm gonna *kill* ya!" came through bloody fingers as Sarah clambered over jagged refuse toward the door. Mack put his hands down, glanced at the blood on them, and stood waiting outside.

Behind him two panting men dressed in grey suits and fedoras appeared with pistols in hand beside a tall woman in a smartly tailored coat and matching grey skirt. She tossed a long brown braid over her shoulder, yanked off her coat, and wiped sweat from a high forehead. Beverly took off her sunglasses and blinked in the glare. Mack glanced over his shoulder, growled, and bolted toward Sarah as she took aim at his face with the two-by-four.

"Hey, cocksucker!"

Mack spun around with a roar. There was a pop, and Mack clutched at his throat as sunlight glinted off the short barrel of the engraved Smith and Wesson in Beverly Davis' hand. Her red lips curled in a smirk as she lowered the gun to point at his crotch. There was an orange flash and another pop, and Mack dropped like a sack of sand onto the top of the wall to lie shuddering on the fake blue stones as his blood turned them purple.

"Kill *my* girls, you pieceashit!" Beverly strode over to Mack and gazed into his face as a torn wail oozed out of him in a braided rope of pain and he gripped a hissing windpipe. Beverly cocked the gun, tapped it against his forehead three times, and fired into his eye from an inch away. A pink nimbus of blood filled the air as Mack stiffened like an electric shock had run through him and went limp. "Goddamn asshole." Beverly put a foot against his bulk, rocked him on the edge of the wall, and rolled Mack off it headfirst. It seemed like forever before there was a thud far below.

"Good shootin', Bee," the shorter of the two men said and tipped his fedora.

Blood sparkled as the plaster drank it in to become a royal purple as it melded into blue. Sarah dropped the two-by-four, limped over to Bee, and hugged her hard.

Beverly pushed Sarah back to arm's length with her hands on her shoulders, "Jesus, Sarah, you look like shit. Can you make it down okay?"

Sarah nodded, and one of the men put his grey suit coat around her shoulders.

* * *

"Bee," Dolores cried, "how the hell did you find me?"

Beverly unfastened the binding on Dolores' leg and helped her off the slab, then wrapped arms around her and gave her a lingering kiss accompanied by keening sounds from Dolores' throat. Beverly ran a finger down Dolores' nose, "That's not important now, sugar, getting a big fat dead lug taken care of and your asses out of here is." Beverly had a bemused expression on her face as she watched Sarah unbuckle the straps on Olive, who moaned and tried to sit up. "What the fuck are you two doing here anyway?"

"These are the guys who were helping Warren kidnap and kill girls!"

"Obviously, hon. I was on to them for a while but I couldn't tell you two, and I thought someone was watching over you but I guess she left it up to you. I apologize, but Ollie is a hell of a talker and you're still kind of an unknown in these parts. Looks like the moxie we both saw in you came through anyway. You ladies need to get some clothes on, by the way." She glanced at the two men behind her with their eyes darting over three naked girls. "These are my chums in the police. No names necessary, ladies," Beverly ran a hand across Dolores' throat, scowled at the bite mark on her breast, hugged her again, and spoke to the cops over her shoulder, "you boys know what to do."

The shorter of the two nodded, and they tipped their hats and stepped outside.

Sarah lifted Olive and gingerly carried her into the sunshine with short painful steps. Olive pressed her cheek against Sarah's. Sarah let out a brief gasp of acknowledgement to her own pain, set Olive on her feet with an arm around her to steady her and glanced at the broken fence, "But what about Ed? He got away."

Beverly examined the fence, "Damn, that was something. He drove right through the goddamn thing. Bet Bill's McFarlan isn't so pretty now. Somebody'll square up with him don't worry. That pieceashit is finished one way or another. Now, you three have to get out of here so our friends can dispose of this mess," she chuckled, "this isn't the first time I've had a limo full of naked girls," Beverly glanced at the walls above them, "they'll probably tear down this whole shebang to put things jake I bet."

Sarah lifted Olive again, who wasn't heavy at all, into the limo. Olive clung to her neck and whimpered, "I thought the Swami's fortune came true, Sarah. . ."

"Oh stop it."

Beverly Davis brushed hair away from Sarah's forehead and put a palm to her cheek. The corners of Bee's mouth spread into a grin that retreated but lingered in her green eyes, "Welcome to Babylon, toots."

XXVIII.

"You really are something, Sarah," Beverly sipped iced tea through a paper straw, "more moxie than any girl I've met since Frisco, and you've been around for what, a week? And now you've got an offer that's something a girl dreams of. Ask any of my girls who came here for the same reason. You're on your way, kid, and with your connections in Vancouver, we can make a killing when Prohibition comes. You really should consider it after the dues you've paid."

Sarah stretched her legs in the sun watching three beautiful young women splashing in the impossibly blue water of Belmore's pool. Their shrill laughter reminded her of her childhood at the seashore on Vancouver Island with Angeline and her brother Paul, running in the sands of Wreck Bay, climbing mysterious castles of drift logs to play hide and seek, hunting for Japanese glass floats and other treasures. Occasionally they'd found the carcasses of sperm and killer whales, rushed home to get their father, and he had sold the ivory. Her nose wrinkled at the memory of their smell. She sipped her iced tea, pushed the sunglasses back up her nose, leaned back, and stared at the tops of date-laden palms rustling in a soft Pacific breeze.

"I'm not sure about the flickers, or staying here… or working with anybody at all right now Bee."

"Really?"

"No," Sarah tested the flagstones with her bare feet. They were hot, and she slipped into her sandals before standing.

Beverly slid a thick brown envelope off the little marble-topped table beside her, "This is for you. Ed had quite a bundle in a safe at his bungalow in Pacific Palisades and my sometimes friends in the police managed to not grab all of it for themselves, since I insisted on going with them. You'll need more than that piece of jewelry around your neck and it's just a taste of what waits for you here. I thought you could use it. Goodness knows, you've earned it." She handed the envelope to Sarah.

Sarah examined the two-inch-thick stack of bills inside and dropped it in her lap, "Any news?"

"Bill's got the coppers after Ed for forging a bunch of his checks and robbing his bungalow on Alvarado. Paramount kept it out of the papers, just like our friends in City Hall kept that little event at Babylon on the Q-T. They're tearing it down," Beverly yawned, "I'll kind of miss it. It's been a landmark for the last three years. Anyway they'll let news about Ed being a thief out in good time and sweep the really bad stuff under the rug. I'm sending money to the families of the girls I knew that bunch killed, so are some other people around here. We're not all heartless, Sarah," she shook her head, "the temperance sisters and revival preachers would have a field day if they got wind of that."

Sarah drained her glass with a rattle, "Like it never even happened."

Beverly nodded, "You get good at that around here. It's for your own survival, toots. By the way I've made an appointment for you at my doctor's."

"Thank you."

Beverly put her chin in her palm and stirred her drink, "What are your plans?"

"I really don't know, Bee," Sarah felt her teeth in her lower lip. She closed her mouth, inhaled, straightened, and fixed Beverly in the most forceful gaze she could muster, "I know that you know. Who… who were those horrible people working for?"

"There are some things I can't tell you Sarah for your own safety. Perhaps someday. You could take over an operation like this yourself eventually and would have to know it all and I'm willing to wager you could deal with it. I really think you've got what it takes, but Prohibition's coming and he's right up there in City Hall. He could be Mayor sooner or later, and he's recruited quite an army of veterans from the War and put them in the Sheriff's office. I've got my own bunch in the Police but I don't want to start a fight I could lose. Besides, I've got the goods on him now. He'll have to come to terms and play by my rules if he wants to keep his ass out of jail or the gallows, but I can promise that there won't be any more of those kind of murder flickers, at least while Beverly Davis is around."

"You're not afraid yourself?"

Beverly Davis, Violet Adair, or whatever her name was responded with a remarkable smile. It was one of total acceptance, even love, and the openness of it paralyzed Sarah for a moment. It touched Sarah's oldest memories, like the smile of her own mother, and would stay with Sarah long after Beverly was gone. "I've been walking on the edge of a knife for as long as I can remember Sarah and I really don't know what else I'd do. Besides, I think I'd be bored."

"I understand."

Beverly fell silent and watched the girls in the pool where Sonya had been listening to their conversation intently with her chin resting on her hands at the edge of it. Sonya caught Sarah's eye and launched herself into the blue water to cross the pool in a backstroke. Beverly played with her braid and gave Sarah a sadder smile, "People make it look easy here but there are big tradeoffs to it I don't have to tell you. We can only use rotten lugs like Warren, Ed, and their ilk to our own advantage after stopping them when they go too far hopefully," Beverly's green eyes were pale and depthless in the glare of afternoon sun, "you do so remind me of myself love. You've got the intuition as well as the looks, and we share the knowledge of someone who is so much older than we are who knows our struggles. If you ever--"

Sarah stood up and held out her hand, "It's been an education Bee, thank you for the money."

Beverly sighed, crossed her legs, and studied her painted toes, "Ollie called."

"Of course."

"You're part of her crowd now in more ways than one. Lots of secrets, a well-earned share of respect, maybe the world by its rather unclean balls, if you want to take that job at Paramount. I'm not saying it'll all be easy street, but everything's jake now and it's a hell of an opportunity. Bill's got Zukor ready to put you in a feature. He can't believe what you went through when we told him the whole story, at least as much as he could believe, and he'll do everything in his power to make you a star," Beverly winked, "he wanted to anyway. It wouldn't have been like him not to once he saw you but why pass it up? No chorus lines or one-reelers for you girl."

Sarah shrugged, "I suppose."

Beverly stared at her for a moment. She ran a ring-covered hand across her face and laughed, "Even the attitude."

* * *

Beverly's limo took Sarah to the corner of Maryland and Alvarado, where William Desmond Taylor had a residence in a lovely court surrounded by gardens with a pavilion of Greek columns bedecked with flowering vines. She thanked the driver, handed him a silver dollar, and walked between beautiful two-story homes that were nothing like the low rambling types poorer people referred to as bungalows. She stepped up to the door of the third house on the left and knocked.

A balding black man wearing a tweed jacket and a white shirt with a starched collar opened the door. He looked her up and down before he frowned and sighed theatrically, "Yes?"

"Is Mister Taylor home?"

"Sarah," Bill Taylor appeared over the shoulder of the man, "I've been hoping you'd show up. By all means, Henry, let the lady in."

Henry nodded and stood holding the door.

Sarah stepped into the crowded living room. To her left was a shiny roll-top desk that had been open for a long time from the looks of its crowded compartments and papers strewn across its top. Pictures of various young women including Mabel Normand and a young blond Mary Minter were on top of it with their feminine handwriting scrawled across the bottoms. A portrait of Mary Pickford hung on the wall similarly inscribed. To the right was an overstuffed couch. Tall glass-walled cabinets stood on either side of the room beyond that, dividing the living room and dining room. A dark wooden table was strewn with papers that were golden in the soft glow of sun through the beige blinds over windows on the west. A kitchen was beyond, and a stairway ran up the left side of the living room upstairs. It was a bachelor's home: cozy, but none too neat.

"Henry, get the lady a drink. Scotch?"

"No, thank you, but something cold would be nice."

"Iced tea? Soda? Beer? Orange juice?"

"Orange juice please."

Henry stepped into the kitchen and reappeared with a tall glass of orange juice and a scotch and soda on a teak tray. He placed them on doilies on the coffee table as Sarah sat down on the maroon couch.

Bill sat on the chair by the desk without turning it around and put his arms across the top. He rested his chin on his forearm, stared at Sarah for a long moment, and grinned, "Heard you thought I was a killer, or some such."

She felt the blood come to her face but kept a hand away from it, "That's why I came, Mr. Taylor, I wanted to apologize."

"Well, obviously I'm not angry. Did Ollie or Bee tell you about that part I want to give you a shot at? Ollie, Mabel and Bee all think the world of you, Sarah. I heard about that stunt work you did for Ince too."

"Yes, yes, and it's wonderful, Mr. Taylor."

"Bill, just Bill."

"Bill, but I'm afraid I have other plans."

Bill ran a hand across his chin, leaned against the desk, and shook his head, "Remarkable! You don't *want* it!" He sat up straight, edged the chair closer, reached toward Sarah's right hand, and slowly put his left over it, "Sarah, you're someone who can accomplish great things here. I can see it, and I'd be honored to assist you in that endeavor should you care to try. Actually I was very much looking forward to working with you," his grey eyes skipped off her legs, and rose with effort to her eyes.

"Seems like you've already got your hands full Bill, what with Mabel Normand and Mary Miles Minter in your life."

"Mabel shall always burn a candle for Mack Sennett, as I think you've gathered, and Mary worships me in a child's way Sarah, but you and I could do great things together. I mean… in the pictures."

She pulled her hand away and stood to gaze out the window, "I've only been here a week and so many things have happened in that time. Terrible things, wonderful things, things I've done myself that I never thought… I never *dreamed* I'd do have happened here. The whole world has turned upside down in a way. I just need time to decide what I'm going to be a part of and what not is all." She took a sip of orange juice, then a gulp, and put it down in the middle of the doily. It burned in her chest. "I really thought you had something to do with murdering those girls Bill, and I can't begin to tell you how ashamed I am. When I saw how you cared about Mabel, I knew I was wrong, yet I--"

He held up a long-fingered hand, "I'm ashamed and embarrassed as the dickens myself, thinking I had a murderer right here in my own home and driving me around town," he slapped a fist in his palm, "I thought that he really... he was just using me to meet girls, like all the rest of the help in Hollywood! They're looking for him in regards to the thievery, and when they catch him, his other crimes shall be dealt with in one way or another I assure you. You've seen the kind of pull Bee has I believe. The studios can't afford to have such horrid things divulged to the general public however. Can you imagine what people would say? What with Prohibition coming and the Temperance Movement trying to shut us down saying we're the root of all evil and that the flickers are the road to Hell? Good Lord! Ed Sands probably isn't his real name anyway. Nobody here has one."

"How about you?"

Bill shook his head, "Me neither Sarah, we've all reinvented ourselves I suppose," he sighed, "and it shall no doubt catch up with those of us who aren't fast enough on this treadmill we've made," he gave her a shy grin, "but it sure is fun when things are going smashingly, don't you think?"

"Ed was so close to you, running your errands, carrying on your private correspondence with Mabel and Mary. Mabel told me that by the way... and you and Ed--"

Bill's mouth became a thin line, "Some things one's reputation can't survive from Sarah. I'd rather not speak about it."

She ran a hand across her lips and glanced at the man Hollywood held up as its cleanest product, "Were you even in the Canadian Army?"

"Oh yes, a Captain, and my father was a Major in the British one. But I didn't see the action people think I did, and a portion of my exploits are due to my own embellishment I must admit."

"I can't stop thinking about those girls, and that no one ever will know what happened to them. I can't believe nobody trusts the law here, at least those that they don't happen to have in their own pockets. What's one to do when things get so horrible? In Canada the Mounties are considered of a higher order, they're utterly trustworthy, and their word is their bond."

Bill stared at two young women in thin silk blouses picking flowers from vines wreathing the pavilion, and Sarah followed his gaze until he spoke. "I was in the Klondike myself and know of what you speak. We've given up much for what we are getting. It's a Faustian bargain I suppose. You're the most mature young lady I've met for a long time by the way, and we could use you at Paramount simply for your earnestness. Perhaps you'll become a rock like Mary Pickford, unsullied by the tides of greed, lust, and avarice washing over us like a rising sea to be purchased a nickel at a time at the box office by the masses as escape from their own travails."

"Good God, Bill, I'm not that pure."

"Yes, but after all you've been through, you still seem decent and hopeful, which is astounding. Besides, neither is she. It's all an image you know," Bill grinned, "I know about you and Ollie by the way. The girl is a chatterbox as you are no doubt aware of by now, but I must say that she adores you utterly at the moment."

Sarah blinked and rubbed her hands together as she examined a broken nail. Ed's handsome face popped into her mind with a wicked smile, and she winced.

"How will you break it to her... I mean leaving?"

Sarah looked up, "Thank you for asking. You actually are the nicest man I've met here, even with your trysting young Mary."

"I hope I'm not too nice. Those fellows never win."

They laughed.

"But you let Ed get the best of you."

Bill stared at the carpet for a moment and looked up with what might have been an attempt at a smile, "And Ollie was your paramour, who took you in while in your hour of need, so perhaps you understand." He ran a hand across his face as his pale blue eyes examined her, "Sarah… did you actually kill Warren?"

Something jumped in the pit of her stomach. Sarah choked on the next swallow of orange juice, and she coughed and put a hand to her mouth, "Excuse me."

Bill was staring with the same fascination she'd seen in Olive's, Bee's and Mabel's eyes, but with the smile her father had at times when she'd done something foolish or headstrong like climb a tree she was afraid to climb down. It made her want to trust him. She thought of Mary Minter.

"Don't worry about it. Like I said Ollie is a talker, and Mabel trusts me with the knowledge also for which I'm honored, and as far as Warren goes, the foul dastard deserved it. I wanted to do it myself after I found out about his dealings with Mabel. He got her right back into the dope after she took the cure back East. Her body can't take it, Sarah. You know how she's prone to the consumption. I'm cursed that I love her and she still loves Mack. Warren was a greedy sonofabitch who wanted to supply her fatal longings along with all his other nefarious dealings. If I'd known about the actual kidnappings and murders, I assure you that I *would* have killed him if I could have gotten away with it. I admire you beyond words, actually," Bill leaned back in the chair, "tell me, how did you do it?"

Sarah's eyes became unfocused as her own furious detour into sex and drugs rose up and laughed at her from far too close. What would Bill think of her if he knew that? Then again, it was most likely nothing strange to him at all. She examined the soothing expression on his face one more time, brushed back her hair, and let out her breath, "With a magnum of scotch."

Bill slapped his knees and roared with laughter.

"Rather appropriate, eh?"

XXIX.

Duke was licking pomegranate juice from Sarah's fingers on the marble steps at Wilshire when Olive's canary yellow Locomobile bounced into the driveway. Olive sprang from the car with a squeal of delight, about to embrace Sarah, when she eyed the crimson stains on her hands.

Sarah put the sticky knife down she'd opened the pomegranate with and crushed the last few seeds between her teeth that burst to release their sweet yet bitter juice. She wiped her mouth with the back of a red-stained hand and scratched Duke's chest with the other.

"Gosh Sarah, you look like a killer with blood all over you."

"Always wondered what these things taste like."

"I don't think that one's quite ripe."

Sarah picked Duke's red hair off her fingers and rubbed a patch off the goddess hanging from her throat with her thumb, "Better a killer than a victim anyway."

"Did Bill give you the part?"

"I turned it down."

Olive's face went blank, and after a long pause, she managed a, "Huh?"

"I'm not staying, Ollie."

Olive's face melted like a little girl told a most awful truth. In moments tears welled in her eyes. She stamped her feet on the flagstones, sniffed, and sobbed. She looked up, put ring-covered fingers to her face, and hiccupped. Olive peeked out between purple painted nails, examined Sarah between her fingers, exhaled, dropped her hands, and for the briefest moment her violet eyes and elfin features unleashed a scathing stare, "Why!"

"I don't belong here. You do I suppose, although to tell the truth I'm awfully afraid for you. It was only luck that you and I are alive right now. Your husband Jack belongs here with friends like Wally I guess. You don't even love him anymore, but there he is, and I think he still loves you. Bill Taylor surely does. He loves playing the director, making flickers, and having his pick of girls... and I believe it doesn't stop at girls either."

Olive's mouth fell open, "He told--"

"I figured it out," Sarah shook her head, "and Jack's sister Mary has thrived and does wonders here. She's founded her own movie company with Griffith, Chaplin and Doug Fairbanks, and seems to be stronger than anyone when it comes to getting something done. I truly admire her and I suppose I should be dazzled by the money but I need to live another life is all," Sarah ran her hands around Duke's muzzle as he licked her fingers clean. She ran a fingertip across his nose, and his long pink tongue tried to follow it, "I'm taking this dog however. I owe him."

"But what will you go back *to,* Sarah? Your family is dead, and... how can you make any money? You're my best friend. You proved the Swami wrong and saved me from death!"

"Bee did. I almost died too Ollie."

Olive paused and took a breath, "Jesus, Sarah, we've been *lovers!* People will love you just like they love me, I know it. You're an amazing person and we need you here. Don't worry, it's all safe now and I'll show you the ropes. God, I never even had a chance to take you to a *filming!* It's not all play. I work really hard too and I'll share that with you I swear. You'll have so much money you won't be able to spend it with all these beautiful fellas at your beck and call. Me and Mabel were going to take you out Saturday to Nat Goodwin's in Santa Monica with our girlfriend Virginia Rappe. Christ... it's all planned!" Olive stamped a sandal on the marble steps, "I've already picked out your dress, so just stay for that please. I'm not jealous, honey, we can share the fuckin' men. Valentino was just a start and you can put that awful Warren and Ed thing away forever and forget it. I know you're bothered by it, but the whole world is waiting for you, Sarah. You've paid your dues. You can be rich and famous, and we can have so much fun, and there's so much to do here and so many people to meet that you won't ever have to regret anything at all because there's always another--"

"I want to go home, or at least find wherever that might be, and I want to regret some things Ollie, *and* remember them. I even regret killing Warren even though he was going to kill me. I always will. I mean, he was a baby in someone's arms once." Tears began to well at the corner of Sarah's eyes, and Olive reached out to wipe them. Sarah gulped air, shook her head, and pushed her hand away, "I mean... I don't know, but that's how life was meant to be, at least it's how mine was. You know, about life itself and the taking of it. There are older souls watching and I can't..." Sarah swallowed, examined Olive's expression, and started over, "it's always the same here as far as I can see, like an endless summer where everyone just... good God is it really November? Perhaps this is paradise for some but I think I'd tire of it. It's just not real for me, what with all these beautiful people dancing the night away while bodies are piling up in a pit somewhere and fakers and swamis are telling them utter nonsense about their lives. It's like they're waltzing on top of Hell and laughing about it. In my world summer needs a fall and fall needs a winter. Last winter and the flu was the worst in my entire life but it sure made spring worth looking forward to... and what about those girls? You knew some of them from Bee's, right? What if one had been Dolores? You've been her lover too. Don't you feel for them? They came here with big hopes and died for what, someone's entertainment? I can't get their faces out of my mind, or the ones I'll never know the faces of. Some of them are still on film somewhere in their agony, on *film,* and they're in my dreams, Ollie. They'll follow me wherever I go or whoever I'm with, and some of those people who did it are still out there and it sounds as if they'll be quite successful around here yet. Some of them are probably in charge even. How can I go anywhere knowing some smiling fellow I meet might have gazed upon a girl that he tortured and murdered, or me when I was unconscious up there at that god-awful fucking house?"

"Wow," Olive laughed, "I never heard you say fuck before, Sarah."

Sarah choked on a laugh and wiped at the hair on her hands, "And I don't want to be one more toss on the sheets or whatever for people like Bill Taylor or Mack Sennett either, *or* Valentino. Or a partner for Bee, even though I do feel safe there and respect her more than anybody else I've met here. I don't--"

Olive's face fell into a lower gear of misery than Sarah had ever seen before, "But... don't you respect *me?*"

Sarah swiped at her hair and smeared juice across her cheek, "Oh Ollie of course I do, but as far as Bee's offer goes, I don't want to be procuring girls and pouring whiskey down the throats of people who might rather be killing me. I remember that look Ed Sands gave me at your house on Lankershim. I've felt others like it that are the same and just because I respect her doesn't mean that I can be like her. People like Bee can deal with that. I won't. I know it's over with those kidnappers, but who will ever know them... I mean the girls? Or speak for them?" She stared into the branches of the pomegranate tree and shook her head, "It's just the way I am I suppose."

Olive's upper lip trembled and she slapped the step with a moan. Her face was streaked with tears.

Sarah put a red-stained palm to Olive's cheek, "You could escape this too and come with me."

Olive's violet eyes widened as she shot Sarah a look as if she had gone totally insane.

"Oh well, Ollie, you've got the whole world here anyway."

Olive fell to her knees and grasped Sarah's sticky fingers. Duke licked her ear as she clutched Sarah's hand to her breast, staining her yellow summer dress red in the heat of November. Sarah could feel Olive's heart beating beneath her palm. Olive stared hard until she gave up the effort, blinked the most beautiful eyes in Hollywood, sighed, sat with a rustle of skirts on the marble steps, brushed immaculately curled ringlets of hair away from a child's face, stared into the branches above her, and let out a long exasperated sigh, "But... where will you *go?*"

"North."

The End

Epilogue

Olive Thomas, born Olivetta Elaine Duffy in Charleroi Pennsylvania in eighteen ninety-four and widely regarded as the most beautiful girl in Hollywood during its first decade, made *The Flapper* the following year, popularizing the name at the dawn of the Twenties in her second to last film. She died September tenth, nineteen-twenty after ingesting poison at the Hotel Ritz in Paris just one month shy of her twenty-sixth birthday while her sometimes husband Jack Pickford was trolling the all night cafés for heroin. Olive lingered for four days in agony, blinded, with her vocal cords burned away, as the mercury bichloride Jack was using to treat a case of syphilis ate away her insides. The incident was called accident, suicide, and murder by various voices of the press, and provided grist for the scandal sheets for decades.

Of course in the early hours to which she was accustomed, she simply may have been trying to get high, the label on the bottle was in French, and, after all it was Olive. Except for *The Flapper* and *Everybody's Sweetheart,* not one of her twenty-two films has survived in its entirety. Some exist in some partial form as for many of her contemporaries. The Argentine artist Alberto Vargas' nude painting of her in nineteen-twenty became known as the *Vargas Girl,* beginning a series that continued over half a century and into the first twenty years of *Playboy* magazine. He kept it in his bedroom until his death in 1981. It's said that producer David Selznick, the son of Myron for whom Olive last worked, who made *Gone With the Wind,* took the middle initial "O" in her memory. Her ghost is said to haunt the New Amsterdam Theater in New York, where she began her career with Ziegfeld. She's buried in Woodlawn Cemetery in Brooklyn under the name Pickford, across the lawn from Jack and a safe distance from the rest of Mary's clan. Mabel Normand bought most of her jewelry at auction.

Jack died in 1933 in Hollywood from his alcohol and morphine addictions, as did his buddy Wallace Reid, who was publicly committed beforehand, as his stoned antics on film sets, bars, and the streets of Tijuana were by then notorious. That sparked the first Hollywood drug exposé film with the production of *Human Wreckage* in 1923, giving Wally's seldom seen and longsuffering wife her fifteen minutes of fame also.

Thomas Ince died aboard William Randolph Hearst's yacht in 1924. Rumor had it that Hearst was shooting at Charley Chaplin, who was bedding Hearst's mistress Marion Davis, and hit Ince in the head instead. The yacht docked along the coast of California near Hearst's estate for a quick and well-paid autopsy by the San Luis Obispo County authorities under Hearst's sway. It recorded natural causes before a hasty cremation and that was that.

The much publicized death of Valentino in '26 is well known.

Weakened by twenty years of high living, cocaine, fighting Bill Taylor's murder investigation in nineteen twenty-two, and defending close friend Roscoe 'Fatty' Arbukle, who was found with the body of Olive's party girl starlet friend Virginia Rappe in his San Francisco hotel suite exactly one year after Olive's death, Mabel Normand died at the age of thirty-eight from tuberculosis on February 23, 1930. Her big Hollywood funeral was paid for by Mack Sennett, whom she never did marry.

William Desmond Taylor, a.k.a. William Deanne Tanner, who deserted a wife and daughter in New York and lied about his age (he was actually in his fifties at the time of this novel) was shot in the back in the living room of his bungalow in Alvarado Court on February 1, 1922. The list of suspects included Mabel Normand, Mary Miles Minter his teenage lover, Mary's controlling stage mother Charlotte Shelby, Henry Peavey his gay butler, Ed Sands his mysteriously absconded chauffeur and reputed lover, Hughie Faye, another drug dealer name Mad Mose, and about a hundred others. The murder was never solved, and was further fodder for endless Hollywood tabloid stories right up until the Sharon Tate murders by Charlie Manson and his little family eclipsed it in people's minds at the end of the sixties.

District Attorney Woolwine, who ordered the destruction of the crumbling ruins of Babylon on Sunset Boulevard, was widely suspected of covering up aspects of the crime, just as he'd done for countless other criminal events concerning the studios. Years later he was finally convicted of corruption and bribery and jailed.

Ed Sands, wanted for robbing Bill Taylor, eluded a nationwide manhunt after his murder. Ed was finally found a few years later stretched out on the banks of a river in Connecticut with a bullet in his head. No one was ever charged with that either.

Beverly Davis, a.k.a. Violet Adair, Isabel Dubois, and perhaps her actual name unknown, ran several high-class houses of prostitution in Los Angeles during the teens, beginning in the Hampshire district on what was then South Belmore, and later was involved in bootlegging throughout Prohibition and the Depression to retire in the late thirties at the age of forty-eight a very wealthy woman who credited her amazing luck to a Goddess. She's also credited with coining the term *call girl* in the American lexicon, and made another fortune with her autobiography, *Call House Madam,* written in nineteen thirty-nine and published in nineteen forty-one. With the admirable reserve of the age, she managed not to mention a single client's or connection's name that was yet alive and was considered the greatest Madam in the history of Hollywood. The book sold a half-million copies until

Pearl Harbor frightened Americans into more urgent endeavors. She disappeared afterward. It has long been out of print.

John Barrymore was one of her best customers just as he was for Jessie Hayman, Bee's flame-haired six-foot mentor in the Tenderloin of San Francisco, where Beverly started at fourteen after fleeing a convent in Los Angeles, and where she survived the earthquake and fire to become the proprietor of her own house on Davis Street at sixteen.

Sarah Mae McCallum returned to the Klondike, opened a roadhouse with Ed Sand's money, never married, and changed her name. Her daughters have passed down a peculiar stone she wore until her dying day and her descendents are scattered throughout the North.

Finis

Acknowledgements

For my editors at Montag Press Collective; Charlie Franco who goes beyond his limits, Mara Renee Brianna Hodges whose exemplary work I could not do without, Niall Patrick Gray, artist and bulwark against chaos, and Hugh Hefner for remembering Olive as fondly as I do.